COLE'S swarthy face darkened, his eyes narrowing into ice-cold slits. "But you're going to have to kill me, Sukey," he said softly, "there's no other way." His smile was lazy, taunting. "And I don't think you will, Sukey, so be a good girl and put down that gun before you hurt yourself."

There was an explosion in her ears at the same time she felt the derringer jerk in her hand. She would never forget the look of stunned surprise on Cole's face, the bright red patch of blood staining his white shirt front.

Nor would she forget the blue-green eyes blazing full in her face, the anger contorting Cole's features. "I should have let Bella have you," Cole said softly, swaying, as he took a step toward her. "Next time I'll kill . . ."

His voice fell away; his eyes closed and he crumpled slowly to the ground at her feet. . . .

Also by Marcella Thum:

ABBEY COURT
FERNWOOD

THE WHITE ROSE

by Marcella Thum

FAWCETT CREST • NEW YORK

THE WHITE ROSE

Published by Fawcett Crest Books, a unit of CBS Publications, the Consumer Publishing Division of CBS Inc.

ISBN: 0-449-24316-8

Printed in the United States of America

First Fawcett Crest printing: August 1980

10 9 8 7 6 5 4 3

John Ford's newest theater in Washington, the Atheneum, was filled to capacity this sultry spring evening. Although for two years the country had been locked in a bloody civil war which had dealt the North one bitter, humiliating defeat after another, Washingtonians still flocked to their music halls and theaters.

Even the latest Union defeat suffered at Chancellorsville only a few weeks before, and the rumor that General Lee's Army of Virginia had started north for Washington, didn't interfere with the audience's enjoyment of the romantic farce being played on the stage. In the rear of the theater, rowdies shouted appreciative, if obscene, comments and covered the floor with tobacco juice and peanut shells, while gold-braided Army and Navy officers and elegantly dressed ladies seated in the front rows of the theater roared with laughter at the antics of the leading lady, Maggie Mitchell.

The impeccably dressed dark-haired gentleman who occupied a seat in the third row of the theater, next to a vacant aisle seat, and whose mind should have been on more important matters, found himself watching the stage show, too. It was not the popular leading lady, Maggie Mitchell, however, who caught and held Cole Sinclair's attention. It was the ingenue who played a minor role in the drama. Although disguised in a young man's clothing, with a ridiculous mustache painted on her face and a plumed hat covering her black hair, there was no doubting the young lady's femininity. The trousers fit snugly over the seductive curves of her slim hips and softly rounded buttocks, and when the young actress crossed the stage, she walked with a flirtatious, naughty swagger that snared the attention of more than one male in the audience.

Studying those gracefully rounded curves through narrowed blue-green eyes that at the moment looked sleepily relaxed, Cole had the nagging feeling that he had met the girl somewhere before. He looked down at the program notes for her name—Rosalind LaSeur. A stage name, no doubt, which meant nothing. Even the girl's large, lustrous dark eyes, although heavily made up now for the stage, had a vague familiarity about them.

Cole prided himself on his memory for faces. In his particular line of work, it could mean the difference between safety and a hangman's noose. Still, the memory of where he could have met the girl eluded him. He listened closely to Rosalind's husky, seductive voice when she spoke her lines, but the voice, like the name, revealed nothing. Finally he settled back, resigned to leaving the mystery unsolved for the moment. In any case, he decided with arrogant amusement, he had certainly never bedded the girl. As many as the young ladies were who had quite happily shared Cole Sinclair's bed, he was sure he would not have forgotten the disturbingly beautiful young girl on the stage.

Then, without turning his head, he became aware that the vacant seat next to him was now occupied. The late arriver, a gray-haired man in his forties, had an air of nervousness about him; beads of perspiration stood out on his high, sloping forehead. Glancing jerkily to the right and then the left, he fumbled with the program and dropped it to the floor.

Both men bent to retrieve the program. The gray-haired man whispered quickly, "You've seen this play before?"

"Yes, before the war, in Richmond," Cole answered softly. And then, as the two men bent forward, the programs of the two men unobtrusively changed hands.

Cole had started to straighten when the second man's voice stopped him. Still a whisper, yet it held a note of frightened desperation clutching at Cole. "I'm

6

sure I was followed. Laf Baker's detectives, at the exits. They mustn't see us together."

Cursing the man silently, Cole Sinclair quite agreed. The fact that Lafayette Baker, chief of the War Department Detectives, did not know Cole's face had saved his neck more than once. He had no intention of giving up that advantage just because this Confederate double agent was stupid enough to allow himself to be followed.

When he settled back again in his seat, though, there was no hint of his annoyance on his face. His blue-green eyes beneath slashing black brows were, if anything, sleepier than ever. Only those close to Cole Sinclair had discovered, often to their sorrow, that the sleepier he looked, the more dangerous the man became. Lazily now he surveyed the audience and the two exits from the theater. There was no difficulty in spotting the detectives standing rather obviously blocking the dimly lit doorways. It was only a matter of time, he knew, before they found where his companion was seated. They had probably already inquired at the box office for the location of the seat. Once they moved in, anyone found seated in the vicinity of the man would be suspect and searched. Cole thought grimly of the incriminating papers he now carried within his own program notes, the latest breakdown of the Union Army's cipher.

"What should we do?" the second man whispered hoarsely.

"Shut up."

Cole spoke quietly, but the icy menace in his voice made the man next to him pale.

Damn bloody amateurs, Cole scowled, disgusted. Still the agent beside him had been useful in the past. He had delivered vital information from Stanton's files, even after the Secretary of War had bragged that he had closed all the "rat holes" in his department through which military information had slipped south to Richmond. If the man didn't lose his nerve, they both might yet escape this trap and the agent could continue to be useful in the future.

Once again Cole's gaze drifted slowly around the theater. In any case, the cipher hidden within his program notes was too important to lose now. Within a few days the Union Army would undoubtedly discover their cipher had been broken and replace it with a new one. But those few days of being able to read the Union Army's ciphered messages could be invaluable to Lee in moving his army from Fredericksburg toward Washington.

"They'll throw us in Old Capitol," the man beside him whispered, terrified. "Baker will see us hanged."

Cole reached down and withdrew the long, thin knife from the pouch he had strapped to his leg and in the darkness placed its point firmly against the man's soft paunch.

"I said, be quiet."

As much as he would regret it, Cole thought dispassionately, it might be necessary to kill his companion. Laf Baker wasn't noted for his kind treatment of spies in Old Capitol Prison, and the man would surely fall apart under questioning. Not that he would be able to tell his captors much about Cole's carefully maintained underground courier route south from Washington to Richmond, the Confederate capital. Each courier in the chain, for his own protection, knew as little as possible about the next link. Still, the man had seen Cole's face. He might even know about Bella. . . .

Cole glanced once again toward the exits and saw, his nerves tightening, that the detectives were no longer there. They must be moving down the dark aisle now, heading for the front-row seats. In a few more seconds, escape would be cut off. Cole thought quickly. There was always the old ploy of yelling "Fire!" Pandemonium would surely result. Everyone knew the theaters in Washington were tinderboxes.

Still he hesitated. He had seen the terrifying results when an audience the size of this one panicked—women and men would be trampled underfoot in their

8

desperate flight toward the exits. Cole had led troops of cavalry into battle many times, had killed men indiscriminately himself. But it was another thing to murder innocent men and women, even in wartime.

In the split second while he hesitated, he had forgotten all about the stage play. Then all at once he became aware that something unusual was happening onstage, and a murmur was sweeping through the audience around him. He glanced toward the stage. The young actress in a man's clothing had stepped to the center front of the stage. As part of her role, she had begun singing a song, accompanying herself on a banjo, its ribbons flung over her shoulder.

The rest of the stage was darkened, and the footlights were fully upon her slim, dark beauty. Her rich, husky voice carried clearly to the rear of the theater. The song had started out to be a light, teasing love song, but suddenly the words and music changed, became taunting, defiant:

> *"And here's to our Confederacy!*
> *Strong are we and brave;*
> *Like patriots of old*
> *We'll fight our heritage to save,*
> *And rather than submit to shame*
> *To die we would prefer*
> *So cheer for the Bonny Blue Flag*
>   *that bears a single star!*
> *Hurrah, hurrah for Southern rights, hurrah!*
> *Hurrah for the Bonny Blue Flag*
>   *that bears a single star!"*

By the time she had reached the chorus of what had almost become the Confederacy's national anthem, the murmur of outrage in the audience had grown to a roar. A few Southern sympathizers cheered, but the predominantly Northern audience sprang to its feet, shouting disapproval, hurling curses and threats, hissing at the girl on the stage and stamping their feet.

Several men rushed toward the stage down the aisle; women screamed. The aisles filled with people.

On the stage the girl stood quietly now, still holding the banjo, facing the audience with a triumphant smile on her mocking lips, then two stagehands hurried out to pull the young actress off the stage, lowering the curtain.

The gray-haired man in the third row had sprung to his feet, too, listening aghast to the traitorous Southern song being sung in the very midst of the Federal capital.

"Did you hear that?" he cried, excited. "Old Baker will throw away the key when his detectives get their hands on that girl."

There was no answer from his companion. The gray-haired man turned, puzzled. The seat next to him was empty.

It was almost midnight as the military carriage moved slowly through the streets of Washington, but Pennsylvania Avenue was still thronged with people. Night or day, nothing stopped the feverish business and social whirl of Washington. Almost overnight the war had changed the capital from a sleepy Southern town into a busy, bustling metropolis. The city was overcrowded with government clerks and copyists, politicians, legislators and soldiers, as well as a multitude of civilian contractors and merchants who had shrewdly discovered that if the North couldn't win the war, at least money could be made from it. Along with the other speculators had come a flood of painted and gaudily dressed young women, imported by madams from as far away as St. Louis to fill the hundreds of brothels in the capital city, the more luxurious establishments located only a stone's throw from the White House.

The military carriage stopped to allow a row of lumbering ambulances to pass, and the girl in the carriage leaned forward to watch them, her dark eyes somber. The ambulances were now as much a part of the Washington scene as the earthen forts and breastworks bris-

10

tling on the hilltops surrounding the city, but she could never get used to them, or to the thousands of maimed and wounded soldiers who poured daily into the capital, overflowing the regular hospitals into makeshift hospitals in churches, warehouses and schools. Even the magnificent new Patent Office building had been pressed into hospital service; its marble floor was stained red with the blood of the wounded and dying.

After the ambulances passed, the carriage gave a lurch and started forward again, turning down First Street and finally stopping before a dingy brick building. Once the home of the Congress of the United States, the two-story building with its impressive portico and arched windows now had the dismal air of a dignified dowager gone to seed. The walls were grimy, and all the windows were defaced with horizontal slats of wood. There were no merrymakers on the street here. The sidewalk was deserted except for armed sentries who patrolled the streets around what was now Old Capitol Prison.

From within the carriage, Rosalind LaSeur studied the bleak facade of the prison and suddenly shivered, as if an icy hand had passed over her flesh. Only a few feeble rays of light showed through the boarded windows. She could well believe the stories which circulated through Washington about the prison. Men and women who disappeared behind its walls were often never heard from again, and pedestrians passing by the prison at night told tales of terrifying screams coming from the rambling low annex built onto the prison.

The young actress straightened and gave herself a mental shake. She was being foolish, she told herself briskly. Such stories were only rumors. Heaven knows, ever since the war began, Washington had been filled with more than its share of wild, unsubstantiated stories.

The Army lieutenant who had escorted Rosalind to the prison had opened the carriage door and was waiting patiently for her to descend. He had arrived at the Atheneum that evening shortly after her performance

11

had caused a minor riot in the theater. With a troop of three men he had searched her dressing room, then formally placed her under arrest.

"On what grounds?" the actress asked indignantly.

He held out a sheaf of letters he had found hidden behind her dressing-table mirror. "These letters are to rebels in Richmond. It's against the law to hold correspondence with the enemy." A spark of amusement touched the lieutenant's face. "And you must admit your choice of songs this evening was, at the least, imprudent?"

Now he studied his prisoner within the carriage and cleared his throat uncomfortably. It didn't sit well, arresting a woman, especially one as young and beautiful as this one. Still, he reminded himself sternly of that other "secesh" girl, Belle Boyd. She was young and pretty, too, they said, but her spying for Jeb Stuart and Stonewall Jackson in the Shenandoah Valley had caused the death of countless Union soldiers.

Rosalind allowed the lieutenant to help her from the carriage, casting him a disdainful glance as he did so. Nevertheless, as she lifted her skirt above the mud in the street, she couldn't resist showing more than was absolutely necessary of her trim ankles beneath her white flounced petticoats.

The lieutenant took her into an anteroom of the prison, where several other prisoners waited, and then, after a few minutes, escorted her to a small rear room on the second floor, its one tiny window overlooking the prison courtyard. The only furniture in the room was a blue-calico-covered straw bed, a wooden chair, a washstand and a broken mirror on the wall.

The girl glanced around, unable to hide her dismay at her rude surroundings. Even the lieutenant looked embarrassed, mumbling, "Sorry, miss, but it's the best room we have. The notorious spy Rose Greenhow stayed here for a year in '61."

A year, the young actress thought, shocked. How could anyone stand living in a little cubicle like this for a year? And she remembered reading that the socially prominent Mrs. Greenhow, turned Confederate spy, had had her little daughter in prison with her the whole time.

She sat down gingerly on the edge of the bed, then murmured with an appealing helplessness, "Perhaps if I could have some warm water and soap."

"Of course," the lieutenant said quickly. "I'll see to it right away. If there's anything else you need, let me know."

His reward was a ravishing smile that dazzled the lieutenant with its brilliance and made the girl's lustrous dark eyes glow even brighter.

After the lieutenant, still murmuring apologies, stumbled from the room, the young actress giggled, delighted. Well, perhaps it wouldn't be too awful after all, being incarcerated in Old Capitol. She'd never played the role of a prisoner before. It would be a challenge to her acting ability.

The warm water was brought to her, and she bathed as best she could. Then, loosening her hair so it fell in a blue-black cloud over her shoulders, she stretched out on the straw bed, still fully clothed. She had put out her candle and almost drifted off to sleep when she heard the door to her cell open quietly. Instantly awake, she sat up in bed, groping in the darkness for the candle.

"Who's there?" she demanded.

"I'd prefer we do without the candle, Miss Appleton." The voice held a familiar harsh, grating twang to it. Her hand fell away from the candle. She gave a sigh of relief. "Oh, it's you, Mr. Baker."

By the moonlight filtering through the slatted windows she was able to distinguish the man's features, reddish-brown hair and full beard. A pleasant-enough-looking face, she thought, until you looked into the man's cold, searching gray eyes. It was then you remembered that Lafayette Baker was considered one of the most ruthless and powerful men in Washington, responsible only to the President, and with a sinister

13

reputation and web of detectives in his employ that reached out into all corners of the capital.

He pulled the chair up to the bed and sat down, his gaze surveying the room quickly. "I'm sorry the accommodations couldn't be better," he said. "But you understand you had to be treated as a regular prisoner."

"Of course." She smiled mischievously. "I should be honored. I've been told that this is the room the Rebel Rose occupied."

Lafayette Baker nodded dourly. "And caused more trouble than any dozen other prisoners. Even while she was imprisoned here, she somehow managed to send stolen military information through her couriers to Richmond. Every decision of Lincoln's cabinet, even copies of war plans, thanks to Rose Greenhow and her influential friends, were known in Richmond within twenty-four hours. And it was her message to General Beauregard about the position of Union troops that helped bring about that disastrous rout at Bull Run."

The girl on the bed said softly, "I only hope I can do as well for the Union cause."

Gazing at the beautiful young girl sitting on the bed across from him, Lafayette Baker hoped so, too. He had little liking for using female spies, but he had very early discovered the truth in the old adage that the female is deadlier than the male. His women agents had often proved twice as valuable as the men in his employ. Certainly he was well aware that the Confederacy relied heavily on intelligence gathered by Southern women spies, and from the very first days of the war, the rebels had been much more skillful in their spying than the Union. How else was it possible for Southern generals like Lee and Stuart and Jackson to know exactly the movement and strength of the Northern armies so that the outnumbered rebel troops always managed to strike at the weakest points in the Union lines?

Still, spying was a dangerous, dirty business for men or women, and, having been a close friend of Major

14

Matthew Appleton, Laf Baker felt a responsibility toward the major's daughter.

"It isn't too late, you know, for you to change your mind," he said now.

Lucinda Appleton stiffened. Behind heavy, fringed lashes her dark eyes, which could change in a moment from the softest, seductive velvet to the hardness and luster of ebony, gazed coldly at her visitor. "I have no intention of changing my mind. Why should I? I've brought you useful information these last months, haven't I? And it went well tonight, didn't it? By tomorrow all of Washington will believe I'm a dyed-in-the-wool rebel."

Baker nodded reluctantly. He had no intention of telling the girl that he hadn't used the information she had secretly sent him; that it had taken several months of cautious waiting before he had become convinced that the girl was, in fact, loyal to the North. He couldn't afford to take any chances, even though he knew for a fact that Major Appleton, despite his Virginia origins, had been a staunch abolitionist and had raised his children to respect and share his beliefs. There were too many double spies in the city, and there was no one in Washington, except the President himself, that Lafayette Baker trusted absolutely. He was certain there were rebel spies still working in the War Department, even within his own section.

"And you know I can shoot and ride as well as any man," Lucinda continued, an impish grin suddenly lighting her face. "Remember that time at the trading post when my brothers and I raced with the Indian boys and won?"

Baker smiled in memory. It was at an Indian trading post in northern Michigan several years before that he had first met Major Appleton and his two sons and daughter. The fourteen-year-old Lucinda had already been a handful, half tomboy, half blossoming beauty, slim and strong as a boy but with a body and provocative face already dangerously stirring to the senses of the trappers and Indian lads who visited the post. It was no wonder, Baker thought wryly, that the major had decided to send his headstrong daughter back East to a young ladies' finishing school.

"My brothers taught me to hold a gun and ride a horse, almost before I could walk," Lucinda said proudly. "By the time I was ten I could outshoot and outride almost any man in the Virginia Valley."

For a moment her dark eyes shadowed with pain, her young face looking suddenly childishly forlorn. Lafayette Baker asked gently, "You haven't heard then from young Matt?"

She shook her head. Tears sparkled in her lustrous eyes, and she thrust the tears away angrily with the back of her hand. "It was bad enough losing the major at Shiloh. At least he died in battle, and he never got over Mother's death anyway. But then to watch my brother Charles die in agony by inches after he was wounded at Antietam! And young Matt! He had just turned sixteen when he enlisted. The last letter I had from him was six months ago. I'm terribly afraid he's dead, too."

"He might be wounded in some Southern hospital," Baker said.

But he knew his words were little comfort. Southern hospitals were less well equipped with medicine and doctors than Northern military hospitals, and Union medical care was deplorable enough. And if young Matt had been captured by the enemy ... well, the horror stories that had reached the North of Southern prisoner-of-war camps were enough to chill the blood of the strongest man.

To change the subject, he said curiously, "I'm surprised you didn't return to Virginia after your father's death, and live with your relatives at Black Oaks."

"Never!" Lucinda's eyes flashed angrily. "Aunt Clare was all right, but I never got along with Uncle Joseph, even as a child. Neither did the major, no matter if they were brothers. They were always quarreling over slavery and how the plantation should be run. My

16

father was grandfather's favorite, but Grandfather Jacob always sided with Uncle Joseph when it came to slavery. I haven't been back to Black Oaks since the day Father took us away. I don't even know if my uncle and aunt are still alive—or if Harry is."

"Harry?"

"Aunt Clare's son from a first marriage. I don't suppose he went into the Army. He was born badly crippled. He's probably running the plantation now."

"I don't know about your aunt or stepcousin, but your uncle is very much alive—at least he was six months ago," Baker said. "He has a high position in Richmond in Jefferson Davis' cabinet."

"Trust Uncle Joseph not to be in the fighting," Lucinda said bitterly. "I only wish I could be there to see his face when Union troops march into Richmond."

"That might be a while," Baker said, his voice dry, "at the rate President Lincoln hires and fires generals. The North has been peculiarly unfortunate in not coming up with general officers of the caliber of Lee and Longstreet and Jackson."

Lucinda was no longer listening. She had risen to her feet and went to stand at the slatted window, looking out into the deserted prison yard. Memories that she had kept out of her mind for years suddenly and painfully swept back over her at thought of Black Oaks and the childhood years she had spent on the plantation in the Shenandoah Valley.

One memory in particular. Dora Lee. The young black girl Lucinda had grown up with, more like sisters than mistress and slave, sharing each other's secrets, getting in and out of mischief together. Then those last few months at Black Oaks, Dora Lee had changed, became sullen, withdrawn. Lucinda had planned to find out what was wrong, but then unexpectedly her grandfather had died, and a few weeks later her father had taken Lucinda and her brothers to visit her mother's relatives in New Orleans. When she returned home, Dora Lee was gone. It was her Aunt Clare who nervously told Lucinda that Dora had been sold south.

The major had promised his daughter to look for Dora and buy her back, but under the terms of Jacob Appleton's will, his entire estate had been left to his youngest son, Joseph. The two brothers had had a violent argument, and rather than stay on at the plantation living off his brother's charity, Matthew Appleton had left Black Oaks abruptly and begun a new life as an Indian trader in Michigan. Lucinda had never seen Dora Lee again, although she had grieved for her for years.

Now she realized belatedly that Mr. Baker had asked her a question, and she said, her thoughts returning to the present, "I'm sorry. I was thinking of something else."

"I was wondering how you happened to go into the theater," Laf Baker asked. He didn't need to add, although his expression did, that a stage life was hardly the usual occupation for a well-reared young lady.

Lucinda shrugged indifferently. "I didn't have much choice. I spent what money Father left me nursing Charles, and the school wasn't interested in keeping me without my paying tuition. Then a theatrical troop came through town. The manager liked me, and gave me a small part. I found I had a gift for the work, and here I am." She smiled smugly. "Oh, I know I'll never be a great actress, but I have a knack for mimicking people and memorizing lines, and I sing passably well. And the life's more exciting than teaching or nursing." She giggled with sudden delight. "I guess it's the excitement I like most." Her eyes widened innocently at Mr. Baker. "Why? Don't you think an actress makes a good spy? Look at Pauline Cushman. She was an actress and one of your best secret service agents."

"And she was captured in Shelbyville with stolen documents and sentenced to be hanged. She would have been, too," Baker added grimly, "if Federal troops hadn't reached Shelbyville in time and driven out the rebels. It was Miss Cushman's own fault," he growled angrily. "She'd been warned never to carry incriminating papers or letters on her, to memorize any information she discovered, but she disobeyed instructions."

It was Baker's considered opinion that that was the trouble with using actresses as agents. They treated the deadly game of spying as if it were a stage play and they were the leading actresses in the drama.

"But Miss Cushman was very brave, wasn't see? As brave as any man?"

"Oh, yes, she was brave." Her visitor jerked irritably to his feet. "But a dead spy is of no use to anyone. Remember that, Miss Appleton. Gathering information from the enemy, exposing Southern sympathizers, is a dangerous business, with little glory or honor attached to the job. I know the newspapers have made a great deal of Miss Cushman's exploits, but the valuable agents, the ones who have done the most good for the Union cause, operate in secrecy. They're never written about, never known. Many have been shot or hanged by the enemy, sometimes betrayed by their own people. If I have any word of advice for you, Miss Appleton, it's this. Trust no one. And remember the shadow of the noose hangs at the end of every trail for a spy."

The girl was listening closely, but if there was any fear in her heart, it didn't show in her pale oval face, or large expressive eyes.

Considering her slim figure and the childish excitement that he could sense coiled within her, Baker was once again assailed by doubts. How old was she? he wondered. Eighteen, nineteen at the most. It seemed sheer lunacy to send an untried child into the assignment he had in mind. God knows, she was beautiful enough, with that mass of black hair and silky, peach-white skin, to charm any man into rashly revealing secrets. And he had no doubts of her bravery. But she would need the wit of a serpent to survive the pit of vipers into which he was throwing her. If only he had any other agent as well suited for the job. . . .

As if guessing what he was thinking, Lucinda said quietly, "I'm sure you didn't have me go through that

19

charade on stage tonight, and end up being thrown in prison, simply to lecture me on the perils of spying, Mr. Baker." She smiled coldly. "If you're concerned about me, you needn't be. I'm capable of taking care of myself. And if young Matt is...is dead, then..." She couldn't help shrugging dramatically. "Whether it ends with a rope or a bullet, at least there'll be no one to grieve for me."

"No one?" Lafayette asked, startled. Surely a girl as beautiful as this one had many lovers waiting in the wing.

For a moment the face of Cole Sinclair slipped unwillingly into Lucinda's mind, but then quickly she thrust the memory away. That was long ago, she told herself, a girlish crush long outgrown and better forgotten. "No one," she said firmly.

Lafayette Baker made up his mind. It was a long chance, using the girl, but it was the only one he had. He sat down stiffly and asked, his voice brittle, "Have you heard of Mrs. Arabella Von Bruck?"

Lucinda's eyes widened, surprised. "The lavender countess? Everyone in Washington has heard of her."

Baker smiled thinly. "The possibility that Mrs. Von Bruck is a real countess is extremely doubtful. We do know she came to this country from Germany before the war and married Herman Von Bruck, who made a fortune in the South in banking and land. He had large holdings in Virginia, a plantation near Richmond. When the war began he decided his loyalty lay with the Union, and he moved to Washington, where he died shortly after the war began. His widow bought the old Van Ness house and remained in Washington after her husband's death, entertaining and being entertained widely. Almost every important figure in Washington has been a guest in her home at one time or other."

"You suspect Mrs. Von Bruck of being a Southern sympathizer?" Lucinda asked, startled. "Why, she's given thousands of dollars to buy medical supplies for our hospitals."

"We are positive her sympathies are with the South," Mr. Baker said sharply. "Her home is part of the Southern courier line between Washington and Richmond. Information she secures from her informants in the War Department, from indiscreet remarks dropped by guests at her parties, goes south to Richmond almost daily."

"But if you know all that, why don't you arrest her?"

"For one thing we have no proof, no papers, no documents linking the countess with a spy ring, and she's too important a person to be arrested without some semblance of evidence. And for another, it's not the countess we're interested in. She's simply a dupe, an agent of the real person in charge of this particular courier route."

"You mean there are other routes, too?"

Baker flung out his arms, exasperated. "Washington has more spies than a dog has fleas. As soon as we scotch one group, another springs to life. In addition to Jefferson Davis' spies reporting directly to him in Richmond, almost all the Southern generals have their own spies, or scouts, as they call them, reporting directly to them. And the damnable clever part is that each intelligence ring operates independently from the others. But the silver fox, who operates out of the Von Bruck home, is the most dangerous of the lot."

"The silver fox!" Lucinda giggled. "Now who's being overly theatrical? Surely he has a name."

Baker frowned grimly. "If he has, we don't know it, nor what he looks like. All we know is he slips in and out of Washington as easily as a greased pig. Every foot of the Potomac River is patrolled, and yet he manages to cross without being discovered. We suspect it's information the silver fox brought to Jackson that helped him outflank and defeat General Hooker at Chancellorsville."

"Why haven't you placed an agent in the Von Bruck home before this?"

Lafayette Baker hesitated a moment. Still the girl was entitled to know so that she would be prepared.

21

"We did," he admitted slowly. "He was found two days ago, his body horribly mutilated, floating in the Potomac River, near the Von Bruck home."

"And I'm to take his place?" the girl asked.

Mr. Baker nodded, his face intent. "It's essential we have someone within the house to keep a careful watch on visitors, to find out anything we can about how the ring operates and to accumulate sufficient documentation of traitorous activities so we can arrest Mrs. Von Bruck. Most important, we need more information on the silver fox, what he looks like, his name if possible."

"If I could get such information," Lucinda said slowly, "how would I pass it along to you?"

"There's a peddler who brings fresh fruit and vegetables to the Von Bruck mansion each week. He's one of our best agents. You'll be given the necessary pass phrase so he'll recognize you. He'll bring your information back to me."

"And how do you propose to get me inside the Von Bruck home?" Lucinda smiled faintly. "An actress like Rosalind LaSeur would never be invited to one of the parties the lavender countess gives."

Baker leaned back in his chair. "No, I have another idea. You told me when we first met that you had played in a road show of *Uncle Tom's Cabin*."

Lucinda nodded, puzzled. "Yes, I played Eliza, and once I played Topsy. Of course, it was just a small company that toured the small towns. We never reached Washington or New York." She stared at her chief, her dark eyes sparkling. "Now I see. So that's why you arranged for my arrest and had me brought to Old Capitol."

Baker nodded again. "To all intents and purposes, Rosalina LaSeur—and Lucinda Appleton—have dropped out of sight. You will remain here in this room, completely isolated, learning your new part, perfecting your role. Anything you need will be provided, including our cipher book, which you will learn by heart, then destroy." His eyes narrowed thoughtfully. "I thought of the name Sukey. How does that suit you?"

"Sukey." The girl repeated the name softly, then nodded, pleased. "I like it."

Baker got to his feet. "Good. I'll leave you, then. I know it's rushing things, but will a week be long enough for you to prepare? Frankly, there are spies even here within the prison, and the less time you spend here, the safer you'll be."

"A week will be fine," the girl assured him. Then she grinned, an imp of amusement in her eyes. "I told you, Mr. Baker, I'm a quick study."

Her visitor halted at the door. "I won't be seeing you again until your job's completed. At the end of the week, you'll be slipped in with the rest of the contraband housed in the left wing of the prison—colored men and women who have fled here to Washington and have nowhere else to stay until they find employment. Mrs. Von Bruck must have a hard time keeping servants. Her butler comes here at least once a month looking for gardeners, stable boys and house servants. They tell me he has an eye for a pretty face, so I'm sure he'll have no trouble finding you, Miss Appleton."

Behind him in the darkness, he was startled to hear a low, husky Negroid giggle. A light, almost childish voice asked plaintively, "Who's Miz Appleton, marster?" He turned, surprised. In the pale moonlight filtering through the boarded window, the girl's features were the same, but there was an almost imperceptible difference in her posture, in the way her head hung submissively as she clutched her skirt with her hand, curtsied awkwardly and said, "Mah name is Sukey, suh . . ."

2

Arabella Von Bruck was in a foul mood. Everything had gone wrong. The violinist who was to perform at her masked ball the following Saturday had been unexpectedly conscripted into the Army. Her gown for the ball which she had ordered from Worth's in Paris six months before had yet to arrive—the ship it was on had probably been captured by a Confederate blockade runner. The final blow to arrive with her morning coffee was the news that her personal maid—whose skills at hairdressing had made Arabella the envy of every matron in Washington—had run away during the night and was not to be found anywhere.

"If I ever lay hands on the little bitch, I'll whip her to within an inch of her life," the countess stormed as she sat before the mirror at her gold ormolu dressing table. She was wearing a lavender satin peignoir, almost the exact shade of her violet eyes, and the ecru lace at the neck of the gown had fallen open, revealing the snowy whiteness and rosy nipples of her full, deep breasts.

A slight, pretty Negro girl, her complexion the color of the countess' café au lait but her eyes a pale hazel green, brushed gently at Arabella's intricate mass of tangled curls.

"Ouch!" The brush had snagged painfully in a curl.

Arabella snatched the gold-embossed hair brush from the girl's hand and savagely struck the maid full across the face with the back of the brush. The blow sent the girl reeling against the bedpost, then down on her knees.

Staring at the cowering figure at the foot of the bed, Arabella felt her first pleasure of the day.

"Come here, Jane," she said softly. The threat implicit beneath the softness made the girl hesitate, staring in wide-eyed fear at her mistress.

In the same soft voice but with a smile playing across her exquisitely delicate features, the countess murmured, "Or would you rather I sent for Caesar?"

An ugly bruise forming on her right cheek, the girl approached Arabella and stood mutely before her. Still smiling, her mistress slowly raised the brush and struck the girl deliberately, but just as savagely, across her left cheek. This time the girl staggered but did not fall, helpless tears filling the pale hazel eyes.

An excitement began to fill Arabella, a pleasurable warmth that made her breasts rise and fall rapidly. She raised the brush again when a sound in the doorway made her turn.

A tall, muscular black man, resplendent in full lavender satin livery, and a pretty dark-brown girl in a simple cotton shift stood in the doorway. Although they both must have seen what had happened, only the young girl looked shocked. The man's heavy, coarse features were wooden, his glance indifferent; only for a second his eyes licked greedily at the sight of Arabella's breasts now tumbling completely out of the robe from her exertion.

"Yes, Caesar," the countess said irritably. "What is it?"

Her majordomo indicated the girl at his side. "It's the new maid I picked up at the Old Capitol this morning, madam. I thought you'd want to see her."

"Oh, yes." The countess looked curiously at her new employee. "Come here, girl."

The maid cast a nervous glance toward the other girl in the room and hesitated.

The countess laughed lightly. "Don't be afraid, child. I won't hurt you." Her voice hardened. "As long as you behave yourself and do as you're told, you'll have no problems, and I pay the best wages in Washington. Now come here and let me look at you."

Slowly the girl approached her, her head cast down.

The countess lifted the girl's chin, studying closely the oval, golden-brown face and large, black-fringed eyes. "She is a pretty thing, isn't she, Caesar?" she said and gave the man a knowing glance. "But then she would be, if you picked her, wouldn't she? What is your name, girl?"

"Sukey, ma'am." The girl had the slightly thick Negroid voice, but Arabella noticed at once that the delicately formed mouth was not full enough for a pure Negro and the bridge of cartilage that divided the nostrils of the girl's short, straight nose was too narrow. There was mixed blood there, Arabella decided. Still, a mulatto, when properly trained, often made the most intelligent servant. "Where are you from, Sukey?"

"Virginia, ma'am. Ah belongs to Black Oaks Plantation."

"That's the Appleton place, isn't it?" Arabella said thoughtfully. "My husband and I visited the Appletons before the war." Her mouth tightened. "I suppose you ran away."

The girl's eyes widened. "Oh, no, ma'am! The Yankee soldiers caught me and drug me along...to freedom, they said." Her voice dropped, childishly bewildered. "But ah needs someone to look after me. Ah don't need freedom, ma'am."

The countess studied the girl for a moment longer, then, satisfied, turned back to the dressing-table mirror. "I suppose she'll do, Caesar. Just make sure she behaves herself and minds her own business," she added sharply. She handed the hairbrush back to her maid, ordering, "Hurry and finish my hair, Jane. I've a dozen errands to do this morning."

The maid lifted the brush, her face miserable, when suddenly the new maid, Sukey, piped up eagerly. "Ah'm real good at fixing ladies' hair, ma'am. Ah always took care of Miss Clare, and folks said she had the prettiest hair in the county."

The countess shrugged. "Very well, you can try."

Gratefully, Jane handed the hairbrush to the new maid with a timid smile of relief. Lucinda worked quickly and deftly, silently blessing the fact that in a small theatrical company she had often had to act as hairdresser to the leading lady. Within a few minutes she had twisted a dozen wiry golden curls around her finger, then pulled them into a chignon, catching them within a braided golden coil. A few curls were allowed to escape, as if by chance, and hang in carefully ordered disarray down the nape of Arabella's slender white neck.

The countess preened at her now faultless gold-and-white beauty reflected in the mirror and smiled in grudging approval at her new maid. "Very nice, Sukey. If you're a good girl, I'll think about making you my personal maid."

The girl grinned and dropped a pleased curtsy. "Thank you, ma'am. Ah'd like that fine."

The countess glanced, frowning, at the girl's shapeless cotton shift. "You'll need different clothes. Jane will take care of that. You're much the same size. And she'll show you where you're to sleep."

"Yes, ma'am. Thank you, ma'am." And then, puzzled, "Ah always slept on a pallet outside Miss Clare's door."

Arabella's violet eyes narrowed, her face all at once as cold and hard as porcelain. "In this house," she said sharply, "you will never come near my bedroom unless I ring for you. And there will be no loitering in the hallway outside the door. Do you understand?"

"Yes, ma'am," the girl said, ducking her head, frightened. She scurried out of the bedroom after Jane, following the maid down a spacious hallway, then through a baize door at the end of the hall into a dark, narrow staircase that wound up to the attic of the house. The long attic room was warm and fetid, with only two tiny windows letting in any air, the ceiling uncovered so that great oak rafters could be seen overhead. Thin pallets upon which the servants slept in one long dormitory were flung on the floor, but there were several closed rooms at one side of the floor. The new maid asked curiously, "Who sleeps there?"

"No one," Jane answered. "Miss Arabella stores things in them, trunks and satchels mostly."

One of the storerooms, Lucinda noticed, was directly over the bedroom of the countess. She made a mental note of the information for future reference as Jane showed her to a pallet at one end of the attic. "You can sleep next to me if you like," Jane offered, smiling shyly.

When the maid smiled, her face brightened, and with the sadness gone from her eyes, she looked almost beautiful—except for the two angry bruises forming on either side of her full, pink mouth.

"You should put cold water on your face to take the pain away," Lucinda said sympathetically. Then, impulsively, "Why do you stay here when she treats you so bad? Why don't you run away?"

A numb misery settled over Jane's face, draining it once again of all beauty. "I have to stay," she said wearily.

The new maid looked puzzled. "Why? I heard President Lincoln ain't allowing white folks to have slaves any more."

"Folks in Virginia still have slaves. And Miss Arabella has my two babies at her plantation. If I run away, she swore she'd have them beaten and sold away from me. She would, too." A helpless fury filled the soft young voice. "She's always hated me because my mother was Mist' Herman's favorite for years before he married the countess. Afterwards, he wouldn't sell my mother or me, no matter how Miss Arabella begged him. He wouldn't sell his own blood, he always said. Mist' Herman, he raised me almost like a daughter, teaching me how to speak proper. And when I turned sixteen he let me marry my Troy and gave us our own little cottage. He always promised to give us our freedom, too, when he died, but he wasn't cold in the ground when Miss Arabella sold my mother south to be a field slave."

"I'm surprised she didn't sell you, too."

"She would have, 'cept for Troy. She wanted him so

28

bad it was like an itch she couldn't scratch and it drove her crazy. But Troy never would touch her and I was the only hold she had on him."

Lucinda's eyes widened, shocked. "You mean she wanted..." Her voice fell away, embarrassed. She had, of course, heard whispered stories about white men taking black women. Jane with her hazel-green eyes was undoubtedly the product of just such a liaison. But for a white woman to seek out a black man...

Jane found one of her dresses, a lavender-and-white-striped cotton with a white apron, and handed it to the new maid. "When Miss Arabella favors a man, she's not particular what color he is." Jane's head lifted with unconscious pride, a deep sweet passion pouring into her voice. "And you ain't seen my Troy. No man on the plantation was as big and strong and handsome as my Troy. He could break a man's neck with one hand like it was a twig, and yet pleasure a woman in bed till he pulled the very heart out of you. All the young gals cut their eyes at him, but it was always me Troy wanted, no one else. Only Miss Arabella she wouldn't let him alone."

The girl's eyes shadowed in memory. "She had to be careful when Mist' Herman was alive, but he wasn't dead a week and Miss Arabella had Troy up at the house, making excuses to get him into her bedroom. And there she'd be lying in bed, stark naked. When he still wouldn't so much as touch her, she had him tied and beaten with a cow whip till his back was raw."

Jane's pretty face tightened, but she smiled, almost triumphantly. "No matter how she tormented him, though, my Troy never gave in to her. Until she told him that if he didn't crawl into her bed, she'd have me whipped, too. And that night, Troy ran away. But he'll come back for me someday," Jane said fiercely. "I know he will. If he's alive, he'll come for me and our babies. And that's why Miss Arabella is keeping me, waiting for Troy to come back for me."

Listening to the young slave's story, Lucinda felt her heart ache with sympathy. She reached out and squeezed the girl's hand. "The war can't go on forever, Jane," she said. "And the newspapers say the South lost one of its best generals when Stonewall Jackson was killed at Chancellorsville—"

She broke off abruptly, conscious that her companion was staring at her curiously. "How come you know so much about white folks and what's going on in the war?" Jane asked suspiciously. "Ah never heard tell of a slave reading newspapers."

Lucinda berated herself silently. How could she be so stupid, forgetting so quickly the role she was playing, like the most amateur ingenue in some third-rate production?

She tossed her head saucily. "Well, you ain't the onliest one brought up proper. Miss Clare taught me my letters. As for wa' talk, don't you think I got ears? What else do white folks ever talk about?"

"You'd better not listen too closely to white folks, not in this house," Jane warned sharply. "Or you'll end up in the cellar, like . . ." She fell silent.

"Like what, Jane?" Lucinda asked innocently.

"Never you mind what." The girl frowned. "Just mind your own business. And stay clear of Caesar or you'll be sorry. That man's mean, clean through."

"Oh, ain't no man I can't handle," the new maid said, giggling coquettishly.

Nevertheless, remembering the deliberate way the man's eyes had flicked over her body in the Old Capitol courtyard, making her feel as if she were standing before him without a stitch of clothes on, Lucinda had every intention of staying out of Caesar's way.

The next morning, though, as she was leaving Miss Arabella's bedroom after helping her mistress with her morning toilette, Caesar was waiting for her in the hallway. Smiling broadly, his arms reached out to encircle the girl's tiny waist. Before she could slip away, he crushed her slim body against his great purple-satin-covered chest. Then two things happened in rapid succession. The girl's knee jerked upward, bringing a howl of pain from the majordomo, and at the same moment her hands clawed at his face, leaving a streak of blood dripping down one cheek.

Caesar's hands fell away. He stared, at first dumbfounded, then enraged, at the tiny slip of a girl who stood defiantly before him, her hands on her hips, a taunting smile on her face.

"Ain't no man touches me, less'n I wants him to," she said sweetly.

Unaccustomed to being thwarted, the majordomo lunged forward like an angry bull, his hand lifted, curled in a massive black fist. Then behind him in the doorway, the countess drawled, amused, "It seems our little kitten has claws, Caesar."

She was drawing on a pair of short lavender kid gloves which matched the moire gown she wore, the great crinoline skirt and tucked bodice delicately embroidered with sprigs of lilac. Several golden curls fell artfully from beneath her velvet lilac bonnet with its brim of white bengaline, framing her beautiful heart-shaped face.

"The li'l she-cat needs to be taught a lesson," the man mumbled indignantly, glaring at Sukey.

"Perhaps," the countess agreed indifferently. "But not now. I need you to do an errand with me in town this morning, Caesar." She gave the man a sharp glance. "And don't think I don't know why my last maid ran away. I saw the bruises on her body from your courting, Caesar. I want Sukey to stay awhile. Do you understand?"

When her majordomo continued to glare murderously, his mistress repeated her words, this time a razor's edge to her voice. "Do you understand, Caesar?"

He turned toward her, his eyes still blinded with rage, but he nodded obediently. "Yessum, I understand."

She laughed lightly, reaching up to brush his scratched cheek with her daintily gloved hand. "There, there, Caesar, don't sulk. Perhaps later you can have your fun. Now come along or I'll be late for my appointment."

Caesar cast one last malevolent glance at Sukey, then followed his mistress as the countess glided gracefully toward the staircase, leaving behind her a fragrance of lavender which hung like a cloud in the hallway. Now that the danger was passed, Lucy discovered she was trembling.

In a few seconds, however, she had recovered sufficiently to hurry to the hall window and watch the countess mount into her silver-and-lavender carriage, while Caesar sat up beside the coachman, who was clad in purple velvet livery.

As soon as the carriage had disappeared down the road, the girl rushed up to the attic and slipped into the trunk-storage room. Shoving aside a trunk and several carpetbags, she knelt on the dusty floor and began to jab and poke at the wooden floor with a heavy knife she had stolen earlier from the kitchen. The wood was dry and rotten with age, but it was an hour's work before she reached the gold-flaked, rococo plastered ceiling in the countess' bedroom. The work of digging the hole went more quickly then, the plaster crumbling beneath her knife blade.

As soon as she had finished the hole, she returned to the second floor, and after making sure there were no servants in the hall, she darted into Arabella's bedroom. The second-floor maid had not cleaned the room yet. The room was in tumbled disarray. Pearl powder was spilled on the dressing table, rouge pots stood open, while a sheer-as-a-spiderweb nightgown was dropped on the floor by the bed.

As she had expected, the digging at the gilded ceiling had left small mounds of plaster on the flowered lavender rug. She gathered up the debris and flung it out the window. She debated making a quick search for incriminating documents hidden in the bedroom, then decided it would be too risky. The countess might return at any minute, and the cleaning girl was due shortly, too. Lucinda decided she would do her searching of the room the night of the masked ball, instead.

She had already been told she would be expected to

help serve the guests at the ball, but she was sure she could slip away during the festivities without her absence being noticed. In the meantime, she would see what she could discover, keeping an eye on Arabella Von Bruck's bedroom. Since the countess was so insistent that all servants stay out of the room without her express permission to enter, Lucinda was convinced that the bedroom must be the place where the countess kept her rendezvous with Confederate agents.

An eager anticipation coursed through Lucinda, a smile curving her lips, as she descended the servants' stairs. If only she could be the one who unmasked Mr. Baker's special *bête noir*, the silver fox. What a feather in her cap it would be! And it would show Mr. Baker that she could be just as useful and effective an agent as any man, she thought, her dark eyes sparkling, before she adjusted her face to a properly demure expression and entered the kitchen to join the other servants.

Each night for the rest of the week, after she was sure the other servants were sound asleep on their pallets in the attic, Lucinda crept silently to the trunk room, easing the door quietly shut behind her.

It was uncomfortable, stretched out on the hard, dusty floor, her eye pressed to the small opening. Lucinda fervently hoped that the mice she could hear skittering about the rafters above her would not descend to the floor. However, aside from discovering that the countess liked to roam her bedroom naked as a jaybird, and that her full white breasts had a tendency to sag, Lucinda could discover nothing damaging happening in the room.

Then the third night, her muscles cramped and aching from lying on the attic floor and watching Arabella sit at her desk writing industriously for more than an hour, Lucinda had her first success. Arabella folded the papers she had been writing, then lifted the rug beside her bed, exposing the hardwood floor beneath. Counting a half dozen boards over, she pressed the edge of one dovetailed board in the floor. The board lifted in her hand, revealing a small opening beneath the floor. The woman inserted the papers into the opening, then replaced the board and rug.

For a change Arabella had been wearing a hyacinth-colored silk robe in her room, although it was a warm, humid night. Now she let the robe drift to the floor as she went to the wall and tugged at the embroidered bellpull. Almost immediately, as if he had been waiting outside the door, Caesar came into the room.

Arabella yawned and stretched out upon the satin coverlet of the bed. "I wanted to make sure that everything was ready for the ball tomorrow night ... and our special guests. Did you pick up the boots?"

"Yessum." Caesar stood, his face impassive, gazing down at his mistress.

"And some of Herman's French champagne, I think, to make our French guest feel at home." She made a contemptuous mouth. "I've no doubt the fine wine will be wasted on the Englishman. Still, it's important we make a good impression on our guests. God knows the South needs the money."

"What time will they be here?" Caesar asked.

"I have no idea. You know he never gives me any details. It's safer that way." She laughed softly. "Probably they'll be brought into the house as part of the guests during the ball. I imagine that's why he wanted me to have this masked ball, so no one would notice our visitors."

She stretched again, lazily, her body moving sensuously against the pale-lilac silk coverlet. As she raised her hands languidly above her golden head, her breasts lifted, the rosy nipples growing taut. The violet-shaded eyes glittered as they watched the man standing beside her bed. Caesar's body was immobile, as if carved from ebony, except for a flaring of the thick nostrils. At last Arabella smiled and beckoned arrogantly. "Now, Caesar."

In almost one movement, the man shed his shirt and trousers. Before Lucinda could turn her horrified gaze away, the black muscular thighs and hips were cov-

34

ering the soft white body, legs spread apart, waiting, on the bed. Just before the black body descended upon her, Arabella's pink-nailed hand flashed out and ripped cruelly down Caesar's cheek, drawing blood. She laughed lightly, teasingly. "That's so you'll bear my mark, too."

With a mingled moan of rage and passion, the black body bore down upon the bed, the powerful hips thrusting cruelly as if hammering a spike into the soft whiteness writhing beneath him. Lucinda, her face red-hot with embarrassment, tore her gaze away and stumbled to her feet and back to her bed.

From the next pallet, Jane muttered sleepily, "Something wrong?"

"No," Lucinda whispered, a sour taste in her mouth, desperately fighting the queasiness in the pit of her stomach, as if any moment she might be sick there in that hot, foul-smelling attic.

The next morning the whole Von Bruck household was a beehive of activity. Servants scurried in all directions, readying the house for the ball that night. All the furniture was removed from the drawing room so that it could be used for dancing, and then buckets of colored sand were spread over the polished floor and arranged in a delicate mosaic of flowers and birds, a beautifully designed work of art which would be destroyed by the first sweep of crinolines dragging across the floor.

The summer kitchen was in an uproar, with the cook shouting orders and taking an impatient broom handle to scullery maids who did not move fast enough. In the midst of the hubbub, the new maid, Sukey, slipped quietly out the back door. A peddler with a load of produce piled upon hay in his wagon was waiting not far from the summer kitchen.

As Sukey walked toward the wagon, she stopped and casually plucked a white rose from a bush rambling over the icehouse. She tucked the rose into her shining blue-black hair, then cast a flirtatious smile at the peddler.

"Does you have any peaches?" she asked, rising on tiptoe to peer into the wagon.

The peddler was a tall, rangy man, his rust-colored beard stained with tobacco, his skin like leather dried too long in the sun. One eye was covered with a black eyepatch, but the other, the color of gunmetal, seemed to bore right through her.

"Too early for peaches, missy," he drawled. Then he showed a row of yellowed teeth as he smiled and said softly, "That's a pretty rose you have there. Almost as pretty as you are."

Sukey replied carefully, "They say white roses stand for freedom."

The peddler answered in the same soft voice, "And red roses for union." Then, making sure they were alone, he asked, "Anything to report?"

"I'm not sure. I heard Mrs. Von Bruck talking about some special guests slipping into the party tonight, a Frenchman and an Englishman, and something about money. Does that mean anything to you?"

The peddler nodded. "They'll be the representatives from France and England, sent to talk to the government in Richmond about negotiating a loan to the Confederacy. We heard they were coming from our agents in London and Paris."

"I thought England and France were neutral."

Her companion spat a stream of tobacco expertly into the grass beside him. "Don't know about the froggies, but the mills in England need Southern cotton badly."

"How will the men manage to make their way south through our lines?" Lucinda asked, puzzled.

"A Southern courier will take them, maybe even the silver fox himself." The peddler's face hardened. "Now, that's a fox I'd like to trap. As for getting through our lines, all sorts of people do every day, lots of them with secesh sympathies. All they have to do is take the loyalty oath to the Union."

"You'll be able to stop them now, though, won't you?"

"Mebbe," the man said cautiously. "But there was

36

a terrible hullabaloo raised when we grabbed Mason and Slidell off that British ship back in '61. Maybe old Abe won't want to ruffle the feathers of England and France again by snatching their envoys, even unofficial ones."

"If the men do show up," Lucinda asked, worried, "how will I let you know?"

"I've got a place in the woods behind the house. I stay there most nights. If you put a candle in the north attic window, I'll see it."

He looked over his shoulder to make sure they were still alone, then asked, "Anything else?"

She hesitated. "There's something strange about the cellar in the house. The servants are afraid to go down there. They say they've heard groans and screams coming from there. They think it's haunted. I sneaked down there the other morning, but I couldn't see anything, except an empty room that has bolts in the walls, as if it was used to chain people, maybe slaves in the old days."

Despite the warmth of the June day, a shiver passed through Lucinda, remembering the chill of terror she had felt in that room, a miasma of fear that she could feel in her bones, as real as the dank noisome air imprisoned in the room. She couldn't wait to leave, to hurry back up the stairs to the warmth and light of the kitchen.

The peddler studied the young girl's face and asked gently, "Are you afraid, missy?"

"No," she said quickly, then sheepishly, "Yes, I reckon I am."

"Ain't no shame in being afraid," the man said gruffly. "Shows common sense. If you want to, you can pull out right now."

Lucinda took a deep, steadying breath and smiled faintly. "No. No, I'll stay. I made a peephole from the attic into Mrs. Von Bruck's bedroom. I'm sure, whoever the men are, they'll be meeting there tonight after the party. Oh, I almost forgot. I saw Mrs. Von Bruck hide some papers under the floorboards by her bed. Would

37

you pass the word along to Mr. Baker? I'm going to try to find out what they are tonight, during the ball."

The man nodded soberly. "Be careful, missy. I've heard of that Von Bruck female. She's a bad 'un, cut your heart out while she's smiling like an angel all the while." Then, without even a break in his tone, he continued, only more loudly, "Pretty little gal like you, be glad to bring you peaches next time I come, if I have to go clear to Georgia for them."

Lucinda turned and saw Caesar bearing down upon them, his face baleful as he glared suspiciously from the peddler to the new maid. "Whuffo you hanging round with this peddler man?" he demanded of Sukey. "Ain't you got 'nuf chores in the house to keep you busy?"

"Was just fetching some melons for you, Mr. Caesar," the girl said, smiling flirtatiously at the majordomo. "Cook says you've got a powerful craving for melons."

Put off guard by the radiance of that provocative smile, Caesar muttered darkly, "Ain't melons I got a craving for, girl," and made a grab for the enticing young maid with the wide velvet eyes and supple body, its curves barely hidden by the simple cotton dress she wore.

The girl twisted gracefully out of harm's way, then, giggling, tossed the melons toward the man. "Catch, Caesar!" And while he fumbled to catch the melons before they struck him, she laughed lightly and darted away toward the safety of the house.

The rest of the day Sukey was kept too busy with her duties as personal maid to have time to think about the two mysterious guests who would be appearing at the party that evening. Arabella began dressing for the ball two hours before the first guests were to arrive. First she soaked in her Italian-marble bathtub, liberally splashed with perfumed oils, then her whole body was gently massaged with rose water and glycerine, before she donned lace pantalets, muslin corset cover and the hoopskirt like a webbed cage, flattened in the front and billowing out in the rear, held together by steel wires and tapes.

Then she clung to the bedpost, her waist encircled by a small whaleboned corset, and cursed loudly in German as Sukey tugged and jerked with all her might to pinch Arabella's twenty-inch waist to a painful eighteen inches. After that came several layers of flounced silk petticoats and finally the ball gown itself, miraculously arrived from Paris only the day before.

The watered-silk gown was the color of lustrous amethyst, brocaded in purple velvet. The tight-V-necked basque was cut so low that Arabella's ample breasts were in danger of spilling out of the bodice if she curtsied too deeply. A necklace of amethysts and diamonds circled her softly rounded neck, and amethysts and diamonds glittered in teardrops from her earlobes.

At the last moment the French hairdresser, François, from Madame Delarue's, arrived at the Von Bruck mansion. The small, nervous man was flushed and out of breath from rushing to a dozen other fashionable homes that evening, arranging the hair of guests who had been invited to the ball. Although Arabella was furious that he was late, she was forced to hold her temper, because it was well known that François, who had once dressed the royal heads of Europe, had a fiery temperament to match her own.

Swiftly now he brushed glittering gold dust through Arabella's lemon-yellow hair, then attached a frame of horsehair to the back of Arabella's head. The golden hair was then brushed smoothly over and under the frame in the waterfall coiffeur so popular in wartime Washington. A diamond-studded invisible hairnet was slipped over the waterfall to hold it in place, and several small diamond hair pins were also tucked into the silken coronet arranged above Arabella's smooth white forehead.

At last finished, the hairdresser stepped back and

murmured approvingly, "The Empress Eugénie could not look more beautiful, madame."

Studying her reflection in the mirror, Arabella nodded in agreement, her violet eyes sparkling beneath the delicately winged eyebrows. Tonight, she thought, a familiar half-painful, half-pleasant ache spreading through her body in anticipation, she should have no trouble coaxing Cole into her bed. The fact that he had held out against her manifold charms in the past would only make the triumph tonight more delicious. She might, she decided, smiling to herself, even make him beg and grovel a little before allowing him to possess her, just to pay him back for making her wait so long.

"Thank you, monsieur," she said, smiling graciously and handing the hairdresser a half dozen gold coins before sweeping with regal dignity from the room.

Most of the guests had already arrived, the carriages standing two deep outside the portico of the mansion, when the maid, Sukey, her blue-black hair covered by a snowy kerchief and wearing a pale-lilac cotton uniform, was sent from the kitchen to help with the serving. Black-frocked diplomats, senators and representatives, military officers in gold braid and scarlet sashes, none below the rank of general, along with distinguished citizens crowded the great hall of the Von Bruck mansion. The women guests' rainbow-colored gowns bedecked with flowers and jewels swirled in a kaleidoscope of color through the hall.

Sukey circulated among the guests, carrying a silver tray with crystal glasses filled with champagne punch, and listened closely to catch a French or English accent that might reveal behind their masks the foreign agents on their way to Richmond. Or perhaps the carelessly dropped rash words of a Southern sympathizer hidden behind a Union face.

Snatches of conversation came her way:

"My dear, you should have seen her gown at her last levee, so garish and vulgar ... and they say she makes Mr. Lincoln's life a perfect hell with her shrewish temper ..."

"...saw the dispatches myself...Lee's already crossed north into Maryland...rebel guerrillas skirmishing across the Potomac from the capital...all Fighting Joe Hooker does is retreat...Washington will be a sitting duck for Lee...."

"Vicksburg should fall any day...that Grant ...now there's a fighting man...of course, they say he's drunk half the time..."

"Did you hear what old Abe said the other day? He only wished he had a half dozen more generals who drank, as long as they could fight like Grant!"

At eleven o'clock Mrs. Von Bruck, on the arm of Secretary of War Stanton, led the way into the dining room, where a long, gleaming table groaned under the weight of platters of turkey, ham, duck, pheasant and lobster. In the center of the table was one of the spectacular spun-sugar masterpieces concocted for Washington hostesses by Gautier. The countess' magnificent creation was a copy of the American frigate *Union* with forty guns and all sails set, supported by nougat cherubs draped in the Stars and Stripes.

As soon as the guests began eating and she was sure Arabella was busily occupied with supper companions, Lucinda slipped out of the dining room and up the back staircase to the second floor. Caesar, she knew, would not be patrolling the hall before Arabella's bedroom tonight. He was still in the dining room, as proud as a peacock in his purple satin livery, keeping a watchful, important eye on the dining-room activities.

Nevertheless, she removed her shoes before she stepped into the darkened bedroom—Arabella's scent still hung in the air like an invisible presence—and did not dare to light a lamp. Someone might notice the light beneath the door. Her feet made no sound on the deep carpet as she swiftly crossed the room toward the bed. Then suddenly she stopped short, a pulse in her temple pounding. An unreasoning but frightening conviction gripped her that she was not alone in the room. She heard it then, a soft whispering sound behind her,

41

and whirled—too late. A hand suddenly descended over her face and pressed tightly, suffocatingly against her mouth.

3

The more Lucinda fought against the hand clamped over her mouth, the tighter its grip became. In addition, an arm had circled her slim waist like a steel band, squeezing the breath out of her. She struggled frantically for air, her lungs straining, a darkness roaring in her head. Gradually, as her struggles weakened, she heard a man's voice, as if from a great distance. "Don't cry out and I'll let you go."

She nodded and was released so suddenly she swayed and fell to her knees on the countess' thick-carpeted floor.

"Let's have a look at you."

She could not see the man's face in the darkness, but his voice—there was something disturbingly familiar about that soft, dispassionate drawl.

He had lit the rose lamp beside Arabella's bed, and now he lifted it, the light shining fully down into Lucinda's face. His own face was half hidden in the darkness behind the lamp. Even so, she recognized him at once and felt a shock, as if she had been plunged suddenly into icewater. It had been six years since she had last seen Cole Sinclair, but it might have been yesterday so indelibly was his face imprinted in her mind—the narrow blue-green eyes, the slashing black brows, the short dark curly hair lying flat against the skull. The face was older than she remembered, and harder, as if the years between had beaten all the softness out of it, the high, sharp cheekbones almost cutting through the bronze skin. The long-boned, broad-shouldered body was thinner than she remembered, too, with the hard muscular thighs and taut whipcord look of a man who spent much of his life in the saddle.

He was smiling down at her, a lazy, sardonic smile, and, oh, how well she remembered that smile. How it could turn her bones to cotton, fill her gawky, coltish body with painful, vague yearnings—hopeless yearnings, of course, because to Cole she was simply Charles' baby sister, tagging after him, always in the way. She thought she had outgrown those foolish, childish yearnings. Now as those aquamarine eyes traveled slowly over her face and body, she could feel her breath come faster, and those same bittersweet longings spread a delicious warmth through her body, as if nothing had changed. Nothing at all.

Then, belatedly, she realized it was not Cole's face that should concern her; it was her own. Had he seen the look of shock that must have been there when she recognized him, heard her faint, whispered "Cole"? And even more damaging, could he possibly have recognized her, even through her disguise?

Apparently not, for there was no flash of recognition in his face or voice as he ordered curtly, "Get up."

She scrambled slowly to her feet, ducking her head as she pretended to straighten her skirt over her slim hips, adjust the snowy kerchief on her head, snatching those few seconds to compose her face and thoughts. When she lifted her face again to the man, it was only that of a frightened, not too bright, pretty black girl, who stammered softly, "Please, suh, don't hurt me."

"That depends," Cole said grimly. "What the hell are you doing in Countess Von Bruck's bedroom?"

"Ah works here. Ah'm Miss Arabella's personal maid."

"I've met Arabella's maid. Her name is Mary, and she's a good foot taller than you."

Lucinda shrugged. "That gal, she done run off a week ago."

Cole scowled. "That still doesn't explain what you were doing, sneaking into the bedroom. Did the countess give you permission to come up here, alone?"

The maid poked her toe into the thick flowered carpet, her eyes cast down, her voice a whimper. "No, suh, she never did." Her wide dark eyes were bright with tears as she lifted her gaze pleadingly to the man. The

44

tears were real enough, for she discovered she was frightened, frightened to death of this man who was not the Cole Sinclair she knew, but a menacing stranger towering over her. "Please, suh, you won't tell her you caught me here. She'd beat me sure if she knew."

"And I'll beat you for sure if you don't tell me the truth," Cole said irritably. "And stop sniveling! What's your name?"

"Sukey, please, suh."

"Where are you from?"

"Virginny." She hesitated a split second. She was taking a fearful chance, but she had no choice. The countess would be sure to tell Cole if he asked her about Sukey's former owner, and it would be worse if she were caught in a lie. "Ah belonged with the Appletons at Black Oaks till the Yankee soldiers carried me off."

"You're lying," Cole snapped. "I know the Appleton place. I've never seen you there."

Lucinda thought quickly. She couldn't recall Cole's visiting the slave quarters on his visits to Black Oaks, nor could he possibly know by sight the more than one hundred slaves that worked on the plantation. And surely the war would have kept Cole too busy for any neighborly visits to Black Oaks lately. Now that she thought of it, why wasn't Cole in uniform? She remembered hearing that Cole had enlisted the day Virginia had left the Union. For that matter, what was Cole doing in Mrs. Von Bruck's bedroom?

She took a deep, tremulous breath. Well, she'd think about that later, she told herself. Right now, all that mattered was that Cole believe her story. "It's the truf, suh," she insisted stubbornly. "Ah worked for Miss Clare and Mist' Joseph before the war."

"Who else lived at the big house?"

The black eyes widened innocently. "Well, there was Mr. Harry, Miss Clare's son. He had a bad arm, so I reckon the Army didn't want him." Her brow furrowed in thought. "There was some other white folks at Black

45

Oaks, Mist' Joseph's brother and his fam'ly, but they left before the war."

It was possible, Cole thought. The girl could have been a slave at Black Oaks. He frowned, uncertain. Something about the girl still didn't ring true. "You haven't explained yet what you're doing here, sneaking into your mistress' bedroom."

Lucy cast her eyes down submissively, allowing a childishly wistful note to creep into her voice. "Miss Arabella's perfume, suh. Ah wanted to put a dab on. It's a powerful love potion. But Miss Arabella, she wouldn't like my touching her perfume, so I waited till supper was served. Miss Arabella tol' me she wouldn't need me to undress her tonight after the party, so I didn't spec' she'd ever know." The quick tears returned. The dark eyes behind the fringe of thick lashes shone as if stars were caught in their depths. She gazed anxiously up into the man's cold, masklike face. "You ain't goin' to tell on me, are you, suh?"

Cole hesitated. The story sounded plausible enough. And the girl evidently was acquainted with the Appleton plantation. Still, an instinct which had never betrayed him made him wary. After all, Union spies had been known to blacken their faces and pretend to be Negro servants. And someone could have told the girl about Black Oaks. Most importantly, Cole Sinclair did not underestimate Lafayette Baker. He was sure that Baker would try to plant a spy in the Von Bruck household.

"Take off your clothes," he said coldly.

The girl's eyes widened, startled. "Wha ... what for, suh?"

He smiled lazily, but the smile did not touch the wintry blue-green eyes. "Because I say so. Or would you rather I sent for your mistress?"

A flush rose beneath the girl's golden-brown skin. Her small hands moved tentatively toward the buttons that ran in a neat row down the front of her gown. She gave the man an imploring glance from her great dark eyes. "Please, suh ..."

"I won't ask again," he said, his voice dangerously soft as he reached for the embroidered bellpull beside the bed.

The girl's graceful brown hands moved quickly then. In a few seconds the buttons opened and the dress fell with a soft whispering sound around her feet, followed by a thin cotton shift. She wore no other undergarments. For a moment her arms moved as if to cover her nakedness, then they fell to her side. She stood, willow-slim and proud before him, her young breasts softly rounded and carried high, the nipples a pale pink against the golden-brown flesh.

Cole Sinclair felt a sudden, sharp stab of pleasure gazing at the girl. She was a rare beauty, no doubt of that. Lifting the lamp higher so that its light fell full upon the slim figure standing before him, he saw that there was also no doubt that the pale-brown skin, the sheen of satin with rich undertones of gold, was the same shade on the tempting breasts and seductively curved hips and thighs as it was on the girl's face.

He reached for her hand. She started to pull away, then quietly let him take her hand and hold it closer to the lamp so that he could see the bluish half-moons at the base of the fingernails.

Well, she was a Negress then, Cole thought, but there was white blood there, too. It could be seen in the delicacy of the girl's features, the soft blue-black tendrils of hair that had escaped from her kerchief and curled around the lovely oval face.

He was surprised to discover that the small hand resting in his own was trembling. Looking up, he found the wide, lustrous dark eyes staring at him were filled with a mixture of fear and rage. Yet he was aware of something else gleaming in their depths, pinpricks of desire like golden flecks, that stirred an answering warmth in his loins and reminded him, forcefully, of how long it had been since he'd held a woman in his arms. Too damn long, he decided suddenly.

Placing the lamp on a table beside him, he reached out for the girl. She tried to twist away from him, but he moved quickly and lithely as a cat, and the next moment she was imprisoned again in his arms. His mouth covered hers, at first gently teasing against her lips, then caressing slowly the sweep of silken lashes, the warm hollow in her throat where a pulse beat rapidly, then back to linger on the soft curves of her lips, waiting for her passion to mount and match his. When she remained strangely passive, unresponsive in his arms, with her lips pressed tightly shut against his, his left hand suddenly caught her two hands behind her back while his right hand snatched off the snowy kerchief. Then his hand fastened on the neat black coil of hair resting on the nape of her neck and yanked her head cruelly back so he could see her face. Her eyes looking up at him were black, opaque pools in a face that was terribly still.

He laughed softly. "So it's coaxing you're needing," he murmured.

Still trapping her arms behind her with one hand, he used his other hand to trace slowly, expertly, a path from the soft furry blackness beneath the gentle curve of her stomach, trailed the fingers upward to the swelling of her breasts, firm and yet soft as feathers as he cupped them in his hand. Gently then he caressed a pale-pink nipple while the narrow sea-green eyes never once left her face, waiting until he heard the sudden, sharp indrawn breath as the nipple grew taut beneath his hand, saw the golden flecks swimming closer and closer to the surface, until finally, almost against her will, the cry of pleasure parted her lips and he pulled her roughly to him. This time her lips were not closed but open and eager beneath his as his tongue explored their silken softness, then thrust within, again and again, as he lifted her in his arms and placed her on Arabella's bed.

"One minute, Sukey, my sweet," he whispered, as he pulled free of the hands clasped tightly around his neck.

As he stripped off his shirt and loosened his trousers, the girl on the bed stirred, almost drowsily. Sukey?

48

Who was Sukey? Like a veil pulled abruptly, rudely away, memory returned. She shivered as if a cold wind had passed over her body, cooling the fever that had set her blood on fire, her flesh burning at Cole's touch. She was Lucinda Marie Theresa Appleton, not some poor helpless slave girl whose body could be used by any passing white man for his amusement. What was happening to her? How could she have forgotten that it wasn't herself, Lucinda Appleton, that Cole desired? It was a pretty colored girl named Sukey.

In the darkness she heard him moving again toward the bed, saw the gleaming white of his flat, muscular body where the bronze skin of his sunburned face and neck ended. Terrified now, her body icy cold at the thought of what was about to happen, she rolled over, twisted off the bed and made a desperate dash for the door.

She had almost made it when once again she felt an arm whip out, circle her waist and pull her, kicking and clawing, to the floor.

"No! Please ... don't. ..."

A hand clamped down again over her mouth, while another arm across her breasts pinned the girl's struggling body to the floor.

"Hush, Sukey." Cole's voice was lazily amused. "As much as I'm sure I'd enjoy it, we've no time for games. And I have no desire to have your mistress find us together. Arabella has a short temper."

His hand loosened on the girl's mouth. "Now be a good girl, and—"

An oath suddenly exploded in the silence of the room as the girl's teeth closed, hard, upon Cole's hand, drawing blood. Her hands, freed, reached up to claw savagely at his face.

Just in time he caught the hands, pulled them above her head and pinioned them against the rug with his one hand. Then, before she could lift her legs to kick, he had rolled over on top of her.

"Why, you little vixen!" His voice was still amused, but there was a core of anger there now. "So you're two

49

of a kind, you and your mistress. It's the rough bit you like, not the sugar. Well, you shall have it."

Roughly then he thrust her legs apart while his hand moved freely, cruelly over her body, bruising the soft breasts, the silky thighs, until she moaned with mingled pain and passion, the two so intermingled it was impossible to tell where one began and the other ended.

Then, to her horror, she suddenly felt an unfamiliar hardness between her thighs. Frantically she tried to roll her hips away, but the hardness pressed against her, found the entrance it was seeking, then thrust all at once inward. Her body arched upward against his. There was no more wild passion then, only a surge of pain splitting her body. A scream rose to her lips but was smothered by his mouth covering hers, drawing the breath out of her body.

Then when she was sure she could endure the pain no longer, it was over. The weight of his body was gone, and she lay, limp, too exhausted to move. After a few minutes she heard him get to his feet, pad over to the table and return with the lamp in his hand. He placed it on the carpet beside her, the light limning her lovely golden-brown body, and he saw the shine of unshed tears in her wide, staring eyes gazing up at him.

He knelt down beside her and touched her cheek gently, his voice gruffly tender. "Sorry, Sukey . . ."

When his lips lightly caressed the heart-shaped mole beneath her left breast, she flinched. His eyes narrowed to angry slits, not at the girl but at himself. But how could he have known she would be a virgin? he thought, baffled. A young slave, as exquisitely lovely and desirable as this one—how was it possible that some black buck or white man hadn't had his way with her before this? And it wasn't that she hadn't wanted him, at least in the beginning. She had been as eager as he. He could still remember the shape and feel of her mouth, moving warm and ardent beneath his, her slender body clinging to him as if she couldn't be close enough.

His eyes once more traveled over the girl's disturbing beauty, the skin with a soft satin sheen, flawless, except for the beginnings of dull, purple-black bruises where his hands had punished her. And for the first time in years, gazing at the girl, Cole Sinclair felt the stirrings of tenderness and compassion, emotions which he had thought the brutal war years had ruthlessly driven out of him. It was uncomfortable, he discovered, allowing himself to feel again. Uncomfortable, he thought grimly, and dangerous. There was no place in a war, or in his job, for pity or affection. They could destroy him.

Quickly now he got to his feet and pulled on his clothes. When he came back to the girl, she had staggered to her feet, but her eyes were still blurred and frightened.

He handed her her clothes. "Get dressed," he ordered brusquely.

Obediently, without a word, she pulled the shift and shapeless cotton dress over her head and slipped on her shoes. When she had finished, he nodded toward the door. "Now I'd suggest you leave, at once." A note of wry amusement crept into his voice. "And keep your mouth shut, Sukey. Your mistress would take a whip to you, for sure, if she learned what took place here this evening."

With her clothes safely back on, Lucinda could feel the fear leaving her, and a white-hot, blazing rage taking its place. Never in her life could she remember feeling as angry as she felt at that moment as she pulled the tattered remnants of her dignity about her and stalked to the door.

At the door, Cole stopped her and pushed several gold coins into her hand, smiling at her with the old lazy arrogance. "Buy yourself a pretty new dress, Sukey," he said absently.

She stared down at the coins in her hands, and her anger rose, like gall, in her throat. "Keep your damn money!" she hissed, and flung the coins as hard as she could into his hateful, smiling face. Then she turned and ran from the room, slamming the door behind her.

51

It was only when she had reached the attic and flung herself down on the straw pallet that a torrent of weeping shook her like a summer storm. The tears weren't only from shock and pain, but something more, the loss of a precious, romantic illusion she had cherished from the first moment she had laid eyes on Cole Sinclair, as a young girl. Finally, wearily, she pulled herself to her feet, filled a bowl with water and washed herself thoroughly from head to foot.

When she had finished, she studied her face curiously in the small, cracked mirror above the washbasin. The girls at the finishing school had always sworn that you could tell afterwards, in a girl's eyes, when she'd lost her virginity, but she couldn't see any difference. All she could see in her eyes was the anger banked there, burning like a golden flame deep in the lustrous blackness. The same anger burned inside her. She nourished the anger, as if the flame cleansed her of the humiliation and degradation she felt, in the same way that the cooling basin bath had removed the feel of Cole's touch from her skin.

But not completely, she thought, shivering, remembering against her will the breathless excitement that had possessed her when he first kissed her, her treacherous body responding eagerly, as if it could not get enough of his touch, his caresses, the wonder that Cole Sinclair, whom she'd worshiped from afar for almost as long as she could remember, was actually holding her in his arms, making love to her.

She stepped away from the mirror, giggling a little hysterically. No, not Lucinda Appleton. It was a black maid named Sukey that Cole had held in his arms. No gentleman would ever treat a white woman the way Cole had treated Sukey, taking her brutally, callously, without warmth or affection, then just as indifferently tossing her aside. And for the first time, Lucinda began to sense how a colored woman must feel at the hands of her white masters, the frustrated rage, the humiliation and helplessness. Well, it must change, she thought fiercely, pacing up and down the narrow passageway between the empty pallets. When the North won the war, and slavery was finally ended, it would change.

What had happened between Cole and her was over, and perhaps in time she would forget. But what wasn't over was her mission here in this house. She had already wasted valuable time indulging in futile self-pity, crying over a lost, childishly romantic dream. There was too much to do. And she might already have been missed downstairs. She didn't dare let Caesar start wondering where she was.

She straightened her dress, retied the kerchief over her hair, then hurried back downstairs to slip into the kitchen for a tray of drinks, then mingled once more with the guests. The ball was at its peak, the musicians playing a gay schottische, the dance floor like a garden of flowers with the swaying, colorful hoopskirts of the women dancing. Drinks had already been liberally consumed by some of the male guests, who tried to grab at Sukey's tiny waist as she passed, or a softer, more tempting part of her body. Skillfully, giggling coquettishly, she managed to elude their grasps. After midnight the guests unmasked, but although Lucinda studied each face, she could not find Cole's among the guests.

The questions she had had no time to consider earlier returned. Why? Why wasn't Cole in uniform? And if he was a guest at the ball, why was he hiding out in Mrs. Von Bruck's bedroom? All at once, she stopped short, almost spilling her tray of drinks. Suppose, just suppose, Cole was the silver fox! After all, why not? He knew the Shenandoah Valley and the land between Washington and Richmond as well as he knew the fields and woods of his own plantation of Gray Meadows. And her brother had always said that Cole had more courage and cunning than any other man he'd met. It would explain also his being in civilian clothes and not wanting to put in an appearance at this ball he had had Arabella so carefully arrange. It was important that he keep his face and name unknown.

53

"What you standing there for, gal, like a ninny?" Caesar growled behind her. "There's a gentlemun wantin' punch over there by the piano." And then, suspiciously, "And where you been? Ah looked for you before."

She smiled demurely. "A gentleman asked me to step outside in the garden with him." Her eyes widened, innocently. "Ah couldn't say no to one of Miss Arabella's guests, now could I?"

Caesar glared at her warningly. "You'll get yourself in trouble one of these days, foolin' 'round with white men, you hear?"

The girl swallowed hard, remembering those moments in the bedroom with Cole. Could Caesar possibly know? All the pain and shock she had felt then washed back over her, so that for a moment she was afraid she would be sick.

Fortunately the majordomo mistook the maid's stricken silence for obedience and said grandly, "Anytime you need hugging and kissing, you come to me, gal," before strutting proudly away, leaving Lucinda weak with relief.

It was three o'clock in the morning before the ball ended and the last guest departed. Wearily, along with the other servants, Sukey made her way to the attic dormitory. Although she lay down on her pallet next to Jane, she didn't allow herself to fall asleep, pinching herself on her arms and legs to keep herself awake.

When she was sure by the sound of Jane's soft, steady breathing and the noisy snoring of the other servants that her companions were asleep, she crept quietly out of bed and into the musty-smelling storage room. A light was on in Arabella's bedroom; she could see its reflection faintly through the small hole she had made in the floor.

Quietly, her bare feet making hardly a sound crossing the wooden planks, she stretched out flat on the dusty floor, and placed her eye at the opening and looked down into the bedroom. As she had expected, the countess was not alone in her bedroom. There were three gentlemen with her. Two of the men Lucinda recognized as having been guests at the ball earlier; the third man was Cole Sinclair.

From her vantage point Lucinda could only glimpse the back of Cole's head, so she could not see that he was struggling to hide his impatience as he listened to Monsieur Duclair, who in broken English was protesting Cole's announcement that the trio would be leaving the Von Bruck house within the hour. The hour was late, Monsieur Duclair pointed out with asperity, the weather had turned rainy, and after a full evening at the punch bowl, he was in no mood for travel.

Cole waited till the man had finished, then shrugged indifferently. "I'm sorry, monsieur." His voice was polite but chill. "It's important we leave as soon as possible. There's no way of knowing if your arrival here in Washington has been noted. Patrols guarding the roads in and out of the city have already been doubled. And night is the best time to cross the Potomac without being discovered."

The Englishman, who had been listening to his colleague without speaking, now asked, his voice curious, "And how do you propose to leave the city without being discovered?"

"The same way I came in," Cole drawled. "In a woodcutter's wagon. I have a pass signed by the provost, and the patrols are accustomed to my coming and going at odd hours. You'll be hidden beneath a false bottom in the wagon."

"And the river—do you propose we swim across?"

"That won't be necessary. There's a Yankee sergeant at the river who'll look the other way if he's bribed sufficiently."

"With Yankee gold, I assume," the Englishman said dourly, "not Confederate dollars."

A flush rose beneath Cole's deep tan, but he pretended not to hear the remark as he turned to Arabella. "Are their boots ready?"

She rang the bellpull beside her bed, and immediately Caesar came into the room, carrying two pairs of boots. Cole took the boots and gave a hard jerk to the wooden heel of the right boot in each pair. The heels turned, revealing an opening inside the wood. "It's too dangerous to carry documents on your person," he said. "You might be stopped and searched before you reach Richmond. You'll keep your identification papers in here until your meeting with President Davis."

The Frenchman looked up, alarmed. "But surely, Monsieur . . ." He hesitated, evidently not knowing Cole's name, then continued, "Surely Monsieur will be accompanying us to Richmond."

Cole shook his head. "Only across the river. Another courier will meet you and take you the rest of the way." He smiled tightly. "Don't worry, monsieur. All my couriers are well trained. I can assure you that you'll reach Richmond safely and that President Davis is most anxiously awaiting your arrival."

Before the Frenchman could protest further, Arabella swept forward, smiling graciously at both men. "My majordomo will show you to a bedroom where clothes more suitable and comfortable for traveling have been laid out for you. If there's anything you need, please don't hesitate to ask Caesar." She held out her hand. The Frenchman kissed it lingeringly; the Englishman, with a wry look of amusement in his eyes. "My prayers and hopes go with you, gentlemen," she murmured, showing them to the door.

As soon as the door closed behind them, she flew to Cole's side and flung herself into his arms. "You don't really have to leave so soon, my love. We haven't had a moment alone together."

"You know it's not my choice, Bella," Cole answered, reaching down to kiss her lightly. But before he could pull away, she had her arms tight around him and was returning his kiss with a passion that left them both flushed and breathless when Cole finally pushed her firmly away. "There isn't time, Bella."

The violet eyes glittered as she whispered teasingly, "How much time does it take, *mein Silberfuchs?*" Then she pouted prettily. "And you haven't even told me that you liked my new gown."

"It's ravishing, as you well know, and so are you, but if I don't get our two friends underway tonight, they may never make Richmond. And the Confederacy needs all the gold and help it can get after Chancellorsville."

Arabella stared at him, surprised. "But Chancellorsville was a great victory for the South."

"Oh, yes, we won, all right," Cole said, frowning. "But the Union troops we came up against this time weren't frightened plowboys any longer, or helpless city clerks carrying a gun for the first time in their life. They were trained, professional soldiers who've learned how to fight, and how to die. I saw a regiment of Vermonters stand off Early's men in hand-to-hand combat. All the North needs now is a general who's not afraid to use those soldiers as they should be used in battle."

"Oh, pooh." Arabella's face was disdainful. "Everyone knows any one of our brave Southern boys can whip ten bluebellies."

"Except there are always ten more bluebellies to take their place," Cole pointed out grimly. "And the South is scraping the bottom of the barrel for men. Those we do have, have a habit of heading merrily for home between battles or joining guerrilla troops like Mosby's, to get their share of the spoils of war."

Arabella, however, wasn't interested in talking about the war. Of course, she wanted and expected the South to win. The thought of defeat was impossible. If the North won and the slaves were freed, her whole comfortable, gracious way of life would disappear; the Yankees might even take over her town house in Richmond, and the Von Bruck plantation on the James River. At the moment, though, Arabella's thoughts were on a more personal sort of combat.

She smiled coaxingly up at Cole, then turned and murmured, "Well, at least before you go, you can undo

57

me. I sent my maid, Sukey, to bed and I can't manage the hooks by myself."

Deftly Cole began to unhook the dozens of tiny clasps that were almost hidden down the back of the watered-silk gown. "Sukey?" he asked, his voice carefully bland. "I thought your maid's name was Mary."

"Sukey's my new maid. Caesar picked her up at Old Capitol Prison after Mary ran away."

"What do you know about her, this Sukey?"

Arabella shrugged. "What is there to know?" The clasps undone, the gown fell in a shimmering lavender cloud around her feet. Casually she stepped out of it, discarding her petticoats and pantalets, just as casually. "She's pretty and young and willing enough. Why?" Once again she turned her back to Cole, ordering sweetly, "The corset, too, please."

Almost absently Cole undid the fastenings on the girdle, which soon followed Arabella's corset cover to the floor in an untidy heap. He spoke thoughtfully. "I've been informed that Laf Baker has a new woman spy in his employ. No one's seen her, so we don't have any description."

All her clothes now lying in disarray on the floor, Arabella stretched luxuriously and sinuously. Then, stepping closer to Cole so that her full breasts pressed soft and warm against his chest, she moved her body slowly, coaxingly, against his. "Let's not talk about my maid, darling," she murmured. "Anyway, you needn't worry about Sukey. If she's a spy, Caesar and I will take care of her, the same way we took care of the other one."

Cole's hands gripped her arms so tightly that she gasped with the pain. "What other one?" he demanded, his voice an icy drawl that sent a sudden shiver of fear through Arabella.

She laughed, a little breathlessly. "Darling, don't look so fierce. It was just a man pretending to be a coachman. Caesar discovered him snooping around, and so we . . ." Her eyelids lowered, a flicker of a smile at the corners of her tiny mouth. "We sent him away."

58

She's lying, Cole thought dispassionately. The man's dead. He only hoped the poor bastard's end was swift, but knowing Arabella and the streak of cruelty that he suspected lay beneath her soft, inviting beauty, he doubted it. And suddenly he found himself imagining that lovely, shimmering brown body he'd held in his arms only a few hours earlier broken and mutilated under the countess' less-than-tender mercy. His hands moved deliberately from the round white arms to rest on either side of Arabella's slim regal neck.

"I want you to watch the girl, nothing else." The hands tightened a little, the thumbs pressing at the warm hollow in Arabella's neck, as he smiled lazily down at her. "Is that clear?"

He saw her eyes widen, not with fear but excitement, her breasts rising and falling rapidly so he could feel the tautness of the nipples burning his skin through his silken shirt, touch and fall away, touch and fall away. A dreamy, sensuous smile curved Arabella's rouged lips. "Of course, darling," she said, her voice thick, slurred, her mouth reaching up hungrily for him. "Whatever you want, anything you want..."

She wants me to hurt her, Cole thought, startled, as his hands moved automatically, caressing roughly the generous satin creamy curves of hip and thigh pressed against him. He knew all he'd have to do was spread her legs now and she'd be moist and warm and ready for him. She moaned softly as his hand tightened on the soft, pillowlike breasts, her body winding tightly around him, suffocating him, her carmine-streaked mouth insatiable beneath his, demanding more and more pain to fill her special, perverted desires. Not wanting him at all, just the pain...

Sickened, he thrust her away from him so abruptly that she staggered and almost fell to the floor. Her violet eyes were glazed, puzzled, staring at him, not understanding. "What is it?" she whispered. "Surely you're not leaving now..."

But the bedroom door had already closed behind him.

4

In the musty darkness of the attic, Lucinda stole back to her pallet, trying to blot out of her mind the picture of Cole's black curly head bent over Arabella's mass of golden hair, to forget the treacherous twist of agony she had felt watching Cole embrace the woman. Angrily, she pushed the memory away. What difference did it make to her if Cole made love to a dozen women? Instead she forced herself to remember what the countess had called Cole . . . *"mein Silberfuchs."*

Her suspicion had been right, she thought, shivering with excitement. Cole was the man Mr. Baker had called the silver fox, the Southern agent he was determined to destroy. And now she was pledged to destroy, too, she realized, just as surely and ruthlessly as Cole and the countess would dispose of her if they discovered the truth about her. And although the air in the attic was oppressively warm, she felt a sudden uncomfortable chill.

Picking up the stub of candle by her bed, she lit it, then carried it to a small open window at the north end of the attic. Not a breath of air stirred. The candle burned with a steady, golden flame in the darkness, sending its betraying beam out into the night. If the peddler was watching for her signal, and Lucinda had no doubt he was, he would be waiting for Cole and the two envoys when they left the Von Bruck house. Staring at the candle flame, the girl suddenly found herself remembering what Mr. Baker had told her—"the shadow of the noose hangs at the end of every trail for a spy." Was that how Cole would die when the peddler captured him? she wondered. Shuddering, dangling at the end of a rope?

Almost she reached out to snatch the candle back from the window. Then fiercely she reminded herself

of the countless number of Union boys Cole Sinclair
had undoubtedly killed with his stolen information,
perhaps even her own brothers, and of how many more
he would kill if he weren't stopped. Her hand fell to
her side, her wide, dark eyes bleakly, coldly determined. When she quietly returned to her pallet, however, and pulled the thin coverlet over her, she found
she was trembling once more, a chill striking deep into
her bones, as if she would never be warm again.

If Arabella was worried about the possibility of
Cole's capture or the taking of the French and British
envoys, she showed no sign of concern the next few
days. She was as gay and charming as ever as she
entertained at suppers and dinners, went on her numerous shopping trips along Pennsylvania Avenue in
her lavender-and-silver coach, or visited the Senate
gallery with other women, fanning themselves and
whispering as they listened to the senators arguing
bitterly about the way the war was being waged and
lost.

One senator beat angrily at his table and shouted,
red-faced, "Where's our Army, I ask you? The rebels
are almost within spitting distance of Washington, and
where's Hooker hiding out?"

For everyone in Washington was aware by now that
Lee's march north through the Shenandoah Valley was
no longer a rumor. The rebel cry of "On to Washington"
struck dread in every heart. Each day new and more
frightening stories raced through the capital city. Jeb
Stuart's cavalry was sweeping through the passes of
the Blue Ridge Mountains, heading for Maryland and
Pennsylvania; the Union forces had been routed and
fled from Winchester, Virginia.

June 15, a stifling hot day, the servants at the Von
Bruck house gathered in small groups, whispering the
latest news heard through the ever-busy Washington
grapevine. Lee's Army of North Virginia had crossed
over into Maryland and Pennsylvania at Hagerstown
and Chambersburg. The governor of Pennsylvania had

appealed to the Federal government for help, and President Lincoln issued a proclamation calling for 100,000 militia to march to the aid of Pennsylvania. The Capitol blazed with excitement, and the lights in the White House burned late into the night.

Now when the countess went shopping, her carriage was stopped by troops of sunburned, bearded veterans, their sabers rattling, as they rode up 14th Street, bound for the Susquehanna and Pennsylvania. One afternoon a troop of jet-black Negro soldiers, solemn-faced, in perfect step, marched by her halted carriage. Despite her feeling of revulsion that the North should sink so low as to recruit and arm black men, Arabella couldn't resist studying their ranks eagerly. Was it possible Troy could be among them? As always when she thought of the slave and his magnificent body, like that of some Nubian god, and of the special, infinite pleasures that body and those powerful arms could bring her once she broke him to her will, a dreamy, angelic smile touched Arabella's face, and a moist warmth gathered between her thighs.

The following Sunday morning, Arabella awoke in her lavender-scented bedroom to the distant thudding sound of artillery fire from the south, toward the Bull Run Mountains. And before the end of the day ambulance trains filled with the wounded and dying once more poured into the city.

In her attic room, Lucinda had heard the sound of the distant guns as she dressed and hurried from the room. She glanced at the storage room as she passed it, but although she was tempted to eavesdrop on the countess on the chance she might learn something of Cole, she did not stop. The evening before, as she had watched at the peephole, she had heard, dismayed, heavy footsteps pausing outside the storage-room door. For several seconds she had lain, as if paralyzed, on the floor, sure that the sound of her heart pounding could be heard through the quivering stillness.

Finally the footsteps had moved on, and she had quickly fled back to her pallet. Not a half hour later the footsteps had returned, and a lamp was raised above her pallet, its light shining down upon her sleeping form. Even with her eyes shut, feigning sleep, Lucinda knew it was Caesar standing there, checking to make sure she was where she should be.

She was well aware that she was being watched constantly now. If she left the house, Caesar was never far behind her. She would look up suddenly and find him staring at her from across the room, while Arabella's violet eyes following her held an amused malevolence that was more frightening than Caesar's watchful, impassive face.

It was almost the end of June before she was able to slip out of the house to talk with the peddler, and only then because the cook was making a frightful row with Caesar about the dinner the countess was giving that evening for Secretary of War Stanton.

The peddler studied the small, dark face, the black eyes shadowed with fatigue, and asked softly, "You look poorly, missy. Is something wrong?"

She shook her head, her voice strained. "Did you see my signal?"

He nodded. "Yes, ma'am, I did."

"Did you . . . did you catch them?"

The peddler's leathery face was glum. "No, ma'am. My orders were to stay with you, so I sent another man after them. He lost them."

The relief that flooded Lucinda left her weak. She swayed, and the peddler quickly reached out a supporting hand. "Are you sure you're all right?"

"It was the silver fox," she murmured. "I'm sure of it."

The peddler spat, disgusted, into the grass. "Yes, ma'am, I figured as much, the easy way he gave us the slip. Don't worry, it's not your fault. You did fine. We'll catch him next time."

"Is it true?" the girl asked, low-voiced. "Lee's in Pennsylvania?"

"Yes, ma'am, although no one knows for sure where, nor where Jeb Stuart is for that matter. One thing's

63

sure—a big battle's shaping up. There's hardly a trooper left in the city. They've all gone to join Meade's forces in Pennsylvania."

"Meade?" Lucinda asked, startled. "What about General Hooker?"

"He's resigned, forced out more than likely." The man spat again. "Let's hope Meade's got the guts to stand up to Lee."

His voice suddenly dropped. "That big black buck's got his eye on us. You'd best go back to the house."

"Yes," she said, her voice taut. Caesar was not coming toward them. He was simply leaning against the summer kitchen, watching them, his face glowering darkly.

The Union agent in the peddler's rags felt a stirring of uneasiness. There was something wrong here. He could smell it. As the girl started to turn away, he said quietly, "If you need me, put the candle in the window. I won't be far away." Then, loudly, "Tell your mistress, got some fine cherries today, almost as sweet as you are, missy . . ."

At the door to the house, Lucinda hesitated, a wild impulse gripping her to turn and run away from the house, as fast and as far as she could. It took a tremendous effort of will to reach out and open the door, to force herself to step inside the cool, dark hall, its brocade curtains pulled against the morning sun. She told herself she was being ridiculous. What use was she to Mr. Baker if she turned and ran like a frightened rabbit every time she felt afraid? But the fear was still there, like a hard knot in her stomach, as she went about her chores, laying out Mrs. Von Bruck's silvery lavender gown for the dinner for Mr. Stanton, filling the hip bath with hot water and fragrant bath oil, then wrapping Arabella's creamy white body in an oversized towel as she stepped out of the tub.

The woman lifted an amused eyebrow. "Your hands are like ice, Sukey. You're not sick?"

"No . . . no, ma'am," the maid stammered softly.

Arabella rubbed her body dry slowly, caressingly,

then tossed the damp towel carelessly to the maid. "You don't have to wait up for me tonight, Sukey."

The maid quickly cast her glance down so that her mistress couldn't see the spark of interest she was sure had flashed into her eyes. It was always when Arabella was expecting a male visitor that Sukey was given the night off. Perhaps it was Cole returning. A pulse in Lucinda's temple began to throb.

The dinner party in the Von Bruck drawing room was under full sway when Sukey slipped up the servant staircase to the second-floor hall. She opened the baize door an inch and peered out into the empty hall, wondering if it was safe for her to investigate the hidden cache in the floor of Arabella's bedroom. She had taken a quick look into the room earlier through her attic peephole, and it was empty. She took a step toward the hall, and then a hand touched her shoulder gently. She spun around, startled, then giggled, relieved. "Oh, it's you, Jane. You gave me a scare."

The maid put a finger to her lip and beckoned with her other hand toward the attic stairs. Puzzled, Sukey followed her up the steps. At the top of the staircase, Jane whispered urgently, "You've got to go, right away."

Sukey's eyes widened. "Go? Why?"

Jane cast a nervous glance over her shoulder. "I overheard Caesar and Miss Arabella talking before the guests arrived. They found that peephole you made in the storage room. Don't waste time." The girl's soft voice trembled. "You don't know Caesar, how he'll hurt you. Won't matter you're white."

The fear Lucinda had felt earlier that day swept back over her in a dark wave, fear and surprise, as she gazed at Jane, puzzled. "You've known about me ... all along?"

A smile crossed Jane's dark face fleetingly. "You make a passable colored gal, only there was a stain I noticed in the washbowl you used. Wasn't dirt. Took hard scrubbing to get it out."

Lucy touched her skin with her fingertips. "They

told me it wouldn't fade, not for weeks, but I'm sure I'm getting lighter," she said, worried.

Jane tugged at Lucinda's hand. "No use fussing about that now. Come along. There's not much time."

At the downstairs door, Lucy whispered, "Would you do me one last favor? Put a lighted candle in the north window of the attic."

Jane nodded, then, impulsively, took a necklace from her neck and slipped it over Lucinda's head. The chain of the necklace was thin strips of leather, intricately plaited, holding a delicately carved flower made from bone. "I want you to have this. My Troy made it for me when we first got married."

"I can't take something that means so much to you," Lucinda protested.

"It'll help keep you safe," Jane insisted stubbornly. "And my Troy will carve me another when he comes back."

Just for a moment the two girls tearfully embraced, then Lucinda slipped out into the darkness. The drawing-room windows were open, and she could hear the musicians readying their instruments for the musical program they would be presenting before the dinner. The curtains at the open French windows billowed softly in the evening breeze. There was a sweetness caught in the night air as Lucinda made her way through the garden, the scent of damask roses and jasmine.

Cautiously, she made a wide circle around the summer kitchen, where she could hear the bustle of activity as preparations for the evening meal were being completed. She had no idea where she would find the peddler man, but there was a whistle Mr. Baker had taught her, two high notes, then two low notes. Once she reached the woods that stretched behind the Von Bruck estate, she could only hope the peddler would locate her if she gave the proper signal.

She was near the icehouse now, and she paused a minute to look back toward the house. Thankfully, she saw a candle flame flickering fitfully in the window of the attic. Jane had kept her word. Now if only the peddler saw her signal...

Then, without any warning, a twig snapped behind her. Before she could turn or cry out, once again a hand descended over her face. But this hand, she knew instinctively, was not Cole's, and it had no intention of letting her go, no matter how she struggled and fought against its bruising, suffocating hardness. The darkness pounded in her head as she struggled for breath; her struggles gradually weakened, finally stopping all together. And there was only the darkness, nothing else.

She did not know how long she had been unconscious, probably not more than a few minutes. When she came to, she was lying on a hard-packed dirt floor. The air around her had a dank, disagreeable smell, but she welcomed it, taking gasping, grateful breaths past the rawness in her throat. It was only very slowly as she became aware of her surroundings—rough brick walls, a crude wooden chair and table upon which a lamp burned—that she became also aware that someone had removed all her clothes. And somehow the shock of her nudity was worse than the knowledge of where she must be—the cellar of the Von Bruck mansion.

She blinked, groggily, into the lamplight and saw the countess standing next to the table. She held her silver-lavender gauze gown daintily away from the dirt floor. The woman looked so incongruous with her delicate white-and-gold beauty standing amid the filth and squalor of her surroundings that for a moment Lucinda couldn't believe she wasn't dreaming, or having a nightmare.

Until Arabella spoke, her voice lightly, maliciously amused. "I warned you, didn't I, Sukey, what would happen if you ran away?"

Sukey, Lucinda wondered, dazed, the pounding in her head confusing her. Who was Sukey? Then, her breath catching painfully in her throat, she remembered. A shudder passed through her slim body. It was only her training as an actress that kept her from betraying herself, that made her answer in a frightened, childish voice, "Please, Miss Arabella, Sukey ain't running away, jest getting a breath of fresh air—"

"Don't lie to me! Caesar found the hole you made in the attic floor and the candle in the window." Lucinda didn't even see the quirt in the woman's hand until it lifted and slashed downward, cutting like a knife into the soft skin of her arm. Unable to help herself, she cried aloud with the pain.

The hand lifted again, the whip poised deliberately above the girl crouching on the floor. Instinctively Lucinda shrank back. Arabella saw the terrified movement, and the violet eyes gleamed softly with pleasure.

Then the quirt descended slowly to her side, and she said, almost purring, "The whipping will come later, Sukey, if you're a stubborn, disobedient girl and don't tell us the truth. First, though, I promised Caesar he could have his turn. He's waited, you know, very patiently, and I'm afraid you've treated him badly." She laughed lightly. "Caesar doesn't need a whip. He's very skillful with his hands."

Lucinda hadn't seen the majordomo in the darkness of the room. He stepped out of the shadows and was suddenly standing before her. His face as always was wooden, almost blank; only his eyes glistened, as if polished, their brightness caught in the lamplight.

There was no time for the girl to scramble away before the powerful black hands lifted her to her feet, effortlessly, as if she were a broken doll. At first the large black hands were gentle, stroking her soft young body, almost as if he were making love to her. Then suddenly, shockingly, they changed. The breath left Lucinda's body in a whimper of pain as the hands pinched and squeezed and twisted her soft flesh, as if they knew exactly where to be placed to bring the cruelest agony. She had promised herself she would not scream, would not give them that satisfaction, but she could not stop herself. Vaguely she had the impression that Arabella was standing to one side, watching, smiling, her exquisite angel's face holding a greedy, almost sensual look. Then mercifully the darkness invaded her mind once more, and she once again lapsed into unconsciousness.

When she came to a second time, she was stretched on the floor, dirt pressed against her cheek, the putrid smell of rot and·mildew in her nostrils. But this time she did not move. She had no wish to draw attention to herself. And gradually she became aware that there was a fourth person now in the cellar room to whom the countess was speaking. Her voice was worried. "I didn't expect you so early. It isn't safe. There are soldiers guarding the house because of Stanton's being here."

"I know. That's why I came down here rather than chancing your room. I wouldn't have come at all, but I need money and a fresh horse. I've got to find General Stuart." Cole's voice lifted, tense with excitement. "My God, Bella, this is the chance we've been waiting for. Washington's stripped itself of its defenses to fight off Lee in Pennsylvania. All they've got left guarding the city are clerks and old men. Jeb Stuart can't be far off. If I can find him in time, his cavalry can gallop straight into Washington, capture Lincoln and his cabinet, and make the White House his headquarters. We could end this war with one bold stroke!"

Then, for the first time glimpsing the small dark figure slumped in a corner of the room, his voice changed, hardened with anger. "I thought I told you I didn't want that girl hurt."

"She's not hurt," Arabella said hastily. "She's just fainted. She was trying to run away and Caesar caught her. He had to stop her from crying out and rousing the soldiers."

Dimly Lucinda was aware of footsteps approaching her, of somebody kneeling down beside her. She thought a hand touched gently the raw cut the quirt had left on her arm.

"She wasn't just running away, you know," Arabella
69

continued angrily. "Caesar found a hole she made in the attic floor, looking right into my bedroom, and a candle burning in the attic window. She has to be one of Baker's spies."

Cole had risen to his feet and moved away from the girl on the floor. "The hole could have been there long before she came," he said skeptically. Then, his voice indifferent, "Still, it's your business. But won't your guests miss you?"

"I slipped away during the musicale. And this shouldn't take long. Caesar has been well trained in handling disobedient slaves."

"Too bad it can't wait until after your dinner party," Cole drawled lazily. "I was hoping we could have a few minutes alone together, Bella." His voice took on a husky, intimate quality. "I've missed you, my sweet."

The countess laughed a little breathlessly. "It serves you right, after the mean way you treated me last time. Anyway, there really isn't time—"

"As you once said, how much time can it take?" Cole asked softly. Lucinda could hear a silken, rustling sound in the darkness as if Arabella's silvery gauze gown was being disturbed by questing hands. Then silence for several seconds.

When Arabella spoke again, her voice was slurred. "Perhaps the girl can wait till after dinner," she murmured. "But we'll have to hurry, darling. It wouldn't do for me to be rude to the Secretary of War by being late to my own dinner."

Lucinda could hear the gown rustle again as the countess moved to the door with Cole.

Were they going to leave Caesar alone with her? Lucinda wondered, terror turning her blood to ice at the thought. But Arabella had no intention of leaving her servant to his pleasures without giving herself the satisfaction of watching. At the door, she said sharply, "Come along, Caesar. I'm sure they need you upstairs."

It was only after she heard the door close behind them, the metallic sound of a lock being put into place outside the door, that the girl pulled herself painfully

70

to her feet. They had taken the lamp with them, and the windowless room was pitch-black. Desperately she felt with her hands along the rough brick wall, although she was sure she remembered from her brief former visit that there was no other exit from the room. She did find her clothes in a crumpled heap on the floor, and she pulled them on slowly, her body one long throbbing ache.

How long, she wondered, before Arabella and Caesar returned? The dinner party wouldn't last more than a few hours. And then ... She began to shake as if with the fever at the thought of those hands touching, tormenting her body again. How could Cole, even as changed as he was since she had first known him, callously leave any woman, black or white, to the merciless tortures those hands could inflict?

Whether it was reaction from the fear squeezing at her insides or the painful knowledge of Cole's betrayal, she began to retch and for a few minutes was dreadfully sick to her stomach. Afterward, she found the chair in the darkness and rested her head on the table, feeling oddly almost at peace, as if terror had finally mercifully numbed her mind and emotions.

She only hoped and prayed it would be over with quickly and she wouldn't betray Mr. Baker's faith in her courage. Exhausted, she drifted off into a half-sleep, for how long she didn't know, but the door opening behind her, its hinges creaking rustily, brought her to instant, terrified wakefulness.

"Sukey?"

It was Cole's voice. She got to her feet and stared through the darkness incredulously, too surprised to answer.

She heard him come into the room, then stop and light a candle, his face suddenly flaring up before her in the darkness. His blue-green eyes searching her face were both worried and impatient. "Are you all right? Can you walk?"

She nodded.

He thrust the candle into her hand, his voice brusque.

"Well, then, get the hell out of here. And in the future leave spying to the white folks."

She couldn't resist the temptation, her eyes widening innocently as she asked guilelessly, "You reckon I'm a spy, suh, and you're letting me go free?"

Cole scowled and shook his head. "I don't know what you are, except you're too pretty by far for your own good. And if you really are a Union spy, then the country's in worse condition than I thought it was!"

"Thank you, suh." She rose on tiptoe to place a grateful kiss on his lips, but suddenly it was much more than that. The candle fell to the floor as Cole's arms tightened around the slim body, wondering bemused how she could smell so sweet, like apple blossoms in spring, in the midst of the squalor in which she stood. Her mouth moved warm and eager beneath his, her hands lifting, tightening in the wiry black curls, pulling him still closer.

At last, almost angrily, he pushed her away. Then, finding the candle, he relit it, handed it to her and gave her a shove toward the door. "And don't let me catch you spying again, you hear? Or next time I'll take a whip to you myself."

"Yes, suh," she said, laughing softly. "Goodbye, suh."

Then she was gone, slipping like a shadow through the garden, then running, without once looking back, toward the shelter of the woods behind the estate. It was only after she reached the tangled grove of pines and sapling oaks that she paused to catch her breath, her eyes searching the darkness around her. Then, softly, she whistled two high, two low notes, and was startled when almost instantly a reply came from the brush only a few feet away. She didn't hear a twig break or a footfall, but suddenly the peddler was standing beside her.

She laughed shakily. "You move as silently as an Indian."

"Yes, ma'am," he said gravely. "I lived with the Osage for a while in Missouri." Then, worried, "Are you all right, ma'am? I thought I saw a light in the window earlier, then it was gone, and I wasn't sure."

"They were on to me," she admitted. "They locked me in the cellar."

"I was afraid that's what happened." The man's voice turned curious. "How did you get away?"

"It was..." Lucinda couldn't bring herself to name Cole, and she finished in a rush, "It was the man you call the silver fox. He let me go."

"I see, ma'am." A new note crept into the peddler's voice, a coldness she had never heard there before. "That will be the man I saw riding away from the house a few minutes ago, like the devil was after him."

"He's gone to find Stuart," she said, reluctantly, but knowing she had to tell the peddler the truth. "With Washington defenseless, he's sure Stuart and his cavalry can take the city easily."

"And he'd be right, too," the peddler said bitterly. "Those pencil pushers manning the barricades around the city don't know one end of the rifle from the other. Stuart's cavalry will eat them for breakfast." He turned abruptly away when she caught his arm, holding him.

"Where are you going?"

He sounded surprised. "After him, of course, ma'am. He's got to be stopped before he can get to Stuart."

"You'll kill him, won't you?"

"Yes, ma'am. That's my idea exactly," he said grimly.

"Take me with you."

He shook off the pleading hand. "Begging your pardon, but you'd just be in the way."

"I can ride and shoot as well as any man," she said stubbornly. And then pointed out, "Besides, you don't know what he looks like. I do."

"That's true, ma'am." And then, grudgingly, "I have another horse. But if I find you're holding me back, I'll have to leave you, you understand."

She took a deep, relieved breath. "Yes, I understand. Don't worry . . . I won't hold you back."

It was after midnight. The dinner guests had long since gone, and all the lights in the Von Bruck mansion were extinguished except for a lamp burning low on a wooden table in a cellar room of the house.

Its faint yellowish light barely touched the body of the maid, Jane, curled in a ball on the mud floor. Where the gown had been stripped away from her back deep gashes had been cut in the soft brown skin. Several of the cuts were bleeding, and there was blood on the leather thongs of the whip Caesar held, motionless now, in his hand.

Arabella was seated on the table, one leg swinging impatiently beneath her silken robe, as she stared, annoyed, down at the maid. "It's foolish of you to lie, Jane. We know you helped Sukey escape."

"No, ma'am," the girl moaned softly. "Ah swear ah didn't."

Arabella nodded to her majordomo. The whip lifted, then descended with deadly accuracy, flicking wider one of the gashes across the girl's back, cutting neatly into the edge of a breast. The slender body jerked beneath the lash, then was still.

"Admit it, Jane," Arabella said petulantly. "We know you were friends with that little black bitch. You helped her get away."

"No, ma'am, it wasn't me. I was in the kitchen all evening with the servants. Ask anyone . . . they'll tell you . . . "

"You're lying!" Arabella sprang to her feet, her pale creamy face flushed an ugly red with fury. She snatched the whip from Caesar's hand and raised it above her head. Then a soft knocking came at the cellar door. It was Caesar who opened the door and listened to a servant's frightened words. He turned quickly back to Arabella.

"There are soldiers at the front door," he said. "They got a search warrant and orders to arrest you."

"They wouldn't dare," Arabella screamed, furious, then when Caesar said nothing, only stared at her woodenly, waiting for her orders, she forced herself to calmness. "I'll take care of it," she said coldly.

Caesar nodded toward Jane. "What about her?"

Arabella was already at the cellar door. "You know what to do," she said curtly. "I'll delay the soldiers as long as I can. You take my jewels—and Jane—in the wagon back to the plantation. Wait for me there." She smiled contemptuously. "They won't dare hold me long. I've too many friends."

Then she swept up the stairs, and without bothering to change from her satin robe, she opened the front door of the house herself. The soldiers crowding behind the captain at the door gawked at the sight of the lavender countess, herself, standing in the doorway, her luxuriant curves concealed, and yet so artfully revealed, by the clinging satin robe.

"Good evening, captain," she said, smiling coolly and dropping him a graceful curtsy. "You wanted to see me?"

5

It was sunrise when the peddler and his companion stopped their horses near a small wooden building in a village in Maryland. A faded tavern sign swung above the front door.

"We'll stop here, ma'am, to rest a bit."

Lucinda, slumped forward in the saddle, lifted her head wearily, too tired to talk. Every bone and muscle in her body ached, not just from the punishment it had received at Caesar's hands, but from the five hours she had spent in the saddle. It had been three years since she had ridden so hard and so continuously. After crossing over into Maryland, they had had to leave the turnpike on which they had been traveling north from Washington. The road had become so clogged with troops, quartermaster wagons, equipment and supplies, the tail end of the Union army heading toward Pennsylvania, that it was impossible to move at more than a snail's pace.

"Our friend wouldn't have taken a Federal supply road anyway," the peddler said, as he led the way off onto a narrow and heavily wooded side road cut across by numerous rocky streams. "A civilian riding toward a battle area alone would be sure to be challenged."

Several of the streams they forded were flooded, the water rising as high as Lucinda's saddle. The icy spring-fed current was strong enough to snatch off one of her shoes as with her knees and hands she struggled to keep her horse from floundering on the slippery rocks underfoot.

Her cotton dress was still soaking wet, clinging damply to her body, as the peddler helped her dismount. She protested faintly, "No need to stop ... my account ..."

"No, ma'am," he smiled gently, as he eased her to

the ground. "We're not stopping on your account. This tavern's run by a widow, Mrs. Surratt. She and her son are secesh; their tavern's a rendezvous for passing rebel spies. I figure our friend's sure to have stopped here to rest his horse and see if he could get any news on Jeb Stuart's whereabouts. Maybe I can find out which direction he's heading."

"Why would they trust you?"

While they had been talking, the man had slipped an arm around her waist, helping her to a nearby massive oak tree, its branches almost overhanging the tavern. Gratefully Lucinda sank down on the mossy grass beneath the tree. Solid earth had never felt so good to her before. Then she drew back, startled, as her companion slipped a rope around her wrists and tied her deftly to the tree.

"Sorry, ma'am," he said ruefully. "That's why the Surratts trust me. I've been through here before. They think I'm a slave snatcher. You're runaway contraband that I'm hauling back to your rightful owners."

In her weariness, Lucinda had forgotten that her skin was still stained brown for her role of the Negro girl, Sukey. She reached up uncertainly to touch her face. "Am I . . . do I look all right?" she asked anxiously. "It's not supposed to wash off, but it does."

"You look fine," the peddler assured her. "Maybe a little cut up around the edges."

He had started to turn away when she asked, "What is your name?"

He hesitated, then said, "Jephthah, ma'am, and maybe, if the occasion arises, we'd better call you Sara. Baker's men should have picked up the countess by now, but she might have sent word to Richmond about Sukey's escape, before her arrest."

Lucinda frowned, puzzled. "But if Arabella could get word to Richmond about Sukey, why couldn't she let Richmond know about Washington's lack of defenses?"

"It would take too long, ma'am," Jephthah explained patiently. "Richmond would need to telegraph the information to some point in the Shenandoah Valley.

From there flag signals and scouts would have to carry the message the rest of the way to Lee's headquarters. And the truth is, ma'am, I doubt if even Jeff Davis knows the exact location of Lee's headquarters. He's been moving too fast these last weeks. No, Stuart and his cavalry are what our friend has to get hold of, and soon, too, if his information is to be of any use." He took an oilcloth cape from his saddle and spread it on the ground beside Lucinda. "You rest now. I'll send someone out with food."

Shortly after he disappeared into the tavern, a middle-aged woman came out and crossed the yard to where Lucinda sat. "Brought you something to eat," the widow Surratt said. Her round, motherly face filled with sympathy as she gazed down at the bound girl. "Why, you're not much older than my Anna."

She loosened the ropes on the girl's wrists so Lucinda could eat the cold biscuits and drink the hot chicory coffee, then retied the girl to the tree, but loosely enough so that she could stretch out on the oilcloth. It seemed to Lucinda she had just fallen asleep when a hand shook her shoulder firmly. She looked up drowsily into Jephthah's lined, leathery face.

"Sorry, ma'am, we've got to move."

"What is it?" Sleep fled from her mind. "Did you find out anything?"

"Our man's not far ahead of us. Stuart raided Fairfax yesterday, heading north toward Pennsylvania."

"Fairfax?" Lucinda said, her face worried. "That's only fifteen miles from the capital."

"Yes, ma'am," Jephthah said grimly. "But at least Stuart's still headed away from Washington, so we know our friend hasn't reached him yet." He untied Lucinda's wrists, but when he helped her mount, she bit back a cry of pain as her weary muscles protested returning to the saddle.

"Are you able to travel, ma'am?" Jephthah asked.

She forced herself to smile brightly. "Of course. A little nap was all I needed." She touched the spurs lightly to her horse. "Let's hurry, Jephthah, or we'll miss him."

After they left the village, though, they found it was impossible to hurry. There were no more back roads they could take to avoid the heavily traveled supply road. Time and time again they were delayed by Union troopers, with drawn carbines, suspicious of a civilian and a Negro girl traveling together. It was too risky for Jephthah to reveal his true identity and mission and Lucinda listened, amused and impressed, at the ease with which the man invented a fictitious name and logical reason for being on the road, never once betraying his impatience or irritation at the delay.

"You should have been an actor," she murmured after the third trooper who had stopped them, finally satisfied by Jephthah's answers, waved them on their way.

Jephthah smiled crookedly. "No, ma'am, just a natural-born liar. Comes in handy in our line of work."

It was almost dark when they reached, at last, the outskirts of Rockville. Lucinda was swaying with weariness in her saddle. Even through her sleep-dulled eyes, though, she could see the thick black smoke rising above the low hills before the town. When they reached the crest of one of the hills, she saw the cause for the smoke. A quartermaster wagon train filled with supplies for Meade's army, food, oats and corn, had been looted and left burning in the road. As she and Jephthah spurred their horses forward to the train, she saw a dozen dead Union troopers lying in grotesque, twisted positions in the road. The soldiers, like the wagons, had been looted, too, stripped of their boots, trousers and coats.

Jephthah cast a professional eye at the bloody gashes in the fallen men. "Sabers," he said dourly. "Cavalry raid."

Lucinda took one look at the dead men, then lifted her eyes, staring straight ahead, determined she wasn't going to shame herself by fainting in front of Jephthah.

79

A young boy, sitting on a rail fence by the road, was warily watching their approach. His face was smoke-grimed, and he looked close to tears.

"Wait here," Jephthah ordered. "I'll find out what happened."

He returned in a few minutes, his face grim. "It was Stuart's cavalry, all right. They came through early this morning, hid out in Rockville and caught the wagon train by surprise. There's no way one hundred and fifty wagons and mules, loaded down with supplies, could outrun or outfight cavalry. Stuart took off with more than one hundred of the wagons and burned the ones too badly damaged." Jephthah scowled and spat, disgusted, into the weeds beside the road. "Damn fool thing to do, loading himself down with wagons. Bound to slow him up."

The boy was still sitting on the fence, gazing, frightened, at Jephthah.

"Did he ... did he see what happened?" Lucinda asked.

Jephthah shrugged. "Half the town did, and cheered Stuart's troopers on. They're mostly secesh around here. Before they left, the boy was told by a couple of Stuart's men to keep the fires going or they'd split his head open when they returned. Not that Stuart's likely to come back," Jephthah growled. "He must be halfway to Pennsylvania by now, and he's not stupid enough to double back. His scouts know this whole area will be swarming with Union troops before long, on the lookout for the raiders."

Lucinda took a deep, thankful breath. "Washington's safe, then? Cole—" She flushed and broke off abruptly at Jephthah's quick, questioning glance. "The silver fox won't reach Stuart in time?" she asked instead.

"No, ma'am. He didn't miss Stuart by more than a few hours, though. I reckon he wasn't too happy about that."

"How do you know?"

Jephthah jerked his chin toward the boy. "He told

me. A civilian on horseback came up to him no more than an hour ago, wanting the same information we did. He said the man had dark hair and was wearing a slouch hat. I figure that was our man."

A sweet relief coursed through Lucinda's body. It was over, then. There was no need to pursue Cole further. "He went on to join Stuart, I suppose," she said.

Jephthah shook his head. "No, ma'am. The boy told me the man rode east, toward the Potomac. Probably heading for Richmond or maybe the Shenandoah Valley." He gazed at Lucinda curiously. "That's where your home is, ain't it, ma'am, in the valley?"

"Was," Lucinda said stiffly. "Not any more." And then, searching her companion's face, she asked uneasily, "You're going after him, aren't you?"

Jephthah nodded. "Why, yes, ma'am. Ain't no question about that. The boy said the man's horse was limping. Won't be hard to track him. This time I have the feeling that the fox's luck has run out."

"Then I'm going with you."

"No cause for you to do that, ma'am. You'd best head back to Washington."

"I'm going with you," Lucinda insisted, her softly rounded chin setting stubbornly. "You still don't know what he looks like. I do. And I haven't held you up, have I?"

"No, ma'am," Jephthah admitted grudgingly. "You ride as good as any trooper, better than most."

"Well, then..." As if that settled the matter, Lucinda picked up her reins and nudged with her knees at her horse.

Jephthah reached over and took the reins firmly from her hands. "We'll talk about it in the morning, ma'am. The boy said his father wouldn't mind our using their barn to bed down in. We'll spend the night here."

"But he'll get too far ahead of us," she protested.

"He'll cross the Potomac tonight, all right, but then he'll have to rest, the same as we do, ma'am." Jephthah smiled crookedly. "Don't know about you, but I'm a mite tired."

81

Lucinda was too exhausted to object any further. When they reached the barn, Jephthah once again helped her dismount. She watched, swaying with fatigue, as he pitched piles of hay into pallets for beds.

"Ain't fancy," he said, grinning, "but beats the hard ground."

Gratefully, Lucinda sank down into the hay. "I've never felt anything so comfortable," she murmured and then was already asleep.

She awoke at the first light the next morning and saw that Jephthah had already saddled their horses. He took a sausage and some hardtack from his bag and handed them to her. "The sausage is courtesy of our host," he said. "And so are these."

He tossed a well-worn pair of trousers, a shirt, straw hat and a much-used pair of boots on the hay beside her.

"You still want to come with me?" he asked.

She nodded, gazing puzzled at the clothes.

"They belong to the boy we met yesterday. Figured they would just about fit you. Makes more sense my traveling with a young Negro lad than a pretty colored girl. Draws less attention, too."

And more comfortable, too, Lucinda decided, as Jephthah tactfully left the barn and she discarded her torn, bedraggled dress for the trousers, shirt and boots. Her long black hair she coiled tightly in a braid, and she clamped the hat over her head so that only a small part of her face was revealed and none of her hair. Gazing down at her bosom, she decided there was not much she could do to hide the revealing curves beneath the shirt. Well, the oilcloth cape would hide that, she decided, even if it was a warm July day to be wearing one.

Jephthah nodded approvingly when he saw her. "You make a right smart boy."

"Thank you, suh." Lucinda lowered her voice an octave, then walked past him with the open-gait swagger of a young boy. Suddenly she giggled at the picture she must present. Her whole life people had been trying to change her from a hoydenish tomboy, first her mother, then her Aunt Clare and her teachers at school. Now here she was, gambling her life that she could act the part of a boy.

Jephthah reached into his saddlebags and pulled out a small silver-plated derringer. "Won this in a poker game," he acknowledged sheepishly. "Never had much use for it, but maybe you'll find it handy."

Lucinda examined the short-barreled pistol. Her father had once had a matched set of derringers much like the one she held in her hand. It wouldn't shoot far, she knew, but it would shoot straight. She flashed her companion a pleased smile, slipping the gun into her saddlebag. "Thank you, Jephthah."

He flushed, then growled uncomfortably, "And don't go flashing a smile like that at any man we happen to meet, unless he's blind!"

"Yes, Jephthah," she said demurely, and without waiting for him to help her this time, she swung into the saddle by herself. Her muscles were still sore, but there was nowhere near the pain that she had felt yesterday. The horse Jephthah had given her was a roan mare and well gaited. As she followed Jephthah's lanky hunter, keeping a respectful distance behind him as a colored stable boy would do following his master, she began to relax, enjoying the pleasure of once again having a fine horse beneath her.

She had learned to ride astride from her brothers, and when she and Jephthah reached the banks of the Potomac, she was glad she had. The river was flooded from the late-June rains and the crude bridge crossing Jephthah had planned to use had been destroyed by Stuart's cavalry. Gazing at the swift current, Lucinda doubted she could cross the river riding sidesaddle.

Two hours were wasted while Jephthah searched and finally found the least dangerous spot to ford the river. Even riding astride, Lucinda had a hard time controlling the mare as it plunged into the water. The river rose quickly to her thighs, then her waist. The horse scrambled and fought for footing, finally swim-

83

ming, the rushing, churning spray from the current splashing into the face of horse and rider alike.

When the mare at last reached the rocks and sand and river willows of the far shore, Lucinda was soaked to the skin, but the day was blazing hot, and within an hour her clothes were dry again.

For the next two days she and Jephthah continued traveling south, then turned west, following Cole's trail through the Glasscock Gap in the Bull Run Mountains.

"Not Richmond then," Jephthah grunted, his gaze never seeming to stop its restless sweeping of the countryside around them.

They were in country held by the enemy now. Lee's Army of Virginia had swept the Federal forces out of the valley in his march north. Although there were families in the valley still loyal to the Union, Jephthah had no way of knowing which ones they were, so they stayed clear of main traveled turnpikes and all farms and homes.

Several times, always managing to hear the sound of approaching hoofbeats long before Lucinda's ears picked them up, Jephthah signaled Lucinda to pull her horse off the road into the woods, and they waited quietly, hidden among the trees, as a brevet of rebel scouts rode by.

Each day her respect for the skill and wit of her traveling companion rose higher. His eye for tracking was as good as that of any Indian scout she had met, but he never forgot they could easily become the pursued, as well as the pursuers. Not even the smallest detail passed him by. Almost as soon as they had crossed the Potomac and were on Virginia soil, she noticed that Jephthah had switched from chewing short-cut tobacco to plug tobacco.

"Folks in the South favor plug tobacco," he had explained when Lucinda questioned him. "If we get stopped and questioned, some smart lieutenant might just notice if I was chewing Northern short-cut. One thing I learned, it's the little things that can tie a noose around your neck."

"What will you tell them about us if we're stopped?" Lucinda asked curiously.

"Small dirt farmer on the track of bushwhackers who ran off his stock," Jephthah said promptly. "That shouldn't be hard to believe," he added dryly, gesturing around him. "Between regular Army men, like Mosby's guerrillas, and the bushwhackers, deserters and just plain ne'er-do-wells who steal from everybody, Union or rebels, the valley's being picked clean."

Lucinda had noticed as they rode along how the fields they were passing through had been stripped bare or trampled down. Jephthah and she had had to halt three or four times a day to find sufficient graze for their horses. And the country roads they traveled were torn up by the passage of heavy artillery and countless wagons, while burned houses and barns and even blackened fence posts could be seen along the roads.

Nevertheless, as each day passed, she was aware of a growing familiarity with the countryside. The deep hazy blue of the Shenandoah mountains glimpsed in the distance, the neat white farmhouses fortunate enough to be left untouched by raiders, rail fences covered with morning glories and trumpet vines, lush valleys filled with apple orchards, the softly rolling hills around her, all brought back nostalgic memories of her childhood when she had roamed, wild as a fawn, through a countryside much like this.

And Cole, she thought, a sudden sharp pain below her heart. It was impossible to remember her youth at Black Oaks without including Cole in those happy, sunshine-filled memories. Quickly now she thrust such memories away. She had made her choice when she had put the candle in the attic window of the Von Bruck house. No matter the gratitude she felt for Cole's releasing her from the Von Bruck cellar, there was no turning back now. Her hand slipped into the saddlebag, tightened on the silver-handled derringer. She would use it if she had to, she thought coldly, remembering the dreadfully butchered soldiers by the burning wagon

85

train, one young lad no older than her brother Matt. She had her loyalties, her duty, the same as Cole had his.

Still, as five days passed and they seemed no closer to catching up with Cole than they had when they left Washington, she began to hope that perhaps Jephthah was wrong. Perhaps Cole was too wily and would escape even a skilled tracker like Jephthah.

Then one morning they saw a great cloud of dust rising in the distance behind them. Hastily leaving the road, they made for a wooded hill, pushing their way through the brush and scrub trees to reach the top and gaze back down into the road.

Jephthah took out a spyglass and after looking down at the dust cloud, handed the glass to Lucinda. At first all she could see was the cloud of dust hanging in the air. Then gradually she could make out green-flagged, rough wooden wagons crawling southward, jouncing over the rutted road, the wagons stretching as many miles back as her eye could see.

"Rebel ambulances," Jephthah said. "Must have been a big battle up there in Pennsylvania with so many wounded." His leather face softened as he gazed down at the seemingly endless ambulance train. "Poor devils. The lucky graybellies are the ones they buried."

Lucinda shuddered, imagining the agony of being wounded and then to endure days of jouncing in a springless uncovered wagon over rutted roads, beaten by rain or in a constant shroud of dust under a blazing sun.

Both she and Jephthah were quiet as they left the hilltop and cantered down a side road, finally coming to the first unburned farmhouse they had seen for almost an hour.

"I'll see if I can rustle us up some food," Jephthah said, sliding from the saddle and handing Lucinda his reins. "And some fresh water." She noticed that he loosened the flap of his pistol holder as he warily approached the house. Farm families, alert to the ever-threatening presence of raiders and bushwhackers, were apt to shoot strangers first and ask questions later.

It seemed an eternity but was only ten minutes before he returned, grinning broadly. "No food, but I got us a piece of interesting information. There was a big battle a few days ago near a small town called Gettysburg. From stragglers who've been drifting back this way, it sounds like the rebels finally met their match. Pickett and his men were smashed to pieces at a place called Cemetery Ridge, and Lee's retreating back into Virginia."

He swung up into his saddle, still grinning. Lucinda, who had become well acquainted with this taciturn mountain man the last few days, studied that grin suspiciously. "There's more, isn't there?"

"Yes, ma'am. The lady of the house told me a man rode by not an hour before us, a dark, curly-haired man, handsome fellow, I gather from her flutters." He gave Lucinda a sidelong glance. "Sound like our friend?"

She nodded, unable to speak, as if a stone had suddenly lodged in her throat.

Jephthah nodded, pleased. "That's what I figured. The lady let him switch horses for a fresh one from her stable. Reckon she would have accommodated him even more if he had been interested, but it seems he had to press on, wanted to make Ashby's Gap by nightfall."

He touched a spur to his horse. "Let's ride, ma'am. It looks like we've finally run the fox down."

The road, after it left the farm, wound through a wooded area, finally petering out into what was little more than a narrow track which might have been a logging road at one time. Lucinda tried to keep up with Jephthah but she was continually ducking her head to avoid being struck in the face by overhanging branches and found herself falling farther and farther behind. Her horse moved quietly over the marshy path, thickly covered with leaves. She was straining her ears to hear Jephthah's horse ahead of her when a branch suddenly struck her full across the face. She felt herself sliding off her horse, landing, with only her dignity hurt, on the soft path. Annoyed, she got to her feet and, grabbing the roan's bridle, decided to walk for a while.

She had gone only ten minutes on foot when she heard voices through the trees ahead of her. Startled, she stopped short. Jephthah? No, the voice was deeper than his, a familiar lazy drawl that made her breath suddenly catch in her throat. Tying her roan to a tree, she took the derringer from the saddlebag and made her way quietly through the thick brush until a rocky clearing suddenly appeared before her.

Crouching low, so she was hidden behind one of the large boulders on the edge of the clearing, she could see the two men clearly. Jephthah was facing her, his leathery face yellow with repressed fury, his pistol in the dust at his feet. Facing Jephthah with his back toward Lucinda was Cole Sinclair. His pistol was leveled at Jephthah's chest and his voice was coldly amused. "You've been following me for days. What's your business with me?"

Jephthah said nothing, spitting into the grass at his feet.

Cole shrugged indifferently. "No matter. You're either one of Baker's spies or one of Major Moore's scouts. I'd take you into Richmond, but I've no time to bother with prisoners. Anyway I expect you'd prefer a bullet to dancing at the end of a rope."

Jephthah nodded. "You're right, sir. I'd take a bullet kindly rather than dancing a sunset jig." For a split second, Lucinda thought that the gunmetal-gray eye had glanced in her direction, had seen her half hidden behind the rocks. But when he spoke again, his voice was placid. Only Lucinda guessed he was stalling for time. "I admire the trap you sprung on me, sir. I don't s'pose it was chance, your telling that woman back at the house where you were heading."

"I don't believe in chance," Cole said coolly. "And I was growing weary of your company. You're a good tracker, though. I'll give you that. I'm truly sorry it has to end this way."

Lucinda saw Cole's hand lift the pistol a quarter of an inch, his knuckles whitening.

She stood up. "Don't move." Her voice trembled, but the derringer was held steadily in her hand.

Cole half turned, his face blank with shock, as he saw a young colored boy holding a derringer within a few inches of his face.

"What the hell!" The blue-green eyes studied the small dark oval face beneath the slouch hat. "Sukey!"

"Yes, suh," she murmured shakily. "Don't move, suh, please. I don't want to have to kill you."

Cole's swarthy face darkened, his eyes narrowing into ice-cold slits. "But you're going to have to kill me, Sukey," he said softly. "There's no other way." His smile was lazy, taunting. "And I don't think you will, Sukey, so be a good girl and put down that gun before you hurt yourself."

He took a half step toward her, the man forgotten in his surprise at seeing the girl and the pistol leveled at him. Out of the corner of her eye, Lucinda saw Jephthah move, as quietly and swiftly as lightning, reaching for the pistol at his feet, leveling it at Cole's back.

There was an explosion in her ears at the same moment she felt the derringer jerk in her hand. She would never forget the look of stunned surprise on Cole's face, the bright-red patch of blood staining his white shirt front.

Nor would she forget the blue-green eyes blazing full in her face, the anger contorting Cole's features. "I should have let Bella have you," Cole said softly, swaying, as he took a step toward her. "Next time I'll kill . . ."

His voice fell away; his eyes closed and he crumpled slowly to the ground at her feet.

6

The derringer dropped from Lucinda's nerveless hand. She gave a little cry and knelt down beside the unconscious man, cradling his head in her lap, caressing the wiry black curls.

"Cole, oh, my God . . . Cole," she moaned, and glanced up at Jephthah, her eyes wide with anguish. "I had to shoot. You would have killed him."

"Yes, ma'am. I sure planned to." He hunched down beside her, examining the blood-soaked wound.

"Is . . . is he dead?"

For a moment, the gunmetal gaze softened as he looked into the girl's stricken face. Then he shook his head, his voice dry. "No, I reckon you're as good a shot as you claimed. You only winged him." Suddenly he cocked his head to one side, listening, his face all at once wary. "Horses, ma'am, coming fast. They must have heard the shot. We'd best get out of here."

Lucinda could hear the horses too, now, at least a half dozen or more judging from the sound of the thudding hooves. She placed Cole's head gently back on the ground. "We have to dress his wound," she protested.

Jephthah grabbed her arm, pulled her roughly to her feet. "There ain't time. That lady back at the house said there were bushwhackers in the neighborhood. If they find us, they'll strip us clean and leave us for the buzzards. We've got to ride . . . now!"

"My horse. He's back on the trail."

Jephthah cast a disgusted glance at Cole's horse. "That farm nag couldn't outrun a mule." He glanced toward the trees surrounding the clearing. "Get back into the woods and stay out of sight. I'll try and lead them off. If I get away, I'll double back for you."

Lucinda nodded, but reached for her kerchief to press it down upon Cole's wound to stanch the bleeding.

Jephthah yanked her aside, thrusting her toward the woods, his voice rasping angrily. "I said hide, and stay hidden! If those bushwhackers catch you and don't kill you, you'll wish you were dead. I've seen what they've done to women."

Frightened, the girl scuttled off into the woods, found a thick clump of underbrush and crept into it, pulling the branches around her. She heard Jephthah riding off. The other horsemen must have heard him too, for a man's voice yelled, "This way . . . he's getting away!" Then the sound of hoofbeats pounding, dying away, then silence.

Lucinda curled up uncomfortably in her hiding place. It was a hot, muggy day, and thorns from a wild rose bush dug into her arms. Soon her leg muscles began to cramp painfully from her crouched position. She didn't know how much time had passed since Jephthah had left; it seemed forever. A bee buzzed at a wild rose blossom near her, its buzzing stitching through the silence.

Then through the stillness, she heard another sound, a faint groan. Cole. A hand squeezed at her heart. She could glimpse him in the clearing through the trees. The sun beat down full upon his prone, unconscious body, the red stain on his shirt front spreading, discoloring the dirt beside him.

Without thinking further, only knowing she couldn't leave him like that, no matter what Jephthah said, she scrambled to her feet. And surely by now Jephthah had led the raiders off. Cole's horse was still standing patiently nibbling at the grass when she came to the edge of the clearing. She found a canteen of water on the saddle, and tearing a tail off her shirt, she dampened it from the canteen and wiped Cole's face. Then gently pressed the wad of material down upon the wound.

Lifting Cole as best she could, she saw, relieved, that there was an exit wound in his back, so the bullet at least had gone straight through his body. She wished she could move him into the shade, but she was afraid she would open the wound further, even if she could

91

manage to lift Cole's heavy weight. All she could do was shield him from the sun with her own body as she bent over him, stroking the wiry curls that clung to her fingers as if they had a virile life of their own.

"Cole," she whispered, lightly caressing his lips with her fingertips, "it's all right, darling. You're going to be fine."

For a moment, his eyelids opened, his eyes staring up at her but not really seeing her, his voice weakly raging, as if he were back in that dark, dank cellar of the Von Bruck home. "Sukey, damn it, what have they done to the girl! Sukey..." His voice died away, his eyes fastening bewildered upon her, then they closed again, and she realized as she touched his forehead that his skin was burning hot.

Frantically, half sobbing with fear, she tore another piece from her shirt, soaked it in water and bathed his face again. She had to get him in the shade, she decided, even if she did open the wound.

She put her arms under his shoulders, braced herself and pulled. Cole was a dead weight in her arms. She tried again. This time she managed to move him a few inches, but a voice suddenly drawled above her, "Well, now, ain't that a touching sight."

She straightened, startled. A tall, rake-thin man in worn dirty gray trousers and a blue jacket lounged against a boulder, watching her. He had a black, straggly beard and a drooping mustache, the mustache so long its greasy ends disappeared into the beard. She could smell him almost before she saw him, a rank, sour odor as if he hadn't bathed in months.

"That's what I like to see, a nigger that stays with his master, not running off like a scared weasel." He walked slowly toward Lucinda, grinning viciously. "But you got a new master now, boy."

For a moment she stood frozen, then turned and darted for the woods. As swiftly as she moved, he was faster, his long arm catching her easily, pulling her, kicking and screaming, away from Cole.

"Hush your fuss, boy!" The man's voice sharpened
92

with anger as he tried to hold the wiggling, twisting colored boy in his arms. "Or I'll give you something to fuss about."

The rough, bony hands tightened their hold around the small waist, reached upward for a firmer grasp on the squirming body, then loosened, surprised. "Well, what do you know!" The man swung his prisoner around, keeping a firm hold around the slim waist with one hand and snatching the cotton shirt front open with the other. The small yellowish eyes ran hungrily over the girl's firm young breasts; the grin widened. "Well, now, ain't you the pretty one. Let's see if the rest of you is just as pretty."

The bony hand reached out, tightened on the waist of the trousers. Lucinda lifted her free hand, clawed at the man's face and kicked at his shins. He gave a surprised yelp, tried to get a tighter hold on the girl, but she kicked at his legs again, this time tripping the man. They both fell, struggling, to the ground, rolling over and over as the man tried to get a firm hold on a kicking arm or leg.

They were both so engrossed, the girl in trying to free herself, the man in trying to sit on her to hold her down, that they didn't hear the troop of horsemen returning, pulling up their horses and gazing curiously down at the scene, the man and the colored girl fighting in the dust at their feet.

Several of the men guffawed, and one man jeered loudly, "What's the matter, Lem? Ain't you man enough to handle one little nigger gal?"

"Need some help, Lem?" another man offered. "Looks like she's going to tear you to pieces."

"That's enough!" A short, heavy-set man with the swaying stride of an ex-sailor got off his horse and pulled Lucinda to her feet by the scruff of her neck. The man Lem, his face flushed, shot Lucinda a furious glance as he climbed more slowly to his feet. "She tried to run off, cap'n. I found a roan tied to a tree back down the trail. I figured there had to be another one hiding near the one who took off, so I waited to see. She snuck out to tend him."

He poked his thumb toward the unconscious Cole. The leader of the men scarcely gave the wounded man a glance. "Get his boots and any valuables on him," he said shortly. "And get mounted. Ain't many hours of daylight left."

Lucinda tried to pull free from the hand pinching her neck. "You can't just leave him," she protested, outraged. "He'll die."

"Reckon he will," the man agreed equably.

Fury pounded in the girl's temples. She glanced contemptuously at the mounted men, the dirty, ill-fitting uniforms they wore, gray Confederate trousers, blue Union jackets. A few of the men were dressed like farmers. "What kind of soldiers are you?" she asked bitterly. "What kind of monsters would leave a wounded man?"

The man holding her scowled. "Mosby's men," he said shortly. "And we don't waste bullets on a dying man." He released her suddenly, a hamlike hand cuffing her across the face so that for a minute the world spun dizzily around her and she fell sprawling again in the dust. "And we don't take sass from nigger gals," he finished coldly.

Mosby's men! Fear gripped at the girl's very soul. Even in Washington, she had heard about the dreaded rebel leader Mosby, and his so-called rangers, small groups of guerrillas on horseback. Mosby, who struck like a gray ghost without warning, murdering and plundering without mercy, then disappearing as if the earth had swallowed him up. During the time the Federal troops had held the valley, Mosby's men still had dared to attack supply trains and railroads, even once invading a heavily guarded Union camp and kidnapping a Yankee general from his bed, carrying him off as a prize of war. In the North, Mosby was considered little better than a horse thief, a murdering cutthroat, but in the South he was a hero. Stories of his daring deeds were whispered around the fireside at night.

Lucinda felt herself being yanked to her feet. "Where's Sam?" the man bellowed.

The largest black man Lucinda had ever seen rode forward, holding extra horses on a long rope. Like the rest of the troop, he wore bits and pieces of uniforms, but all the clothes he wore were too small for him, as if he had never been able to rob a man his size. Although his skin was a burnished blue-black, his hawked nose and sharp, high cheekbones reminded Lucinda of the Indians she had met on the frontier.

Lucinda was pushed toward the black man. "Tie her on a horse, Sam," the captain commanded. "Keep an eye on her."

Lem stepped forward anxiously. "You ain't forgettin' she's mine, cap'n? She'll bring me a good price in Richmond."

"You know the rules, Lem," the captain said sharply. "We share the booty equally in the troop."

The black man lifted Lucinda into the empty saddle as easily as if she were a down pillow, then without a word tied her wrists tightly to the saddlehorn. The movement pulled open her torn shirt, exposing her taut, upthrust breasts.

One of the troopers, younger than the others and with a clean-shaven face, pushed his horse next to hers, leering down at the girl. "Now that's one prize I can't wait to share, cap'n," he said, grinning fatuously.

"Later," the captain said, although his own eyes lingered for a moment on the soft swell of breasts between the torn shirt. "The one who got away may be sounding the alarm, and we got work yet to do."

So Jephthah, at least, had escaped, Lucinda thought gratefully, as the black man took her reins in his hand and, waiting till the other troopers rode ahead, brought up the rear.

"Where are we going?" she asked her black captor.

The man said nothing, keeping his eyes straight ahead, as if she hadn't spoken.

She glanced at him curiously. "You b'long to these white folks, Sam?"

His eyes flashed defiance. "Ah don' b'long to no one 'cept myself."

She brought her horse closer to his, flashing him a radiant smile. "You got a gal, Sam?"

He did not even glance in her direction, much less answer.

Her voice dropped coaxingly. "Help me get away, Sam, and I'll be your onliest gal."

"Shut your mouth, gal," he said fiercely, "or I'll shut it for you."

Then he dug his knee into her horse's flanks so that it sprang forward as the troop ahead picked up speed on the open road. Glancing around, Lucinda saw that the men were simply retracing the route she and Jephthah had traveled earlier that day. Within a half hour they were near the farmhouse where Jephthah had stopped and picked up the information about Cole from the farm woman. The captain motioned to the men, and they spread out into the low hills surrounding the house. Sam pulled Lucinda's horse with his up to the crest of the hill, where they could look down upon the peaceful farm in the valley below.

But not peaceful for long. With a series of fearful yells that lifted the hair on Lucinda's arms, the half dozen mounted men rode down upon the house, whooping and yelling and shooting. There were answering gunshots from inside the house. One of the troopers swayed on his horse but straightened and continued riding directly for the front porch of the house.

Three of the riders turned off toward the barn, and after they brought out three horses and several cows, Lucinda watched horrified as they set fire to the hay in the barn. Soon the roof and walls of the building were consumed in flame. Keeping safely at a distance from the flames, the men immediately set to work butchering and quartering the cows.

Then a wild crescendo of screams tore her eyes back to the farmhouse. A woman and man had been dragged from the house, the man gray-haired, his head bloodied. Two of the bushwhackers tied the man to a fence post and with the butts of their guns began systematically to beat the man until he slumped, motionless, in his bonds.

The woman, who had been forced to watch, and who had never stopped screaming the whole time, suddenly pulled free of the arms holding her and ran toward the man. A shot rang out. The woman's apron fluttered in the breeze and she half-turned, then fell slowly, almost gracefully, to the ground.

"Dammit, Lem," one of the men shouted angrily. "You had no call to shoot her. Now we'll never find out where they buried their money."

Lucinda, swaying forward in the saddle, shut her eyes against the horror of the scene, wishing she could as easily shut out of her mind the sound of the woman's screams, echoing and reechoing in her head.

After a few minutes she was dimly aware that her horse was moving, going downhill. She felt the heat from the flames of the burning barn, and now the house went up, too, tongues of flame reaching toward the soft cloudless blue sky overhead.

While Sam loaded the freshly cut meat and other supplies dragged from the house before it was set to the torch, the rest of the men dug with pitchforks and sticks into the ground.

"Here, cap'n, looks like the dirt just been dug up.... No, dammit, nothing here but rocks. Try the well; the last place they hid their gold in the well bucket...."

It was almost twilight before the men, disgusted, gave up the search for the money. Lucinda, gazing dully around her at what had once been a simple homestead, wondered if the couple had ever had any. As she watched, the roof of the house collapsed in a shower of sparks, and flames once again leaped upward in the growing darkness, throwing grotesque shadows over the scene of carnage around it.

She turned her gaze away from the murdered man

and woman, the butchered cattle, the burning house, barn, hay ricks and hen run. Anger stiffened her spine as she demanded in a soft, fierce voice of Sam, "Mosby's a Southerner. How could his men kill their own people?"

Just for a second a look of contempt flickered in Sam's haughty black face, the rich, deep voice filled with scorn. "Mosby wouldn't give this scum camp room."

The captain had swung into his saddle. "Let's light out," he yelled. "Time's wearin'. We want to make the gap by full dark."

The next hours passed in a merciful blur to Lucinda. The troop rode at a gallop now, only stopping occasionally to rest the horses before racing onward through the night. Several times she would have fallen from the saddle despite her bound wrists if Sam, riding beside her, hadn't reached out and grabbed her arm, jerking her back upright. Gradually she became aware that the ground beneath her horse had changed, was rougher, rockier. They had left the road and were climbing, following a narrow path that meant they had to ride single file. Even through the darkness she could feel the forest on either side of the path closing in, and the higher they climbed into the mountain, the cooler the air became. During the heat of the day, she had longed for coolness. Now she found herself shivering in her cotton shirt and trousers and wishing for some of that heat back. To add to her discomfort, it began to rain—not a heavy rain, but the chill wind, caught within the narrow limits of the pass, groaned loudly and threw the rain back into her face, no matter how she tried to duck her head. The men pulled on ponchos and oilskin cloaks which had been rolled tightly to their saddles, but no one thought of Lucinda's misery. Finally Sam took a poncho from his roll and flung it around her shoulders.

"Thank you," she whispered.

He shrugged his broad shoulders, his voice flat. "A

98

dead slave ain't bringing any price in Richmond, and I shares the booty with the rest of them."

After they penetrated deep into the gap, the rain stopped, and evidently deciding they were out of reach of pursuit, the captain called a halt for the night. They made camp in a cleared, sheltered area where Lucinda could see evidence of old campfires, as if the troop had used the clearing before. There was a small natural cave in the mountainside at one edge of the clearing, and Sam carried Lucinda inside it and deposited her on the ground. The cave had a musky scent, as if animals had used it as a lair, but at least it was dry. Lucy gratefully stretched her cramped, aching limbs.

"Couldn't you untie me, Sam?" she asked pleadingly.

He hesitated, then shrugged. "Reckon so. You ain't going nowhere, not in these mountains."

After he untied her, he left her to tend the horses. Then he started a fire and began fixing food for the men, who had already started warming themselves with nips from a bottle of peach brandy that was handed around from one man to the next. After the men had eaten, Sam brought Lucinda some food and water in the cave and left her alone.

Although she was famished, she had to force the barely cooked meat and stale bread down her throat. As she ate, she noticed faint patches of white on her hands. She wondered if the stain was beginning to wear off anywhere else on her body. She hoped not.

She had already seen how the troop of men treated a white woman. At least as a comely black girl, she was worth money on the auction block and would be kept alive. Then, too exhausted even to be kept awake by the sounds of merriment from the camp fire as more peach brandy was passed around and a deck of cards was brought out, she curled up on the poncho and fell asleep.

She was awakened by a hand fumbling with the buttons on her shirt and a man's voice, jocular, half drunk, in her ear. "Wake up, gal. Ain't no fun with you asleep."

She was completely awake then, panic racing through her. In the dim half-light of the cave, she recognized the young man they called Cal leering drunkenly at her. She sat up, pulling away from the hand groping inside her shirt for her breast, and darted out of the cave. The man's hand still grasped her shirt, and it ripped off in his hand. He came weaving out of the cave after her, waving the shirt and shouting blearily, "Hey, gal, where you goin'?"

In her eagerness to escape those fumbling hands, she had forgotten the men sitting playing cards around the campfire. As she stumbled half-naked out into the clearing, a half-dozen pair of eyes ogled appreciatively the young, rounded breasts and silken golden-brown skin gleaming in the firelight.

One man shouted raucously, "If you can't handle her, Cal, let a full-grown man show you how."

Another man said hoarsely, "I'll give you twenty dollars for your turn, Cal."

The young man shook his head. "No, sir, I won her fair and square. You get your chance at her tomorrow night."

Dazed with horror, Lucinda realized then the meaning behind the cardplaying—she was the prize for the winning hand. Her glance flew to the woods surrounding the clearing, searching for a path of escape through the half circle of men lounging around the campfire. She saw Sam standing to one side of the group, his body half hidden in darkness, his arms crossed relaxed over his chest. His eyes, too, were staring fixedly at her breasts, but it wasn't lust she saw in his face. Just for a second another emotion appeared there, shock, or was it anger, dropped like a rock into a deep black pond, disturbing for a moment its stillness.

But she had no time to puzzle over Sam's reaction. The young man named Cal was weaving drunkenly toward her, a vacant smile on his face, arms outstretched. Knowing it was useless, but knowing she had to try, she ran for the woods. One of the men lazily stretched out his leg. She tripped and fell to the ground, the breath knocked out of her. Before she could rise, the man who had tripped her was on top of her, his moist mouth covering hers, his rough, greasy beard scratching her skin while his hand tore at the waist of her trousers.

As in a nightmare, too terrible to be real, she felt herself jerked roughly from one man's arms to another, as the men gathered in a circle, laughing and shouting, eagerly, almost merrily, passing the girl from one man to the next. A mouth smelling of brandy and tobacco would briefly crush against hers, hands fumbling, eagerly seeking her soft, warm body before another man claimed his turn.

Then an explosion suddenly split the night.

Cal stood, swaying, pistol in hand, glaring at the men, his voice boyishly shrill with anger. "Dammit, let her go. She's mine. I won her, didn't I?"

The captain, who had joined in the fun as lustily as his men, nodded regretfully. "The lad's right. It was a fair game. Let the gal go."

Lucinda, suddenly released, swayed dizzily on her feet. She had the odd sensation she had stepped outside her body, had become a stranger, all emotions numbed, standing to one side, watching the proceedings, her body, everything that was happening to her, no part of her at all.

She was thrust forward into Cal's arms, and she docilely allowed him to lead her back into the cave, made no protest as he lowered her onto the poncho she had spread earlier on the ground. She watched almost with disinterest as the young man hastily pulled off his clothes, exposing a rangy body, all hard muscle and long bone. She only whimpered a little in protest as his hand tugged awkwardly at her trousers, finally managing to slide them off her body. Then he stopped to take a long drink from the bottle of brandy. Wiping his mouth with the back of his hand, he handed the girl the bottle. "Here, take a swig of this. You'll feel better."

He stuck the bottle to her lips, but she turned her head away, vaguely sensing that drinking the peach brandy might take away the blessed, saving numbness, make her start feeling again, and that would be disastrous.

The light from the campfire cast shadows against the wall of the cave, flickered faintly over her body and that of the man leaning over her. His pale-brown eyes, glazed from the brandy and from wonder, as if unable to believe his good fortune, traveled delighted over the soft, golden-brown curve of hip and thigh, the pink-tipped swell of breasts awaiting his pleasure.

"Ain't never seen anything so pretty," he muttered thickly.

His hand reached out to caress the tempting softness of a breast, then his mouth—she could feel the painful, feral sharpness of his teeth on her tender nipple—and she tried to turn her body away. "Please, no..." she moaned.

He lifted his head, his hands moving feverishly over her body, thrusting her legs apart, his voice hoarse, excited. "Don't worry, I ain't aimin' to hurt you, gal. I'm not like Lem. He likes to hurt niggers."

Dimly, repressing a giggle of hysteria, she sensed that he was actually trying to be gentle with her. Or perhaps it was only that he was unsure of himself and had not known many women. In any case, it was over with more quickly than she could have imagined possible. The weight of his body on top of her was gone as he sighed deeply and rolled over on his side, one arm and leg still sprawled across her.

She waited motionless for several minutes, terrified that any movement on her part might rouse him. Then slowly, carefully, she pulled her body free of his. Then, looking into the boy's face, she saw that she needn't have worried. She had seen her brothers once or twice in the same condition from imbibing too freely at the punch bowl. It would be hours before Cal regained consciousness.

Shivering, she pulled on her clothes, her hands trembling. Odd, whimpering sounds came from her throat as she crept to the opening of the cave and peered out into the darkness. The campfires had burned low. She could barely distinguish the figures of the men stretched out around it.

Gradually, with a wrenching physical effort, she pushed the hysteria deep inside her. From the sound of the snores disturbing the silence of the night, she suspected that the men were in much the same condition as Cal. If she were to make her escape, it would have to be now, she realized. Whatever terrors the dark woods and towering rocks of the mountain held, they couldn't be worse than the terrors she faced here in this camp.

Quietly now, walking in her own footsteps with the soundless Indian stride she had learned at the trading post, she edged her way toward the black fringe of pine trees surrounding the clearing. She had circled the dying campfire, the sprawled, sleeping men, had almost reached the safety of the trees, when a hand suddenly clamped down on her shoulder. A gasp of fear rose to her lips when a voice behind her whispered sharply, "Shut your mouth!"

She had forgotten Sam, she realized, despair bringing tears of frustration to her eyes. She remembered now that the men hadn't offered the black man any of the brandy. She should have guessed that they expected Sam to stay sober and act as night guard for the camp, the same way he was expected to tend the horses and do the cooking.

Then, to her surprise, instead of forcing her back to the cave, she was being pushed toward the trees. Pine needles, still wet from the early evening rain, brushed damply at her face. She stumbled over a log and would have fallen, but the hand still clamped painfully on her shoulder, numbing her arm, pulled her roughly to her feet, thrust her forward again deeper into the stand of pines.

Then abruptly they halted in what appeared to be another, smaller clearing. She could not see Sam's face in the thick darkness surrounding them, but his voice came harshly at her out of the blackness. "Can you ride bareback?"

She stared up at him, too startled to speak.

He shook her roughly, like a terrier with a squirrel in his mouth. "Can you?" he repeated impatiently.

"Yes."

"Wait."

She did not hear him leave or return, but suddenly he was back. Her eyes had grown more accustomed to the darkness and she could make out his massive figure, the shine of his eyes, the whiteness of his teeth, when he spoke again. "Take the roan. She's used to you."

She saw then the two horses he had brought back with him, the roan mare the bushwhackers had stolen from her, and a big black bay the captain had been riding. The horses were bridled but without saddles, and their hooves were encased in soft leather to dull the sound of hoofbeats. Quickly obeying his nod, she stepped into his clasped hands, and as she swung astride the roan, memories of her days on the Michigan frontier returned when she and her brothers had been taught to ride bareback by their Indian friends.

Sam watched her mount with grudging approval. "Where'd you learn to ride, gal? Ain't never met any slave gal can ride like that."

Then, not waiting for an answer, he swung astride the bay and, taking the lead, led the way up an almost invisible track through the woods. At first they walked their horses, which, even with their hooves covered, made soft thudding noises in the night. Lucinda held her breath, waiting for some sound to come from the camp behind them, for one of the men to wake up and discover that she and Sam were missing, to hear the cries of angry pursuit behind them. But except for the occasional cry of a sleepy bird, the rustle of some small animal passing through the brush, the night was silent. They had ascended the mountain for almost fifteen minutes when they came to a small stream with a cliff rising precipitously on the other side of the water.

Sam stopped his horse, gesturing toward the cliff. "That's where we're going."

The black night was dissolving into a gray dawn that brought with it a fine chill mist. Lucinda stared, disbelieving, at the solid wall of stone before her. "How can we climb that? There's no path."

"There's a path all right—more like a goat trail. Hang on tight and follow me."

The bay splashed across the creek with the roan mare following. There was no question of Lucinda hanging on; there was nothing else she could do but hang on for dear life, her arms flung around the roan's neck, her knees digging into his flanks as he lunged and fought his way up the narrow, stone-covered path. Once the mare stumbled and fell to his knees, neighing with terror. Lucinda took one look down the cliffside, a straight hundred-foot drop down to the creek, a thread of silver far below her, and closed her eyes and said a silent prayer. Then she felt someone grab at her bridle, Sam's voice soft as velvet, soothing, calming the frightened animal, coaxing the roan again to his feet. Another five minutes and they were safely at the crest of the cliff. Here the forest cover was skimpier, and with the sun almost fully risen, Sam cast an eye at the sky and said, "We'll hole up here for a couple of days, till they get tired of looking for us."

He led both horses through a ravine, where a brook made a waterfall on its downward course. Behind the waterfall was a narrow opening in the side of the mountain, almost invisible, like a crack in a fold of rock. Lucinda slipped off her horse, her legs wobbly beneath her, following Sam as he took the reins and led the horses through the opening. Once inside the crack, the passage widened, became almost the size of a small cabin.

Lucinda gazed around her, surprised. "How did you know this was here?" she asked Sam.

He shrugged. "I hid out in these mountains most two years before I joined up with those bushwhackers." He removed the haversack he had slung across his back and took out some cold meat and a bottle of brandy. "Can't take a chance on a fire, not yet. Smoke can be seen a long ways."

Lucinda refused the meat; her stomach turned over at sight of its congealed-grease exterior. But she swallowed a little of the brandy, welcoming the delicious warmth it sent coursing through her body. The combination of the chill mist dampening her clothes and hair and her exhaustion and shock had started her shaking, and she couldn't seem to stop.

Sam studied the exhausted girl, the shudders shaking the slender body so that even her mouth was trembling, and taking a thin blanket from his haversack, he tossed it to her. "Take off those wet clothes and wrap this around you," he ordered brusquely.

She reached to remove her shirt, then stopped, staring pleadingly at the man. He scowled and strode from the cave, returning in ten minutes with a load of pine boughs. She had removed her wet clothes and wrapped the blanket around her like a cocoon. Now she sank gratefully down on the makeshift bed her companion had prepared from the boughs.

Even with the pine boughs beneath her and the blanket wrapped around her, she couldn't stop trembling. Every bone and muscle in her body ached. She longed for sleep, but her nerves were stretched taut and she couldn't relax. Not just her own tension, she realized all at once. She could feel as well the repressed anger flowing toward her from the black man, who hunched on the floor watching her, like a volcano on the verge of erupting.

Then suddenly, as if he could no longer contain himself, he had crossed the cave to her side in one lithe stride and dropped down beside her. A wicked long narrow knife was in his hand, and before she could move, he had placed the point of the knife against the soft hollow of her throat.

"Now," he said fiercely. "Now I wants the truth."

Lucinda gazed up at him blankly, too terrified to move. "I . . . I don't understand," she stammered. "What . . . what truth?"

His free hand caught at the braided leather necklace around her neck and jerked it free. "This," he cried hoarsely, dangling the necklace before her eyes, his own eyes shining with a wild fury. "Where did you get it?"

"It . . . it was a present," she said, bewildered.

Then gasped, as the knife pricked painfully at her throat, drawing blood. "Don't lie!" he whispered hoarsely. "My Janey wouldn't give my necklace away. She's dead, isn't she?"

Understanding burst upon Lucinda. With a strength she didn't know she still possessed, she pushed the hand with the knife away and struggled to sit up. "No! No, she's not dead. I left her not more than a week ago in Washington." She studied the man's painfilled face and said quietly, "You're Troy, aren't you? Jane's husband."

The knife fell from the man's hand. He stared at her suspiciously. "How come you know about me?"

"Jane told me. She told me all about you."

"She's alive . . . you're sure?" he persisted.

"I'm sure." She nodded. "I was a servant in the Von Bruck home in Washington with Jane."

"Washington." The man's shoulders slumped, his face a mask of despair. "That's where she's gone to. I snuck back to the plantation two months ago. I was going to steal her and the young 'uns away, no matter what, but she wasn't there. And the babies were too little to take with me, to run with me and hide in the mountains. I joined those no-count men, hoping to make some money to buy my babies and Janey." His voice turned bitter. "If that she-devil will ever let them go."

"That's why you helped me escape, because you recognized the necklace?"

He nodded impatiently. "Why else? You ain't nuttin'

to me. Why should I care if that trash wants to pleasure themselves with you?"

Lucinda studied the brooding, hawklike face and smiled faintly. "I don't believe you, Sam," she said, shaking her head. "I believe you meant to help me, even before you saw the necklace. You wouldn't be the man a woman like Jane could love, otherwise."

Then she sank back on the boughs with a sigh. She was too tired to talk any longer, too tired to think or even feel. Her very bones ached with weariness. But the sleep that finally possessed her was not a peaceful sleep, and she jerked awake, shaking with cold, her teeth chattering.

Although she made hardly a sound, Sam, on his pallet of pine boughs near the entrance to the cave, came instantly awake. He rose to his feet and padded over to stare down at her, frowning as he watched the girl's helpless, violent trembling. Then, without a word, he lay down on the pallet beside her and wrapped her in his powerful arms. Startled, still half asleep, she tried to push him away. It was like trying to move a mountain with her bare fists.

"Be still," he commanded harshly.

At first she felt only the shock of his hard, muscular body pressed against hers, then a sensation of warmth began to flow from his warm flesh against her ice-cold skin, like the heat from a wood stove, deliciously warming her. She cuddled closer to that warmth, finally drifting off to sleep.

When she awoke in the morning, she was alone in the cave. She dressed quickly, grateful to discover her clothes had dried. The chill was gone from her body. Instead she felt uncomfortably, blazing hot, her throat raw. When she tried to walk to the entrance of the cave, her legs gave way beneath her and she sank dizzily back down on the pine boughs. When Sam came back from making sure the horses were fed and watered, he insisted she eat. Although she forced the cold greasy meat down her throat, she instantly retched it up again. The brandy fared no better.

"You'd best rest," Sam said, worried. "Wish I could make a fire, but we can't chance it, not yet. The cap'n ain't goin' to take kindly to losing a slave gal worth five hundred dollars on the block and his prize black bay."

"I'll be all right," Lucinda said, lying back on the pine boughs, wishing her head would stop pounding, the cave stop whirling around her. "Just... need... sleep."

Sleep brought her no rest, though—only nightmares. She was freezing cold and stark naked, running through a dark woods, pursued by ragged men with greedy, lust-filled faces, like Lem's. Then she was burning hot, the trees around her a blazing inferno. In a clearing in the midst of the burning woods, Cole lay, helpless and bleeding, his blue-green eyes staring at her accusingly as she tried in vain to reach him through the flames.

There were other, more peaceful moments from her childhood at Black Oaks. Fox-hunting with her brothers and Cole, reading in Black Oaks' dim, cool study, laughing with her slave friend, Dora Lee, at a trick they had played on Aunt Bessie, the cook.

Then Black Oaks disappeared and she was back in the cave, and an icy darkness, like a great weight, was pressing down upon her so that she gasped and struggled for breath. Dimly she was aware that Sam had built a fire after all. Great clouds of steam seemed to be rising from it, filling the cave, easing the pain in her lungs. Then once again the clothes were being stripped from her body. She felt something harsh, like rough wool, rubbed against her flesh, bringing warmth to her skin, until her flesh felt on fire. Then the darkness once more descended over her, pulling her down into nothingness.

7

It was a blue jay calling raucously to its mate that roused and finally held Lucinda's attention. She lifted her eyelids, which felt strangely heavy, and stared at a window curtained in pale-yellow dimity. The yellow curtains turned the sunshine pouring through the window into the color of rich cream as it spilled across a highly polished wood floor. Colorful rag rugs were scattered over the floor, and the walls of the room were painted the same pale yellow as the curtains.

Lucinda stared around her apprehensively. For such a long time, it seemed, she had been locked into a dark, pain-filled world, her body cramped and chilled one minute, burning hot the next; voices and faces rushing at her through the darkness then receding into a gray mist. For a moment she was afraid she was still caught up in that frightening, alien world; that if she closed her eyes all the warmth and comfort around her, the feather-filled coverlet over her, the down-filled pillows beneath her head, would disappear.

Her hand reached out tentatively to cup a stray sunbeam in her curled fingers. Her gaze drifted bewildered from the red mahogany posters of her bed to the lowboy dressing table and huge, carved wardrobe in a corner of the room. Odd how it all somehow seemed vaguely familiar, as if she should know this room, had been here before. Even the gnarled branches of a Judas tree, almost thrusting through the open window, had a familiar look about them.

"Lucy."

The voice was soft, hardly a whisper, yet it was familiar, too.

She turned her head toward the gray-haired woman seated beside the bed. "Aunt Clare?" Lucy's eyes widened, surprised. "What are you doing here?"

Her aunt brushed tears of joy from her childishly round blue eyes. Leaning forward, she squeezed Lucy's hand gently. "You're going to be all right now, dear. We've been so worried about you."

Memory returned to Lucinda then in a rush. This was her room, the bedroom she had grown up in at Black Oaks. She stared at her aunt, dazed. "I don't understand. How did I get here?"

"Don't think about that now, dear. Drink some of this broth. You haven't kept any food down in days, but I'm sure you'll be fine now."

Obediently Lucy swallowed the warm chicken broth. She had many more questions she wanted to ask, but her eyelids still felt weighted and it was too much of an effort to talk. Once again she slept. This time, though, it was a deep restful sleep. And when she awoke again, she knew, even before she opened her eyes, where she was.

The sun was still streaming into the room, the blue jay scolding from his perch in the Judas tree. Did he never get tired? Lucinda wondered, stretching luxuriously. For several seconds she simply savored the familiar scents of beeswax and lemon polish that had always filled her bedroom, even as a child. Nothing, she thought, delighted, had changed. It was almost as if she had never been away. Even the jagged crack in the wall that she and Dora Lee had made during a pillow fight that had gotten out of hand was exactly the same.

The door to the bedroom opened, and her aunt bustled in, carrying a tray. Aunt Clare hadn't changed either, Lucy thought fondly. The pink round face was a shade plumper, but her slim, girlish figure was the same, and the gray, carefully waved wig her aunt always wore was, as usual, just a trifle askew. Her aunt had lost much of her hair during a siege of typhoid fever when Lucy had been only a small girl and had worn wigs ever since.

"How are you feeling, Lucy, honey?" she asked, anxiously.

"I'm fine, Aunt Clare. And I hope that's more than broth on the tray, because I'm starved."

Her aunt settled the tray beside the bed, her small hands fussing over the plate and snowy napkin. "It's just eggs and corn bread, I'm afraid, darling. I wish you could have bacon, but we haven't had any since the quartermaster's men came through and took our last sow and the ham we had stored in the smokehouse. Of course, I'd do anything for our dear soldiers, but I can't help being glad that Harry managed to hide the milk cow and the chickens."

The war, Lucinda thought, flinching, as memory swept back. Too many memories. Those terror-filled hours riding with the bushwhackers, the sickening horror of those moments in the clearing by the cave, hands grabbing at her, thrusting her from one man's arms to another, making her feel less than human, Cal's eyes shining greedily, his hands fumbling at her body. And Cole ... dear God, Cole! Cole lying bleeding to death, beneath the blazing sun. And she had killed him.

Her throat tightened, and for a moment she couldn't swallow. Misery was like a dagger slowly, agonizingly turning in a spot just below her breastbone.

"What is it, Lucy? Are you feeling ill again?"

Her aunt's voice reached out to her, pulling her back to the present.

Lucy forced herself to smile reassuringly into her aunt's worried face. "I'm all right, Aunt Clare." She studied, bewildered, her hands holding the fork. How strange to see the skin was white, not tawny gold. She had become so accustomed to seeing herself, thinking of herself, as Sukey, a small brown slave girl, that it was difficult to realize that girl was gone.

"Eat your eggs, Lucy," her aunt urged, "before they get cold."

Lucy discovered she was ravenous, and she did not speak again until, with a contented sigh, she pushed her clean plate away from her and asked curiously,

"You haven't told me yet, Aunt Clare. How did I get here to Black Oaks?"

Her aunt's plump cheeks flushed. She studied her niece uneasily. "You don't remember . . . anything?"

Lucinda frowned. There was Cole and Jephthah facing each other in the clearing . . . the bushwhackers and Cal . . . and Sam! How could she have forgotten Sam? Her face cleared. Of course. He must have brought her here. But how had he known about Black Oaks?

"Where is he?" she asked, struggling to sit up. "Where is Sam?"

"Is that his name?" her aunt asked. "He wouldn't tell us a thing, not even his name. He just arrived one morning with you, more dead than alive, tied to one horse and him on another."

"Where is he now? He didn't leave?"

Her aunt bit her lower lip nervously, not meeting Lucy's gaze. "No, he's still here. Harry . . . that is, we both thought it best to hold the man until you regained consciousness. He's locked in one of the slave quarters."

At Lucy's look of outrage, her aunt continued apologetically, "Sam's perfectly all right, dear. Naturally, we had no way of knowing what had happened to you. . . ." Her voice trailed off tactfully.

"Sam saved my life," Lucinda said. Then, as her aunt waited patiently for her to continue, she improvised rapidly, knowing there was very little of the truth she could tell without shocking Aunt Clare out of her wits. "I was working in Washington—as a nurse—when I became ill. With Father and Charles gone—and I haven't heard from young Matt in months—I decided to return to Black Oaks."

Tears filled her aunt's soft blue eyes, spilling unheeded down her gentle, grief-stricken face. "Oh, my dear, I'm so sorry about your dear father and Charles. We heard about your cruel loss. Such a terrible waste."

"Yes." Lucy couldn't bear to dwell on the deaths of her father and brother and hurried on. "I hired Sam to drive me from Washington to Black Oaks."

"Through the enemy lines?" her aunt asked, shocked. "Wasn't that taking a dreadful chance, my dear? Suppose the Yankees had caught you?" She gave a delicate shudder of horror at the thought.

Lucinda shrugged impatiently. "The Yankees aren't two-headed monsters, Aunt Clare. They're men, just like . . . like our Southern boys. And it isn't that difficult passing through the lines if you have the proper papers. But going through Ashby's Gap, we ran into bushwhackers. Sam managed to get me away on horseback, but we had to leave the wagon and all our supplies behind. Then we got caught in a rainstorm, and I guess . . . well, I don't remember the rest except I suppose I must have been very sick. Sam must have decided to get me home any way he could."

She pushed back the coverlet and got to her feet, swaying dizzily and clutching at a bedpost for support. "I want to see Sam. He must be released at once."

"Of course, dear." Gently her aunt coaxed her back into bed. "When you're stronger. I'll speak to Harry about Sam. We both will want to thank him for bringing you home."

Home. Lucy found herself blinking back tears at the word. No matter how much she had resented her father's being cut out of her grandfather's will and how firmly she had turned her back on the plantation and everything it represented, whenever she thought of a home during the last years, it was always the faded red brick walls of Black Oaks that came immediately to mind. She had been born in this house. Her roots were here deep in the softly rolling fields and rich red valley soil.

Then she shook her head sadly. "Black Oaks isn't my home, Aunt Clare, not any longer."

Her aunt's plump face crumpled in distress. "You mustn't say that, child. Of course this is your home. I'm sure if my dear husband were alive, he'd say the same thing."

Startled, Lucinda noted for the first time that her aunt was wearing widow's weeds. "I'm sorry, Aunt

Clare. I... I didn't know." She reached out a hand in sympathy. "How did Uncle Joseph die?"

Her aunt took a white lacy handkerchief from her sleeve and dabbed at her eyes. "There was no way you could have known, darling. It happened just a month ago, in Richmond. Mr. Appleton was attending a cabinet meeting, and he had a stroke, the doctor said. He died almost at once. They had such a lovely service for your uncle in Richmond. I wish you could have been there. President Jefferson Davis said Mr. Appleton died as bravely in the service of his country as any soldier struck down in battle."

She sighed tremulously. "Poor Harry. Joseph's death was terribly hard on him. They were very close, for a stepfather and stepson." She shook her head wistfully. "The whole war's been hard for Harry. He tried several times to enlist, but with his... his affliction, they wouldn't accept him. They said he was needed here at Black Oaks, raising food for the Army. Heaven knows, that's difficult enough, trying to raise a crop with almost all our servants and field hands run off or taken by the Army to help build fortifications around Richmond."

She gave her eyes one last wiping, then tucked the handkerchief briskly back into her sleeve. "There, now, listen to me run on, burdening you with my problems. I should be grateful that we still have a roof over our heads. When I think of Gray Meadows and the families like the Sinclairs..." Her voice trailed off unhappily.

Lucy sat up abruptly. "What happened to Gray Meadows?"

Her aunt rose to her feet. "I'll tell you some other time, child. I'm sure I shouldn't be upsetting you this way with sad stories. You need your rest."

Lucinda caught her aunt's hand before she could move away. "Tell me, Aunt Clare. Please, I have to know."

Clare Appleton hesitated, studying, thoughtfully, her niece's face. "I'd forgotten, Lucy. You were very fond of Cole Sinclair, weren't you?" The soft blue eyes hardened as she spoke, and Lucinda all at once remembered that her good-natured aunt, for some unknown reason, did not approve of Cole.

"Alice Sinclair died over a year ago," she said tautly. "And Cole didn't come home, not even for his mother's funeral."

Lucy remembered how Cole, an only child, had loved Gray Meadows, almost as much as he had idolized his frail, invalid mother. At his father's death, when he had been only eighteen, Cole had worked as hard as any field hand building Gray Meadows into one of the most prosperous plantations in the valley, while Alice Sinclair had made their home into a showplace filled with priceless art objects, as well as the warmth and glow of a home that is deeply loved.

"How did Mrs. Sinclair die?"

Her aunt sighed and sat down again beside the bed, spreading her skirt carefully over her ankles. "It was last year," she said reluctantly. "Our gallant General Jackson had driven the Federal troops out of the valley. There was a skirmish not far from Gray Meadows. Some stragglers from the Yankee Army came across the house. When Mrs. Sinclair refused to give them money, they put a torch to the house and all the outbuildings. Fortunately, several of the servants managed to get Mrs. Sinclair out of the house before it burned to the ground. Afterwards, the poor woman collapsed. I had her brought to Black Oaks, of course, but there was nothing I could do. She never recovered from the blow of seeing her home burned down before her eyes. She died in my arms, praying to see her son one last time. We had sent for Cole at once, but he never came," Clare Appleton finished bitterly.

"Perhaps he couldn't come," Lucinda said slowly. Knowing the shadowy world of the spy in which Cole must live, she could well believe there were days, even weeks, when it would be impossible for even his superiors in Richmond to reach Cole.

"Perhaps." Her aunt's voice was skeptical. "He did come home two weeks after we buried his mother. They say he rode up to Gray Meadows, took one look, then turned and rode away again without a word to anyone."

No wonder Cole's face had seemed that of a cold, merciless stranger, Lucy thought, heartsick. She was sure that Cole, feeling as he did about his mother and Gray Meadows, would never forgive or forget what the enemy had done, murdering his mother, destroying his home. Just as Cole would never forgive her? she thought, with a sudden shiver of fear, if, pray God, by some miracle he was still alive.

Noticing the bleak look on her niece's face, Lucy's aunt was instantly alarmed. "There, I have upset you," she said anxiously. Glancing down at the gold watch hanging on her bodice, she frowned unhappily. "Oh, dear, and I forgot. I promised Harry he could talk to you for a few minutes this morning. That is, if you're feeling up to visitors?"

"No," Lucinda blurted. She felt unsettled enough without facing her cousin Harry. Even when she had lived at Black Oaks, she had always felt uncomfortable around her stepcousin. Then, afraid she might have hurt her aunt's feelings, she added quickly, "I am tired, Aunt Clare. I think I will rest now."

"Of course." Her aunt started to tiptoe from the room.

At the door, Lucy called after her drowsily, "And you won't forget about Sam?"

"I won't forget, dear," her aunt promised.

For two days, pleading weariness, Lucy was able to avoid seeing her cousin. The third day, however, when her aunt came to her bedroom, she saw her cousin Harry standing in the doorway behind his mother.

"I'll only stay a minute, Cousin Lucy," he said, smiling thinly. "I wouldn't want to tire you."

Only that morning her aunt had washed and toweled dry Lucinda's hair. Now it fell in a night cloud over her shoulders, with the delicately etched bones of her face pale as a lovely cameo against its luxuriant darkness. Although there were still dark shadows beneath

117

her eyes from her illness, they only served to emphasize their velvety blackness behind long, sooty lashes. She was wearing a white India muslin nightgown borrowed from her aunt. Its folds covered her demurely from neck to ankle, but still she had the uneasy feeling that Cousin Harry's oddly yellow-shaded eyes with their smoothly smiling glance were well aware of every soft curve beneath the gown.

He came closer to her bed. "So this is little Cousin Lucy. Mother was right, my dear. You've developed into a beauty. It's hard to imagine you're the same awkward tomboy, all arms and legs, that I remember."

Cousin Harry had changed, too, Lucy saw. He had lost the unattractive obesity that she remembered from the days when Harry had first come to Black Oaks, a pimply, sullen boy with a twisted, useless arm. His face was still heavyset, with thick jowls, but age had set well on her cousin, Lucy reflected. In spite of his handicap, she was sure that many women would consider Cousin Harry a fine figure of a man—if, she added mentally, they didn't look too closely into the cold, yellowish eyes or notice the tight, cruel set of the thin lips.

As a young girl, Lucy had become well acquainted with her cousin's cruelty. He had delighted in plaguing and tormenting her, always, of course, when his mother or her brother wasn't around. One incident in particular she remembered vividly, although she couldn't have been more than ten or eleven at the time it happened.

She had returned alone from an afternoon's ride and, taking her horse into the stable, found to her horror that her Cousin Harry, his face flushed scarlet with anger, was beating his sorrel mare with his riding whip. Even as a child Lucy couldn't bear cruelty to animals, and she flung herself upon the startled Harry, beating at him with her fists and screaming like a demented thing, "Stop it! Let her alone!"

The whip dropped from her cousin's hand, and then, so quickly Lucy had no chance to cry out, Harry's good arm circled her waist and thrust her face down upon the dusty stable floor.

"The mare threw me," he said, his voice cold with fury. "She needed a lesson in manners, just as you do, Cousin Lucy. Do you know how ridiculous you look, riding around the county in pants, making a laughingstock of yourself and the family?"

He knelt down beside her, his knee pressing into her back so that her body was pinned painfully to the floor. He laughed sharply. "Well, if you prefer to dress like a boy, then you shall be thrashed like a boy, cousin."

To her horror, she felt his hand at the back of her trousers, tugging at them, felt cool air sliding over her skin as he pulled her trousers down over her hips. Shocked, she realized that he meant to whip her across her bare buttocks, the way her brothers were thrashed when they misbehaved.

In vain, she fought to free herself, tasting the stable dust in her mouth as she struggled. Then a voice drawled from the stable door, "That's enough, Harry. Let her up."

She felt her cousin stiffen. "This is family business, Sinclair," he said curtly. "Stay out of it."

Cole Sinclair's voice took on even more of a lazy drawl, but Lucinda could hear sharpness, like a deadly stiletto thrust, beneath. "I said, let her go."

She sensed her cousin's hesitation, then his hand slowly left her trousers, and she hastily pulled free, stumbling to her feet.

Cole flicked a glance in her direction. "Are you all right, Lucy?"

She nodded, too embarrassed to speak.

A note of contempt crept into Cole's voice as he looked back at Harry, his glance disdainfully traveling over Harry's plump body. "Instead of a horse or a small girl, Harry," he drawled, "Why don't you try beating a grown man? Or aren't you man enough for that?"

Lucy saw her cousin's good hand unconsciously reach over to grip at his useless left arm, hanging at his side. In spite of herself, she felt a twinge of pity.

Then she saw the icy malevolence in her cousin's pale-yellow eyes, staring at Cole, and instinctively she stepped back. It was the first time she had ever seen naked hatred in a man's face.

For a long moment the gaze of the two men locked. Then a sneering smile touched Harry's thin lips and he shrugged indifferently. "Some other time, Sinclair, and I'll oblige you. That's a promise."

Well, there was no touch of malice in Harry's smile now, Lucinda thought, reaching for the coverlet and wishing that her cousin would stop staring at her hungrily as if he were a starving man who had just had a plate of petit fours placed before him.

To change the subject, she asked quickly, "How is Sam doing?"

"Sam?" Cousin Harry frowned. "You mean that big black buck who brought you to Black Oaks? He's too uppity for a slave by far. He needs to be taught his proper place."

"Sam is not a slave," Lucy protested, and almost asked if they hadn't heard that President Lincoln's Emancipation Proclamation had freed the slaves. Except, of course, she reminded herself wryly, that such a proclamation meant little in Virginia, which no longer owed allegiance to the United States.

"Are you saying that Sam is a free black?" Cousin Harry asked, amused. "Surely you've noticed the chain marks on his ankles and the whip scars on his back. Oh, he's a runaway all right." He gazed at Lucy thoughtfully. "As a matter of fact, I heard the other day that one of the men running with that bunch of bushwhackers holed up in Ashby's Gap is a black man. They say he's a magnificent specimen, much the size and build of your Sam."

Lucinda lowered her eyelids, hoping her face didn't show the dismay she felt. Aunt Clare had no doubt told her son the story of Sam's and her escape from the bushwhackers. Now she found herself wondering uneasily how much of the story her cousin believed. She might be able to fool sweet, trusting Aunt Clare, but she didn't underestimate Cousin Harry's intelligence. Nor his greed, she decided hopefully. Harry wasn't about to turn over to the authorities for hanging a strong, healthy field hand.

"I owe Sam my life," she said firmly. "I would have died without his help. I won't have any harm come to him."

"Of course, Cousin Lucy," Harry said agreeably. "Sam is welcome to work here at Black Oaks for his keep." He continued smoothly, "Just as you are welcome, Cousin Lucy, to stay here as a guest at Black Oaks for as long as you want."

Guest! Lucy felt her face grow hot with indignation. Glimpsing the smugly complacent look on Harry's face, she knew he had chosen the word deliberately. Well, it was true, she told herself angrily. She was only a guest. With Uncle Joseph's death, Aunt Clare had inherited the house and plantation, and to all intent and purposes that meant Harry was the new master of Black Oaks now.

How Grandfather Jacob would be twirling in his grave if he knew who was the new owner of his beloved plantation, she thought bitterly. Her grandfather had been fond of Aunt Clare, but he had never trusted or cared for Clare's son by her first marriage, even though her Uncle Joseph had legally adopted Harry and given him the Appleton name.

"It's not his twisted arm that bothers me," her grandfather had muttered darkly to the young Lucy one day as he watched Harry stride across the front lawn of Black Oaks. "It's what's twisted inside that boy that bothers me."

Lucy was sure that cutting his eldest son out of his will for his abolitionist sentiments had been an impulsive act on her grandfather's part, one that he would undoubtedly have reversed had he lived.

Aunt Clare glanced unhappily from Harry to Lucinda. As usual she jumped in to smooth the waters that her son seemed to delight in stirring up. "It would be a great favor, Lucy dear," she said coaxingly, "if you

121

could persuade Sam to stay on. The only servants we have left are Aunt Bessie and Uncle Joe, and the wheat will rot in the fields if we don't find help to harvest it soon."

Lucy hesitated, then agreed reluctantly, "I can't promise, but I'll talk to Sam."

It was several days, though, before she felt strong enough to get dressed and walk out to the slave quarters with Cousin Harry. At one time she remembered the whitewashed cabins had been well cared for, with neat vegetable gardens growing around the cabins. Now the gardens were knee-high in weeds and doors were sagging on leather hinges, the whitewash all flaked away.

The hut in front of which Cousin Harry stopped was in better shape than the others, with a new lock on the door. As Harry took out a key and unlocked the door, Lucy turned upon him angrily. "Aunt Clare said Sam was to be free."

Harry shrugged. "I'm afraid Mother is too tender-hearted. You don't suppose your man would have stayed around for a day if I hadn't kept him locked in here?"

When he opened the door, Sam got lithely to his feet and came to the door, blinking against the brightness of the sunlight after the darkness of the little hut.

"I want to talk to him alone," Lucinda said.

Her cousin's narrow mouth pursed disapprovingly. "That may not be safe, Cousin Lucy."

"For heaven's sake," she exploded. "Sam brought me all the way here without killing me. Why should he harm me now?"

Her cousin hesitated, then nodded grudgingly. "I'll be right over there, under the trees, if you need me."

After Harry withdrew, Sam ducked his head and stepped outside the door. Lucy had forgotten how tall he was, towering over her, the breadth of his shoulders as wide as the door. Yet he walked lightly, and she remembered well the gentleness of his hands when he had tried desperately to keep her body warm back there in the cave.

"I'm sorry." She gestured helplessly toward the hut. "They had no right to lock you in there."

Sam's hawk face was expressionless as he gazed down at her. "It don't matter." For a second a glint of amusement leaped into the deep-brown eyes as he glanced scornfully at the hut. "Ain't no chicken coop like that can hold me, 'less I want to stay."

"Why?" Lucy asked curiously. "Why did you stay? Why didn't you run away?"

He didn't answer her.

"How did you know to bring me to Black Oaks?"

"You talked, in your fever, about Black Oaks," he said finally. "Before the war, I drove a carriage for the Von Brucks. They visited Black Oaks once."

Lucy remembered the countess mentioning that she knew the Appleton home. It seemed so far away now—Arabella, the horror of the fetid cellar room. Even the war seemed far removed from peaceful Black Oaks, with the sun shining down upon the rose-red brick walls, the fields of wheat beyond the slave huts, ripe and heavy-headed, rippling in the sunlight like a golden sea.

"My cousin and aunt want you to stay here at Black Oaks," she said. "They need help with the harvest."

To her surprise, Sam shrugged indifferently and said, "I'll stay."

She said, feeling suddenly awkward, "You . . . you don't have to, you know. And I should warn you, I think my cousin suspects you were with those . . . those bush-whackers. I don't think he'll turn you over to the authorities, not as long as you remain here at Black Oaks. But I don't trust him. If you want to get away, I'll help you. I owe you much more than that."

His proud hawk's face held an unconscious dignity as he studied her face for a long moment, then asked, "You want me to go?"

At first, Lucinda didn't understand. Then all at once she found herself remembering that night in the cave

123

when Sam had lain down beside her and held her in his arms to keep her warm. Only it was a black girl he thought he had been holding, she realized. It occurred to her that it must have been a shock for Sam when his ministrations had removed the stain from her body and he discovered he had been sheltering a white woman. Was it possible, she wondered now, that he thought she was humiliated by the memory of a black man holding her in his arms and that she wanted him out of her sight so she wouldn't be reminded of that night?

"Don't be foolish," she said, exasperated. "Of course I don't want you to go."

He shrugged again, his face once more an impenetrable polished ebony mask. "I'll stay then," he said.

8

Lucy stared moodily out of the second-floor hall window of Black Oaks, a dustcloth held listlessly in her hand. It was still early in the morning, but the day had already grown warm with a stagnant August heat, the brassy smell in the air foreshadowing a storm before the day was finished. Despite the oppressive heat, the men were hard at work in the fields, harvesting the wheat. From the window she could see Sam, stripped to the waist, his body lifting and bending without a wasted movement, his skin shining with perspiration as if it were wax-polished.

Not far away, and despite his useless arm, Harry was doing his awkward best to help gather and tie the sheaves of wheat.

That morning at breakfast Lucy had offered to join the men in the field, but her aunt had been horrified at the suggestion. "You're not strong enough yet, Lucy. Anyway, your skin would be ruined by the sun."

Aunt Clare frowned unhappily. "It's bad enough poor Harry's working in the field, but he said it's absolutely necessary that the wheat be harvested as soon as possible. Harry says the merchants in Richmond are offering a fortune for wheat. Food is so short that they even had bread riots in the city in April. President Davis himself had to calm the people."

Lucinda lifted a puzzled eyebrow. "Richmond? I would think the Confederate quartermaster would want to buy the wheat for the Army."

"Well, yes, of course." A pretty pink colored her aunt's cheeks. "Only Harry says the merchants will pay in gold while the quartermaster pays in scrip. Harry says he has enough scrip now to wallpaper the house." She made a fluttering gesture with her small hands. "I'm only a woman, so naturally I don't understand such business matters. But I'm sure Harry will do what's right."

Lucy hid a smile. Trust Harry. A shrewd business-man, he knew if the South lost the war, Confederate scrip would be worthless, but win or lose, gold held its value. She shrugged mentally. Well, Harry wasn't any worse than the Northern contractors who sold the Union Army shoes with cardboard soles that fell apart in the first rainstorm and rancid tinned beef.

Restlessly she rose from the table. "I have to do some-thing, Aunt Clare. I can't just sit around the house."

"You could help with the dusting," her aunt offered. "Aunt Bessie does her best, but her eyesight's failing, and she misses more dust than she sees."

So, dustcloth determinedly in hand, Lucy roamed through the spacious rooms of Black Oaks. At first, she enjoyed becoming acquainted again with the nooks and crannies of the house, all the memories it held for her, the front parlor with the precious set of Chippendale chairs, one of which still bore marks carved on its leg by her young brother, Matt, with the new knife he had received for Christmas. She wandered into the study, where her grandfather had loved to sit in the wing chair by the fireplace with the Adams mantel and the huge brass-balled andirons. It was a young heartbro-ken Lucinda who, six years ago now, had found her grandfather dead of a heart attack in the study. He must have struck his head against a corner of his desk when he fell, and in her mind's eye she could still see her Grandfather Jacob sprawled on the floor, as if a mighty pine had toppled.

In the dining room she admired the beautiful rose-and-white Sèvres china in the sideboard, which her mother as a bride had brought with her from Louisiana, as part of her dowry. She even dusted the gold frames of the family portraits lining the wide upstairs hallway. In childhood, she remembered, the portraits had fright-ened her, staring so grimly down at her as she passed. Now, studying them more closely, she could see her grandfather's nose on a great-uncle's face, her own arched cheekbones on a rather arrogant elderly lady, her brother Charles' merry blue eyes on another ancestor. Somehow, looking into the faces in the portraits made the hurt of losing her father and brother easier to bear. Her own children might someday have her father's nose, her brother's eyes.

Thinking of marriage and children, however, reminded her of Cole, and she hastily turned her thoughts away. The memory of Cole, very possibly dead at her own hands, was still too painful for her to handle, like a raw wound that refused to heal.

After a week, though, the chore of dusting began to pall on Lucy, and as she stood gazing out of the window this morning, she could feel a restlessness tightening inside her like a spring. It wasn't that she didn't love Black Oaks and being with Aunt Clare again, but the truth was, she was bored to tears.

As terrifying as her experiences these last months had been, working as a secret service agent for Mr. Lafayette Baker, at least she had felt challenged and alive. The thrill of the ever-present danger, the excitement of walking a tightrope between life and death, was, in its own way, as intoxicating as strong drink. And, Lucy suspected, just as habit-forming. Now she felt as if she were merely existing, each day monotonously the same as the one before.

She roamed downstairs, stopping to take a look at herself in the great gold-framed pier mirror by the front door. She was pleased to see she had gained back the weight she had lost while she was ill. The dresses her aunt had lent her were already beginning to fit too tightly through the waist and across the bodice. And her flesh was no longer a dull white but held a sheen like creamy, pink-toned silk.

She pinched at her cheeks to bring color into her face, thinking absently that she could do with some exercise. Perhaps explore the county a little. She had been housebound too long, she decided.

At lunchtime she broached the subject to her aunt.

"Do you have a riding habit I can borrow, Aunt Clare? I thought I'd go for a ride this afternoon."

"Why, yes, I believe so." Her aunt's forehead wrinkled anxiously. "Are you sure you're feeling well enough to ride?"

"I'm fine," Lucy said, a little impatiently. "And I imagine the roan and the bay Sam and I brought with us could stand some exercising." She glanced across the table at Harry. "By the way, Harry, where are the horses? I haven't seen any in the stable."

Her cousin hesitated a moment, then said stiffly. "We keep the horses in a corral in the woods to make sure they're not stolen by ... by any Yankee soldiers that might happen by."

Or Confederate soldiers, Lucy thought, amused, knowing that the rebels needed good horses even more desperately than the Union troops and wouldn't hesitate to commandeer any horses they found, no matter to whom they belonged.

"Where do you plan to ride?" her cousin asked. "I'm not sure you should ride alone. There are too many ne'er-do-wells roaming around the countryside these days."

"Oh, I won't go far," Lucy assured him, making her voice purposely vague.

That afternoon, though, as she rode away from Black Oaks on the roan mare, she knew perfectly well where she was going. Taking a short cut through the pine woods bordering the western boundary of Black Oaks land, she came out after a half hour's ride on the outer fields of Gray Meadows. It was another fifteen minutes' ride through fields overrun with broom sedge before she came to the curving, oak-shaded road that led to the Sinclair home.

Like the fields, the road was untended, overrun with weeds. The crushed oyster shells that had once neatly covered the road had long since disappeared, leaving only muddy ruts in the dark-red ground. Although the roan was eager to run after its weeks of inactivity, Lucinda kept the mare to a slow trot. She wasn't sure, after all, if it was wise for her to visit Gray Meadows. All she knew was that she had to see Cole's home again, a compulsion without rhyme or reason. Next to Black Oaks, she had always loved Gray Meadows the best. Its serenity and gracious charm had always had a way of soothing her spirits as a young rebellious child. And being in the presence of Cole's gentle invalid mother had always made Lucy feel like a young, perfectly behaved lady for all her hoydenish ways—perhaps because Mrs. Sinclair invariably treated Lucy as if she were a young lady.

The row of oak trees on either side of the road, the branches meeting like the dark nave of a cathedral overhead, hid the house from view as it always had in the past. But beyond the next curve ... Lucinda pulled her horse in abruptly, a cry of anguish rising to her lips. She had expected to find the house destroyed, but she still wasn't prepared for the tragic scene that met her eyes. Blackened and twisted columns fell across what had once been a wide, lovely veranda. The soot-covered stone foundation of the house and two towering chimneys were all that remained of what had once been one of the loveliest homes in the Virginia Valley. Even the outbuildings had not been spared. Barns, corn ricks, stables, slave quarters—all had been burned to the ground.

Tears pricked at Lucinda's eyes, blurring the blackened ruins before her, as she dismounted and walked slowly up to the house. Then she sank down on the cracked, marble-flagged floor of the veranda and wept uncontrollably, not sure whether she was crying for the charred and ugly ruins behind her, or for Cole and herself and the long-cherished dream that had died back there in the sun-lit clearing.

Finally, she was exhausted, and the wild sobs died away. Wearily Lucy pulled herself to her feet and walked back to the slave quarters and the well that had always been there. The water was still pure and sparkling. She lowered and pulled up the bucket, then

129

cupped the water in her hand and splashed her face until all trace of the tears was washed away.

"A sad sight, isn't it?"

Lucy glanced up, startled. She had been so wrapped up in her own private misery that she hadn't heard the sound of Cousin Harry's footsteps as he approached her, leading the black bay. For all that he was a large man, she noticed that Harry could move very quietly.

Idly he slapped the reins of the bay against the palm of his hand as he surveyed Lucinda, as closely as she was studying him. There was a glint of malice in the pale-yellow eyes as he asked abruptly, "Or is it Gray Meadows you're crying for, Cousin Lucy?"

She dried her hands with her handkerchief. "How did you know I was here?" she asked curiously.

Harry shrugged, his voice jeering. "With that schoolgirl's crush you had on Cole Sinclair, where else would you go?" Then, eyeing her speculatively, "Do you suppose Cole is still alive, Cousin Lucy?"

Lucy felt her blood run cold. Was it possible that Harry had somehow learned about her shooting Cole? She lowered her eyelids quickly so that Harry couldn't see the dismay she felt. "How would I know?" she asked, with careful indifference.

Harry's thin lips curled disdainfully. "Cole's the type that would die a hero's death. I can see him storming the ramparts, leading a daring, futile charge against the enemy."

"At least he'd die fighting," Lucinda said, gazing contemptuously at her cousin. And then was instantly ashamed when she saw Harry's right hand tighten, almost instinctively, against his useless arm. "I'm sorry," she murmured. "I had no right to say that."

Harry smiled mirthlessly. "There's no need to apologize. No doubt my dear mother would be shocked, but the truth is I have absolutely no desire for combat or living with a lot of unwashed, ignorant soldiers." And then, reflectively, almost as if he were talking to himself, he added, "There are other, better ways of winning a war."

130

"What do you mean?" Lucinda asked, puzzled.

Harry ignored her question. The pale-yellow eyes traveled slowly, deliberately, from the tip of her boots to the full young breasts straining against the too-tight bodice of Aunt Clare's riding jacket, then lingered at her face, at the soft mass of black hair pulled back from her forehead and caught at the nape of her neck in a chenille net. "I'd hoped you'd outgrown your foolish, childish crush on Cole Sinclair," he said, and then cruelly, "You're much too beautiful a woman, Cousin Lucy, to waste your affections on a man who never gave you a second thought."

Although his words were only too true, Lucy felt her face flush angrily. "Cole was my friend," she said fiercely.

"Oh, yes, Cole was a friend to a great many women, young and old, white and . . . black," Harry said mockingly. "Surely you remember poor Dora Lee?"

"Of course I remember Dora. What has she got to do with Cole?"

Harry shrugged. "It was because of Cole that Uncle Joseph was forced to sell the girl. I'm afraid Uncle Joseph was rather straitlaced. He didn't approve of mulatto babies in the slave quarters."

"Dora Lee!" Lucy said, shocked. "She couldn't have been carrying Cole's child. She wasn't much more than a child herself."

"She was old enough . . . for Cole."

"I don't believe you! Cole wouldn't—" Lucy fell silent, suddenly remembering a scene from so long ago she hadn't thought about it in years. It was the day before she and her father and brothers were to leave for New Orleans. She had been riding near Gray Meadows, and she had seen a man and girl in the pine woods together. The girl was crying and the man was holding her in his arms. She had dismounted and walked closer, close enough to determine that the girl was Dora Lee and the man was Cole Sinclair. Then before they could discover her, she had returned to her horse and ridden quickly away.

She had meant to ask Dora Lee about that scene in the woods, but with her family leaving the next day, there hadn't been time. And when she had returned from her trip, Dora Lee was gone.

Watching her face as she struggled with disbelief, Harry said smugly, "Ask Aunt Clare if you don't believe me. She knows all about Dora Lee and Cole."

Lucy, however, was remembering something else now. She was reliving those moments on the flowered lavender carpet in Arabella's bedroom, when Cole had taken her, ruthlessly and yet casually. And why not? Wasn't Sukey a pretty black girl, fair game for any predatory white man? Why should it have been any different for Dora Lee? she thought bitterly.

Harry reached out and took her chin in his hand, his voice no longer taunting, almost gentle. "I'm sorry to have been the one to tell you, Cousin Lucy. I assumed you had guessed. You and Dora Lee were so close."

"No . . . no, I didn't know." She wished uneasily that Harry would remove his hand from her face, that his pale-yellow eyes didn't suddenly remind her of the faces of the bushwhackers around the campfire, the same oily gleam in their eyes licking greedily at her face and body.

She tried to pull free, but Harry's hand tightened on her chin, pulling her unexpectedly toward him. She had forgotten how strong her cousin was, despite his crippled arm.

"Lucy," he muttered hoarsely. "My beautiful Cousin Lucy."

Then his mouth covered hers. His lips felt strangely cold and leaf-dry as his hand slipped down and imprisoned her tiny waist. At first, she was too shocked, and in a way too embarrassed, to move. Then Harry's mouth was forcing her lips apart and the hand had left her waist. Before she realized what he was doing, he had nimbly undone the top buttons of her jacket. It was when she felt the hand slide inside the jacket and fondle her breast that she fought back, swiftly and effectively.

She lifted her hands and caught her cousin's blond hair in her fingers and jerked as painfully hard as she could.

With a sharp cry, Harry's mouth abruptly left her lips. Then his good arm slipped again to her waist, tightened deliberately, squeezing the breath from her body. He smiled coldly down at her. "There's no need to put on a display of maidenly modesty for me, Cousin Lucy. You see, I know all about you."

If he had wanted to shock her, he had succeeded. She gazed up at him dumbfounded.

Harry smirked triumphantly at her dismay. "After we heard of your father's death at Shiloh, mother insisted that I must go north and find you and bring you back to Black Oaks to live. Your father had written that you were in a school near Boston, and when I found the school, they directed me to the boardinghouse where you lived after you left the school. It was the boardinghouse keeper who told me about Charles' death and how you'd run off with a traveling theatrical company immediately afterwards." He pinched her waist, smiling roguishly. "I'm sure a girl who makes her living on the stage is well acquainted with men . . . taking liberties."

Lucinda almost breathed a sigh of relief. So Harry didn't know about her joining the secret service and spying for Mr. Baker, or that liberties had, indeed, been taken with her person. Not by the members of the theatrical company, though, who had always scolded and watched over and protected her from the men who visited the stage door after performances.

Harry took her silence for consent, and once more his hand began to roam familiarly above her waistline, his voice taking on a righteously pompous tone. "I'm sure you realize, Cousin Lucy, that most gentlemen would hesitate to take a woman of your theatrical experience for a wife. Soiled goods, shall we say? Still, I pride myself on being more liberal than most. And, after all, you were alone, without family or friends. In time, I've no doubt I could forget . . ."

133

Lucy hadn't really been listening to Harry. Now she thrust him away from her, blurting anxiously, "You didn't tell Aunt Clare about my being on the stage?"

Harry lifted a startled eyebrow. "Naturally not. Mother would have had a nervous collapse if she learned the truth. I simply told her I was unable to find you. And after we're married, there will be no need for her to know about your unfortunate past."

"Married?" Lucy stared up at her cousin blankly. Was Cousin Harry really proposing to her?

"It's what Mother's always wanted," Harry continued, "that you and I should marry. Ordinarily there would be a period of courtship, but under the circumstances, and with the war, I see no need for us to wait."

Marry Cousin Harry! How absurd. Lucinda felt a giggle of amusement rising in her throat at the thought. Why, she'd die a dozen times an old maid first. Almost she spoke the words aloud but caught herself in time. It would be stupid to make an enemy of Cousin Harry, she realized practically.

She lowered her gaze and fluttered her eyelashes demurely. "I'm flattered, of course," she murmured, remembering the rote they had taught her at Mrs. Ellen's Finishing School for Girls, for when a young lady received an undesirable proposal of marriage. "And I'm well aware of the honor you wish to bestow upon me. But this is all so sudden. Perhaps at some future date, when I've had more time to consider the matter..." She gave a soft, tremulous sigh. "Now if you'll excuse me, Cousin Harry, the ride tired me more than I realized. I should be returning to Black Oaks."

Cousin Harry inclined his head stiffly. "As you wish, Cousin Lucy." He escorted her to her mare and helped her mount. But when he handed her the reins, his hand suddenly gripped painfully around her wrist. "Take all the time you want, my dear," he said softly. "Only make no mistake about it. We *will* be married."

As soon as Lucinda returned to Black Oaks, she went looking for her Aunt Clare. She found her aunt in the kitchen, preparing a tea tray. Before her aunt could speak, Lucy burst out unhappily, "Is it true, Aunt Clare? Was Dora Lee carrying Cole's baby when she left Black Oaks?"

Her aunt's round face flushed a bright pink, and her voice was flustered. "Really, dear, I don't think its proper for a young lady to discuss such—"

"Oh, for heaven's sake, Aunt Clare," Lucy interrupted impatiently. "Don't you suppose I know by now where babies come from? Was it Cole's baby?"

Her aunt wiped her hands on her apron. "Yes, dear," she said unhappily. "I'm afraid it was."

"I don't believe it."

"I don't want to believe it either, but Dora Lee told me herself."

So it was true, Lucinda thought, and then, furiously, How could Cole? Not just seducing, perhaps even raping, poor helpless, guileless Dora Lee, but allowing the girl carrying his own child to be sold south. If life in Virginia could be hard for a slave, how much worse it was to be sold south to work in the malaria-ridden rice fields of Louisiana.

Her aunt had removed her apron and was tidying her hair as she sighed and took a last, worried look at the tea tray. "Oh, dear, I do wish we had some of Aunt Bessie's pound cake to serve with the tea. Bread and butter seems so inhospitable."

For the first time Lucy noticed that the tea tray bore Aunt Clare's best lusterware cups and saucers and flat silver spoons. "Are we having company?" she asked, surprised.

"Didn't I tell you that we have a guest?" her aunt said, pleased. "Such a pleasant gentleman, a Confederate chaplain on his way to join General Stuart's headquarters at The Bower. He lost his way and stopped to ask directions to Martinsburg. Why don't you change, dear, and join us on the veranda? I thought I'd serve tea there where it's cooler."

Lucy was not much in the mood for teatime conversation, but visitors to Black Oaks were a rarity and a Confederate officer might at least have some news of the outside world. She changed quickly into a pale-green-and-white-striped challis gown. Studying herself in the mirror, she realized she hadn't noticed that the bodice of the dress was cut so low in the neck, much too low for an afternoon frock. The swell of her breasts could plainly be seen above the heart-shaped neckline. Well, there wasn't time to change again. She only hoped she wouldn't shock the chaplain, she thought, amused.

When she came out onto the veranda, Aunt Clare was seated at the tea table, and the chaplain, a tall man in a sober straight-breasted coat of black cloth, was standing with his back to Lucinda. He turned as Lucinda approached. For a moment, seeing the man full face, she faltered, then she came forward quickly.

Her aunt looked up, smiling. "Oh, there you are, dear. I'd like you to meet the Reverend Major Robert Bailey. My niece, Lucinda Appleton."

"A pleasure, ma'am." The major bowed low, smiling.

Lucy returned the smile as she settled herself demurely in a chair beside her aunt. Then she couldn't resist asking, "Have you been a chaplain long, major?"

For even with his beard shaved off, his hair clipped neatly, and the black patch gone from his left eye, she had recognized Jephthah at once.

"No, ma'am," he drawled, a spark of laughter in his gun-metal eyes. "You might say the call came upon me suddenly."

Aunt Clare handed a cup of tea to the major. "I'm sure you're a great comfort to our dear, brave boys."

"Yes, ma'am," he said gravely. "I do my best to encourage, elevate and spiritualize the men with my sermons."

"The major has brought some distressing news, Lucy," Aunt Clare said unhappily. "Not only has Vicksburg fallen to the enemy, but Port Hudson, too. My dear, late husband was always fearful of such an event. He said it would be disastrous if the Mississippi River should ever be completely controlled by the North; that it would split the Confederate States in two." She sighed to herself, then straightened her rounded chin determinedly. "Still, we mustn't despair, must we? I'm sure our gallant General Lee will come up with some plan to hasten our victory."

"Yes, ma'am," the chaplain agreed soberly. "I'm sure he will."

"And God," Aunt Clare said firmly, "is on our side."

"God is always on the side of the oppressed and suffering, ma'am," the major said quietly.

Lucy saw her aunt's round blue eyes widen, a little uncertainly, as she gazed at her guest. Lucy got hastily to her feet. "Perhaps you'd care to see the gardens, major?"

"Thank you, I'd enjoy that. With your permission, ma'am?"

The major cast a polite glance toward his hostess. Aunt Clare bit her lower lip nervously. The major seemed rather more attractive than she thought a man of the cloth had a right to be. Then, ashamed of her suspicions—he was a minister, after all, she reminded herself—she smiled at her niece. "Run along, child, but don't tire yourself."

As soon as they had left the veranda and walked down into the lower level of the garden where a shrub border of rhododendrons shielded them from view, Lucy flung her arms around her companion. "Oh, Jephthah, I'm so glad you're safe."

For a moment Jephthah's long arms tightened around her, then he held her away from him, studying her face before nodding, relieved. "You're all right, then? When I doubled back for you and found you gone, I could read by the tracks what had happened. I started after you, but I lost the trail in the rain. I didn't catch up with those bushwhackers till two days later." He smiled wolfishly in memory. "Three of those scum won't be doing any more thieving and killing," he drawled. "One of them, before he died, told me that a black man, named Sam, had taken you away the night before."

He reached out a hand awkwardly to touch her wrist,

his face flushing painfully. "Those men . . . they didn't hurt you?"

She walked quickly away from his too-searching gaze. "I'm fine, Jephthah, really I am." Then, taking a deep breath, she turned around and blurted, "The man, Jephthah? The man I shot. Was he still alive when you got back to the clearing?"

"I couldn't say, ma'am," Jephthah said slowly. "He was gone when I got there."

"Gone?" Lucy's voice lifted happily. "Then he's alive!"

Jephthah's gruff voice softened as he looked into the girl's suddenly vividly alive face, her black eyes radiant with hope. "I can't say that for sure," he said gently. "Someone else might have come along and found him . . . and buried him."

"Yes." The brilliance in Lucy's face was gone, like a candle suddenly snuffed out. Her voice was bleak. "I suppose it is foolish to think he might still be alive."

"You did the right thing," Jephthah said sternly. "Don't ever think otherwise."

"Yes," she said wearily. But the knowledge didn't make her sense of guilt any easier to bear, not any easier at all.

She and Jephthah continued strolling down the path, which wound by a lichen-covered statue of Diana, the huntress. With no more gardeners at Black Oaks, the flowers in the brick-lined beds were fighting a losing battle against the weeds. Clumps of marguerites and asters had survived, but the stout, leafy stalks of nightshade had completely taken over one of the flower beds. Something about the nightshade's cluster of violet flowers reminded her of Arabella Von Bruck, so beautiful and yet so deadly.

"What happened to the countess?" she asked. "Did Mr. Baker's men arrest her?"

"Yes, ma'am." Jephthah's long face grew glum. "They found the evidence against her, too, right where you told them it would be. But the last I heard she was only in Old Capitol a few weeks when she was sent to the South, exchanged for some Union prisoners."

Lucinda stopped and gave her companion a quizzical glance. "Don't you think it's time you told me why you're here, Jephthah? You didn't really lose your way, did you?"

"No, ma'am," the scout admitted sheepishly. "I remembered your telling me your home was at Black Oaks here in the valley, and I figured if you were still alive, you might have ended up back here. I was in the neighborhood, so I took a chance and dropped by."

"You're still working for Lafayette Baker?"

"No, my face got a mite too familiar in Washington. I'm working for General Sharpe now. His headquarters is here in the valley." Jephthah's glance roamed over the green fields and golden hills around the gardens of Black Oaks, to the stark, rugged beauty of the Blue Ridge Mountains in the distance. "This is where I figure the war will be won or lost, right here in the Shenandoah Valley," he said soberly. "The South desperately needs the valley, its meat and grains to feed Lee's army. And until the North controls the valley, Richmond can never be taken." Jephthah scowled darkly. "It won't be easy, fighting a war in this valley. We'll be fighting on the enemy's home ground, and his spies and scouts are everywhere. Some of the agents operate out of Stuart's headquarters, some out of Richmond, and some are just Southerners, men and women who live here. They watch every move the Federal Army makes and report to Lee's or Stuart's headquarters, or one of Mosby's guerrilla bands."

Jephthah's mouth twisted, disgusted. Lucy suspected, amused, that he missed his plug tobacco, but chewing tobacco was hardly in keeping with the role he was now playing.

"Sometimes I think General Meade can't sneeze and Stuart's headquarters don't hear about it," he grumbled.

139

"That's why you're here—to locate and expose Confederate spies?"

"That and do a little spying of my own," Jephthah admitted, with his wolfish grin. "A chaplain with properly forged papers can move from camp to camp without any trouble. And it's gratifying how talkative troopers can be around a minister. Still, what we really need is someone inside Stuart's headquarters, someone above suspicion. Jeb Stuart is General Lee's eyes and ears, and whenever Lee makes his move, Stuart is sure to be there with him. General Sharpe wants to know when Stuart is ready to move and how strong a force he has."

He glanced sideways at Lucinda, drawling innocently, "I hear tell Jeb Stuart can't resist a pretty lady. Women flock to his camp like bees to honey. And wherever his headquarters is, there's always music and dancing and parties." He added casually, "Stuart's headquarters is at The Bower, just south of Martinsburg, near the Dandridge plantation. I don't suppose you know any families in that area?"

Lucy thought a moment, then said, "The Jaspars have a home near the Dandridge plantation. Mrs. Jaspar went to school with my aunt, and I used to be friends with Sally Jaspar." Lucy plucked a purple flower from the poisonous nightshade, shredding its petals absently. So that was really why Jephthah had come to Black Oaks, she thought—to recruit her again into the secret service.

She lifted her gaze slowly to her companion. "It would be very dangerous, wouldn't it?" she asked. While she had worked for Mr. Baker in Washington, at least she had been in the federal capital. At General Stuart's headquarters she would be surrounded on all sides by the enemy, with nowhere to run if she were caught.

"Yes, ma'am," Jephthah agreed at once. "Reb pickets caught two of our couriers last month. They were both hanged at Castle Thunder in Richmond within the week. Don't rightly know if they'd hang a woman, although General Bragg sentenced Pauline Cushman to hang."

"It isn't the danger I mind so much," Lucy said thoughtfully. "Not that I'm all that brave," she said, smiling, "but there is an excitement in playing a role and knowing if you're not letter-perfect, it won't just be rotten eggs they'll be throwing at you from the audience!"

Unlike Lafayette Baker, Jephthah understood at once what Lucinda meant. He nodded, grinning. "I reckon most of us in this business feel the same. Tweaking the nose of old man death can be gratifying."

Lucy gestured helpelssly around her. "What does matter is my turning my back on this—Black Oaks, Aunt Clare, the valley." It was one thing, she thought, to spy in the North, among strangers. It was another to know that she would be spying on her own people, perhaps even betraying relatives and friends. She turned hopefully to Jephthah. "Is it really necessary? With the defeat at Gettysburg and the fall of Vicksburg, surely the war can't go on much longer."

"Yes, ma'am, it's necessary," Jephthah said, his long mouth settling into a grim line. "Oh, the South will lose in the end. They're running out of supplies. Sooner or later, they'll run out of men. They're already conscripting boys who've never shaved, old men with gray beards. Still, they manage to hang on. In the meantime there'll be more slaughters like Gettysburg. Thousands of men from the North and South, dying for a cause that's already lost. If what I'm doing can bring the war to an end one day sooner, I figure it's worth it."

When Lucy remained still, staring unhappily out across the fields, he said quietly, "No one can blame you for turning me down. You've done more than your share. Lots of people are tired of the war and want it to end. The draft riots in New York showed that."

"What riots?" she asked, startled.

"I reckon you haven't heard yet. Happened a couple of weeks ago in New York City when they started drafting men for the Army. A mob of men burned and looted and pillaged, hanging any black man, woman or child they could find, killing any policemen or firemen who tried to stop them. The riot lasted four days, and it took calling in the Federal troops to end it."

Lucinda shivered. "No, I didn't know. How terrible."

Jephthah pulled a watch from his pocket. "I hate hurrying off, ma'am," he said regretfully. "But I have a piece to go before Martinsburg. I'd appreciate it if you'd say goodbye to your aunt for me." He held out his hand, Lucy's tiny hand disappearing into his large, bony grasp. Then he stepped back, saluted her gravely, and turned and began to walk away.

Lucy stared after him, frowning slightly. Jephthah had gone only a few steps when she called after him, "Jephthah, wait!"

He turned, and by the amused twitch at the corners of his long mouth, she knew he had guessed all along that she would not let him go.

She smiled wryly. "You didn't tell me, Jephthah. When I get to General Stuart's headquarters, who will my courier be?"

9

"Lucy, aren't you dressed yet?" Sally Jaspar knocked impatiently at the bedroom door. "Hurry up, Lucy, the dancing's already begun."

Inside the bedroom, by the light of a tallow candle, Lucinda wrote with a tiny quill pen upon a small, tissue-thin sheet of paper. That afternoon General Jeb Stuart had held one of his "spread-eagle" grand reviews at his headquarters at The Bower. The brigade band had led the way across the field with band instruments flashing in the sun and kettledrums rolling. Behind the band had followed the 1st Virginia Cavalry, red battle flags flying proudly. Although the troopers' uniforms were faded and ragged—some were wearing Union blue uniforms captured at Chambersburg—their sabers, carbines and spurs had sparkled silver in the sunlight.

General Stuart himself had been resplendent in a gold-braided uniform, the long black ostrich plume on his slouch hat flowing in the wind as he inspected the ranks. As the general rode by, displaying as always his superb horsemanship, a cheer rose from the crowd of people on the parade ground. Dozens of young women rushed forward, throwing bouquets of flowers, adding to those already fastened to the general's hat and coat and tied in a wreath around the neck of his favorite charger.

Lucy had joined in the cheering, but she had also been busily occupied in mentally counting the number of troopers, horses, caissons and guns attached to the horse artillery passing in review. Now, before she forgot the numbers she had memorized, she was writing down the information, using the special colorless ink Jephthah had given her. All trace of the script disappeared from the tissue paper before she had finished writing the last word. Then, quickly folding the paper inside a small piece of black silk, she tucked the silk beneath the blue-black shining coil of hair she wore in a neat coronet like a tiara around her head. Finally, she lifted her crinoline skirt and returned the vial of ink, the tiny quill pen and the remainder of the tissue papers to a velvet bag tied around her waist.

After glancing around the bedroom to make sure she hadn't forgotten anything, she opened the door and, retreating to her mirror, called out gaily, "Come in, Sally. I'm almost ready."

Sally Jaspar came sweeping sideways into the room, barely making it through the door without crushing her green-and-white sprigged crinoline skirt. She was a short, plump girl with bright-red hair, milk-white skin, and a sprinkling of freckles across her cheerful face.

There was only the slightest touch of envy on that face now as she gazed at Lucinda and sighed, "You look simply beautiful, Lucy. Every girl at the dance tonight will want to scratch your eyes out!" She studied Lucy's gown, the flounced scarlet skirt looped up on one side to display a ruffled red-and-white striped petticoat beneath. Cherokee roses from the Jaspar garden were tucked into the tiny red-velvet-belted waist.

"Is that really what fashionable ladies are wearing now?" Sally asked, fascinated. "Do they pull up their skirts that way and show their petticoat?"

Lucinda nodded, pinning several scarlet and white roses expertly into the waterfall of black, glistening curls cascading down the nape of her neck. "It's the latest style from Paris."

"Oh, dear, I do miss keeping up with the new fashions," Sally said unhappily. "Every girl in the South is going to look like a frump by the time the war's ended. I haven't seen a new *Godey's Lady's Book* since Manassas." A look of bewilderment crept into the girl's face as she gazed at her friend. "I thought your Aunt Clare wrote my mother that you lost everything when you got away from those bushwhackers. Yet you've worn a different frock practically every day these last three weeks, each one prettier than the last."

Lucinda gave Sally a conspiratorial wink. "Don't tell anyone, but I found a whole trunkful of my mother's gowns that Aunt Clare had packed away in the attic and forgotten. She wanted to cut them up for bandages, but I talked her into giving them to me instead." She made a wry mouth. "Of course, the gowns were dreadfully old-fashioned, but one thing I learned at that boarding school up North was how to sew."

"How awful for you to be sent to school in the North," Sally said sympathetically. "Before the war, Papa wanted to send me to school up North, but Mama said she wouldn't have me picking up coarse Yankee ways, and anyway I didn't have to know how to speak French or parse Latin to catch myself a husband." The redheaded girl preened in front of the mirror, running her hands over a waist so tightly boned and corseted that if she took a deep breath, she turned giddy. "Mama was right, too. I'm sure Lieutenant Richardson is going to propose to me tonight."

It was Lucy's turn to stare, bewildered, at her companion. "I thought you were already engaged to an officer in Wade Hampton's troop."

"Oh, I am," Sally said, tossing her head airily. "And a captain in Fitz Hugh Lee's cavalry and a lieutenant on General Longstreet's staff."

"You're engaged to four men at once?" Lucinda asked, amused.

"Why not?" Sally said, practically. "After all, the chances are they won't all come back from the war, and I don't want to end up an old maid, do I?" Her full lower lip quivered in sympathy. "Anyway, how can I refuse a soldier going off to battle? It would be too mean not to make his last weeks happy."

Lucy shook her head, unable to keep from laughing. "Sally, you're impossible. You should be ashamed of yourself."

Her friend gave her a sudden troubled look. "Oh, I don't know, Lucy. At least I don't flirt with every man in sight, the way you do. You've broken the hearts of more men here at The Bower than any girl, and the truth is I don't think you care about any of them, or the war either for that matter," she added shrewdly.

"Oh, pooh." Lucinda reached into her jewel box and tied a narrow black velvet ribbon, to which a gold locket in the shape of a heart was attached, around her slim, graceful neck. "What's the harm in a little flirting? I can't help it if a beau takes me seriously, can I? The war's dreary enough. I'm not going to let it spoil my fun."

"You've changed, Lucy," Sally said slowly. "You used to care—about a lot of things." Then, going to the window, she added sadly, "But then I reckon the war's changed everything." She gestured to the dancers gathered on the green turf outside the house. Bonfires had been placed around the area set aside for dancing, and their fire cast a wild, romantic shadow over the scene, the brightly gowned girls, the exotically uniformed Zouave officers. "Before the war, Mama would have had a fit before she'd let me attend a dance like this, unchaperoned. Now all the girls, nice, respectable girls, come to dances at The Bower and no one thinks anything about it."

Lucinda knew what Sally meant. Aunt Clare had been hesitant at first about allowing Lucy to visit the Jaspars and join in the festivities at Jeb Stuart's headquarters. "I know how dull it must be for a young girl here at Black Oaks, and I'm sure General Stuart is a fine, Christian gentleman, but one does hear stories." She sighed nervously, two tiny frown lines etched between the childish blue eyes. "Oh, dear, I do wish that Harry hadn't accepted that position in President Davis' War Department. I'm proud he was offered the position, of course, but it's so difficult for me with him away in Richmond so much of the time."

Lucinda, however, was secretly delighted that Harry was safely in Richmond. She suspected Harry wouldn't approve at all of her going off alone to The Bower. Aunt Clare, though, she could always manage to twist around her finger, especially when she assured her aunt that Sam would accompany her to the Jaspars in case she should run into any trouble on the road.

"I can't imagine why you're so worried, Aunt Clare," she protested. "After all, I'll be staying at the Jaspar home, and Virginia Jaspar is one of your oldest friends."

Finally, reluctantly, Aunt Clare had agreed.

Now Lucy joined Sally, who was leaning out the wide bedroom window, her crinoline billowing out behind her as she watched the dancers below. A merry reel was being played on the banjo, fiddle and bones by General Stuart's favorite black musicians, who traveled everywhere with him. Caught up in the gaiety of the music, Lucy found her own feet happily tapping time. For a brief moment she forgot she was playing a role here at The Bower. She was no longer the heartless, beautiful coquette, bewitching every man in sight, artlessly coaxing her beaux into talking more freely than they should of military matters. She was simply Lucy Appleton, young and carefree, with nothing more on her mind than a soft summer's night of music and dancing.

Sally leaned further out the window. "Oh, here comes General Stuart." She gave an enraptured sigh. "Isn't he the handsomest thing, Lucy?"

Lucy had to admit that Jeb Stuart's flowing mustache, cinnamon-shaded beard and trim, athletic body made him the very picture of a gallant cavalier. She gave a little giggle. "No wonder they called him the Beauty at West Point."

"Marian Wilds told me she saw the general kissing you on the Dandridge veranda yesterday afternoon," Sally said.

Lucinda shrugged indifferently. "Oh, he kisses all the girls. You know that. It doesn't mean anything." She laughed at a memory. "One of his aides told me about the time the general rode into Upperville and dozens of women rushed up to him, kissing his uniform and his gloves. Finally the general complained, "La-

147

dies, your kisses would be more acceptable on the cheek!"

Sally joined in the laughter, then said, "I'm glad General Stuart has come tonight. Lieutenant Tilby, the general's aide, was telling me only this afternoon that the general might be late arriving at the dance—that he had some important business to attend to first."

Immediately Lucinda was alert, all thought of enjoying the evening forgotten. Business delaying the general could mean orders had been received from General Lee. General Sharpe would want to know about any such dispatch to pass the information along to General Meade. Lucy's wide dark eyes took on an added sparkle of excitement. She would have to be especially nice to Lieutenant Tilby at the dance tonight, she decided. Snapping her black lace fan shut, she turned eagerly to her friend. "Come along Sally. We don't want to be late to the party."

It was no problem singling Lieutenant Tilby out at the dance for her special attention. The rather homely, pompous aide was already smitten with the beautiful Lucinda Appleton and was overjoyed when he discovered that she had saved most of her dances for him.

His partner was light as thistledown in the lieutenant's arms as they danced, her long black lashes fluttering over her dark lustrous eyes as she cast languorous smiles up at her escort. In the light from the bonfires, the skin above her tightly laced, low-cut scarlet basque glowed like pearls with a faint pink undertone. The heart-shaped locket dangled just above the shadowy, enticing cleft between her breasts. It was an effort for the lieutenant to tear his gaze from the locket, to listen, bemused at his good fortune, as the lovely creature in his arms actually asked him if she might go riding with him the next day.

Lucinda smiled demurely up at her dancing partner. "But then I'm sure the general must have all sorts of tasks for you to do tomorrow. You'll be much too busy to spend any time with me."

"No . . . no, not at all," the lieutenant stammered

happily. "I'll be delighted to ride with you tomorrow afternoon."

Lucy thought coldly that if Stuart had received orders from Lee, it evidently didn't include the 1st Virginia Cavalry leaving camp tomorrow. But the smile she gave Lieutenant Tilby was as innocent and flattering as always. "And the party Saturday ... I'm counting on your being my partner."

The lieutenant's face clouded unhappily. "I'm afraid not, Miss Appleton. We ... I mean, I'll be otherwise engaged Saturday."

Lucy made a disappointed mouth. "Oh, dear," she sighed prettily. "It's another girl, isn't it? You're taking someone else to the dance. Well, I'll just have to find myself another partner."

"No, that's not it," the aide said desperately. "There's no one else. We ... that is, none of the brigade will be here Saturday!" he blurted. Then, flushed, he added hastily, "I'd appreciate your not mentioning to anyone what I just said, Miss Appleton. It's not common knowledge yet."

He fell silent, suddenly, belatedly realizing that his partner was no longer hanging with rapt attention to his every word. In fact, her whole body had become strangely stiff in his arms. Glancing puzzled down into her face, he saw that her skin had drained as white as the Cherokee roses she wore in her hair. She looked so pale that the lieutenant was afraid that she might faint. His arm tightened around her tiny waist, and, flustered, he asked, "Miss Appleton ... Lucinda ... are you all right?"

She did not answer him. Her night-black eyes were staring, as if mesmerized, at the musicians gathered at the edge of the lawn. Curious, he turned to follow her gaze. General Stuart was standing by the musicians with several officers, but only the general was lustily joining in the singing of "Old Dan Tucker," which the musicians were playing. Lieutenant Tilby frowned. It never seemed dignified to him, a general officer singing with his black musicians, the way Gen-

149

eral Jeb Stuart loved to do. Still, there were quite a few things Jeb Stuart did which the lieutenant didn't consider at all proper.

"Who is that black-haired major with the general?" his companion asked.

The lieutenant returned his gaze to his partner, relieved to see that the color had once more flowed back into her lovely face. If anything, her cheeks were too flushed, and he noticed a slight tremor beneath the rich, sweet voice.

He didn't need to ask which officer she meant. He'd had a run-in with that particular major only that afternoon, and he wasn't likely to forget the incident. "That's Major Cole Sinclair, chief of Stuart's scouts," he said stiffly. "He arrived this morning on a special mission for the general."

The girl in his arms gave a little breathless gasp. "You mean the major's a spy? How exciting!"

The lieutenant experienced an undignified stab of jealousy. "It's not work I'd enjoy," he said stiffly. "And hardly the sort of work for an officer and a gentleman, prying into people's private lives, trusting no one, imagining spies behind every bush, even here at headquarters."

His companion's eyes widened as she stared, apparently fascinated, at the lieutenant. "Is the major actually looking for a spy here at The Bower?"

Lieutenant Tilby nodded reluctantly. "A few days ago, a brevet stopped a man a couple of miles from our camp. When he tried to escape, they shot and killed him. They found papers on his body. I don't know the whole story, but evidently a chemist in Richmond discovered secret writing on the papers, military information the man must have gained from someone here in Stuart's headquarters."

Vaguely, the lieutenant realized he was talking too freely, but he had never before had a beautiful young woman hanging with such flattering interest on his every word. Anyway, his interview with Major Sinclair still smarted. The brazen effrontery of the man! Why,

150

he had practically accused the lieutenant of negligence in his duties, as if the information the dead spy had been carrying had come from his tent. He had thought about calling the major out, but there had been something unnerving about those icy blue-green eyes staring through him, a lazy menace behind the smile that had made him hesitate.

Now he saw uncomfortably that the same penetrating gaze was fastened upon him and his partner, a look of almost puzzlement gathering on Major Sinclair's face as he studied the lieutenant's dancing partner.

Lucy Appleton gave a soft sigh and rested her hand lightly on the lieutenant's arm. "I'm feeling a little faint, Lieutenant Tilby. If you, perhaps, could find me a place where I can sit down?"

"Of course." The lieutenant was instantly solicitous. Anyway, he had heard that young ladies often used the excuse of faintness to cleverly get their beaux alone in some secluded corner. He slipped a delighted arm around the girl's tiny waist and escorted her away from the dancers and the lighted bonfires to a wrought-iron bench in the small herb garden behind the house. Lucinda sank down on the bench, her crinoline skirt looking black in the moonlight as it billowed gracefully out around her. Immediately the lieutenant dropped on his knees beside the girl, grasping her small soft hands tightly in his own.

"Do I dare hope, Miss Appleton . . . Lucinda," he murmured boldly, "that you'll worry about me when I'm gone?"

Lucy stared down at him blankly. Her thoughts were racing so wildly that she had forgotten all about the lieutenant. All she could think of was Cole. He was here; he was alive. But the blessed relief that had spread through her body when she had first seen him, making her feel as dizzy as if she'd had too much apple toddy, had been followed just as quickly by a more sobering sensation.

Lucy understood now why her courier hadn't been at their usual meeting place yesterday morning. The

151

man who had been shot with the incriminating papers found on him had to be her courier, carrying the information she had stolen from Lieutenant Tilby's tent. Now they knew there was a spy in Stuart's headquarters, and it was Cole they must have sent to ferret the spy out. She shivered, a terrible fear trickling down her spine like icewater. Surely when Cole took a close look at her, he would recognize her. He would know that she was the black girl Sukey, who had shot him and left him for dead; that she was the spy he was seeking.

The lieutenant mistook the shiver, the rapid rise and fall of the girl's breasts, the icy coldness of her hands in his grasp, as maidenly modesty.

"You do care then, Lucinda?" he asked, gazing happily up into the girl's lovely oval face, the long sooty lashes casting delicate shadows over the arched cheekbones, the satin-soft skin, pale in the moonlight.

When she said nothing, staring at him with that same frozen look, he rushed on eagerly, "If you only knew how I prayed for just such a moment as this, my dear. The thought of leaving you now..."

He dropped a kiss into the palm of her hand, his hands boldly fondling the rounded softness of her arms. At his touch, the blankness slipped from Lucinda's face and a hardness that the lieutenant was too enraptured to notice crept into the velvet black eyes. "Do we have to be parted?" she whispered. "Perhaps I could come to...wherever you'll be. Will the brigade be moving far from Martinsburg?"

The lieutenant was seated beside her now on the bench, his arms twisting her soft body eagerly toward him. When she made no move to resist him, his lips caressed the silken slope of her shoulders, advanced cautiously toward the delicious dark hollow between the warm breasts where the golden locket lay. "Brandy Station," he whispered hoarsely. "We could meet there, my love. I'll send you word—"

"Lieutenant Tilby."

Neither the lieutenant nor Lucinda had heard Cole's

silent footsteps coming across the garden lawn. Although the major's voice was a soft drawl, it cracked sharply as a whip around the tableau in the moonlight. The lieutenant, flushed and furious, jerked to his feet.

"You will place yourself under tent arrest, Lieutenant Tilby," Major Sinclair said coldly.

"Arrest?" The aide stared at Cole, his mouth dropping open in astonishment. "Wh—why?" he stammered. "For what—what reason?"

"You were passing military information along to Miss Appleton." Cole's eyebrows lifted sardonically. "Or aren't you aware that a general's aide is supposed to keep his knowledge of troop movements to himself?"

The lieutenant's eyes bulged. "But surely... you don't think... you can't believe Miss Appleton..."

The major made an impatient gesture with his hand. "I suggest you withdraw, lieutenant. I've no doubt General Stuart will have a few words to say to you."

The lieutenant cast Lucy a last pleading, helpless glance, then stumbled away into the night.

Now that the moment she had been dreading was here, Lucy felt a thrill of excitement racing along her nerves, the way she always felt when she stood on the stage on opening night. As she waited in the wings, there was always the grinding fear like a fist squeezing her stomach, but the minute she stepped onto the stage and was actually facing the audience, the excitement, the challenge of the role, took over. It was how she felt now as she rose to face Cole, her dark eyes brilliant, her voice lightly mocking. "Aren't you going to arrest me, too, Cole?"

The moonlight made the space between them almost as bright as day. She saw his eyes narrow as he searched her face. For a moment she felt as if her heart had stopped beating.

Then he spoke slowly. "You've changed, Lucy."

So he hadn't recognized her as Sukey after all. Her brittle, teasing laugh, she hoped, hid the flood of relief she was feeling. "Heavens, Cole, everybody tells me

153

that. I would have thought you'd be more original. Or did you really expect me to be the same scrawny twelve-year-old I was the last time we met?" She pirouetted gracefully before him, her crinoline skirt whirling around her. One puffed sleeve of her gown, pulled off her shoulder by the lieutenant's passionate, if fumbling, hands, revealed the dimpled softness of her shoulder. "The change is for the better, I assume you'll agree."

"You are very beautiful," he said, smiling that lazy, mocking smile she remembered so well. "But then you've been told that many times before, haven't you?"

He stooped to pick up a white rose which had fallen from her waist as she twirled before him. As he did so, she noticed a slight frown cross his features.

"What is it?" she asked, puzzled.

"Nothing." He handed her the rose. "It's just something Lieutenant Tilby's orderly told me, about a white rose he found on the floor of Lieutenant Tilby's tent."

Lucinda felt her breath catch in her throat. She remembered she had been wearing white roses in her hair the night she had crept into Lieutenant Tilby's tent over a week ago. That was the night she had discovered the information about Jeb Stuart's forming two new divisions of cavalry, along with the size and strength of the new divisions. It was this information she had sent with the courier, the courier who had never reached Union headquarters. Was it possible she could have unknowingly dropped one of the roses in the tent? She took her time readjusting her sleeve over her shoulder so she wouldn't have to meet Cole's glance.

Then she shrugged and said indifferently, "Everyone wears roses. All the girls do. Even General Stuart carries bouquets of roses."

"Yes," Cole said thoughtfully. His narrowed gaze once more probed too uncomfortably into her face. "I'm surprised to find you here, Lucy. With your father's abolitionist beliefs, I would have thought you would be sharing your charms with Union officers."

She tossed her head petulantly. "Good heavens, Cole, what do I care about politics and this tiresome war? And I hated living in the North. It was so cold and gloomy." She gave him a seductive smile, her voice dropping softly. "Besides, the Northern men aren't half as handsome as Southern officers." She stepped closer to Cole, her black eyes gleaming behind the fluttering lashes, the scent of the roses in her hair filling the air around her, her soft lips parted to show the tip of a pink tongue pressed against her waiting lips.

For a moment, Cole thought regretfully of the young Lucy he had known who had tagged annoyingly around after her brother Charles and him. Knobby-kneed and pigtailed, and yet there had been something endearing about the girl. He had been aware of it even then, a hard core of unflinching honesty and courage, a touching vulnerability and innocence. What a shame she had, after all, turned into just another shallow coquette pursuing anything in pants, flaunting a childish helplessness that he knew only too well from past experiences with her kind actually was the helplessness of a morning-glory vine strangling the tree it twined around.

For no reason, looking into Lucinda's wide, lustrous eyes, he was suddenly reminded of Sukey. In her own way he supposed that Sukey was just as venal and untrustworthy as Lucy Appleton, but at least the young slave girl hadn't been a shallow, empty-headed flirt. He remembered those last moments in the cellar when he had held her in his arms. There had been no deception between them then. Her passion had been open and honest, with that touching vulnerability that had once been Lucy's. Now, looking down into Lucinda's lovely face smiling up at him with practiced ease, the carefully calculated fluttering of the lashes, feeling the tempting warmth of her breasts pressing deliberately against his chest, he felt a white-hot anger leap in him. He could not have said whether it was anger against Lucy or against the young slave girl who had made a fool of him, deceived him and almost killed him. With

155

a sudden movement, his arms tightened around Lucinda, pulling her hard against him, his mouth fastening cruelly down over hers. The kiss lasted only a few short moments, his mouth bruising the soft lips, forcing them apart so that his tongue found the softness within.

Then abruptly he thrust her away from him. "That's what you wanted, isn't it, Lucy?" he jeered mockingly. "Another conquest? You see, I've already heard about Lucinda Appleton, the belle of the regiment, who spreads her favors indiscriminately. I don't even suppose it's occurred to you to worry about Lieutenant Tilby—that your silly flirtation with him may have led the poor fool before a firing squad?"

He had released her so suddenly that she swayed, her eyes staring up at him, wide and dazed, reminding him suddenly, uncomfortably, of a child being punished and not knowing why.

"Oh, I'm sorry, Lucy, I didn't know you were ... occupied."

Sally Jaspar stood on the path, staring curiously from Lucy to Major Sinclair. Flustered, she half turned to leave, then Cole drawled, "Don't go, Miss Jaspar. Miss Appleton is no longer occupied. I was just leaving."

Then he turned and strode away, his face as black as a thundercloud. Sally stared after him, then back at Lucy. Her voice admiring, she said, "I don't know how you manage it, Lucy. Major Sinclair's only been here one day and already you have him alone in the garden with you. Not that it'll do you much good," she said practically. "All the girls have set their caps for Cole Sinclair, but I've heard there's a widow in Richmond who has her claws in him for good."

She took a closer, worried look at her friend's face, then asked, frightened, "Are you all right, Lucy? You look ... funny."

For a moment, Lucinda couldn't speak. She had the odd sensation that she was falling to pieces inside, and that her outward composure would shatter as well if she weren't very, very careful. She had been so positive that Cole was dead, and that even if by some miracle he was still alive, she would feel nothing if she saw him again, except perhaps contempt after she had learned what he had done to Dora Lee. How could she have known that it would take only one moment in Cole's arms and all her carefully constructed defenses against him would crumple like papier-mâché; that just the touch of his arms could send all the foolish, futile longings rushing back into her heart?

With an almost physical effort, she took hold of herself, taking a deep, steadying breath. Well, it was certainly over now, she thought ruefully. At least she should be gratified that she had played her role so well. The obvious disdain in Cole's face as he pushed her away from him had proved her performance was a great success. Cole had not connected white-skinned, vain, flirtatious Lucinda Appleton with the pretty brown spy Sukey. If he had, Lucinda had no doubt but that she'd be under arrest right now, just like poor, silly Lieutenant Tilby.

"Lucy?" Sally repeated, uncertainly. "You don't have the vapors, do you?"

Lucinda shook her head. "No. I am a little tired, though. I think I'll go back to my bedroom, Sally."

"Shall I go with you?"

"Don't bother. I'll be all right."

Before Sally could insist further upon accompanying her, Lucy slipped quickly away. Once in her bedroom, she bolted the door and, lifting her flounced skirt, removed the velvet bag from her waist. Taking the tissue paper from its black silk nest in her hair, she added the information about Stuart's cavalry removing to Brandy Station by Saturday. Lee's Army of North Virginia in its retreat from Gettysburg had pulled up around Culpepper, only a few miles from Brandy Station. General Meade would want to know that Stuart and Lee were once again dangerously combining forces.

Then she put the folded tissue paper into her reticule, along with a piece of silver foil from a box of chocolates. Wrapping herself in a dark cape, she hurried from the room. Within minutes she was knocking softly at the slave quarters behind the Jaspar house, asking that her coachman, Sam, be sent out to her.

Almost immediately Sam joined her, and they walked a short distance away from the quarters before Lucy stopped abruptly and faced him. "I have a message that I want you to deliver to Martinsburg tonight, Sam. There's a very good chance, though, that if you're stopped and the message is found, it could go very hard on you. I'd go myself, but I'm sure the roads in and out of Martinsburg are being watched, and a woman alone on the road at night would be too conspicuous."

They were standing under a catalpa tree. The moonlight filtering through the branches threw a shadow across Sam's face so that she could not see his features, only the luminous shine of his eyes.

When he did not speak, she said swiftly, "I'm sorry. I have no right asking you to risk your life. One man is already dead."

"I'll go," Sam said quietly.

Now it was Lucy who hesitated. It would be bad enough, she knew, if she were caught carrying military information. It would be much worse for a black man. Taking the risk he was, Sam was at least entitled to know why.

She took the tiny slip of paper from her reticule and said, "This note contains information about General Stuart's military strength and movements. It's being sent to Union headquarters."

"Yes'm." Sam's voice was flat. "I figured you was spying." At Lucy's start of surprise, he shrugged. "Had to be a reason why a white lady was running around the countryside stained black like a nigger."

"You know what will happen to you if you're caught?" she persisted.

"Yes'm. They hang spies. A black spy, I s'pose they'll come up with something special—that is, if they find that paper on me."

158

"They may not," Lucy said, an impish gleam in her eyes. "Let me see your teeth, Sam."

They stepped out of the shadow of the catalpa into the moonlight, and Sam opened his mouth. She stood on tiptoe to peer inside, then nodded, pleased. "There's a cavity in the back that should do just fine." Taking the piece of tinfoil from her bag, she wrapped it around the tissue paper until it was a small, hard silver pellet. "This should fit nicely into the cavity, Sam." She giggled nervously. "If you're stopped, let's hope they don't think to check your teeth."

In a few seconds the pellet was transferred to Sam's mouth and Lucy was giving him the rest of his directions.

"There's a man staying at the Benton Hotel in Martinsburg named Robert Bailey. Tell him the white rose sent you, and give him the pallet. And, Sam ..." She hesitated, a current of fear running through her voice. "Tell Mr. Bailey to be very careful. Tell him the silver fox is alive and in Stuart's camp. He's Stuart's new chief of scouts. He'll understand."

Something of the fear she felt must have shown in her face, for Sam asked softly, "Will you be safe here?"

She pulled her cape more closely around her as if warding off a sudden chill. "I don't know," she admitted, remembering that probing look in Cole's wintry eyes as he handed her the white rose. Cole might not have recognized Sukey in the moonlight, but in the bright light of day, wasn't it possible that some tone of voice, or tilt of the head, might give her away? Or, she thought, despising herself for her cowardice, wasn't it the real truth that she was too unsure of her own emotions to dare face Cole again?

"I'll be back by sunup at the latest," Sam said. "We can leave for Black Oaks at the first light."

Ignoring the flutters of fear in her stomach, Lucy said coldly, "No. If Major Sinclair does suspect me, my leaving so abruptly will seem suspicious. The brigade's moving out day after tomorrow. We'll leave for Black

Oaks then, after they've gone." Surely, she thought, a little vainly, she was a good enough actress to continue playing her role of flighty, flirtatious Lucy Appleton another twenty-four hours without arousing Cole's suspicions.

When Sam stood, frowning at her, she shrugged with unconscious arrogance and said calmly, "Don't worry, I'll be all right. I've fooled Major Sinclair before. I can do it again."

The next morning, though, as she arose quietly while Sally and the rest of the Jaspar household were still sleeping off the effects of the dance the night before, the flutters of fear were still there, like butterfly wings inside her stomach. She dressed with great care, wearing the handsome riding habit that General Stuart had given her as his honorary aide-de-camp, an honor he reserved for only the prettiest of the young women who flocked around him. The riding habit of gray Confederate cloth, trimmed in black braid with the rank of captain on the collar, fit snugly through the bodice, while the long gray plume of the hat almost hid the blue-black coiled hair from view.

Sam was waiting for her at the stable and saddled her roan mare. There were too many stable boys around for her to question him about his night activities until he led the mare out into the yard. Then as she mounted, she reached down for the reins and whispered, "Any trouble?"

He shook his head. "The pickets stopped and searched me on the road." For a moment his teeth flashed whitely beneath the hawk's nose. "They didn't find nothing." Then, sobering, he said softly, "Mr. Bailey says you should watch yourself. He'll be at Lee's camp at Culpepper, but it'd be best for you to lay low at Black Oaks for a while. If you want to pass information on to him, use Ely's Inn near Cold Brook." Then, seeing the Jaspars' groomsman coming out of the stable, he asked loudly, "You want I should ride along behind you, Miss Lucy?"

Lucinda shook her head. "No, thank you, Sam. I think I'll ride alone today."

She started at a sedate canter, then, as she reached a stretch of fields sloping gently toward the horizon, she let the roan out full gallop, delighting in the crisp October air flowing past her face, the exhilaration of feeling the magnificent horse beneath her. For a while, everything else was forgotten. She was the young, reckless tomboy again, racing with her brothers across the fields at Black Oaks. When a rail fence cut through the fields before her, the roan took the jump effortlessly, horse and rider appearing as one to a small group of admiring observers on horseback, watching from a nearby rise of land.

When she became aware that she wasn't alone, Lucy slowed the roan to a trot and joined the half dozen uniformed men. She saw Cole in the general's entourage but deliberately ignored him while flashing Jeb Stuart a demure smile. "Good morning, general. Lovely morning, isn't it?"

"You ride like a red Indian, Miss Appleton," the general said, his gaze lingering appreciatively on the girl's face, the skin flushed an attractive wild-rose pink, the dark eyes willful and lusty with life. "Not even my Flora handles a horse as well as you."

"Thank you." She fluttered her sooty eyelashes coyly. "But then any aide of yours should ride well, shouldn't she, to keep up with you?"

The general turned toward Cole. "I don't believe you've met my chief of scouts, Major Sinclair."

"We've met." Lucinda smiled mischievously. "As a matter of fact, Cole and I practically grew up together."

"I can't understand any officer of mine letting a beauty like you get away from him, Miss Appleton," the general said gallantly.

Lucinda pouted prettily. "Oh, I'm afraid Major Sinclair doesn't approve of me, general. Last evening I was sure he was going to arrest me just because poor Lieutenant Tilby . . ." She bit her lower lip, tears all at once

shining in her large, lovely eyes as she gazed pleadingly at the general. "Oh, dear, I do feel so badly about
the lieutenant. I'm sure he didn't mean any harm. I'd
hate to think he was in trouble because of my stupidity."

The general cleared his throat gruffly. "There's no
need to upset yourself, Miss Appleton. Lieutanant
Tilby has been transferred back to Richmond on a re-
cruiting detail. It would seem more his line of duty,"
he added dryly.

During the exchange, Lucy had glimpsed a mocking
smile on Cole's face, as if, she thought uneasily, he was
watching a performance which amused him. But he
said nothing until Lucinda thanked the general profusely and rode away. Then he brought his horse close
to the general's and said quietly, "Are you aware that
Miss Appleton's father and brother both fight for the
Union?"

"Of course. Miss Appleton told me when she first
arrived at The Bower." Jeb Stuart scowled. "But then
God knows how many other families in the valley are
split between Union and Confederate sympathies. It's
the most damnable part of this whole war, turning
families against each other." He studied his chief scout
closely. "Are you saying that you think Miss Appleton
is a spy?"

"I'm not sure," Cole said slowly. It could be that Lucy
was just what she seemed, vain, frivolous, interested
only in satisfying her own selfish pleasures. Still, the
instinct which had alerted him so often in the past to
danger was working again. He had, he reflected bitterly, been betrayed already by one woman, and a black
woman at that. He had no intention of letting his defenses down again.

As for Sukey . . . Cole's face hardened, his blue-green
eyes deadly beneath the slashing black brows. Well,
they'd meet again. And the next time, he would take
exquisite pleasure in making that golden, seductive
body pay for making a fool of him. By the time he had

finished with her, little Sukey would wish she had killed him back there in the clearing.

"Have you found out anything about the agent who's been passing information from our camp?" the general asked.

Cole jerked his thoughts back to the present. "Not yet, sir. There's a Union agent who has been operating in the valley for the last months, and goes by the code name of white rose. That's about all we know. Could be anyone, man or woman, white or black."

"A black spy?" the general asked, startled.

Cole shrugged. "Our pickets stopped a black man, named Sam, last night. He was searched thoroughly, but nothing was found on him. He was on his way to Martinsburg, courting a servant girl there, he said."

"One of my black musicians is named Sam," the general said. "But I'd stake my life on the loyalty of Sam Sweeney."

"This man wasn't a musician. He was a big handsome fellow, part Indian, I'd say."

General Stuart frowned. "Miss Appleton's groom is one of the finest-looking bucks I've ever seen. It seems to me she called him Sam." He turned to gaze thoughtfully after Lucinda, galloping back toward the Jaspar home. "I'd suggest you keep an eye on that young woman, Major Sinclair."

"I intend to," Cole said grimly.

10

"Lucy ... Lucy, wake up."

A soft knocking at her bedroom door awakened Lucy. She yawned and stretched luxuriously so that the feather coverlet threatened to slide off the four-poster bed. Quickly she snatched it back against the April chill in the room.

"Come in, Aunt Clare," she called sleepily.

Her aunt bustled into the room, her round blue eyes apologetic. "I'm sorry to disturb you, dear. I know you didn't return from the Pattersons until late last night, but I just received a message from Harry. He's returning from Richmond today, and he's bringing a guest. I'm at my wit's end, worrying what I can possibly serve for dinner. We ate the last of the ham last week, and we need the chickens for the eggs, and it hardly seems proper serving a guest at Black Oaks corn hominy and sweet potatoes."

Lucinda sat up, pulling her robe around her and brushing her hair back from her face. "I don't know why not. From what I hear, they're eating lots worse than that in Richmond these days." Then, holding her hand to her mouth to cover a yawn, she said drowsily, "Sam told me he heard some wild turkeys calling in the woods the other day. If there are any guns left in the house, he can try to shoot one for dinner."

Her aunt's face brightened. "There's an old musket in the attic that belonged to your grandfather. If you'll speak to Sam, I'll see if I can find it."

She half turned toward the door, then stopped, gazing with worried eyes at her niece, at the shadow of unhappiness that had not left the girl's face since her return from The Bower. "You look tired, dear. You're wearing yourself out, visiting so much around the county. Even Harry noticed, when he was home at Christmas—"

She broke off abruptly, noticing the ominously stubborn tilt of Lucy's chin. Oh dear, she shouldn't have mentioned Harry, she thought. When her son had been home at Christmas, he and Lucy had had a terrible fight over Lucy's stay at The Bower. Evidently even in Richmond they'd heard stories about the beautiful Lucinda Appleton and how she had enchanted any number of Jeb Stuart's officers, even the general himself it was whispered.

Of course, Clare Appleton was sure the stories were just nasty gossip. Lucy was simply young and high-spirited, and with her beauty she couldn't help attracting male attention. Unfortunately, Harry hadn't taken such a dispassionate view of the matter. If only, Clare thought, sighing to herself, Harry would learn that he would never get his way with Lucy by ordering her about. There was too much of her Grandfather Jacob in Lucinda for that.

She lifted her hands helplessly. "It's not just the late hours, my dear. I worry about your riding around the countryside, a young woman, alone."

"I'm sorry, Aunt Clare," Lucy said repentantly. "I don't mean to worry you. But I'm perfectly safe. All the fighting is over by Brandy Station and Bristoe and Culpepper. Anyway, I always have Sam along, and you know he won't let anything happen to me."

A flush pinkened Clare Appleton's cheeks. Truth to tell, she wasn't too happy about that situation either. She was sure it was already being noticed that wherever Lucinda Appleton went, the handsome young black giant followed like a shadow. Then she was instantly ashamed of her own uncharitable thoughts. She had never seen the servant so much as glance at Lucy without that blank, impassive look on his face. And with Harry away so much in Richmond these days, heaven knew how she would have managed at Black Oaks without Sam.

To change to a less worrisome subject, she asked, "How was the Pattersons' party? I imagine Sarah is overjoyed, having her son home again, even for a few days. Did you have a pleasant evening?"

"Yes," Lucy said shortly, turning away quickly so that her aunt couldn't see the stain of guilt on her face. She wondered if she would ever stop feeling unhappy about what she was doing. It was so pathetically easy to get a young officer like Tony Patterson to brag about his war exploits to a pretty girl who hung breathlessly on his every word, while hoping all the while that he'd mention just one piece of vital information that might be useful to Jephthah and General Sharpe.

Lucy much preferred the times during the last months when, with Harry safely in Richmond, she could come and go as she pleased from Black Oaks. Sometimes she would pretend to take shopping trips to neighboring towns, while other times she told Aunt Clare she was visiting friends in the valley.

Once she left Black Oaks on those outings, though, Lucy Appleton was left behind. Using the makeup arts she had learned in the theater, she became an Irish peddler woman, eyes red-rimmed and merry, her black hair frowzy and untidy. With a thick Gaelic brogue, she wheedled her way past the pickets at Confederate camps and peddled pies and cakes to the troops, who were only too happy to have a change from military rations. And just as happy to exchange conversation with a cheerful peddler woman, often revealing bits of military information at the same time.

Occasionally she disguised herself as a black woman, but she didn't dare the role of the saucy Sukey again. Instead she became a grizzled bent old mammy, a kerchief wrapped around her head, who took in washing for Confederate officers at their winter quarters along the Rappahannock River. Black laundresses were such a commonplace sight in camp that no one noticed as she lingered longer than necessary, delivering her laundry to the headquarters tents and the officers' quarters. In one such camp, she glimpsed Jephthah on

166

guard duty in a faded butternut uniform, but if Jephthah recognized her, he gave no sign.

Usually such forays into the enemy camps brought her much more vital information than she was able to garner as Lucinda Appleton of Black Oaks, flirting outrageously with officers home on leave and at regimental parties.

Except last night, she thought, smiling to herself. Last night she'd had a bit of luck at the Pattersons'. Shivering, she went to her wardrobe and began to dress quickly, thankful that she had been able to save at least one flannel petticoat from her Aunt Clare, who had turned most of the table and bed linen at Black Oaks, as well as almost all the cotton and flannel petticoats, into lint and bandages for the hospitals in Richmond.

As she pulled a gray merino wool gown over the flannel petticoat, she thought again of Tony Patterson turning to his mother at the dinner table and remarking, "You'll never guess who I saw coming out of General Stuart's headquarters last week, mother. Remember Sally Pollock?"

"Of course, a dear, sweet child, but the Pollocks live in Cumberland, Maryland," his mother said, surprised. "Whatever was Sally doing in the valley?"

"That's what I asked her," Tony said, grinning. "She was pretty cagey, but finally I found out she comes down the valley regularly, bringing military information to Stuart and Lee that she's managed to learn from the Yankees. They say it was word Sally brought Lee that helped us wipe out a whole troop of Custer's cavalry when Meade tried to cross the Rapidan River at Mine Run last November."

"You mean Sally's a spy?" his mother said, shocked. "Why, she can't be more than eighteen! Whatever is her mother thinking of?"

Well, Miss Sally Pollock wouldn't be doing any more spying in the valley, Lucy thought grimly, pulling a shawl over her shoulders and hurrying down the stairs to the warmth of the kitchen. Not if the note she'd had

Sam deliver to Ely's last night reached General Sharpe's headquarters.

Aunt Bessie fixed Lucy's breakfast, grumbling all the while about her rheumatiz. Her legs were wrapped in coal-oil-soaked red flannel against the affliction. "Don't see how Miss Clare 'spects me to cook dinner and clean that back bedroom for Mr. Harry's visitor, not with my legs bothering me so I can hardly stand."

Lucy swallowed the bitter chicory coffee and finished the corn fritters quickly. "Don't fuss, Aunt Bessie," she said soothingly. "I'll do up the back bedroom. You help Aunt Clare with the dinner."

Before she began that chore, though, she went to find Sam. He was chopping wood in the back lot, and for a few moments she stood admiring the apparently effortless way the ax rose and fell, splitting the logs with one stroke as if slicing through butter. As quietly as she had come up behind Sam, he had heard her, and without stopping the rhythmic rise and fall of the ax, he asked, "You want something, Miss Lucy?"

She told him about the wild turkey and asked if he thought he could shoot one for dinner that evening.

"Expect I can. They're old birds, though, and tough."

Lucy glanced around to make sure they were alone, then asked, "Did it go all right last night at Ely's?"

Sam and she had decided that it was better if he acted as the courier, delivering her messages to Ely's. The inn, about a half hour's ride from Black Oaks, was little more that a rough country tavern, and Lucy's presence was sure to cause attention. A black man, however, could slip in and out of the kitchen and drop a note on tissue paper into a special flour bin without anyone becoming curious.

Sam nodded, but Lucy saw the hesitation in his face and asked quickly, "What is it?"

"A peddler's been hanging around Ely's the last couple of days," he said slowly.

"Well?" Lucy asked impatiently. "What of it?"

"Mr. Ely's worried. He thinks the peddler's a Confederate agent. The man's too friendly and spends too much money on drinks, not enough time peddling." Sam stopped chopping, burying the ax into a butt of wood, and turned to face Lucy. He watched the girl's face closely. "And that Major Sinclair that was at The Bower. Mr. Ely says he's been seen in the neighborhood."

Lucy drew her shawl more closely around her shoulders. The April sun was bright overhead, but without any warmth. Thinking quickly, she decided there was no possible way Cole could connect Lucinda Appleton with Ely's. Yet she felt a flicker of fear run through her veins so that her skin prickled.

The rest of the day she was kept too busy airing and cleaning out the guest bedroom, helping Aunt Clare get the house ready for Harry's guest, to worry anymore about Cole. She was dressing for dinner when she heard horses ride up to the front veranda of Black Oaks. Peering curiously out of the bedroom window, she glimpsed Harry and a stranger, a tall, thin middle-aged man who walked with a stoop. When she went down the stairs she saw that the man's mouth had a cynical twist, even when he smiled, and his eyes burned with a missionary's zeal.

Cousin Harry introduced his guest. "Mother, Cousin Lucy, may I present Mr. Clement Vallandigham."

The name sounded vaguely familiar to Lucy, but she couldn't remember where she had heard it before until later, when they were gathered at the dinner table over Aunt Clare's turkey stew. Sam was right. The wild turkey he had shot had been a tough old bird, Lucinda thought, only absently listening to Harry and his guest discussing the war and more particularly President Abraham Lincoln.

"The man's a despot!" Mr. Vallandigham announced, brandishing his fork indignantly. "Innocent men are rotting in dungeons because that tyrant in the White House wills it so. He does not wish to end the war. Lincoln will continue the bloodshed as long as there are any contractors or officers to enrich."

Lucinda gazed thoughtfully at the man, at his face

169

flushed with anger, listening to the hatred throbbing in his voice. Strange for such a staunch Southerner, his voice held a decided Midwestern twang. Of course! She remembered now where she had heard the man's name before. While she had lived in Washington, the newspaper headlines had been filled with stories about Clement Vallandigham, the leader of the Copperheads, as the antiwar Democratic Party was called. The man's speeches against President Lincoln and the war had grown so virulent when he ran for governor in Ohio that he'd been thrown into prison by General Burnside, military governor of Ohio. Facing court-martial, he had been saved from imprisonment by President Lincoln, who had shipped Vallandigham south under military escort, to the arms of the Confederacy.

Aunt Clare looked dismayed at the man's words. "Surely President Lincoln cannot be such a monster," she protested. "Is there nothing that can be done to stop him?"

Lucy saw Harry and his guest exchange a swift, covert glance. Then Mr. Vallandigham dabbed at his mouth with his napkin and began to attack the dried-apple pie placed before him. "The tyrant will be deposed. You may count on that, ma'am," he nodded grimly. "If he's renominated at the Republican convention this summer, he'll be defeated in November. The war's been a costly failure. The people see that now. The North cannot possibly win. Each new Northern general brings only more disastrous, bloody defeats."

Lucy widened her eyes innocently. "Surely you're forgetting General Grant and his Union victories in the west, at Vicksburg and Chattanooga?"

Harry gave Lucy an annoyed glance. "Grant's a vulgar, ignorant dirt farmer, and a drunkard besides. General Lee will deal with him easily if Grant is ever foolish enough to face Lee here in the valley."

Mr. Vallandigham's eyes rested on the silken curve of Lucy's shoulders, gleaming in the candlelight. The narrow black velvet ribbon around her slender, graceful neck matched the velvet-soft black eyes behind the thick, sooty lashes. "Your cousin is much too beautiful a young lady, Mr. Appleton, to understand such things as military strategy," he said, smiling condescendingly. The patronizing tone in the man's voice brought a surge of color to Lucy's cheeks. "I may not understand military strategy, Mr. Vallandigham," she said coldly. "But I recognize a turncoat when I see one!"

There was a shocked silence around the table. Then Aunt Clare took one nervous look at her son's face, which was turning a rich scarlet hue, and got quickly to her feet. "Perhaps the gentlemen would prefer to have coffee alone, Lucinda. I've been saving one last bottle of my dear husband's madeira for just such a special occasion as this, Mr. Vallandigham. I'll fetch it at once."

Casting an uneasy smile at her guest, Clare Appleton headed with more speed than courage to the dining-room door. Lucy, still furious, started after her aunt. She had reached the hall when Harry caught up with her, jerking her around to face him. His eyes were shining with rage, and his fingers bit cruelly into the soft flesh of her arm. "How dare you?" he demanded, his voice low and trembling with anger. "How dare you insult a distinguished guest in my own home? You will return and apologize to Mr. Vallandigham at once."

His home, Lucy thought, enraged, her anger rising to meet his. Harry could live at Black Oaks forever and it would never be his home. He would always be an interloper, a stranger.

She tried to pull free, but the grip on her arm was too strong. "I'll never apologize," she said, fighting back tears of pain. "The man's a traitor. The South should be ashamed to shelter him. He'll only bring dishonor to the Confederacy."

Harry smiled smugly down at her. "No, not dishonor, dear cousin. It's victory Mr. Vallandigham will be bringing us."

Then abruptly, as if aware he had spoken too freely, he released her arm so suddenly that she staggered.

171

His pale-yellow eyes roamed insolently over her slender figure, lingering possessively on the swell of her breasts above the ruffled bodice of her gown. He smiled tightly. "But then I'm forgetting what a rude child you always were, Cousin Lucy. After we're married, it will be my pleasure to teach you better manners. If Mr. Vallandigham and I didn't have pressing matters to discuss, I'd deal with you right now. For the moment, though, I want you to go to your room and stay there until I send for you."

At Lucy's instinctive gesture of rebellion, he stepped forward, smiling coldly down at her. "And don't think for one minute, my dear, that even with only one good arm I can't drag you, kicking and screaming if you like, up those stairs."

Lucy hesitated. She could feel the anger pounding at her temples, but something else, too. Curiosity. What pressing matters did a man like Vallandigham and Harry have to discuss? She shrugged disdainfully and turned away with a careless swirl of her skirt. "I'll be quite happy to go to my room, Cousin Harry. I find my own company far preferable to yours or that of your distinguished guest."

Once in her own bedroom, she waited by the door until she heard the massive sliding doors of the dining room close with that shrill note of protest they always made. Then she hurried down the stairs through the back hallway and into the kitchen. Aunt Bessie was dozing by the wood stove and didn't even hear Lucy slip into the serving pantry between the dining room and the kitchen. There was a swinging door between the pantry and the dining room, and even when it was closed, voices from the dining room could be heard in the pantry.

Cousin Harry was still evidently apologizing profusely to his guest for Lucinda's behavior. "There is no need for apology, Mr. Appleton," Mr. Vallandigham finally interrupted, a note of injured dignity in his voice. "There are many people in the South as well as the North who do not understand the great work that

172

the Sons of Liberty, such as you and I, are doing. We operate in the strictest secrecy, so how can they be expected to understand? The attacks on my reputation, the despicable accusations thrown at me, I can bear with impunity, knowing the glorious deeds we shall soon be accomplishing to bring this terrible war to an end."

"You will be taking part in the operations yourself?" Harry asked.

"I'm on my way to Ontario now to meet with Mr. Hines and Mr. Thompson. Since my face is so well known, it is necessary that we conduct our meetings in Canada. Now that your Secretary of War, Mr. Judah Benjamin, has supplied the necessary money, there is nothing to stand in the way of our campaign. Hines himself will lead the attack in Chicago, first freeing the thousands of brave Confederate prisoners held at Camp Douglass. Along with other Sons of Liberty, and freed prisoners, our small army will sweep through the industrial North, burning and sacking Indianapolis, Buffalo and New York. The new Northwest Confederacy that will be formed from the chaos that will follow will split the North in two."

"Surely Federal troops will be sent against you?" Harry said hesitantly.

"No doubt," Mr. Vallandigham agreed calmly. "But that will mean withdrawing Union troops from here in the valley, dividing the Federal forces. General Lee will have no trouble handling the small Army of the Potomac left behind in the valley."

"Suppose the people of the North won't rise and join with the Sons of Liberty?" Harry asked, worried. "Such an undertaking must have the support of the common people to succeed."

"Oh, the people will rise against the tyrant," Mr. Vallandigham said confidently, his voice taking on the ringing tones of the accomplished orator. "The draft riots in New York show how weary the people are with this war, how anxious they are for a negotiated peace, which Lincoln has refused them. Once the Sons of Liberty begin the attack, the rest of the country will follow. There will be rioting in the streets, mark my word. King Lincoln will tremble on his throne!"

"It was my stepfather's dearest dream," Harry said. "Uncle Joseph was always convinced that the North must be attacked from within if the South were to succeed. Ever since I accepted the position in the War Department, I've been trying to convince Mr. Benjamin that the Northern cities must be put to the torch, if we are to win the final victory."

Harry must have had more than a few glasses of Uncle Joseph's cherished madeira, Lucy decided. His voice was beginning to sound thick and maudlin. She had been standing frozen in the pantry, afraid to move for fear that the men on the other side of the door might hear her. Now she allowed herself to lean forward a little so that she could peek through the slit in the door.

The madeira in the bottle was half gone, and the two men at the table looked more like middle-aged tipplers than grand conspirators. Was it possible? Lucy wondered, frowning, trying to make sense of what she had overheard. Could such a plan possibly succeed? Or was it all only the ramblings of an embittered exile, plotting dreams of glory? Yet even Jephthah had been concerned about the discouragement of the Northern people with the war, she rememberd.

In any case, she thought, edging back quietly toward the kitchen, the soft swish of her skirt sounding like thunder in her ears, Jephthah and General Sharpe should be notified at once of the Sons of Liberty and their plot to overthrow the government.

In the kitchen she leaned over Aunt Bessie and shook her gently awake. "Aunt Bessie, I want you to find Sam for me, right away. Do you understand?"

The old woman blinked sleepily. "He ain't here, chile. Don't you remember? He took your mare to be shod to the blacksmith over at Castletown." Her eyes regarded Lucy suspiciously. "Whuffo you want Sam

174

this time of night anyway? Ain't fittin' the way that man tags after you."

Disappointed, Lucinda turned away. It could be hours before Sam returned, and she wanted her information to get to Ely's this evening. With Vallandigham leaving the first thing in the morning, it was important the message be passed on as quickly as possible.

She started for the kitchen door, Aunt Bessie's scolding voice calling after her, "Where you going without a shawl? You'll catch your death of cold."

"I'll only be gone a minute, Aunt Bessie. Go back to sleep."

She was already out the door and halfway to the stable when she realized that the cook was right. It was a cold night, but, casting an eye toward the sky, she saw that at least there was no moon. It would be a good night to ride unseen to Ely's. After all, there wasn't any reason why she couldn't make the trip herself, she decided. She would be back and in her bedroom before anyone in the house would even know she was gone.

She couldn't go dressed as she was, of course, but that presented no problem. She slipped into the stable and made her way back to the tiny tack room, where she lit an oil lamp. From an old wooden box shoved into a corner under a pile of blankets, she took out a pair of worn trousers and a shirt. Then, shinnying out of her gown and petticoats, she found the bottle of stain she used when she had played the elderly mammy laundress visiting Confederate camps. Although not as long-lasting as the chemical stain she had used in Washington, it was one she had often used on the stage and would last at least until she washed herself with soap and water.

Quickly now she covered her body with the stain, using a long-handled brush to reach the awkward, hard to reach areas, then after strapping a knife to her leg, she pulled on the trousers and shirt, pushing an old

175

hat of Sam's down over her hair so that her face and hair were hidden from view.

The next fifteen minutes she spent writing down what she remembered of the conversation between Harry and Mr. Vallandigham. She didn't have the invisible ink she'd had at The Bower; instead she used the elderberry ink her Aunt Clare had concocted when it was impossible any longer in the South to secure imported ink. The paper itself she hid in the sole of her shoe.

When she was finished, she saddled the bay, who had been pawing restively in his stall, and led him quietly from the yard, not mounting until they were a safe distance from the house. Once in the saddle, she gave the horse its head, shivering, not from the cold, but from the excitement racing along her blood.

Despite the darkness of the night, she had no difficulty following the road to Ely's Inn. It was a well-traveled turnpike, and the sound of the bay's hooves echoed sharply against the still-frozen ground. Patches of ice on the road splintered like shattered mirrors underfoot, sounding unnaturally loud in the quiet chill of the night. As she drew closer to the inn, though, she prudently took the precaution of leaving the main road and followed a lesser-known path through the woods that approached the inn from the rear.

The clouds covering the sliver of a moon, like a torn gray chiffon scarf, parted as she came closer to the inn. She had just glimpsed the two-story wooden building through the trees when a sixth sense made her draw in the bay sharply. It was a Saturday night, a night when the inn was usually filled with roisterers, yet the inn was strangely silent. Surely there should be more noise, music, lights, Lucy thought uneasily, her every sense suddenly alert. She had thought to leave her horse in the woods and slip unobserved into the kitchen of the inn and leave her message in the flour barrel. Now she hesitated, uncertain, remembering what Sam had told her that morning, about Mr. Ely's worries that there was a Confederate spy hanging about the premises.

An icy fear gripped Lucy; her knees tightened on the bay. Sensing a trap, she had jerked at the reins and half turned the bay around when a man leaped out of the shrubbery and grabbed at her bridle.

She lifted her whip and slashed viciously at the man's head. He fell away, but a second man had joined the first. The bay, terrified, snorted shrilly and tried to rear. All at once the night was filled with alarm and confusion, voices calling. A half-dozen men surrounded her, pulling at the reins of the bay, trying to jerk Lucy out of the saddle.

She slashed with her whip to the right and left, laying open the cheek of a burly sergeant, who cursed with the pain. Reaching up, he caught at her arm, wrenching the whip from her hand with a violence that left her wrist numb. Other arms tugged at her legs, at her waist. Overpowered, she felt herself sliding from the saddle. The next minute she had landed on the ground, almost beneath the bay's flailing hooves.

The sergeant, blood welling in his cheek, pulled her roughly to her feet, his voice a low growl of fury. "Use a whip on a white man, will you?"

Then he flung open the inn door and shoved his captive through so that the slight trousered figure went sprawling to the floor. Lucinda had a brief glimpse of the tavern room, dimly lit by grease candles, tables and chairs smashed to pieces, broken glass, and the sour smell of spilled whiskey. Then, slowly, her gaze lifted and took in the body of a man tied to a chair, a surprised look on his battered, lifeless face.

For a moment, looking into the face of the innkeeper, she thought she was going to be sick. With a tremendous effort she choked back the nausea rising in her throat, even as she wondered, panic-stricken, how much Mr. Ely had revealed before he was tortured and killed.

Then she felt herself being pulled to her feet. When

she tried to turn her face away from the dead man slumped in the chair, her chin was taken between the sergeant's pincerlike fingers and she was forced again to look at the dead man.

"See what happens to Yankee spies?" The sergeant grinned. "Take a good look. That's what's going to happen to you if you don't talk and talk quick. Who sent you? What are you doing here?"

"Ah don't know nuttin', master." It wasn't difficult for Lucy to duck her head and feign the voice of a frightened Negro boy. She was terrified.

Staring down at the slender figure in the tattered trousers and shirt, a frown of suspicion gathered in the sergeant's deep-set, piglike eyes. Before Lucinda could move, his hand swept out and knocked the slouch hat from her head. The thick braid of hair she had pinned beneath the hat fell over her shoulder.

The sergeant's eyes squinted, partly in surprise, partly in delight. "Well, whaddya know, a gal!" He once again grasped Lucy's chin, forced the girl to look into his bristled face. "And a pretty one, too. Ain't the major going to be surprised?"

Lucy tried to wiggle from his grasp. "Let me go," she mumbled. "Ah ain' done nuttin'."

The sergeant's face hardened, his small eyes glittering. "You cut my face for one thing, gal. Ah reckon you'll pay for that. No nigger gal's going to use a whip on me." He turned to a young trooper who had followed him into the tavern. "Wait outside, Jenkins," he ordered, giving him a cheerful wink. "This won't take long."

The trooper, who couldn't have been more than sixteen, had a prominent Adam's apple that moved nervously up and down his throat. He asked anxiously, "What you going to do?"

"Going to question this little nigger spy," the sergeant said, chuckling hoarsely. "Time I'm through, she'll be begging to tell me what she's doing here and who she's working for, just like old Ely there."

The young man's face paled. "For God's sake, sergeant, you heard Major Sinclair. He said he wanted any prisoners we took alive, so he could question them when he got here. And look what you did to him!" He jerked his chin convulsively toward the innkeeper. "The major will have your hide for that."

The sergeant gave Ely a disgusted glance. "How'd I know the old fool would die so easy?" He ran his eyes hungrily over the willowy form of the young Negro girl standing before him. "Anyway, ah ain't planning to kill the gal, just have a little fun. This one's no field-hand," he said shrewdly. "She's a quality yellow gal, probably been taught lots of fancy ways of pleasing a man, ain't you, missy?"

Once again his hands reached out, this time dragging Lucy hard up against his chest. His moist, open mouth fastened down over hers so that she couldn't breathe. She tried to keep her mouth shut against him, but he forced her lips apart, his tongue sliding between her teeth. Lucinda bit down upon that tongue with all the strength she had left in her body.

With a yelp of pain the man released her. Then, his nostrils flaring with anger like an enraged bull, he slapped her full across the face so that her head snapped back, hitting the wall behind her. The room swam dizzily around her. She sank to her knees.

She was dimly conscious of the sergeant pawing at her. Dazed, half conscious, she felt rough hands pushing her down to the floor, hands tearing at her shirt. Was it Cal again? she wondered confused. Was she back in the cave? Then through a gathering pain-filled darkness, she heard a voice crack angrily, "What the hell's going on here?"

11

Lucy recognized that voice at once. And wasn't sure if it was joy or terror that coursed through her, so confused were her feelings mingling with the pain throbbing in the back of her head.

Cole's voice became dangerously quiet. "Your orders, sergeant, were to hold any prisoners till I arrived."

"Yes, sir. I know, sir, but the nigger was trying to get away. Jenkins here will tell you." The sergeant was sweating. He had seen that look on the major's face before, and he knew what it meant. The major wasn't noted for his patience or mercy when he was disobeyed. The sergeant had seen brave men break down in tears by the time the major had finished with them.

Cole glanced at the dead man slumped in the chair. A note of sarcasm crept into his voice. "And Ely? Was he trying to get away, too?"

"No, sir," the sergeant mumbled. "I just thought, while we was waiting, I'd see what I could find out from him."

"And did you?" Cole drawled softly. "Did you find out anything?"

"He . . . he died too fast," the sergeant admitted unhappily.

The young trooper felt sorry for the sergeant in his misery and offered uneasily, "At the end, major . . . the old man, he said something . . . it sounded like rose, white rose, I think."

Cole's voice cut like a honed razor at the sergeant, his eyes narrowing to angry slits. "You're a stupid, bungling fool, Hannigan. Ely was our best chance to break the courier route. He was the weak link. He's no use at all to us dead."

"There's the other spy, sir," the sergeant said eagerly. "We caught her trying to sneak in the back way.

And she ain't no ordinary nigger gal, sir. You can see that."

He grabbed Lucinda and pulled her to her feet, thrusting her toward the major. "Take a look for yourself, sir."

It was useless to try to delay the moment any longer. Lucy lifted her head and stared defiantly into Cole's face. She didn't know what she expected to see there—perhaps surprise, or that lazy, mocking smile taunting her. What she did glimpse in the narrowed eyes stunned her. Their aquamarine depths held a savage pleasure as they stared at her, a frightening smoldering fury that she glimpsed for only a moment before hardness settled like a mask over Cole's face. "I was sure we'd meet again, Sukey," Cole said, his voice flat, empty of all emotion, as he gazed down at the girl standing before him.

Then, before she could answer, he turned to the young trooper. "The girl rides with you, Jenkins. And see that she's well tied. We're leaving immediately. And stay alert. There are Yankee patrols in the area."

Lucinda felt herself being unceremoniously bundled onto the trooper's horse, her own horse tied behind them. At least, she thought gratefully, she hadn't been riding her roan mare. Cole wouldn't have overlooked the fact that Lucinda Appleton had also been riding a roan mare at Jeb Stuart's camp.

It was almost dusk the next day when the small troop of horsemen rode into Lee's winter quarters stretched out along the Rappahannock River. Several soldiers, fixing dinner at campfires, stared curiously at the Negro girl tied to the saddle. For her own part, Lucy, pretending sleep, was studying her surroundings beneath lowered eyelids.

Lee's winter quarters were like a city of small, hastily constructed wooden huts daubed with clay, providing scant protection against the unusually bitter Virginia winter which had just passed. As they rode through the camp, Lucy recognized it as one she had

181

visited as a black laundress. The heavy artillery guns were mounted and ready for action, and additional fieldpieces were disposed along the fords at the river's edge. Across the river, unseen, hidden in the brush, she knew Meade's artillery was equally well disposed. The two forces had faced each other across the river during the long winter. Several times Meade had attempted skirmishes across the river, but always the Confederates had driven him back.

Gazing at the Southern soldiers she could see lounging around the campfires as she rode by, Lucy marveled that they had found the strength to stand up to the enemy at all. Many of the men were barefoot, their clothing in rags, except for those fortunate few who had commandeered pieces of Union uniforms from dead Yankee soldiers. But it was their faces that haunted Lucinda; pasty, hollow cheeks, sunken, listless eyes, the aftermath of living for months on the sharp edge of starvation. How many more of the men, she wondered, were huddled in the cold huts, sick with fever and dysentery, and all the other illnesses that beset men in winter quarters on short rations and no medical supplies.

She was so intent on watching the men that she didn't see the tree on the side of the road, the gruesome burden hanging from one of the lower branches. When she did see the hanged man, stripped of his boots and trousers, she gave a gasp and turned her eyes away.

Cole brought his horse close to the young trooper's. "Friend of yours, Sukey?" he asked lazily. "He's a spy we caught yesterday. He was hanged this morning at sunrise."

Lucinda forced herself to look at the discolored, mottled face, the obscene limpness of the body. Not Jephthah, she thought, relieved. Thank God, not Jephthah.

Cole caught the look of relief which flashed for a moment across the girl's face, and frowned as he turned to the trooper. "Take the prisoner to my quarters," he ordered brusquely.

The young trooper blinked, surprised. "Your quarters, sir?" He had expected to escort his prisoner to the guardhouse.

"My quarters," Cole snapped. "And don't let her out of your sight for a minute."

"Yes, sir."

Cole's quarters turned out to be an abandoned one-room farm cabin set off to one side of the camp. The cabin was furnished spartanly, a camp bed with a blanket thrown across it, a chest of drawers, a table and two cane-bottom chairs. The one window in the room was shuttered, and, Lucy noticed, her glance quickly and unhappily taking in her surroundings, there was only one door to the cabin, before which the young trooper awkwardly stationed himself.

A bed of hot embers glowed in the small fireplace, and Lucinda went to it, holding her bound hands out to its meager warmth. She was cold and tired and light-headed with hunger. But most of all, remembering the way Cole had looked at her back there at the tavern, the savage cruelty in his face, the glittering hatred in his eyes, she was afraid, more frightened that she had ever been before in her young adventuresome life, more terrified even than in those moments in the Von Bruck cellar with Caesar. And as she thought about the hanged spy she had seen when she rode into camp, imagining herself hanging from that same tree, the room suddenly spun dizzily around her.

From the doorway, the young trooper saw the girl sway. He crossed quickly to her side, lowered her into a chair. "You'd best sit," he said gently. "I'll stir up the fire."

She gazed hopelessly at the young man. "They'll hang me, won't they?" she asked dully.

The young man flushed unhappily. He had never guarded a female prisoner before, certainly not one as pretty as this young Negress. There was something about the girl, the wide, frightened eyes, the sweetly curved trembling lips, that stirred his sympathy and made him want to reassure her.

183

"Maybe not," he said. "Maybe if you tell the major what he wants to know . . ."

His voice fell away, because he didn't really believe himself what he was saying. General Bragg had ordered that white woman spy in Tennessee hanged. Why should Major Sinclair hesitate at hanging a colored girl?

"I'm sorry," he said, turning away and poking awkwardly at the fire.

Even through her haze of fear, Lucy had been aware of a familiar warmth in the boy's eyes gazing at her. Sitting straighter in the chair, she gazed thoughtfully at the young, fair-haired trooper and felt the first faint stirring of hope. She still had her knife strapped to her leg, she remembered, her heart beating faster. If she could get the boy off guard for just a moment . . .

She said softly, "Please, suh, can you untie me?"

The boy hesitated, then said uncertainly, "Don't suppose it'd do any harm."

As he untied her wrists, she looked up into his face, her eyes wide and pleading. "Ah don' want to die. Please, suh, can you help me?"

For a moment she saw the boy's face soften with compassion, then he sighed and shook his head, "I wish I could, but the major'd have my neck 'stead of yours."

He returned to stirring up the fire, turning his back on the girl so he wouldn't have to feel so guilty looking into that childishly frightened face, the softly beseeching eyes.

Except if he had been watching he would have seen that the eyes watching him were no longer soft, or even frightened, but lacquer-hard and coldly determined. Carefully, stealthily, Lucinda reached down to her leg and removed the knife from beneath her trousers. Still without making a sound, she rose to her feet, lifting the knife in her hand so that it poised between the shoulder blades of the young trooper.

Then, remembering the boy's kindness to her, she hesitated for a moment, staring at the young, defenseless back, all at once reminded of young Matt. It was

184

a moment's weakness that cost her dearly. As she stood motionless, a hand descended over her wrist, and wrenched her arm behind her so sharply that she cried aloud with the pain. The knife fell with a clatter to the floor from her numb fingers.

The trooper whirled, gazing, startled, from the knife on the floor to Major Sinclair's grimly scowling face and the girl struggling like a wild cat in the major's arms.

"Where did she get the knife?" Cole demanded.

The trooper's voice was boyishly shrill. "I . . . I don't know, sir. She must have had it on her."

"Are you saying the prisoner wasn't searched after she was taken?" the major asked, his voice coldly furious.

"No. We didn't think . . . she's just a girl."

Still holding the struggling girl, the major picked up the knife and tossed it to the soldier. "You would have been just as dead, no matter whose hand held the knife," he commented drily. Then at the boy's flushed embarrassment, he felt almost a twinge of pity. After all, he really couldn't blame the boy. Sukey had made of fool of him, too, hadn't she?

"I'm sorry, sir," the boy said, shamefaced.

Cole dismissed the trooper. The boy bolted from the cabin without a backward glance, glad to have gotten off so easily.

Lucy had stopped struggling, standing stiff and still within the tight circle of Cole's arms, but he could feel the tension coiled within the slim body pressed close against him. Too close, he realized angrily, all at once aware of how the softly tantalizing curves of the girl seemed to fit naturally against his own body, like two parts of a whole. And was even angrier to discover that the remembered scent of the girl, the tawny gold of her skin, could even now stir a warmth in his loins, a hunger that had remained with him ever since that first day he had taken her in Arabella's bedroom.

Deliberately he forced himself to remember that other Sukey, the girl who had thrust a gun into his face, shot him and left him for dead, the frozen-faced Negress he had glimpsed a few minutes before with a knife clutched in her hand, ready to bury it in the back of the unsuspecting trooper. He pushed the girl away from him so violently that she staggered and fell into the chair she had only recently vacated.

He stood over her, smiling lazily down at her. For a moment she felt her throat tighten. The smile reminded her of the handsome, teasing Cole Sinclair she remembered from her childhood, her brother's friend whom she had worshipped shyly and from afar. Only there was no gentleness or warmth in the hard, spare lines of Cole's face now; the wintry gaze searching her face was pitiless, as if, she thought uneasily, he was able to probe behind her eyes into her very mind.

"Well, Sukey," he drawled. "What do you have to say for yourself?"

"Please, suh," she said, her voice feigning a childish bewilderment, ducking her head against that searching gaze so that her thick lashes cast dark shadows across her pale-gold cheeks. "What do you want with Sukey?"

Cole laughed grimly. "Oh, no, Sukey, that innocent pickaninny act won't work twice." He reached down suddenly and cupped her chin in his hand, forcing her to look up at him. He studied her face carefully in the flickering firelight that dimly illuminated the room. "Sergeant Hannigan was right about one thing. You're no ordinary servant girl, Sukey. I'm sure you can speak as well as any white girl if you want to. Someone's trained you very well for your job."

She tried to pull free. She said sulkily, "Ah don' know what you're talking about."

"The white rose? That doesn't mean anything to you?"

"It's ... it's a flower, ain't it?" the girl asked, wide-eyed.

"It's a code name for a spy," he corrected her coldly. "Your code name, Sukey, I've no doubt. What were you doing at Ely's Inn?"

"Just passin' by," she said, her thoughts racing desperately. How much did Cole actually know of the courier route, and how much was guesswork on his part?

Cole's hands bit into her shoulders, jerked her abruptly to her feet. The muscles in his face were pulled rigid. "Don't lie to me, Sukey. I've no time for games. You were at the tavern to pass information to the late Mr. Ely, weren't you?" His eyes suddenly narrowed as he gazed speculatively down at the girl. "Come to think of it, Sergeant Hannigan never searched you, did he? Whatever message you were carrying could still be hidden on you somewhere, couldn't it, Sukey?"

By the shocked look of sick despair in her eyes, he knew he had hit his mark. He smiled triumphantly as he caught her wrists behind her back with his one hand. Although she struggled fiercely, she couldn't free herself from his iron grip. "Let's see, Sukey," he drawled. "Where shall we start? The hair? I understand that's a favorite hiding place for female spies." Reaching up with his free hand, he loosened the braid of blue-black hair, running his hand through its glossy tangled softness to make sure there were no hidden combs. "Not in the hair?" he said, lifting a mocking eyebrow. "Well, then we'll have to look elsewhere, won't we?"

His hand moved casually to her shirt, began slowly to undo the buttons. The shirt fell open, and the pale-golden swell of her breasts caught the light from the fireplace. "Buttons are another good hiding place," he said, seeing the fear gathering in her eyes as he slid the shirt off her shoulders, only the quick rise and fall of the small, high breasts betraying her agitation. "A spy I caught not long ago had a whole campaign of Longstreet's written on a piece of tissue paper and hidden in one of his large brass buttons."

Carefully he examined every inch of the worn, homespun shirt, then tossed it to the floor. When he turned back to the prisoner, she saw the glint of amusement in his eyes beneath the black, slashing brows.

He's enjoying himself, Lucinda thought, fuming, her fingers itching to reach out and scratch that mocking

187

smile from his face. Except, remembering the pantherlike quickness with which Cole could move, she was sure her hands would never reach his face and her attack would only bring quick and painful retribution. Instead she contented herself with summoning up as much dignity as she could muster under the circumstances, and lifting her chin proudly, she glared at Cole.

"The trousers next, Sukey," he drawled. And then when she didn't move, standing stiffly, obstinately still before him, he smiled grimly, "Or would you prefer I call Sergeant Hannigan in to remove them? He seemed quite taken with you, back there at the tavern."

A flush rose beneath the pale-golden skin; her eyes suddenly blazed with fury as she blurted, "I wish I had killed you!"

Sitting down in the chair, she removed her shoe, took out the folded piece of paper from between the sole and threw it at Cole. He took the paper closer to the fireplace and read through it quickly, scowling as he took in its contents. He had heard rumors of Judah Benjamin's brainchild, a conspiracy to infiltrate the Northern industrial cities, release Southern prisoners of war and overthrow the Union government from within. It seemed to Cole a wild, fantastic gamble.

Yet, God knew the South couldn't afford not to take the risk. The Confederacy was slowly but surely being brought to its knees. Time and time again Lee had outfought the Union Army, yet the bluebellies kept coming. And now there was the latest disturbing information that Cole had received from his agents in Washington just two days before. General Ulysses S. Grant had been named general in chief of the armies of the United States. Unlike many of his fellow officers, Cole did not lightly dismiss Grant's abilities. Any man who could sacrifice thousands of his men as Grant had done at Shiloh and Vicksburg, and still hang on with a bulldoglike tenacity, still push forward, was not a general to be scorned.

Frowning, he tore the tissue paper to tiny pieces. If only it weren't civilians like Vallandigham involved in the conspiracy, he would be more confident of the plan's success. He had seen how Jefferson Davis and the civilian legislature had hamstrung General Lee with their mismanagement and incompetence so that his troops had gone into winter quarters half starved. Lee had even begged for corn from Richmond and it had never come.

In any case, Cole reminded himself impatiently, the Sons of Liberty and their conspiracy was not at the moment his concern. It was the girl, Sukey, and how she had uncovered the information about the conspiracy. More important, he needed the names of those above her along the courier route so that they could be sought out and destroyed. Soon General Lee would be mounting his new spring offensive. It was vital that his campaign plans not be passed along to the enemy by Federal agents planted in his own camp. With Ely dead, the girl was his last hope of breaking up the spy ring.

He turned back to his prisoner and saw that she had pulled on her shirt again and was tucking it inside her trouser waist. He strode back to her side, his face darkening angrily. "Take the shirt off," he said sharply.

She looked up at him, startled. "I was cold." Then defiantly, "Or do you plan that I should freeze to death before I hang?"

"Are you so eager then to hang?" Cole asked, his voice softly threatening. Before she could step away, he placed his hands, almost caressingly, around the girl's slim neck. His thumbs pressed slowly, inexorably, into the soft hollow of her throat, cutting off the air from her lungs. In a few seconds her head was pounding as she fought for each rasping breath. "What a shame, little Sukey," he murmured, "to have such a pretty neck broken on the rope. Of course, you don't weigh very much. It will take you longer than your friend to die. You may even strangle first, choking, your tongue swelling..."

She lifted her hands, tried in vain to push his hands away from her throat. Horror filled her eyes as she gazed up into Cole's face, wiped clean of all expression. She felt a thundering in her ears, a star-shot blackness exploding before her eyes, when the hands suddenly, abruptly released her. She swayed and caught at the chair, taking a deep, painful breath past the rawness in her throat.

"That's how a noose feels, Sukey," Cole said, smiling coldly. "Not very pleasant, is it? Or perhaps you'll be lucky—perhaps you'll be declared contraband and sold on the auction block." He studied the girl's slim figure thoughtfully. "I doubt if you've ever been near a slave auction, have you, Sukey? Shall I tell you how it is for a pretty young slave put on the block? You stand on a platform with all the gentlemen present ogling you, while the auctioneer discusses your finer points. As the bidding goes higher, some of the prospective purchasers will insist upon examining the merchandise more closely, to make sure it's not ... damaged. You'll be taken to one side, your clothes stripped off. The auctioneer will spread your legs and allow the gentlemen to—"

"Stop it!" The sour taste of nausea rose in Lucinda's throat. "What is it you what?" she cried desperately.

"The truth, Sukey. I want the truth. I warn you not to lie to me. How did you come by the information you were going to pass on to Mr. Ely?"

"A man gave the note to me," she said, her eyes downcast, not meeting Cole's knife-sharp glance. "He gave me a dollar to take it to the tavern, give it to the tavernkeeper. I didn't know what it was ... I swear—"

"The man wouldn't have been that lanky Kentuckian who was with you the day you shot me and left me to die in the dirt?"

Her glance flashed upward in protest. "I didn't want to leave you," she cried. "The bushwhackers came and ..." She fell silent, seeing the steely glint of disbelief in Cole's eyes. What was the use? He would never believe that if she hadn't shot him, Jephthah would surely have killed him.

"The man who was with you that day, Sukey. Where is he now? What is his name?"

Her mouth set stubbornly. "I don't know. He never told me."

"You're lying," Cole said softly, but she could sense the anger beneath the lazy drawl. "I warned you not to lie to me, Sukey. The man's here in this camp, isn't he, Sukey?"

This time when he stepped toward her, his hands circling her neck ever so gently, she did not try to pull away. A tremor of fear shook her, but she forced herself to stand still, knowing it would be useless to try and resist, foolish to antagonize Cole further. Mr. Baker had warned her, hadn't he—the shadow of the noose lay at the end of the trail for spies. If that was to be her fate, well, her father and brother had given their lives bravely as soldiers, believing in the cause they had died for. She could do no less.

She lifted her dark, expressive gaze to Cole. Her face was pale beneath the golden sheen, but her voice was steady. "Caesar hurt me, too. I didn't talk then. Nothing you can do to hurt me will make me speak now."

Staring down into that still, determined face, Cole felt a reluctant admiration for the girl's courage. She meant what she said. He had no doubt of that. He had questioned enough enemy agents to know almost instinctively the ones who would break at thought of the rope and the ones who would remain mute, carrying their secrets to the grave. Pain wouldn't force this girl to talk, he decided, as much as it might please him to pay her back for trying to kill him, and the trooper. Still, there were other ways. He studied the proud lift of her chin, the way she held herself with an unconscious, regal dignity as she faced him defiantly. It was her pride that was her weak point, he suspected, a pride and innate dignity she had inherited—from where? Some dusky African princess? It was her pride he must crush and destroy, the dignity he must strip away, he thought coldly, if he were to subdue her, force her to

191

tell him what he must know of the other agents in the courier ring. The fact that she had such exact details of Vallandigham's conspiracy only proved how dangerous she and her fellow agents were, how close to the inner circle of command they must be.

His hands left her neck, drifted downward, thrust aside the rough material of her shirt to touch and stroke the rounded silken softness of her breast. He remembered she had been a virgin when he had taken her in Belle's room, but he recalled vividly the fiery, eager warmth of that slim body responding to his touch, how ardently, for all her innocence, her lips had moved beneath his. He doubted if the girl herself was aware of the depths of the unawakened passion trapped within her and of how unable she would be to defend herself against the betrayal of the unfamiliar, demanding appetites of her own body.

He saw the golden flecks swimming deep in the wide, dark eyes as his fingers teased and caressed the pale-pink nipple, reaching down to allow his tongue to add its pleasure, until he felt the velvety softness grow taut, heard the sharp intake of her breath.

Then he stepped away from her, laughing softly. "Are you so sure, Sukey?" he murmured. "Nothing I can do will make you talk?"

She stared up at him, a mingled confusion and bewilderment in her eyes as he pulled the narrow camp bed closer to the fireplace and threw back the blanket. Then he lifted her in his arms and placed her on the bed while his hands skillfully and quickly removed the shirt and trousers.

When she reached instinctively for the blanket to cover herself, he caught her hands and held them tightly pulled above her head. For a moment she struggled, then lay still, glaring up at him.

"That's better," he said, smiling down at her. The firelight played across her pale-golden body, gilding the skin and giving it the sheen of richest satin. Flickers of light traced the gentle curve of thigh and hip, the tautly lifted breasts, the dark hollow nested in her

192

throat. Her face was almost completely hidden in shadow except for her eyes blazing up at him.

"It won't matter, no matter how you hurt me," she hissed. "I'll never tell you anything."

The icy blue-green eyes roving over the slim, golden body gave no hint of how stirred Cole himself was at the girl's loveliness, what an effort of will it took for him to steady his own voice as he replied lazily, "Hurt you? Who said anything about hurting you, Sukey, my love? As a matter of fact, you remind me very much of a quadroon I met in New Orleans when I had just turned twenty. She was beautiful, too, like you, with great dark eyes and a body that brought a man pleasure I'd never dreamed existed. She'd been trained very well how to please a man, but she taught me a great deal, too, in the ways of pleasing a woman. There wasn't an avenue of passion and delight that we didn't explore together, not an inch of her body that she didn't teach me how to awaken, to bring her the most exquisite pleasure."

As he talked, Cole's hands moved lightly, caressingly over Sukey's body with deliberate slowness, fondling her breasts with his mouth and tongue while his hands roved gently over the curve of hips and buttocks and the soft well of stomach. His fingers stroked lightly the silken flesh of the inner thighs and the dark shadowy velvet between. He could feel her body quivering beneath his touch, a warmth spreading beneath her skin, and watched her eyes narrow, as if in pain, her mouth parting.

Then, allowing his hands alone to stroke the arching breasts, he dropped light, teasing kisses in the hollow of her throat, the shell-like curve of her earlobe, until finally his mouth brushed her lips, his tongue seeking out the softness within.

For a moment she tried to resist him, her body stiffening, twisting away, but he only held her more tightly. His mouth became more insistent on hers, the hands stroking less gentle, seeking surely, deftly, where they could bring the greatest pleasure.

Until finally she was helpless to resist any longer, and her arms lifted and held tightly around him, pulling his mouth ever closer, her own lips opening, her tongue mingling with his. Waves of pleasure washed over her body so that she felt as if she couldn't breathe, much less think, only feel, as if there were no skin between his stroking hands and caressing lips and the raw nerve ends of her body.

Then abruptly, so suddenly that she gasped, he pulled away from her. She gazed up at him, black eyes glazed with desire. She had expected he would take her as he had in Arabella's bedroom, cruelly, ruthlessly. She had prepared herself mentally to withstand his brutality, but she was totally unprepared for the skilled and gentle exploration of his hands upon her body, for the overwhelming assault upon her senses. Now she stared up at him bewildered, her body aching with sensations she had never known or felt before.

Cole sat down on the edge of the bed, stuck out his long, muscular legs before him, then ordered brusquely, "My boots, Sukey. Quickly." When she lay there without moving, his hand reached out idly, traced a path over her stomach, paused, then swept between her thighs, slowly, with long, lingering caresses. "Or shall I stop, Sukey?" he asked, laughing softly. "Shall I leave you, Sukey?"

She stumbled to her feet, knelt before him. After she had removed the boots, he said coldly, "Now my shirt." Her hands trembled as she undid the buttons until impatiently he thrust her away and slid quickly out of his shirt and trousers. She was once again conscious of the whiteness of his body against the bronze throat and face; the hard length of thigh and narrow hips. She could not see his face in the darkness; the room seemed to be blurring before her eyes. She felt herself swaying, and his arms caught her and pulled her close against him.

This time when his mouth fastened over hers, when, shocked, she felt his manhood hard between her thighs, she tried frantically to pull free, as if reaching out

194

desperately to hold onto some semblance of herself. But it was futile. The arms and mouth tightened inexorably, crushing her in his embrace. She had the odd feeling that she was a slowly diminishing circle, a dot, disappearing into nothingness, her identity gone, nothing left but pure emotion, pure desire pulling her irresistibly closer against that hardness as if she couldn't get close enough.

Once more she felt herself being lifted onto the bed, but this time Cole was lying next to her, looking down at her, while his hand delicately, lightly roamed over her body, between her thighs, bringing her exquisite pain, overpowering delight.

"Tell me, Sukey," he said softly. "Is your friend in camp?"

She frowned faintly, opened her eyes, but his face was too close. She could see nothing but the ruthless icy blue-green eyes. She shivered suddenly, tried to pull away, sensing dimly the trap into which she had been coaxed. She saw a scowl tighten his mouth at her last feeble defiance and with one movement he was on top of her. The crisp black hair on his chest scratched the softness of her breasts, as he fit his body to hers. Then he pulled away just far enough removed so that the hardness brushed teasingly against her, causing a warmth to sweep over her, a burning need like a knife thrust into her stomach.

"Shall I leave you, Sukey?" he whispered.

"No...don't go..." The words jerked from her throat.

Briefly, the hardness, like a gentle, knowing caress, touched her again, teased her to breathlessness, a tension mounting within her, a terrible desperate desire to reach the satisfaction, the relief he was denying her.

"Your friend, Sukey. What is his name?" The demanding voice was inexorable, impossible to refuse. She felt as if there was nothing left in the world but that voice, those hands caressing her, the hardness of his body, so tantalizingly near....

"Jephthah." The word came out in a half-sob.

"Is he here? Is Jephthah in this camp?"

"Yes," she cried. "Yes, he's here."

Her body arched upward, reaching frantically for him, her legs entwining around him.

Perspiration broke out on Cole's forehead. He had planned deliberately, coldly, to make the girl pay for having made a fool of him, so that even the final culmination of her desire would be denied her as a punishment for her betrayal, the last vestige of her pride stripped away.

Only he had overestimated his own iron self-control. Nothing in the world, no desire for revenge, could have stopped him at that moment from possessing her. He was consumed with the same hunger that had goaded her beyond endurance. He hesitated a moment poised above her, then plunged deeply into the waiting soft warmth of her body.

There was no pain for her this time, only a rapture almost too sweet to be borne, lifting her, carrying her away from the last familiar shore of her childhood into a wild, dark sea of emotions and sensations she had never felt before. Vaguely she was aware that Cole was no longer any more in control of what was happening between them than she was.

At the last moment, she thought she heard him whisper hoarsely, "Sukey, my sweet Sukey," and then an explosion of pure delight spread through both their bodies. She moaned, a soft cry of pleasure, her body quivered in one long, last caress beneath his ... and then was still.

12

Afterward, Cole rolled away from the girl, but one arm was still flung across her, the other arm resting beneath her head. For several moments he lay quietly, savoring the memory of the moments that had just passed. It was as if for a short while with Sukey he had found an island of warmth and sanity, after the last terrible years of living in a world filled with the mindless brutality and madness of war.

Finally, though, the chill of the room crept into the narrow bed, and he saw that there were only a few embers left glowing in the fireplace. He found some logs and kindling and prodded the flames back into life. When he turned back to the bed, he noticed that the blanket had fallen to the floor. The firelight cast its dancing shadows over Sukey's slim, golden body, a coil of blue-black hair curving down, almost covering one pale, pink-tipped breast. Regretfully, hating to hide such loveliness but afraid she would catch a chill, he pulled the blanket over her. Her eyes were closed, her face curiously still.

"Sukey," he said softly.

She did not stir. Only by a very slight rise and fall of her breasts could he tell she was breathing. The blank immobility of her face sent a swift stab of remorse through him. He had never before used a woman the way he had exploited Sukey, deliberately forging her passion into a weapon turned against her, betraying her.

Now watching the girl, her face drained of all emotion, his remorse turned to fear. If the passion they shared had shaken him so that he felt as his whole world had been rearranged, what had Sukey felt? he wondered uneasily. He had been so sure that at the end she had shared the same sense of incredible happiness that he had felt. Could he be wrong? Had he gone too far, too quickly, thrusting the girl into a state of shock? She looked so small and fragile lying there, as vulnerable as a sleeping child.

"Sukey," he said, sitting on the edge of the bed, shaking her shoulder gently. "Sukey, are you all right?"

At his touch, she flinched and her eyelids flew open. And he saw at once she was not in a state of shock but consumed by a violent fury. Her black eyes blazed bitterly up at him as she edged away from him as far as she could in the narrow bed. "Stay away from me!" she cried. "Why didn't you kill me? Oh, God, I wish I were dead."

The wild hatred in her face, the anguish in her voice, pulled Cole back to reality, back to the war and its constant unending betrayals and cruelties, which had become his life now. Why had he thought anything had changed? he thought bleakly. Had he really expected that after what he had done to the girl, she would feel anything but hatred and contempt for him?

He got to his feet, moving away from her to the fireplace. When he turned to face her again, his eyes were expressionless, his voice flat. "You're alive because I prefer you that way. You're no use to me dead. And you've only begun to tell me what I want to know about Jephthah."

She watched him warily. "There's nothing more I can tell you."

When he said nothing, his narrowed eyes surveying her with sleepy amusement, she tugged the blanket cocoonlike around her and slipped out of bed, backing away from him. "I swear! I swear there's nothing more I can tell you."

He walked slowly toward her and saw her disappear into the shadows as she stepped out of the circle of firelight. Only her eyes glowed like burnished silver, staring, wide and frightened, up at him.

Reaching out a hand, he ran a finger lightly down her cheek, caught a lock of silky black hair and tugged at it gently. "Are you sure?" he drawled, feeling the shudder pass through her body at his touch. A shiver of remembered passion, he wondered, or revulsion? And was dismayed to realize how much he disliked the thought that his touch should be repulsive to her.

He let his hand drop. "I thought you had learned not to lie to me," he said coldly.

She took a deep, steadying breath, her chin lifting stubbornly. "I'm not lying. You can do what you want. You can't make me tell what I don't know."

Cole studied the defiant face, his eyes half-closed, reflective. Even if he had wanted to, an emotional assault on her body, he knew, would never work a second time. It was the girl's lack of experience, of knowledge, which had caught her unawares the first time. She would never be that innocent, or vulnerable again. All a renewed assault upon her body would do would bring him a perverted sense of vengeance. And suddenly he no longer wanted revenge. After all, he thought wearily, why shouldn't she try to kill him, betray him? She had only been doing the job she had been trained for, the same as he. He was the enemy and she was sworn to destroy him by any means she could. Why should he fault her for that?

In any case, he was convinced that this time she was telling the truth. She couldn't tell him any more about the courier route. He had dueled wits too often with the man she called Jephthah not to have a high respect for the intelligence of the Yankee agent. Jephthah was too clever to let any member of his operation know more than absolutely necessary. That way, if captured, there would be very little they could betray of the overall workings of the courier route. Sukey probably had no more idea than he did exactly where Jephthah was in camp, or what disguise he was using, or how he managed to pass the information out of camp.

Sukey sensed Cole's hesitation, and a jeering note of triumph crept into her voice. "You'll never find Jephthah. He's too clever for you."

He walked back to the fireplace and dressed quickly. "I don't plan to find him. I'll let him find you."

She stared at him suspiciously. "What do you mean?"

He lifted an amused eyebrow. "Come now, Sukey. You and Jephthah spent a great deal of time together, and you must know you're a beautiful woman. I can't imagine that he'd stand by and watch that lovely neck of yours stretched on a rope."

She glared at him, understanding. "You mean I'm to be your bait? You think Jephthah will reveal himself, trying to save me? He never would!"

She stepped forward into the circle of firelight. Even with the blanket clutched around her, Cole could see the lovely, graceful line of her throat melting into the golden slope of her shoulder. Remembering the feel of that tawny skin, soft as silk beneath his hands, he felt a familiar warmth spread through his body. It was an effort to keep his voice steady as he said harshly, "You underestimate yourself, Sukey. I doubt if there are many men who wouldn't gamble their lives to save you from the hangman's noose."

"Not Jephthah," she said, and he felt an irrational sting of jealousy at the pride in her voice when she spoke the man's name.

"We'll find out soon enough," he said grimly. "By tomorrow morning the whole camp will have heard that I'm holding a Negro female spy, including your friend Jephthah."

He walked to the door and spoke to the guard stationed outside the cabin. In a few minutes the man returned with several tin plates of food which Cole placed on the rough wooden table.

He pulled a chair to the table, then glanced up at Sukey. "You're welcome to join me at dinner."

"I'm not hungry," she said sulkily.

He shrugged. "Suit yourself."

She moved a few steps closer, drawn by the sight of food, her stomach forcefully reminding her of the long hours since the scant breakfast she'd shared with Cole's men that morning. "What is it?" she asked, her nose wrinkling distastefully.

"The men call it slosh," Cole said cheerfully. "It's

mostly mush fried in grease with bits of meat added, if they can find any. It's not bad if you're hungry enough."

Still clutching the blanket around her, she sat down across from him, and he watched, amused, as, pretending indifference, she nevertheless began to eat quickly. He was sure she was as hungry as he was.

When she had finished the last morsel on the plate, she said scornfully, "The Yankee soldiers have meat and white bread and drink real coffee in their camps."

"I know." Cole smiled wryly. "I've seen our men trade some of their Virginia tobacco for coffee and sugar from the Yankees on the other side of the river."

"Why?" the girl asked, staring at him, bewildered. "Why do you keep fighting? Your army's running out of everything—food, guns, supplies, men."

"Perhaps," Cole said, his voice grim. "But this is our land, and we'll be buried in it before we give up our rights and let a bunch of Northern politicians run our governments and our lives."

"And your slaves?" the girl flashed indignantly. "You'd die to keep men and women and children in bondage?"

Cole shrugged uncomfortably. "Slavery would have been done away with in the South without a war. It was only a matter of time." For himself he had already decided, even before the war, to free his own slaves at Gray Meadows. The idea of owning another human being had always disturbed him, and, practically, he had long ago realized that slavery as a means of labor was too inefficient to be productive.

He studied the girl across from him curiously. Certainly her life as a slave couldn't have been too onerous. There had been no whip scars on that smooth, satiny back, and the Appletons at Black Oaks had always treated their people well. His dark brows gathered in a frown. Still, it couldn't have been at Black Oaks that Sukey had learned to speak and act with all the manners and airs of a pampered white girl. Where then had she learned? And who had taught her the dangerous craft of operating as a Union secret service agent?

"Was it Jephthah, Sukey? Was he the one who trained you to work for Lafayette Baker?"

She lifted her gaze guilelessly to him. "I don't know any Mr. Baker."

Cole pushed the table away from him so sharply that the plates clattered. Damn the girl anyway. Why must she persist in lying to him now, when it was too late to matter?

"Your belonging to the Appletons," he said shrewdly, unexpectedly. "That's a lie, too, isn't it?"

Lucy felt the color rush to her face, and she hesitated a moment, uncertain. Still, how could Cole prove, without seeing the plantation books, whether or not she had actually been an Appleton slave?

"No, suh, it's the truth," she said stubbornly. "Ah b'longed to the Appletons till Mr. Joseph Appleton sold me, along with Dora Lee." At the last words, Lucy's long, thick lashes lowered to veil her eyes, or Cole would have glimpsed the reckless gleam that all at once appeared there. Lucy continued, as if unable to stop herself, her voice softly, innocently questioning even as she could hear her heart pounding in her ears. "Dora Lee was mighty pretty. Maybe you remember her from when you visited the Appletons?"

"Yes," Cole said slowly. "I remember Dora Lee." He remembered how appalled he had been when he had heard the Appletons had sold the girl. He would have bought her himself, except he hadn't heard of the sale until it was too late to stop it.

"Dora Lee was going to have a baby," the girl continued, in the same soft, ingenuous voice. "A white man's baby. That's why she was sold. But then maybe you know all about that, major, suh."

Cole stared at the girl, puzzled at the derision only half hidden in her voice. He wished he could see her face more clearly. The flickering shadows from the candle he had lit at the table streaked the girl's face darkly like soot. Had she really known Dora Lee, or was it all

202

another passel of lies? He had never met a woman, white or black, who could smile so sweetly and lie so convincingly as this girl, Sukey. Or could make him happily want to throttle her one minute and drag her off to bed the next, he thought wryly, very much aware of that slim, lovely body hidden beneath the rough woolen blanket that she clutched so determinedly.

"If Dora Lee had a child, it wasn't mine," he said curtly. "And the fact that you knew Dora doesn't necessarily prove you were an Appleton slave." There was something wrong here. He could sense it, the same way he could sense the girl was lying to him. But why? Why should she pretend to be from Black Oaks?

He lifted the candle from the table, held it high so that its light poured down into the girl's lovely, oval face, the wide, brilliant black eyes, the delicate curve of her mouth, all as familiar to him now as his own features, and yet ... wasn't there something about her face that was almost too familiar?

He spoke slowly, cautiously feeling his way. "If you lived at Black Oaks, then you must have known Lucinda Appleton."

Lucy felt her skin grow cold. Had her impulsive disregard for danger, her foolish need to find out the truth about Cole and Dora Lee, broken through the thin ice of her disguise? It took all her dramatic training to keep the fear from her voice, to look up into Cole's searching gaze and toss her head with sullen indifference. "'Course I knew Miss Lucinda. Only Dora Lee, she knew her better."

Cole reached out a hand and traced with his finger the arched line of the dark, winged brows, the sweetly curved chin. He should have seen the resemblance sooner, he thought, annoyed at his own blindness. The Appleton features, Lucy's features, in Sukey's face.

"Who was your father, Sukey?" he asked abruptly.

For a moment she didn't understand. Her mind felt paralyzed with dread. Then, understanding, she breathed a silent sigh of relief. With a silent apology to her dead father, she answered in a soft, childish voice, "Ah ain't

203

sure, suh. I expect he was a white man." She cast a quick upward glance at Cole beneath lowered eyelashes. "Marse Matthew . . . he used to come 'round to our cabin to see my ma sometimes," she added guilelessly.

Cole frowned and lowered the candle. It was possible, of course. Lucinda's father had been a young man when his wife had died in childbirth. And he wouldn't have been the first white man to find solace and comfort in a black woman's arms. Sukey could very easily have been the product of such a liaison. Except, for all his abolitionist sympathies, Cole had respected and liked Matthew Appleton. He found it hard to believe that the man would sell his own child away from him. Only, Cole suddenly remembered, Matthew Appleton had been away with his children, visiting his dead wife's in-laws in New Orleans, when Dora Lee and Sukey had been sold. And it was Joseph Appleton, not Matthew, who had had the two girls quickly sold and spirited away, almost overnight. Had straitlaced Joseph discovered the truth about Sukey, his brother's bastard child in the slave quarters, and made sure she was sent away from Black Oaks?

Cole smiled grimly to himself, thinking how shocked Lucy Appleton would be if she knew she had a pretty black half sister. Then, reminding himself it wasn't Sukey's parentage he should be thinking about, but her friend Jephthah, he changed the subject abruptly. "How long have you been spying for Jephthah, Sukey?" And then to his own surprise, he heard himself ask, "Is he in love with you?"

Sukey's eyes widened, then she murmured, a smile playing impishly across her face, "Ah reckon you'll have to ask Jephthah that, major, if you catch him."

"I'm asking you!" Cole stepped toward the girl, scowling angrily.

She rose hastily at his approach, putting the table hurriedly between them, while her hands moved to pull the blanket more tightly around her neck. "You'll never catch him. Never!" she cried tauntingly.

"Well, then you'll hang in his place, sweet Sukey," Cole drawled. "Tomorrow at sunset with the whole camp turned out to watch. Do you care that much for the man that you'd die protecting him? That's what will happen if your friend doesn't give himself up by sunset tomorrow."

"No!" It was a cry of pure terror, wrenched from her lips. Her face was drained pale so that her eyes shone, enormous, drenched with fear.

A knock came at the door twice before either of them heard it. Cole strode to the door and pulled it open. After listening briefly to the guard posted outside the door, he nodded, "All right. Tell the general I'll be there immediately."

When he turned back to Sukey, he said warningly, "I wouldn't think of trying any of your tricks on the guard while I'm gone. It's ex-sergeant Hannigan, and since he lost his stripes, he's not in the best of humor."

After the door had shut behind Cole, Lucy moved unsteadily toward the fireplace. Outside the shuttered window she could hear faintly the sound of soldiers' voices singing the sad refrain of "Lorena," as they gathered around the evening campfires. The music drifting into the cabin tugged at her emotions, emotions that were already dangerously close to the breaking point. Every nerve in her body throbbed with terror and exhaustion, and even more frightening, the too-vivid memory of those moments in Cole's arms when her body had treacherously turned upon her.

Although she had been raised with two brothers, had known the roughness of frontier life, nevertheless Lucinda Appleton had always been carefully protected, first by her father and then the girls' school she had attended, from any improper knowledge of what happened between a man and a woman in bed. Nothing in Lucy's young life, not even those moments when Cole had raped her casually in Bella's bedroom, certainly not the bushwhacker's fumbling gropings at her body, had prepared her for the shocking sensations that had swept over her body in Cole's arms. It had been fright-

205

ening, almost like a small death, and yet she had never felt more alive. Every inch of her body had responded with delicious abandon to the slightest touch of Cole's hands, as if she could not get enough of their caresses, her body aching because she could not hold him close enough.

She suspected that only loose, immoral women behaved as she had with Cole, low, coarse women devoid of all shame and decency. Now she was one of those women. And what was most damning of all, she had betrayed Jephthah. And for that she could never forgive herself.

She sank down upon the cot, burying her face in her hands, her shame submerged in her overwhelming sense of guilt, as painful as a cramp twisting her insides. The pain had gradually dulled to a half-lethargic misery when she heard the voices outside the door of the cabin.

One of the voices she recognized at once as Hannigan's; the other was a man's voice, heavily slurred with drink, so that she caught only snatches of words. "No harm . . . one look . . ."

Hannigan's voice became louder. "You're drunk again, McGraw. Better get back to your hut with that rotgut of yours before an officer sees you."

"Not rotgut," the second man protested indignantly. "Good Virginia bourbon. Taste it yourself."

"You want to get me shot?" Hannigan demanded angrily, but the girl in the cabin could hear the hesitation in his voice.

"One little drink won't hurt. It's a cold night. Keep you from catching a chill. Who's to know, anyway?" the man insisted with drunken persistence. "All I want is to get a look at the nigger spy-gal through the window. What's the harm?"

"The major will have my tail. No one's allowed near the prisoner." There was again that hesitation in Hannigan's voice, then a bottle clinking, changing hands, and silence. Inside the cabin Lucy had grown rigid; her hands clasped tightly at the edge of the bed. That second man. For all its slurred drunkenness, she was sure it was Jephthah's voice.

She moved swiftly to the door, pressed her ear against it. The second man was still cajoling the guard, urging him to have another drink. She heard the sound of drunken laughter, then a lurching noise as if the man had fallen against the door.

"One little look . . . ain't never seen a nigger spy."

"Get away from that door, McGraw!" Hannigan sounded exasperated. "Oh, all right, come around to the window. But one quick look, that's all. Then I get the rest of that bottle."

She heard the sound of footsteps moving around the side of the cabin, and snatching up the candle, she waited. There were fumbling noises at the window shutters as they were unlatched from the outside and pulled open.

She glimpsed Hannigan's beefy red face, and next to him, another man, a leering drunken smile, black greasy hair, shaggy black eyebrows almost hiding his eyes. Jephthah? she thought, uncertain, holding her candle higher so the light fell on the window. Could it possibly be Jephthah?

"Pretty little thing, ain't she?" The black-haired man grinned foolishly at her. "Too pretty to swing for crowbait."

For a moment, the candle raised, Lucy saw the man's eyes clearly, saw the calm, pewter gaze she recognized before the look of drunken senselessness settled over the straggly-bearded face.

"Go away!" she cried, frightened now, more for Jephthah than for herself. This was just what Cole had hoped Jephthah would do, walk into the trap he had set, with her as bait. "Keep away from me!" she cried desperately. "Do you understand? Keep away."

"Ain't no need to fret, missy," the man whined, scratching at his beard. "Won't be long, all your troubles will be over, ain't that right, Hannigan?" He snickered. "Yes, sir, not long at all."

Hannigan was frowning nervously. Even the bottle

shoved inside his jacket didn't make him feel easy about what he was doing, what would happen to him if the major found out. He snatched his companion, shoved him away from the window and slammed the shutters shut. "Now get the hell out of here, McGraw," he ordered. "And keep your drunken mouth shut or I'll shut it for you, for good."

She heard the murmur of retreating voices, footsteps dying away. Slowly Lucy made her way back to the bed. Had Jephthah understood? She was frustrated by her helplessness to warn Jephthah further of the danger he was in. What did Jephthah mean, her troubles would soon be over? Would he really be foolhardy enough to try to rescue her from under Cole's nose? It would only mean he would be caught, too, and they would both end up dancing the sunset jig, she thought despairingly. And it would be her fault.

She prowled the cabin restlessly, trying to think of some way of escape, until, body and mind worn out by the long day, the lack of sleep the night before, she finally returned to the bed. Pulling the blanket over her, she fell at last into an exhausted slumber.

It wasn't a restful sleep. The same frightening nightmare returned. She was running through a thick, black woods, pursued by faceless men. Only this time there was no escaping them. No matter how fast she ran, her breath jabbing painfully into her lungs, her legs aching, she could hear them gaining on her. Then she stumbled, fell, and they were upon her. She felt hands jerking her to her feet. She was being dragged to a tree, the rough hemp of a rope's noose scratching her neck. Then she saw, horrified, there was another body already hanging from the tree, a hanged man with Jephthah's bruised mottled face, Jephthah swaying gently, lifelessly. . . .

Just before the noose tightened slowly, inexorably around her own neck, she could hear herself screaming.

And jerked awake, trembling, her body ice cold, to discover that Cole was seated on the bed beside her.

His arms were around her and his voice was gently soothing, as if speaking to a frightened child.

"What is it?" she asked, confused, staring, bewildered, around her, at the pallet beside the fireplace where she realized Cole must have been sleeping when her screams awakened him.

"You were having a nightmare," he said. "Don't you remember?"

She shuddered, memory of the nightmare returning in a rush. The memory of the rope around her neck was so real that she reached up tentatively to her throat, as if she expected to find rope burns there.

"They were going to hang me," she whispered. "I could feel the rope, see their faces staring up at me, and Jephthah. . . . I could see Jephthah . . . I was afraid, so afraid of dying." She began to shake helplessly and almost instinctively found herself burrowing deeper into the hard protective circle of Cole's arms, even as she bitterly reproached herself for her cowardice. "I have no right," she moaned. "I'm so ashamed . . . I shouldn't be afraid . . ."

Cole brushed the tangled mass of black hair away from her dark, lustrous eyes, blurred with fear. "We're all afraid, Sukey," he said softly. "All the time. Any man who says he isn't is a liar." Slowly, soothingly, he continued talking, while silently cursing the men who had sent this girl, little more than a child herself, into the midst of a brutal war that he had seen destroy the courage and sanity of strong men. Fianlly, he felt the slim body within his arms cease its violent trembling, the dark head resting quietly on his shoulder.

When he loosened his hold and began to pull away, she clung to him, her voice low and fearful. "Don't go," she whispered. She despised her own weakness, but she knew she could not endure falling asleep again with the terrors that were lurking, waiting for her in the darkness.

"The fire's almost out," Cole said. "And your skin's like ice. Once the room is warm, you'll feel better."

209

"No!" Her small hands clutched frantically at him. "Don't leave me."

In the dim light, she could barely make out Cole's features, but she could see the question gathering in the blue-green eyes, the quizzical slant of one black eyebrow. She felt her face flush as she said softly, "I don't want to be alone."

He nodded and in one motion he had lifted the blanket and slid into the cot beside her. The heat of his body against her skin sent a shock wave through her. Then his arms reached around her and drew her close, and she sighed contentedly, cuddling closer to the warmth. She hadn't realized how cold she was, as if her nightmare had drained all heat from her body.

In the darkness, Cole grimaced wryly. He realized it was comfort the girl was seeking, someone to hold her quietly until she fell asleep, but his own needs were quite different. The curve of her hip, the softness of her breasts pressed against him, had caused an immediate reaction in his own body. His hands moved, almost of their own volition, to caress with long, gentle strokes the silken shoulder and graceful inward curve of her back, gradually returning to cup one small, proud breast.

When she did not immediately pull away, when he heard her sharp, indrawn breath of pleasure, he lifted himself upon one elbow, gazing searchingly down at her.

"Sukey." It was not a statement but a question.

She spoke in an embarrassed rush. "I know it's sinful, my feeling this way. But I can't help myself. I don't want you to go . . ."

He said, startled, "What the hell are you talking about?"

Her eyes widened. "What we're doing . . . no decent girl feels this way with a man."

"Who told you such nonsense?" he demanded, half furious, half amused. "The only indecency here is the war," he added grimly. "And that you're caught in the middle of it instead of safely at home where you belong."

She reached up and covered his mouth quickly with her hand. "I don't want to talk about the war," she protested softly. "I want to forget all about the war. Help me forget, Cole." It was the first time she had used his name, and yet, for one brief moment, he had the nagging sensation that his name on her lips had an oddly familiar sound. Then she asked, her voice wistful, "Was that colored girl in New Orleans very beautiful?"

"Ravishing," Cole drawled, smiling teasingly at her. The nagging little mystery was forgotten as his lips found the warm hollow in her throat, traced a path slowly down to the deep cleft between her breasts, finally catching and holding a rosy nipple in his mouth. He caressed its softness at first teasingly, then with more urgency, as he felt a long shiver pass through her body, arching suddenly upward beneath him. Her hands reached up to catch in the black, wiry curls, pulling his head closer to her breast.

He was startled at the fierceness of her passion rising to meet his, the eagerness with which her hips moved with delicious abandon beneath his. Her hands lightly caressed the nape of his neck, her mouth moving with silken softness in slow kisses across his throat and shoulders. When, unable to restrain himself any longer, his own mouth found and fastened roughly upon hers, crushing her lips, she did not cry out, nor when his hands became more demanding upon her willow-slim body, bruising without meaning to the petal-soft skin.

She clung to him hungrily, a hunger in both of them that Cole sensed dimly went beyond the needs of their bodies, had become a desperate, passionate reaching out for life in the midst of death. As if the very closeness of death all around them made their lovemaking all the more precious, life affirming life, driving their emotions to a peak of pleasure he had never experienced before. Cole knew he never wanted the ecstasy to end, and yet couldn't bear for it not to end, her body against his one long, unceasing caress.

Deliberately, a groan breaking through his lips, he forced himself to pull free of her embracing thighs. In the firelight he sought her face in the half-shadowy light. Her eyes were shut so that her lashes lay like fans on her cheek, her hair a black shadow spread over the pillow, a smile curving her lips as she murmured drowsily, "Don't . . . stop . . ."

"Look at me, Sukey," he said hoarsely. "Open your eyes. Look at me."

Her eyelids flew open. In their wide, lustrous depths he saw confusion and for a moment, fear, as memory of what had happened between them earlier returned, the calculating way he had cruelly led her to the edge of desire, to achieve his own ends. Did he mean to torment her so once again?

"No," he said quickly, kissing her lips softly, reassuringly, as if guessing what she was thinking. "It's only that I don't want you to shut any part of yourself away from me. I want to look into your face . . . into your eyes . . ."

"Yes," she said softly, smiling. "I want that, too. I want to remember, always."

And then he found he could wait no longer, nor could she, as their passions met and mingled, exploding into a joyful rapture. He watched, delighted, the joyful wonder filling her dark eyes as she gave herself completely to him. Then the utter contentment that spread across her now relaxed and lovely face as they lay quietly, finally at peace, in each other's arms.

13

It was a peace that was to last less than ten minutes. Even as Cole held the girl quietly in his arms, her breath light and warm against his cheek, the apple-fragrance scent from her hair in his nostrils, he heard the sound of gunfire shattering the early-morning calm.

"What is it?" The girl stirred, her voice drowsy. "Why are they shooting?"

"Those aren't our guns. They're Yankee repeating rifles." Cole had sat up, listening intently. "We're under attack."

Frightened, she reached out a hand to hold him, but he was already gone from the bed, pulling on his trousers, tugging at his boots. She sat up in bed, shivering, pulling the blanket around her. It must be almost dawn, she thought absently. Between the distant dull bursts of the carbines, she could hear, ironically, a mockingbird serenading its mate with low, sweet trills.

Then the only sound was the thunderous pounding of horsemen and the ear-splitting alarm of bugles. Men shouted as they tumbled from their huts, screaming as bullets found their marks. The crack of pistol fire mingled with the ragged, rattling volleys from Federal rifles.

Lucy clutched frantically at Cole. "Don't go! Stay with me." Her fear was not for herself but for him.

He lifted her abruptly from the bed and fitted her snugly into his arms, impatiently pushing aside the blanket to pull her softness closer to him. "Listen carefully, Sukey, my love. We haven't much time." His voice was harsh even as his arms held her tenderly. "You'll be safe here till I get back. Then somehow I'll get you out of this mess. And when I do, there'll be no more spying, do you understand?" He smiled crookedly down at her, a wry amusement in his narrowed eyes. "I can't fight the Yankees and you, too, my sweet Sukey. And the thought of someday finding your lovely body dangling from a tree..." His arms tightened convulsively around her so that for a moment the breath left her body. Then he loosened one hand to imprison her chin, forcing her to meet his searching gaze. "I want your promise. You're out of the spying business for good."

"Yes." She lifted her trembling lips to his. "Oh, yes. But you'll come back. Promise me you'll come back. If anything happened to you, I wouldn't want to live."

"I'll be back." For a long breathless moment they clung together. His hard mouth imprinted itself on the soft curve of her lips as if putting a seal to a promise. Then he was gone and she stood motionless, fighting back tears. She heard the door slam shut behind him, heard his voice calling out, then his footsteps and voice were lost in all the confusing sounds of men yelling, horses galloping by the cabin, dragging artillery, clanking and rattling. Gunfire exploded so close now it sounded as if the fighting were right outside the cabin door.

She stiffened suddenly, staring at the closed cabin door. Above the noise of the gunfire, she was aware of the sound of wood being shattered under powerful blows. The door itself seemed to be disintegrating before her terrified gaze. She had half turned, clutching at one of the iron fire prods to protect herself, when Jephthah, his face smoke-blackened, and holding one end of his carbine like a battering ram, appeared in the smashed doorway.

"Hope you'll excuse my busting in on you this way, ma'am." He grinned widely, exposing his yellowed teeth. "But I reckon we'd better skedaddle, the quicker the better."

She hurried to him, stumbled over the end of the blanket and realized, belatedly, that she hadn't a stitch of clothes on. "My clothes," she said, flustered. "I don't know where they are."

"No time to stand on ceremony, ma'am," Jephthah said. His long arm reached out to yank her after him through the doorway. She felt the blanket fall completely away from her, the damp morning air chill against her bare skin. She almost stumbled over Hannigan, stretched out unconscious before the cabin door, his head bloody. A sulfurous cloud of gray-black smoke hung in the air around her, blinding her. She was caught up in a melee of men in close hand-to-hand combat, sabers flashing, red flashes of gunfire and horses screaming, rearing in terror. Then there was just one horse and Jephthah was lifting her up into the empty saddle and swinging up behind her. A soldier clutched at the bridle, then gaped, startled, at the naked girl in the saddle. Jephthah drew his revolver coolly and shot the man through the head. The soldier fell almost beneath the horse's feet.

Through the haze of smoke, Lucy glimpsed Hannigan staggering to his feet, his rifle in his hand. She saw the man lift his Enfield, and take careful aim. She heard herself scream a warning to Jephthah, soundless in the explosion of noise on all sides of her. Then she felt herself flung backward at the same moment, she felt something slam hard against the side of her head. If Jephthah hadn't grabbed her, she would have pitched from the saddle.

She didn't lose consciousness, but it was as if someone had lain a red-hot poker against her temple. She could no longer see clearly. The early-morning gray fog from the river mingled with the sulfurous haze and drifted over the woods and fields surrounding the camp. Jephthah's arm tightened around her waist in a grip of steel. "Hang on, ma'am," he yelled, as his powerful horse plunged forward through the tangle of men and guns, finally, miraculously unharmed, reaching the safety of the woods.

Once within the barrier of the trees, Jephthah stopped, whipped off his jacket and wrapped it around Lucy. Then he took his kerchief from around his neck and tied it tightly around her head to staunch the flow of blood turning her black hair scarlet.

His gun-metal eyes studied the girl. "Can you go on?"

"Yes," she muttered, clutching at the saddlehorn to keep from swaying. "How far ... ?"

It was full light when Jephthah rode his mud-splattered horse into headquarters. The sentry at General Sharpe's quarters glanced fascinated from a scowling Jephthah to the young colored woman slumped in the saddle before him, a blood-soaked kerchief around her head, a pair of slender, shapely legs revealed beneath a butternut jacket.

Jephthah barked orders and in a few seconds Lucinda felt herself being lifted carefully in Jephthah's arms, carried to a bed in the quarters and deposited on a narrow camp bed covered with several soft woolen blankets. In another few moments an orderly arrived with something warm and steaming in a cup, tasting of tea and honey and enough brandy to send a delicious warmth coursing through Lucy's cold and aching limbs.

The orderly was closely followed by the regimental doctor, who washed the dried blood away from the girl's hair and face, and after treating and bandaging the wound, announced, "If that minié ball had been a quarter of an inch closer ..." He shook his head. "You're a very lucky girl, Miss ..." He hesitated, looking up at Jephthah for his patient's name. When the tall, rangy man simply shrugged and said nothing, the doctor nodded and got to his feet. It hadn't escaped his notice that when he washed the wound, the pale-gold color of the girl's skin had washed away, too.

"You might have a scar, but your hair should cover it, I expect," he said, getting to his feet.

"Everything's blurred," Lucinda said anxiously. "I can't see clearly."

"That will pass in a few days," the doctor assured her. "What you need now is complete quiet and rest."

"And a bath," Lucy said wistfully. "Please." She glanced pleadingly at Jephthah. "A hot bath."

Jephthah frowned, uncertain. "Don't reckon there's any bathtubs in camp . . ." Then he snapped his fingers. "Just wait one minute," he said, grinning.

It was almost five minutes before he returned with two troopers carrying a huge wooden washtub between them, filled with hot soapy water. "Will this do, miss?" he asked triumphantly.

"Oh, yes," she said, smiling blissfully. She could hardly wait for the men to leave before she stepped into the steaming washtub, giving a sigh of contentment as the hot water soaked the chill and aches, as well as the golden stain, from her tired body. Then she dried herself, returned to the bed, and had no sooner put her head on the pillow than she sank into a deep, dreamless sleep.

Several times during the next days she awoke when a knock came at her door and a pleasant-faced black woman who said her name was Mary brought her a tray of food. Lucy always ate ravenously and fell immediately back to sleep. Then one morning when she awoke, the woman brought her not only food but undergarments, stockings and shoes, and a dress of pale leaf green, with a dark-green velvet Zouave jacket and matching stylish porkpie hat, trimmed with gold braid.

"But where . . . ?" Lucy looked inquiringly at Mary. "And they're my size, too," she said, surprised.

The woman smiled. "Marse Jephthah, he's got plenty of lady friends. He told me to tell you if they didn't fit, just let him know. He'd find some other gal to borrow from."

The dress did fit, beautifully, Lucy discovered. Mary laced her into the undergarments, while Lucy giggled as she mentally tried to digest the picture of shy, gangling Jephthah as a lady's man. When she had finished dressing, she removed the bandage from her head and, studying herself in the mirror, saw that the doctor had been right. Not only had her vision completely returned but there was only a very tiny scar near her temple. After Mary brushed her thick black hair, she pulled it

217

back from Lucy's face into several fat curls caught at the nape of her neck by a green velvet bow. Several smaller curls were placed strategically on either side of her forehead so that even the scar was hidden from view.

After she ate her breakfast, Lucy stretched luxuriously, feeling alert and fully aware of her surroundings for the first time since Jephthah had carried her... where? she wondered idly. A Union headquarters, of course, but whose?

"Whose quarters are these?" she asked Mary curiously.

"General Sharpe's."

"How long have I been here?"

"Five days, miss."

Five days! Aunt Clare must be frantic, wondering what had happened to her, Lucinda realized guiltily, remembering how she had left Black Oaks in the middle of the night without a word to anyone.

Then, wondering what story Jephthah had put out to explain her presence here in camp, she asked hesitantly, "How... how did I get here?"

Mary gazed at the girl, surprised. "Don't you remember? You crossed into the lines without a pass and a picket shot you. Not knowing in the dark you wuz a gal," the servant added hastily. "Mr. Jephthah brought you here so the camp doctor could tend you."

"Yes," Lucy said slowly. "Yes, I remember now." A sudden flush rose in her cheeks. And Jephthah's finding her stark naked in Cole Sinclair's quarters, she wondered. How had he explained that?

Remembering the cabin, and Cole, the feel of his arms tight around her those last moments before he left her, all other thoughts were swept from her mind. Was it less than twenty-four hours they had spent together? But the hours they'd shared in the cabin weren't the sort of time one could measure in minutes and days. It was as if those few brief hours had split her life decisively. What went before no longer existed or mattered for her; it was only Cole, the love they shared, their future together, that filled her thoughts and life now.

A dreamy smile curved her lips. Her wide dark eyes grew velvety soft and a delicious weakness spread through her body when she thought of Cole, so that she sat down quickly on the edge of the bed.

"Are you feeling sickly, miss?" Mary asked, worried at how quiet the girl had suddenly become.

"I'm fine," Lucinda said happily. Cole loved her. She was sure of that now. What else mattered? Even the thought nibbling at the corner of her mind that it was a colored girl named Sukey that Cole had held in his arms, not Lucinda Appleton, couldn't destroy Lucy's newfound happiness. She would find a way to set matters straight between Cole and her, she thought, her natural, youthful exuberance taking over. All she needed was a little time.

Mary picked up the breakfast tray and started for the door, pausing to say, "The general said he'd like to see you, miss—that is, if you're feeling well enough."

Lucinda nodded at once and got to her feet, although she dreaded the thought of the meeting. Still, there was no use postponing the inevitable. Sooner or later she would have to tell General Sharpe and Jephthah the truth.

When she walked into General Sharpe's tent, Jephthah was with the general. Both men rose at her entrance. Jephthah smiled broadly at her; the general, a tall, handsome man, put down his cigar and nodded gravely. "I'm pleased to see you looking so well, Miss Appleton." His voice had a slight clipped Eastern accent, and Lucy remembered that General Sharpe was from the 120th New York Regiment. He took her arm and escorted her to a chair. "Please be seated, ma'am. Jephthah tells me you're one of our most valuable and courageous agents. Mr. Baker in Washington also speaks very highly of you. I'm honored to finally have the pleasure of meeting the white rose."

Lucinda's hands twisted nervously in her lap. Her voice was miserable. "I'm not..." she blurted. "I'm not

219

what you think at all, General Sharpe." She cast Jephthah a despairing glance. "I betrayed you, Jephthah, I told Co—I told Major Sinclair you were in his camp. He was planning to use me ... as bait to catch you. When I think of the attack on the camp, the men who were wounded, killed, trying to save me, I'm so ashamed."

The general cleared his throat, breaking in quickly, "The attack on the camp had been planned well before your capture, Miss Appleton. It was, shall we say, providential that in the confusion of the attack, Jephthah managed to free you."

Jephthah took a chair and, turning it to straddle it with his long legs, asked softly, "How did you happen to get caught, ma'am?"

Lucinda remembered, then, the reason for her visiting Ely's Inn, the conversation she had overheard between Cousin Harry and his guest and the note Cole had found in her shoe and destroyed. "I had some new information I thought you should have at once," she said. "Sam was away, so I took it myself to Ely's. Only the tavern was being watched. I was caught before I could get away." Quickly, then, trying to remember exactly what she had written down in her note, she told the two men about the conversation she had overheard in the dining room at Black Oaks.

When she finished, General Sharpe puffed thoughtfully at his cigar for several seconds, then said, "We've heard of the Sons of Liberty and rumors of their conspiracy to overthrow the government. But we weren't sure how deeply Clement Vallandigham was involved in the plot. Mr. Baker, under direct orders from President Lincoln, has already taken steps to break up the ring. I'm sure he doesn't know, though, that Vallandigham is returning North or that the operation is now being financed by the Confederate government. I'll have word sent to Washington immediately."

"Is it possible?" Lucy asked, gazing, worried, at the two men. "Could such a plot actually succeed?"

"It's possible," Jephthah said glumly. "If General

Grant doesn't win a battle here in the valley soon, Lincoln could lose his bid for reelection in November. The people are tired of the war. We have more men, more supplies, more guns than Lee, and yet we can't lick him."

"I thought General Grant was in command in the West," Lucinda said, surprised.

"Not any longer. President Lincoln has made General Grant commander in chief of the armies of the United States." Jephthah grinned, amused. "I thought you'd heard about the promotion. Your young friend Sally Pollock did. She was picked up on April 12th after we received your message about her spying activities in the valley. She had letters on her proving that rebel spies had already learned of Grant's promotion and the plans being made by Grant in Washington to attack Richmond. They even knew exactly how many men he would have with him." Jephthah spat, disgusted, into a brass spittoon by the general's desk. "Not only does Lee outfight us, but his spies always seem to be one jump ahead of us. Maybe you should get yourself a new man, general," he finished grimly.

The general put aside his cigar. "Don't sell yourself short, Jephthah. You've done good work, you and the white rose here. You broke up the operation of Countess Von Bruck in Washington, and thanks to both of you, the silver fox's courier route is no longer in existence from Washington to Richmond. I'm proud of both of you. And once Miss Appleton gets settled in Richmond, I'm sure we'll find out a great deal more about Richmond's defenses to pass along to General Grant."

"Richmond?" Lucy glanced startled from Jephthah to the general. "How would I get to Richmond?"

"Your cousin, Mr. Harry Appleton, is taking you," the general announced. "At least that's what he told me about an hour ago."

"Harry . . . here?" Lucinda said, stunned.

"I'm sorry, Miss Appleton, of course you couldn't have known," the general apologized. "As soon as you had sufficiently recovered, we sent word to your family of your whereabouts. Your cousin arrived this morning to fetch you. He assured me that your violating our lines without a pass was simply a girlish prank; that you had left your home in the middle of the night in a pique after you and he had..." The general gave Lucy an amused glance. "I think he called it a lover's quarrel."

Lucy straightened indignantly. "Harry and I are not lovers!"

"Having met the gentleman, I rather thought not," the general acknowledged. "Nevertheless, I gather your cousin is determined not to let you out of his sight in the future. Therefore he's taking you back to Richmond with him to keep you out of trouble."

"We already have an excellent agent in Richmond," Jephthah said, leaning forward in his chair. "A Miss Elizabeth Van Lew. She has established a courier route between Richmond and our headquarters and has contacts that reach into the Southern White House itself. She'll be waiting for you to get in touch with her once you're living in Richmond with your cousin." He hesitated, then continued slowly, "There's one job in particular in which she'll need your particular assistance."

"I can't!" Lucinda cried, staring intently down into her hands, unable to meet Jephthah's eyes. "I can't spy for you, not any more." A silence descended within the tent, so thick that the low hum of a bee buzzing at a honeysuckle bush outside the tent flap seemed abnormally loud.

When Lucinda finally did force herself to look up, she found Jephthah's gray gunmetal gaze fastened upon her face. "Is it what happened back at the rebel camp?" he asked. "Your telling Sinclair about me?" When Lucy didn't answer, he continued quietly, "Everyone has his breaking point, you know. We can't all be as brave as young Sam Davis," he added, referring to the young Southern spy from Tennessee who had gone to his death rather than betray his comrades.

"No." Lucinda shook her head, a lump of misery in her throat. How could she possibly explain to Jephthah

222

the circumstances under which she had betrayed him, or that she had given Cole her word not to spy any longer against the Confederacy, a promise she had no intention of breaking? "It isn't that I've stopped believing in our cause," she said hastily, her dark eyes pleading with Jephthah to understand. "I just can't betray my own people any longer."

"They're my people, too, Miss Appleton," Jephthah said.

General Sharpe pushed back his camp chair, giving Jephthah a disapproving glance. "If Miss Appleton has decided to leave the service, then that's her decision. The young lady has obviously been through a great ordeal."

Jephthah turned to the commanding officer. "May I speak to Miss Appleton alone, general?"

The general hesitated, then nodded grudgingly, getting to his feet. "Very well."

As soon as the officer had left the tent, Lucinda said proudly, "I'm not afraid, Jephthah. It isn't that."

"No, ma'am. I know." He studied her face, shadowed with unhappiness beneath the jaunty porkpie hat, the dark eyes glistening as if she were forcing back tears. The girl had more courage in her little finger than most men he knew. No, it wasn't lack of courage that had brought her to the decision to leave the service. It was Major Sinclair, of course. He had sensed from the beginning that Lucinda Appleton's feelings for the man ran deep. He had seen the anguish in her face when she had been forced to shoot the major. And when he had broken into Sinclair's quarters, he had taken in the situation at a glance, the rumpled bed, the girl naked as the day she was born, with the softly glowing look on her face of a woman who had been made love to.

"Does Major Sinclair know that the colored girl, Sukey, is actually Lucinda Appleton?" he asked.

Lucinda bit her lip, shaking her head unhappily. "No," she admitted, "not yet." And then hastily, "But

223

I plan to tell him the truth, of course. I'm sure he'll understand."

"Yes," Jephthah said, but his voice was doubtful. The major didn't strike him as the forgiving and forgetting type, especially when it was a woman who had tricked him.

"Anyway, I promised Cole," Lucy said desperately. "I promised I'd give up spying. I can't go back on my word, Jephthah."

"It seems to me you swore an oath to Mr. Baker, too, when you joined the secret service," Jephthah said quietly.

"I know." A flush rose beneath the girl's pale skin. "Surely, though, there must be someone else you can send to Richmond in my place."

"No, ma'am." Jephthah reached into his pocket and pulled out a gold locket. "I reckon you'll know why when you take a look at this picture."

Even before she snapped open the engraved golden lid and looked at the picture of the young girl inside, Lucinda recognized the locket. It was her own locket, her own picture, with her black hair spilling over her shoulders, a younger Lucinda with a girlish, smiling face.

"I gave this locket to my brother, Matt, when he joined the Army," she said, dismayed. "How did you get it?"

Jephthah returned to his chair. "Almost one hundred Union prisoners escaped through a tunnel from Libby Prison in Richmond early in February. Miss Van Lew helped plan their escape, hiding some of the prisoners in her own home. One of the men left this locket with her. He said it belonged to one of the prisoners who was too ill to join them in the escape. He didn't know the man's name. Evidently no one does, not even the prisoner himself. The last time I was in Richmond, Miss Van Lew gave me the locket and told me the story. She located the young man in Libby and seems to have developed a special attachment for him. When I saw the locket..." Jephthah spread his hands. "Well, naturally, I recognized the picture. I thought you'd want to know."

"Matt," Lucinda said, her voice incredulous. "Matt's alive."

Jephthah shook his head quickly. "We don't know that for sure. We don't even know if the prisoner is your brother. Some other soldier could have picked up the locket on the battlefield, or stolen it from your brother."

"Did Miss Van Lew give you a description of the prisoner?" Lucinda asked eagerly.

"Only that he's very young and fair-haired. And," he added grimly, "Miss Van Lew is afraid he'll die if he stays in Libby. From what we hear of the place, it's a wonder any of the prisoners, even the well ones, manage to stay alive." His mouth twisted as if with a bad taste. "Still, I hear some of our Yankee prisons aren't much better."

Lucinda rose to her feet and began to stride, agitated, back and forth. "It is Matt. I know it is." She turned to Jephthah eagerly. "Can't an exchange be arranged?"

"There are no more prisoner exchanges," Jephthah said. "General Grant passed the word. I guess he figured the South needed the men they'd get back and the North didn't."

"What about Miss Van Lew? Can't she do anything?"

Jephthah shook his head again. "She's watched too closely these days."

Tears sparkled in Lucy's eyes, spilled unheeded down her face. "Matt turned seventeen in April," she cried softly. "He's just a boy. I can't let him die." She brushed childishly with the back of her hand at the tears and gazed imploringly at Jephthah. "What shall I do?"

The tall, lanky man rose to his feet, his voice sober. "That's a decision you'll have to make, ma'am. I can't even guarantee you that the lad's alive. I do know, though, we could use you in Richmond."

Lucinda sighed deeply. It had been such a lovely dream, Cole and her together the way they had been that night in the cabin, but like all dreams it was too fragile to last in the cold light of day. A knot of pain settled in the pit of her stomach. She had a feeling that it was an ache that would never leave her. "Oh, it isn't fair," she cried despairingly, her young face stricken.

Jephthah nodded dourly. "No, ma'am. But then there's not much about a war that is fair."

When Lucinda walked out of the general's tent an hour later, it would have taken a very sharp observer to find any trace of the tears that had stained her cheeks, and a much closer look to notice that the dark, lustrous eyes held hidden in their depths a numb look of misery.

Certainly Harry Appleton, as he left the waiting carriage and came forward to greet her, was too preoccupied with his own annoyance at his cousin's latest escapade to notice. Giving her a brief kiss on the cheek, he said hastily, "We'll have to hurry. We're catching the train to Richmond at Welch Junction."

Sam, who had climbed down from the coachman's seat to hold the door open for Lucy, gave the pale face beneath the jaunty velvet hat a quick, searching glance, then asked softly, "Are you all right, Miss Lucy?"

She smiled faintly. "Yes, Sam. Will you be coming to Richmond with us?"

"Yes, ma'am."

Harry gave the servant an irritated glance. He disliked the familiarity in the man's voice when he spoke to Lucinda, and the way Sam looked her straight in the eye when he spoke to Lucy, instead of ducking his head submissively. If it weren't for the fact that a good strong field hand, not to mention a competent coachman, was almost impossible to come by these days, Harry would have taken pleasure in having that annoyingly arrogant air beaten out of the coachman.

"After Sam drops us off at the station, he'll go back to Black Oaks and pick up mother and drive her to Richmond," Harry explained, climbing into the car-

226

riage after Lucinda. "Mother will bring your trunks along with hers."

"Aunt Clare is coming to Richmond, too?"

"Of course." Harry lifted a shocked eyebrow. "It would hardly be proper, your staying in my home in Richmond without a chaperon. After all, our engagement hasn't been formally announced yet."

And it never would be, Lucy thought indignantly, then decided it would be more politic for the moment not to start an argument with her cousin. "Aren't you concerned, leaving Black Oaks untended?" she asked, meekly enough.

Harry settled back in the carriage, a smug look of self-importance in the pale-yellow eyes. "You forget I occupy an important post in the war department, Cousin Lucinda. I can assure you by summer's end, General Jubal Early will have all the Federal troops swept out of the valley." He frowned and added, "In any case, Mother isn't well enough to stay at Black Oaks alone."

So General Early was planning a campaign through the valley this summer, Lucinda thought. She smiled ruefully to herself when she discovered she was already making a mental note of the information to pass it along to Jephthah, then Cousin Harry's words suddenly struck home. "Is Aunt Clare sick?" she asked anxiously.

"She hasn't been completely well since Joseph died," he replied. "She suffered a heart seizure at that time." He gave Lucy a reproachful glance. "And your outrageous behavior these last days hasn't helped her any. She's been sick with worry about you."

"I didn't know," Lucinda said unhappily. "Aunt Clare never said anything about being ill."

"Mother doesn't complain," Harry said, almost indifferently, as if, of course, it was proper that she shouldn't. And then, aggrieved, "I must say your actions have caused me a great deal of distress, too, running off in the middle of the night that way without

227

a word to anyone. You can imagine the gossip that's been going around Richmond about your behavior, the future wife of a man in my position being held prisoner in a Yankee camp for almost a week."

"Well, I could hardly help that," Lucy pointed out, with a touch of asperity. "I'd been shot, after all. And I was treated with the greatest of courtesy."

"General Sharpe did seem almost a gentleman," Cousin Harry admitted grudgingly. "Still, your behavior is inexcusable."

And for the rest of the trip until they reached the railroad junction, Lucinda had to endure a harangue on all the virtues she lacked and the embarrassment her deplorable unladylike behavior had brought to the family. Once on the train, though, Cousin Harry had no more time for scolding. It was difficult enough finding space for Lucinda and himself, let alone the luggage he had brought in the carriage. The train was crowded with refugees intent upon reaching the safety of Richmond, as well as cars filled with wounded soldiers on their way to hospitals in Richmond, and Yankee prisoners of war headed for the dreaded Libby Prison.

As Lucy gazed at the wan faces of the Union prisoners, many with bloody, untended wounds, she asked the sergeant in charge indignantly, "Do they have to be packed in like that, like animals?"

"Yes, ma'am, as long as they keep coming, thicker than lice on a hen and a damn site ornerier." He glanced disgusted at the prisoners. "If I had my way, I'd shoot all prisoners like blackbirds, 'stead of letting them sit in Libby, eating rations our men could use."

Before Lucy could reply, Cousin Harry grabbed her arm and pulled her away. "Come along, Lucy," he said impatiently, "or we'll lose our seats, and I don't intend to stand all the way to Richmond."

Once inside the car, Lucinda was relieved to discover that Harry had not been able to find them seats together. Her companion turned out to be a young woman in widow's weeds, her eyes dull and red-rimmed from crying. She told Lucy she was on her way to Richmond to bring home the body of her husband, who had been stricken with dysentery while serving along the Rapidan River, and had died at a military hospital in Richmond.

Lucinda gazed at the young face behind the black widow's veil. "You couldn't have been married very long," she said sympathetically.

"Two years, but in all that time we were together only two weeks." the woman said. Bitterness made her voice quiver. "The nurse at the hospital said Jim might have been saved if they'd had the proper medicines."

"How terrible for you," Lucinda murmured. "How you must hate this war."

The girl gave her a startled look. "I don't hate the war. I hate the damn Yankees!" She lifted her chin proudly. "Anyway, I had rather be the widow of a brave man than the wife of a coward."

Looking at the young woman, Lucinda was reminded of all the grief-stricken mothers and widows she had met since her return to the South, almost all of them cast in the same mold as this young widow beside her. The Southern women's hatred of the Yankees, she had discovered, was even more virulent than that of their menfolk.

The young woman gave her a curious glance. "Have you a sweetheart in the Army?"

"Yes," Lucinda said hesitantly, then more firmly, "Yes, I have." As she spoke the words, a longing for Cole swept over her so intense that for a moment it was as if an agonizing cramp had gripped her, and she almost doubled over with the pain. Suppose Cole should be killed, she thought. Suppose she never saw him again. Oh, God, I couldn't bear it, she thought frantically, her young face bleak. At least her seat companion had had two weeks with her lover. She and Cole had had only one night. She gazed, marveling, at the young woman beside her. How could she be so brave? I'd die, she thought, if anything happened to Cole.

The thought was too painful to bear thinking about, and she forced herself to concentrate on the scenery they were passing. Not that it was very cheering—charred woods and fields where battles had been fought, empty houses like Gray Meadows with only blackened shells left. But already tendrils of spring green were covering the devastation wrought by men, lilacs blooming by a tumbled chimney, trumpet vines clambering over broken-down fences.

Gradually as they drew closer to Richmond, the train began passing through fortifications. Jefferson Davis had bragged that no Union troops could ever penetrate Richmond's defenses, and as Lucy carefully noted the number and location of camouflaged batteries, open rifle pits, signal towers, lines of artillery and ammunition dumps, the regiments of soldiers and blacks building still more fortifications around the city, she began to wonder if President Davis might not be right. It did seem impossible that any army could fight its way through the miles of fortifications.

Then the spires of Richmond came into view and the foaming rapids of the James River. In the railroad station, Cousin Harry managed to get their luggage unloaded, but as they stood outside the station, their luggage piled beside them, it was clear that hiring a carriage in the busy capital city was another matter.

Cousin Harry's face was once again beginning to turn an angry, frustrated red when a silvery shaded victoria pulled up on the street before the station. While the coachman stopped the carriage, a woman in a stylish, pale-purple poke bonnet decorated with lilacs leaned through the window and asked graciously, "May I give you a ride into town, Mr. Appleton?"

That softly musical voice sent a shock of recognition through Lucy. She turned her head and found herself gazing full into the creamy white face and violet-tinted eyes of Arabella Von Bruck.

14

For a split second, black eyes and lavender eyes met. Lucinda held her breath, hoping the dismay she felt didn't show in her face. Then Cousin Harry was making introductions. "Countess Von Bruck, may I present my cousin, Miss Lucinda Appleton."

Lucy could detect no spark of recognition in Arabella's serenely lovely face, no memory of the small black servant, Sukey, she'd had tortured in the cellar of her home in Washington. Those same lilac-shaded eyes that had watched Sukey's agony with a look of almost sensual delight now rested indifferently on Lucinda Appleton's face, narrowing a little with the automatic dislike that Arabella always bore toward any other beautiful woman in her vicinity. Then her smiling gaze moved immediately back to Harry Appleton.

"I'll be passing Franklin Street," she said. "I'll be happy to carry you and your cousin to your home."

"Thank you, countess. If you're sure it won't be too much trouble."

Lucy noticed, amused, that Cousin Harry's usually brusque voice was almost fawning as he bustled around, directing the placing of their carpetbags inside the coachman's box, then squeezing himself between Lucinda and Arabella in the carriage.

"I heard you were leaving Richmond for the summer, countess," he said, as the carriage rolled away from the station.

"I'll only be gone for a few weeks—some matters at Maywood that require my attention." The countess sighed plaintively. "I'm afraid I have no head for business, and it's so difficult, running a plantation the size of Maywood—a woman, alone." She gave Cousin Harry a helplessly appealing glance.

He immediately leaped at the bait, insisting gallantly, "By your own choice, I'm sure. And if there's any way that I can be of help to you, in your ... your business affairs, countess, I'd consider it an honor."

Through lowered eyelids, Arabella watched Harry Appleton's eyes glisten hopefully as they fastened on her face. She had been meaning for some time to turn her attention upon Harry Appleton. After all, it was common knowledge that Mr. Appleton was one of the shrewdest speculators in Richmond. And if there was any money to be made from the war, Arabella intended to get her hands on a share of it.

She fluttered her eyelashes demurely. "Why, thank you, Mr. Appleton. You're very kind. It's so difficult to know how to manage one's affairs these days with the blockade cutting off our markets in England, and our people running off every chance they get. And the price of slaves these days! Do you know I paid four thousand dollars just last week for a field hand that wasn't worth a cent over one thousand dollars?" Indignation crackled in Arabella's voice at the injustice of it all.

Cousin Harry made sympathetic noises. "Prices for everything are outrageous," he agreed. "My last pair of boots cost me two hundred and fifty dollars. And unhappily our Confederate currency is not as sound as it might be. It's only too true, as you ladies have complained, that you carry your money to market in a basket and bring your provisions home in your purse."

Lucinda was only half listening to the conversation. She had drawn as far away as possible from the countess, but she found she could not escape the lavender scent Arabella wore. The sickeningly sweet fragrance brought back memories of Arabella's bedroom in her Washington home, where that same lavender scent had clung to the curtains and bed linen. And another even more disturbing memory, those moments when she had watched through the peephole in the ceiling of that bedroom, watched Arabella in Cole's arms, her full white breasts crushed against Cole's chest, his dark head bent over her golden hair. Lucinda had never known jealousy before, and she was surprised to discover it had a taste, like unripe persimmons in her mouth.

"Watch out!" Harry's sharp cry to the coachman pulled Lucy back to the present, to the carriage swerving to avoid knocking down a woman who had stepped without looking into the street.

Lucy turned to stare back at the woman, who stood, as if bewildered, on the side of the street, shaking her head and mumbling to herself. It was impossible to tell her age. The small, ornate parasol and old-fashioned bonnet hid the woman's face from view, but she appeared frail and elderly.

"Shouldn't we stop?" Lucinda asked. "She may be hurt."

"Oh, that's just Crazy Betsy," Arabella said coldly. "Drive on, Sampson."

"Crazy Betsy?" Lucy echoed, startled.

Cousin Harry's mouth tightened disapprovingly. "That's what she's called, Cousin Lucy. It's a great tragedy. The Van Lews are an old aristocratic family, but they made the mistake of sending their daughter, Elizabeth, to school in Philadelphia, before the war. Unhappily, her mind was affected. She came back completely changed. She became a rabid abolitionist, freeing the Van Lew slaves, even speaking out against the South. Now she roams the streets like a crazy woman, talking and singing to herself, when she isn't visiting the Yankee prisoners at Libby Prison."

"She's a lunatic—or a traitor," the countess said shrewdly. "I'm not sure which. I've never approved of her being permitted to visit the prisoners, the way she's allowed to bring food to that Yankee scum. I wouldn't be surprised if she played a part in the escape of those prisoners in February."

Cousin Harry laughed nervously. "I agree that Miss Van Lew is a pathetic creature, countess, but I'm sure

General Winder is well aware of Miss Van Lew's activities when she's inside the prison."

A look of veiled contempt passed across Arabella's face. She had her own opinion of a provost marshal who allowed a hundred prisoners to escape almost under his nose.

"No doubt you know best, Mr. Appleton," she murmured, while Lucy turned her head for a last startled look at Crazy Betsy. So that was the woman who was to be her contact in Richmond, who was her only chance of freeing young Matt. Was it possible Cousin Harry was right, and that Elizabeth Van Lew did have an unhinged mind? If so, could she be trusted not to betray any agent making contact with her?

The carriage had pulled up before a two-storied red brick house in what was obviously one of the more affluent sections of the town. Lucy later learned that General Lee and his invalid wife had their home not far down the street from Cousin Harry's.

She climbed out of the carriage and waited, a little impatiently, while Cousin Harry profusely thanked the countess for the ride. Arabella hadn't seen fit to address two words to Lucinda during the entire trip. Now she turned and gave her passenger a condescending smile. "I'm sure you'll have a pleasant visit in Richmond, Miss Appleton. With the great number of soldiers in town, all the young ladies, even the homeliest ones, have no trouble getting beaux."

"Having so many eager gentlemen around must be a great comfort to the older ladies, too," Lucy said, smiling sweetly at Arabella.

A flush of anger made spots of color in the countess' pale cheeks, and she shot a furious glance at Lucinda. Bella was well aware that Harry Appleton's annoyingly beautiful cousin was a good ten years younger than she was.

As the silver Victoria rolled off down the street, Harry frowned, exasperated, at Lucinda. "Really, Cousin Lucy, you do have a knack for offending people. You were extremely rude to the Countess Von Bruck."

Lucy shrugged her shoulders indifferently. "Don't be foolish, Harry. She's no more a countess than I am."

Harry eyed her suspiciously. "How would you know? Have you met Mrs. Von Bruck before?"

Lucy turned quickly away, running up the front steps of the latticework-covered veranda that ran across the front of Cousin Harry's house. "I'm sure I'd remember if I had," she said lightly. "Come along and show me your house, Harry. I'm dying to see inside."

Two days later, in the afternoon, Aunt Clare arrived in Richmond. When she alighted from the carriage, Clare Appleton's usually pink cheeks had a gray pallor that alarmed Lucinda. She insisted that her aunt lie down at once in the cool, shuttered front bedroom she had prepared for her, and she sent one of the servants to fetch Harry from the Spottswood Hotel, where he had spent the last two nights.

While Harry was with his mother, Lucy found Sam in the stable grooming the carriage horses. Quickly she told him of Arabella Von Bruck's presence in Richmond. "You can't stay in town," she said, worried. "She's bound to see you. I'll think of some excuse to get Cousin Harry to send you back to Black Oaks."

Sam continued calmly currying the horse. "No, ma'am, I'm fixing to stay right here."

"You can't! Jane told me about ..." Lucy fell silent, embarrassed, remembering how graphically Jane had described Arabella's desire for Jane's husband.

"I'm staying," Sam repeated, only a muscle jerking in one high cheekbone betraying the emotion he felt. "My Janey might be here in Richmond with that she-devil."

Looking into that stubborn, hawklike face, Lucinda knew it was useless to try to change Sam's mind. "At least be careful to stay out of her sight for the next few days," she said coaxingly. "The countess will be gone from Richmond soon. When she comes back, I'll find out if Jane's with her."

"Yes'm," Sam agreed, then gazed soberly at Lucy. "You be careful, too, miss. Richmond ain't a healthy town for a spy."

"Oh, I've given all that up," Lucy said quickly. It was bad enough, she thought, that she had had to break her word to Cole, without involving Sam again in her spying activities. As dangerous as it would be for her if she was caught, it would be twice as dangerous for a black man, caught spying in the very heart of the Confederacy. In any case, rescuing young Matt was her responsibility. She had no right endangering Sam's life, too.

"Yes, ma'am," Sam said, skeptically.

The next few weeks Lucy threw herself into the feverish social life of Richmond, a beleaguered city which in many ways reminded her of Washington. There were the same bristling fortifications and flickering campfires around the city, the sound of enemy guns in the not too far distance, and the daily clanging of the alarm bell in the square, giving the city an air of being constantly under siege.

The hotels, as well as the private homes, overflowed with refugees. Wealthy planters, speculators, harassed government workers and sleekly dressed blockade runners jammed the restaurants and barrooms while poverty-stricken families, dispossessed by the war from their homes and employment, found shelter where they could. And, as in Washington, a never-ending stream of ambulances rumbled through the streets bringing the wounded to the city's many makeshift hospitals. With only the most primitive of medical and sanitary supplies left anywhere in the South, most of the wounded quickly left the hospitals again. Stripped of their valuable clothes, the dead were buried at Hollywood Cemetery, whose hillsides were already thickly covered with fresh graves.

Although almost all the women Lucy met in Richmond were in mourning for a dead son, husband, or brother, the balls and receptions, charity bazaars and

236

theatrical parties, held nightly, were well attended and filled with a restless, brittle gaiety. The gowns of the belles at the balls might be turned or of the plainest muslin or calico, the styles long outmoded; still, the women danced and laughed and flirted through the summer nights as if they were wearing satin and velvet and the latest fashions from Paris. Their battle-scarred escorts in gray and gold, old bewhiskered men and callow-faced youths, danced and made love with equally desperate abandon. Grant and his massive Army of the Potomac were poised, waiting, along the Rapidan River. Each man was only too aware that a dance with a lady love one night could turn into a dance of death on the battlefield the next day.

As an Appleton of Black Oaks, Lucinda was immediately welcomed into Richmond society. The provost marshal himself signed her pass with a flourish, allowing her the freedom of the city and as far out of Richmond as it was prudent for her to travel. Word of her conquests at The Bower, her shocking escapade when she had been captured by the Yankees, had reached Richmond before Lucy, and she discovered herself to be a minor celebrity.

Parties and balls were given in her honor. Her beauty, striking even in a city noted for its beautiful women, brought admirers flocking around with proposals of marriage, while rumors of her scandalous behavior at The Bower aroused other, less respectful, sentiments in the breasts of some of her escorts.

Almost every night in the flirtation room of a Richmond mansion, Lucinda gracefully fended off proposals and propositions alike, while spending her days dutifully attending sewing circles and charity bazaars with her aunt.

At Aunt Clare's insistence, Lucy also performed her stint of nursing at one of the local hospitals. In the hospital, she soon discovered another sort of feverish activity was taking place. Nurses and surgeons were gathering what little supplies and medicines and empty beds they could find, preparing for a new onslaught of wounded. A battle was already rumored to be taking place north of Richmond at an old deserted mining area of tangled trees and thick underbrush called the Wilderness.

In the middle of a warm May night, Lucinda was jolted awake by cannonfire so loud that it jarred her bedroom window. She could hear the alarm bell clanging in Capitol Square. Artillery and cavalry clattered through the streets of Richmond all night long and into the morning, heading toward the Wilderness to reinforce General Lee. For two days and nights, men fought and died in the junglelike growth of the Wilderness until the fragile violets and spring-green leaves in the undergrowth were stained scarlet with blood. Dry leaves caught fire from exploding shells and turned the woods into a holocaust. Wounded and dead soldiers were caught alike in the raging flames, while the haze and stench of the smoke could be seen and smelled as far away as Richmond.

Within days, ambulances of wounded from the battlefield began to arrive at hospitals in Richmond. Lucinda and her aunt, along with dozens of other Richmond girls and matrons, worked with the wounded around the clock. They were able to snatch only brief moments of sleep as the battle moved south to further slaughter at the Bloody Angle at Spotsylvania and blazed anew, with thousands of men in blue and gray dying at Cold Harbor.

Lucinda did not have to be told that if the Wilderness and Spotsylvania and Cold Harbor had been victories for General Lee, then they had been bought at a terrible price. The burned bodies of the men who overflowed the beds in the hospitals had endured every form of bloody, ghastly wound and mutilation. With no morphine to ease the suffering of their patients, there was little the women could do but walk among the beds and pallets laid on the floors, carrying tin buckets of water and sponges to wash off the blackened bodies. They listened to the screams of agony as surgeons operated, stanched the flow of blood when they could and gently closed the eyelids of the dead.

Each day Lucinda told herself she could not bear the terrible suffering at the hospital, the stench of festering wounds, one more hour. Yet each day she went back, driven by the thought that one of the wounded men might be Cole. What if Cole were lying wounded, helpless, with no one to give him comfort and ease his pain? Or worst of all, what if Cole were one of the thousands killed at the blood bath that was Spotsylvania or Cold Harbor? Each soldier brought into the hospital with black, curly hair made her blood run cold until she could wash away the soot and grime from the face and breathe a deep, guilty sigh of relief. Not Cole. Thank God, not Cole.

Even without the thought of Cole, though, prodding her each day to the hospital, there was the example of her Aunt Clare to shame Lucinda into returning. Quietly, competently, never once complaining, Clare Appleton made her rounds through the wards where the worst of the wounded were kept. Her soft voice soothing, her small hands gently changed bandages on bodies mangled almost beyond recognition. Scolding, teasing, cajoling her patients, she confounded the surgeons by literally dragging men back from the edge of death by the sheer force of her own will, stubbornly refusing to give up hope.

Until one afternoon Lucinda found her aunt slumped, unconscious, across the pallet of a wounded soldier. She revived quickly, insisting that she was only tired. "Don't make a fuss, child," she protested weakly when Lucy insisted that she must go home.

"You're both going home," the matron of the hospital said briskly, coming up behind Lucinda. "You've done more than your share, and the worst seems to be over. At least, there haven't been as many casualties since General Lee stopped the Yankees at Petersburg." When Clare continued to protest, she said tartly, "Stop making a martyr of yourself, Clare Appleton. You're no good to anyone dead." And then in a worried whisper aside to Lucinda, "Take her home and make sure she stays in bed. I don't like her color."

Sam was waiting outside the hospital with the Appleton carriage. As if Lucy's aunt were a child, he picked her up and placed her in the carriage, then carried her up the stairs to her bedroom in the house on Franklin Street.

Lucy sat beside her aunt's bed until her aunt finally drifted off to sleep. Then she returned to her own bedroom. Despite a weariness that made her bones ache, she found she couldn't rest. Sleep, she suspected, would only be filled with nightmares of mutilated bodies and the black, dank smell of death. Without bothering to change her bloodstained dress, she flung a lace shawl over her shoulder and hurried out of the house into the blessedly warm and golden June sunlight.

Walking quickly, as if pursued by invisible demons, she hurried past Capitol Square, where a band was playing to an assembled group of gaily dressed ladies, their parasols and bonnets decorated with home-made flowers. The women waved proudly at a troop of young artillerymen marching by, no doubt on their way to besieged Petersburg. Lucy didn't stop to watch. She'd had enough of young men marching gallantly off to war; she could see the stamp of death already on their young faces. Was it only a year ago, she thought, that she had been so eager to join Lafayette Baker's secret service? She had thought that war was as exciting and glamorous as a stage production, and she wanted a leading role in the drama. Now she wondered if she'd ever get the stench of death from her nostrils.

She walked aimlessly down one street and up another, past lovely fenced gardens, gracious tree-shaded homes. Several people turned to look askance at her bloodstained gown, but she stared, unseeing, through them. Finally, as if coming to an unconscious decision, she found herself climbing Church Hill Street, stopping at last before the aristocratic three-story Van Lew mansion with its broad, white-columned veranda. The formal garden before the house was lush with boxwood, vines and beds of roses, like patchwork quilts.

Gazing at the mansion, Lucy remembered uneasily the stories she had heard of the eccentric Miss Van Lew. Yet where else could she turn? She had made discreet inquiries during the last weeks, and without help it was clear that she could never manage to visit Libby Prison and see for herself the young man who might or might not be Matthew.

As she stood uncertainly before the house, she became aware of the woman working in the garden, carrying a straw basket and wearing an old-fashioned sunbonnet. The woman straightened from her task of heading the roses and stared curiously at Lucy.

Lucinda felt a shock of recognition. It was Crazy Betsy, the woman Arabella's carriage had almost ridden down the first day Lucy had arrived in Richmond. Except there was no trace of mindlessness in that face now, Lucy saw, surprised. In fact, closer inspection of the features revealed a face that must have been beautiful in youth, but the high cheekbones and thin nose had grown sharply spinsterish in middle age. The woman gave Lucy a suspicious glance, her voice abrupt. "What do you want?"

"I'm . . . I'm Lucy Appleton, Miss Van Lew."

"I know that," the woman replied sharply. "I know your cousin Harry. He was a disagreeable boy." She cackled loudly. "Can't say age has improved him." Again she gave her visitor that oddly piercing glance and asked, "What are you doing here?"

Lucy remembered then, as if some stage cue almost forgotten, and reaching out her hand, she touched one of the full-blown white roses. "I've heard white roses stand for freedom," she said softly.

"And the red roses for union," the woman replied, then stepped closer, peering cautiously up at Lucinda from beneath the wide-brimmed bonnet. For all the fact that she was several inches shorter than Lucinda, the girl was aware of a vitality, a power about the

241

woman, a keen brilliance in the blue eyes in the angular face. She's crazy, like a fox, Lucy thought, contrasting this self-assured woman with the mumbling, pathetic creature that she had first seen.

"Took you long enough to get here," the woman snapped.

"I've been busy," Lucy said, embarrassed, not wanting to admit that the woman's reputation had dissuaded her from making contact.

Miss Van Lew tucked her head to one side. "I know. You've been working in the hospital. How many wounded would you say have come into Richmond?"

"I . . . I don't know," Lucy stammered, and then, her voice rising indignantly, "I didn't have time to keep count." But, of course, she understood why Miss Van Lew had asked her question. General Sharpe would want to pass along to General Grant how many men General Lee had lost in the last month's battles, how badly the Confederate Army had been hurt at the Wilderness and the other engagements. "I'm sorry." She shook her head wearily. "I'll do better. It's just been so . . . so horrible." A shudder passed through her body in memory, her hand plucking absently at a dried stain of blood on her skirt.

For a moment the sharp face staring up at her softened. "This is your first time, nursing in the hospitals?"

Lucy nodded. "If only there were morphine or even whiskey to give the men," she said desperately. "But to have to watch them die and there's nothing you can do." Her voice broke as she fought back tears.

"Union soldiers have died, too," her companion reminded her harshly. "Grant lost fifty thousand men during May alone. The newspapers up North are calling him Butcher Grant, and the Wilderness and the Bloody Angle and Cold Harbor, Grant's Funeral March. If Grant doesn't have a victory soon, Lincoln will never be reelected. Then the war's a failure and all the men will have died in vain."

"Have you orders from General Sharpe?"

"He wants all the information he can get on Lee's

movements, particularly how many men he has at Petersburg, which regiments he's sending in and from where. Whenever Lee pulls away men for Petersburg, it weakens his line of defense elsewhere."

"I'll try," Lucinda said. "Are you to be my courier?"

Miss Van Lew shook her head so vehemently the calico sunbonnet was in danger of toppling off her head. "No, and don't come near my home again. It's dangerous, our being seen together. It was foolish of you to come today in broad daylight. I have a farm outside of Richmond. One of my servants brings in eggs and fresh vegetables each morning to sell house to house. If you have any information, put it in her egg basket. You'll have no trouble recognizing her. She has a scar on her forehead and speaks with a stutter. But she's completely trustworthy. She'll see that I get any message." A touch of vanity crept into Elizabeth Van Lew's prim voice. "General Grant will have the information the next day, along with the fresh flowers I send him daily for his table. My courier route has never failed."

"What of my brother?" Lucinda blurted, as the woman started to turn away. "You haven't told me yet about Matthew. When will you take me to Libby Prison?"

The woman turned back, frowning. "You can't go to the prison with me. Haven't I just told you we mustn't be seen together? And I don't know that he is your brother. Surely Jephthah told you that."

"I have to see for myself," Lucy said stubbornly, her own face as sharply determined as Miss Van Lew's. "There must be some way you can get me inside. They say you're the only visitor who's allowed to see the prisoners. How do you manage?"

The woman chuckled softly. "Oh, I have my ways. For a while when Colonel Todd, the brother-in-law of Mr. Lincoln, was in charge of the prison, I'd feed him buttermilk and gingerbread. As for the provost marshal, he thinks I'm a harmless old crackpot. Crazy Betsy, isn't that what they call me?" She shook her ringlets, smiling at Lucy's embarrassment. "Oh, I know what they think of me in Richmond, those that don't threaten to hang me from the highest tree! I don't mind a bit as long as the guards at Libby let me pass without looking too closely at what I carry in and the information I smuggle out. But if I went to Winder and asked permission for you to visit the prisoners, he'd be immediately suspicious. And a pretty young woman like yourself would attract too much attention from the guards."

"I don't have to be young or pretty," Lucy said thoughtfully. "I can borrow one of my Aunt Clare's gray wigs, make myself look and talk like an old woman. Jephthah told you I was once an actress, didn't he? Even General Winder wouldn't recognize me, I promise you."

"It might work," Miss Van Lew said grudgingly. "Do you have any money? Gold, not Confederate. You'll need it to bribe the guards."

Lucy nodded. General Sharpe had given her a plentiful supply of hard currency before she left his camp. "When?" she asked eagerly. "When can I see Matthew?"

But this time her companion did turn and march away with quick, nervous steps, pausing only long enough to say over her shoulder, "I'll let you know."

A week later, when the first light of the sun gilded the James River with a lovely, peaceful radiance, a portly, gray-haired woman, heavily veiled and shrouded in widow's weeds, stopped in front of the grimy four-story building that before the war had been a tobacco warehouse and was now Libby Prison. The sentry who met the woman at the gate immediately passed her along to another guard, but not before some coins had changed hands. The second guard, who had received his bribe earlier from Miss Van Lew, didn't cast more than a passing glance at the woman, except to notice that she had a plump, motherly face, and that her steps were faltering and uncertain as she followed the man down a short corridor.

When they reached the end of the corridor, the guard warned, "Hope you don't get the vapors easy, ma'am. The stink's enough to make strong men faint."

Lucinda had already pressed a heavily scented lace handkerchief to her nose. Not even the terrible smell of the hospital wards compared with the noisome stench of slop, human excrement, and decaying flesh that filled the air in the prison. The floor of the long room into which the guard took her was coated with a black, greasy slime, the walls coated with mold. There were only two windows in the deep, open room, and they were both at one end of the room and heavily barred. For a moment Lucinda stopped short, gazing around her, appalled. It was like a scene from Dante's *Inferno*, the dank, evil-smelling room crowded with prisoners so jammed together there was barely space to lie down. Bearded, filthy faces stared apathetically up at Lucinda, their eyes set in sunken hollows, their flesh putrid-looking. All of the prisoners were covered with vermin, which they picked, some plucking listlessly, some with grim determination, as Lucinda walked by, holding her skirt as high as respectable from the floor.

"It's Private No-name you're looking for, ain't it, ma'am?" the guard asked.

"Is that what you call him?" Lucinda asked, her voice muffled behind her handkerchief. "Was there nothing at all to identify him?"

"Nothing," the guard said cheerfully. "He was picked clean as a hound's tooth. One of the guards claimed they saw a pretty gold locket on him, but when I searched him, I didn't find anything." He stopped beside one of the bunks that lined the wall at the far end of the room, near the windows.

When Lucinda started forward, he held out his hand warningly. "Best not get too close, ma'am. No one knows what's wrong with him. Might be typhus."

Lucinda brushed the hand impatiently aside and stepped closer to the bunk. Sunlight trickling through the dirty, barred windows penetrated only a short distance into the darkness of the room. It was impossible to see the prisoner's face clearly. The man lying in the lower bunk, his face half turned toward the window, could have been any age. His touseled hair, beneath a dirty, bloodstained bandage, looked gray in the shadowy light. Two deep lines, like gashes, ran from his nose to his mouth, and his dark-blue eyes, wide open, staring blankly at nothing, had a vacant look about them.

Lucy did not even know she had swayed until she felt the guard's hand on her arm. "You all right, ma'am?"

"Yes," she said faintly. "It was just the shock, at first, of seeing him."

"You know this man?" he asked, startled.

"Of course I know him." Lucy reached out a hand to caress gently the ravaged face that looked like that of a middle-aged man, but she knew only too well was that of a boy who had turned seventeen on his last birthday.

Her voice faltered, then continued steadily. "He's my . . . my son, Matthew."

15

Cole stood in front of the elegant Von Bruck townhouse on Clay Street, debating with himself whether or not to go inside. The parlor windows were open, and voices and laughter, the tinkling of crystal, the lively plinking of a banjo, drifted out into the soft June night. Cole reached out his hand to the wrought-iron gate, then hesitated. When he had run into Arabella that morning in Capitol Square and she had insisted that he come to her party that evening, it had seemed a good idea at the time. After two weeks in the hospital, imprisoned with his own gloomy thoughts, any diversion seemed welcome. Now he was no longer sure. Instead of lifting his spirits, the sounds of merriment from within the house only made his depression deepen.

Also, knowing Arabella, he had no doubt that the invitation pressed upon him wasn't just to her party but to her bed as well. And the thought of Bella's billowy curves, her moist, insatiable mouth, after Sukey's flower-soft lips, her slim, golden beauty opening beneath him, was suddenly unendurable. Scowling, Cole turned and started to limp away, the pain throbbing in his leg in no way as agonizing as the pain that he had lived with ever since he had learned of Sukey's death.

My fault, Cole thought savagely, as he had so often berated himself these last weeks. I brought her to the camp. It was my fault she died. Oh, it was Hannigan who had pulled the trigger and made the almost fatal mistake of bragging to Cole after the Yankee troops had been driven back across the river. "You don't have to worry about that little nigger spy-gal, major. My ball caught her right in the head, must have blown half her face away."

Cole only dimly remembered smashing his fist over and over again into Hannigan's beefy, grinning face,

247

until someone finally dragged him away. Yet even as he was battering the man's face into a bloody pulp, he was thinking dully, "My fault... my fault." He had promised Sukey he would keep her safe. Instead he had destroyed her, the same way everything he loved and cherished in his life had been destroyed. His mother, his beloved Gray Meadows, and now Sukey. In one second all that incredible beauty, so young and vibrant, turned cold and still. And what little spark of warmth still left within Cole Sinclair, fanned to momentary life by the passion he and Sukey had shared, had turned cold and still, too.

He had gone into the hell that was the Wilderness, hoping for death. Then he had fought like a madman with Ewell's forces at Spotsylvania, where men all around him had been blown to pieces and he had climbed over the dead, like cords of wood, to fight in hand-to-hand combat in the trench line of the Bloody Angle. Ironically, with death all around him, the only wound he had suffered was a minié ball in the calf of his right leg. It must be true, Cole thought, his mouth twisting grimly, it was the soldier who didn't care whether he lived or died who somehow managed to survive.

His bad leg slowed him so he had taken only a few steps away from the Von Bruck house when through the open windows he heard a woman start singing to the accompaniment of the banjo. It was a pleasing voice, rich and husky, but it was not the almost professional quality of the singing that caught and held Cole's attention. There was something familiar about the timbre of that voice. Cole paused, listening. He could swear he'd heard that voice somewhere before, but where?

The song itself was familiar enough. It had been a favorite of the South's latest, fallen hero, the flamboyant, reckless Jeb Stuart, who had been fatally wounded at the battle of Yellow Tavern and died in Richmond only a few weeks before.

*"If you want to catch the Devil, have a good time,
just jine the Cavalry ..."*

There was a wave of applause when the girl finished,
and almost immediately she swung into another song,
this time one every Southerner knew by heart, particularly its rousing last lines:

*"Hurrah, hurrah, for Southern rights, hurrah!
Hurrah for the Bonny Blue Flag that bears a single
star!"*

Cole's face cleared, and he half-smiled, remembering. Of course. The pretty young actress at the Atheneum in Washington the night Laf Baker's men had
almost caught him. Would have caught him, too, if the
girl's defiant singing of the Confederate anthem hadn't
almost caused a riot in the theater, giving him his
chance to escape.

Curious now as to whether he was mistaken, whether
it could possibly be the same woman, Cole retraced his
steps. He had no sooner crossed the veranda and
stepped through the front door of the town house when
Arabella came sweeping eagerly across the hall toward
him, arms outstretched. "Cole, darling, I was so afraid
you weren't coming."

She was wearing a lilac-colored gown, with long angel sleeves that fell away at the shoulders, leaving her
pale-white throat and a provocative expanse of her
breasts bare. When she embraced Cole, he was aware
of the heavy scent of lavender, and even more aware
of the ripeness of the body beneath the gauze-sheer
gown, pressed close against him.

Over her shoulder he tried to look into the parlor
and catch a glimpse of the singer, but the audience had
risen to its feet and was milling around the improvised
stage at one end of the room, hiding the performer from
view. Then, just for a moment, the clusters of people

249

parted. Cole saw a familiar slender figure in a scarlet-flounced dress, the ribbons of the banjo still slung over one bare, rounded shoulder, a mass of black curls piled high on top of the delicately boned, oval face.

"I didn't know Lucinda Appleton had been on the stage," he said, surprised.

"I'm sure she hasn't," Arabella replied. "The Appletons would never allow it." She laughed deprecatingly. "Miss Appleton has a sweet little voice, but it's hardly professional quality. She often sings at parties, like mine, raising money for the hospitals."

Then, when Cole continued staring, as if puzzled, into the parlor, she asked, her eyes glittering a little too brightly, "Are you a friend of Miss Appleton's?"

"We were neighbors," Cole said shortly. "Her brother, Charles, and I were close friends. I haven't seen Lucy since last fall at The Bower."

"I'm afraid all Richmond heard of Miss Appleton's behavior at The Bower." Bella shook her head. "Poor Mr. Appleton is going to have his hands full, being married to that young lady."

"Harry Appleton?" Cole drawled, lifting an amused eyebrow. "You mean Lucy is going to marry her cousin Harry?"

"Well, the engagement's unofficial," Arabella admitted. "Mr. Appleton told me in strictest confidence." Then, never happy talking about other women, Arabella tugged impatiently at Cole's arm, pulling him into a small side parlor. The moment she had closed the door, she flung herself into his arms. "Oh, darling, I've missed you so," she whispered breathlessly. "I wish we could go upstairs right now, but later, as soon as the party's over . . ." Her pouting, rosy lips parted, lifted to Cole, so that he could see the pink tongue nestling, waiting for his kiss.

When he didn't respond at once, his face convulsed with a look of almost pain, Arabella stepped back. Her lilac glance flew to his leg, her eyes widening, appalled. "I heard you were wounded, but you're . . . you're not . . ."

Cole shook his head wryly. "No, I'm not. I took a
250

minié ball in the leg. Otherwise I'm fine. I should be able to rejoin my regiment in a few weeks."

"I thought you'd be assigned to General Winder's office here in Richmond," Arabella said, disappointed.

"I'm no longer with the secret service," he said, his voice all at once harsh. "That's all finished." His hands tightened with an unconscious painful ferocity on her arms as he spoke. Arabella, shivering with delicious anticipation, recognized that savage, ice-cold look in his narrowed eyes. She sensed Cole's need to strike out wildly, to hurt as he had been hurt. What was troubling Cole did not interest her. All that mattered was that their lovemaking would be that much more pleasurable for her because of the terrible anger banked within the man.

The thought of that pleasure caused a prickling of warmth in her thighs, and she stepped back into Cole's arms, her eyes feverishly bright. This time she did not wait for him to kiss her but fastened her moist mouth on his, her tongue darting quickly, expertly between his lips while her soft body moved provocatively against his hard, lean body.

In spite of the emptiness within him, Cole found himself instinctively responding to Arabella's overtures, his own mouth tightening cruelly on the moist lips beneath his, his hands caressing the invitingly plump hips. Why not? he thought bitterly. Perhaps this was what he needed to blot from his memory the slim, golden loveliness of Sukey, who could never be his again, to make him forget for a few moments the agony of losing her, like a knife slowly turning within him.

Yet, it was Cole who first heard the click of the lock at the door to the small parlor, who had already half pulled away from Arabella when the door suddenly swung open and he looked full into the startled face of Lucinda Appleton. He would have pulled completely free of Arabella's embrace, oddly embarrassed by the look in Lucy's wide, lustrous eyes—anger, pain, disbelief—so quickly that accusing look was there and gone, he could not tell. But Arabella clung to him, turning a smug smile to her guest as she murmured, "Was there something you wanted, my dear?"

Lucinda's dark lashes swept down over her eyes, a faint pink showing beneath the pale skin. When, after a second, she glanced again at Cole, he saw only a mocking amusement in their depths. "Please forgive the intrusion, countess. I didn't realize you were ... engaged. I seem to have torn the hem of my skirt. I was wondering if I might borrow one of your maids to do some repair work."

Arabella nodded. "Of course. My maid, Jane, is very good with a needle. She's upstairs." Then, grudgingly, turning to Cole, "I believe you've met Colonel Sinclair, Miss Appleton."

Lucy dropped a quick, graceful curtsy. "I just heard this evening that you had been wounded at Spotsylvania, Cole. I'm glad to see that you seem to be on the road to recovery."

Although Lucy's smile was outwardly cool and composed, inwardly she was raging. It's a performance, only a performance, she reminded herself fiercely. Don't step out of your role. Don't forget your lines. Now you smile at your audience, curtsy again, make an exit right ...

And she was finally, safely out of the parlor, walking in a daze up the stairs, that frozen set smile still on her face as she evaded the grasp of a slightly drunken major who had proposed to her earlier that evening, waved to a friend, moved lightly, quickly down the upstairs hall to the nearest door and opened it.

Once inside the room, Arabella's she was sure, because it smelled so thickly of lavender, she sank down upon a satin slipper chair and buried her face, burning hot, in her hands.

"Are you feeling all right, miss?" a voice asked timidly.

Lucy recognized that soft, hesitant voice at once. She smiled at the young colored girl in a maid's uniform standing before her. Then her smile faded as she took a closer look at Jane's face, at the ugly jagged scar

252

disfiguring the left cheek. "What happened to your face, Jane?" she demanded, dismayed.

The girl flung up her hand, hiding the scar, a flush rising beneath the creamy brown skin. "Was there something I could do for you, miss?" she asked stiffly.

Lucinda got to her feet. "I told Arabella I needed someone to sew my hem, but that was just an excuse, of course, so I could talk to you."

When Jane still stared at her, bewildered, Lucy turned the lamp so the light shone into her face. "Look at me, Jane," she said quietly. "Don't you know me? I'm Sukey. We met at the Von Bruck home in Washington. Don't you remember?"

Jane stepped closer, studying Lucy's face intently, then she clapped her hands with childish glee. "You got away then, miss. How did you ever manage?"

"Never mind that now," Lucy said, frowning angrily. "It was Caesar, wasn't it, who did that to your face? It wasn't because of me, was it?"

Jane shook her head quickly. "Oh, no, it happened this winter. I took my babies and tried to run away, to find Troy. Only Caesar caught me and took me back to Maywood. Mrs. Von Bruck, she had him brand me— R on the forehead for runaway slave. Only I . . . I moved and his hand slipped." The slim body flinched, remembering the agony of those moments, the red-hot iron searing her cheek. A look of ineffable sadness clouded the hazel eyes. "I reckon it don't matter now if I ever do find Troy," she said dully.

"But he's here. Troy's here in Richmond at my house," Lucy said eagerly. "That's why I came to the party tonight, to find you."

"Here?" the girl whispered, disbelievingly. "My Troy's here?"

For a moment, Lucy thought the girl was going to faint, and she lowered her gently onto the slipper chair. "He goes by the name of Sam," Lucy said. "He's our coachman. And Sam and I have a plan to get you and your children away to the Yankee lines."

Jane lowered her head, her voice a mixture of pride

and hopeless resignation. "I ain't having Troy see me, not ugly like this," she said stubbornly.

"You can't mean that!"

Jane unconsciously reached up to hide the scar with her hand, gazing bleakly at Lucy. "He won't want me any more. No man would."

Lucy gave the slumped, narrow shoulders an impatient shake. "Don't be an idiot, Jane. Of course Sam will want you. He loves you. Anyway, you certainly can't stay with Mrs. Von Bruck. One of these days, she or Caesar will kill you, or you'll be sold south. What about your children then? Who will take care of them?"

It was, she knew, the one argument that would sway Jane. She saw indecision struggle briefly on the girl's face, then she nodded, her hands clenching tightly, frightened, in her lap. "All right. What should I do?"

Lucy spoke quickly. "Tonight, after Arabella's gone to bed, come to the Appleton house on Franklin Street. It's not far from here, the red brick house with a big magnolia tree in the front yard."

"I know the house," Jane said. "Mrs. Von Bruck visited Mr. Appleton once, last time she was in Richmond."

"I'll leave the side door unlatched. I'll be waiting for you. Sam and I will take care of the rest." Lucy turned her head abruptly to the bedroom door. She noticed the door was slightly ajar, and she thought she heard a noise in the hall. Going to the door, she looked out into the hall, but the corridor was empty. Frowning uneasily, she turned back to Jane. "We mustn't talk any longer. Someone might notice us together. Only one thing. Where is Caesar? I haven't seen him here at the house."

"He's back at Maywood, making sure no more of the Von Bruck slaves run away," Jane said, and then, wistfully, "You're sure? You're sure Troy will still love me?"

"I'm sure," Lucinda said firmly. She had no doubt of Sam's devotion. Nothing, she was sure, would alter or sway his feelings for his wife. Some men were like that, she thought. And others...bitterness rose like gall in her throat, remembering Arabella snuggling in Cole's arms. How could he forget Sukey so soon? she thought furiously. What a little fool she had been, worrying herself frantic about him, waking up in the middle of the night, wrenched with longing, wanting to die if he were dead, so certain that he felt the same way about her.

"Is something wrong?" Jane asked, studying her companion's pain-filled face.

Swiftly Lucy pushed the humiliation of the scene of Arabella and Cole together from her mind. "Nothing's wrong," she said, forcing herself to smile reassuringly at Jane. "There's just someone . . . someone here at the party that I don't want to see. Is there some way I could slip out of the house without being noticed"

"There's a back door the servants use. I'll show you the way."

Within seconds she had found Lucy's wrap and the two women exchanged whispered goodbyes at the servants' entrance of the Von Bruck home. Then Lucy hurried down the ivy-lined path to the front of the house, and past the vine-shielded veranda. She had reached the front gate when a voice spoke from the veranda.

"Leaving so early, Lucy?"

At first she could not see Cole, only the red glow from his cigar where he sat in the darkness of the veranda. Then he tossed the cigar over the railing and joined her at the gate.

"Which is your carriage?" he asked, gazing at the row of waiting carriages and drowsing coachmen.

"I walked," Lucinda said. She had no intention of letting Arabella possibly get a glimpse of Troy by having him drive her to the Von Bruck home.

"Well, then I must insist upon escorting you home," Cole said cheerfully, taking her arm.

She jerked her arm free from his grasp as if his touch burned her. "There's no need for you to bother." She glanced at the new silver eagles on Cole's uniform.

"Colonel Sinclair. I'll be perfectly safe. It's only a short walk."

"No bother," he assured her, once more taking her arm. This time he held her arm so tightly that she could not pull free without causing a scene. And then drawled, amused, "I'm sure Harry would never forgive me if I let his fiancée walk the street at night unescorted."

"I am not Harry's fiancée," she said, furious.

"I was surprised when I heard the news," he admitted, giving her a sardonic glance as he matched his limping stride to hers. "But then you never cease to surprise me, Lucy. For example, I hadn't realized you were on the stage."

Although he could not see the expression on her face, he felt the muscles in her arm grow taut under his hand. Her voice, however, revealed nothing. "You're mistaken, Cole. Whatever gave you the idea that I'd been an actress?"

They were passing under a gas lamp, and he suddenly stopped and pulled her around to face him. "Because I saw you at the Atheneum in Washington," he said calmly. "You were dressed like a young man and wearing a ridiculous hat and mustache, but your voice made a very definite impression on me. I even remember the song you sang that night, the same one you sang tonight, 'The Bonny Blue Flag.' A patriotic, but not a very wise selection, under the circumstances," he added drily. "I thought you told me you had no interest in politics, Lucy."

She laughed lightly. "I haven't. Two gentlemen friends bet me a large sum of money that I wouldn't sing that particular song that night. And you know me, Cole. I never could turn down a dare."

"I'm surprised you weren't thrown into Old Capitol Prison."

"Oh, I was, but only for a few days. Then they released me. I suppose I wasn't considered a very serious threat to the government."

Cole, listening closely to her voice, not the words,

caught the sound of half-truths and truths, mixed freely, and wondered why she was lying to him. Then he shrugged mentally. It wasn't any of his business. Not any more. He said slowly, "I can't imagine your father, or Charles, for that matter, allowing you to prance around on the stage in a man's tights."

She took a deep, painful breath, then said flatly, "Father and Charles are dead."

His hand dropped from her arm, his voice shaken. "Good Lord, Lucy, I'm sorry. I didn't know. And young Matt?"

She walked quickly out of the circle of pale-yellow lamplight into the sheltering dark, no longer trusting her face not to betray her. "He's... Matt's with relatives in New Orleans."

Misery gripped her so that for a moment she felt tears burn behind her eyes. If it were only true, she thought, remembering Matt's face as she had seen it that morning, the sunken eyes, the bones of his cheeks almost cutting through the parchment-thin flesh. And worse of all, his eyes, staring at her blankly, not recognizing her, as far as she knew not even seeing her, as if he were staring into some private hell of his own. She had bribed the guards to get Matt transferred to the prison hospital. At least in the hospital she could visit Matt each morning, see that he was bathed, bring him clean clothes and a blanket, and the hot nourishing soups which were the only food she could coax him into eating.

The doctor, when she had finally coaxed one into seeing Matt, had offered little encouragement. "It's not the wound to his head, you understand. It's what happened inside the boy, in his mind. I know some of my colleagues think soldiers like your son are just faking, shirking their duties, pretending to have lost their minds, because they're afraid to go back into the line. But I'm not so sure." The doctor shook his head regretfully, gazing at young Matt. "I'm afraid the truth is that medicine actually knows very little about how the brain and emotions can control the body."

"There must be something you can do," Lucinda begged.

The doctor tugged at his beard, unable to meet that pleading gaze. "I'm sorry. Perhaps if you could get your son away from here, somewhere where he can have rest and care, proper food, it's possible he might recover in time. I've seen others, worse than your son, recover miraculously. And others . . ." He shrugged helplessly. "It's as if they simply give up, lose all desire to live, literally will themselves to die."

"Lucy, could you slow down a little?"

Lucinda was jerked back to the present by the sound of Cole's voice. She turned and saw that he was limping badly, trying to keep up with her fast pace.

"I am sorry, Cole," she said penitently, waiting for him to join her. "I forgot about your leg. Is the wound very painful?"

"I've had worse," he growled angrily, discovering, annoyed, that he hated to show signs of weakness before this girl who had followed worshipfully after him as a child. Gazing at Lucy's chiseled, perfect profile, the ringlets of black, lustrous curls falling down her slim, regal neck, he thought wryly, Who would have imagined that knobby-kneed little tomboy would turn into such a beautiful young woman?

Watching Cole, seeing the unmistakable look of admiration warming his eyes, Lucy seethed inwardly. How dare he look at her that way? How could he forget Sukey so quickly? And impulsively, wanting to hurt him as he had hurt her, she flashed her companion a radiant smile and murmured, "I'm sure you've had all sorts of wonderful adventures, Cole. You must tell me about them. Your other wounds, were they received in battle, too?"

She was aware that once again, as if unable to stop herself, she was close to crossing that narrow line separating rashness from a reckless, dramatic love of danger.

Cole shrugged. "I would think you'd be bored to

death with all the war stories you must have heard from all your beaux."

"Now you're being modest, Cole," she said coyly. "At The Bower I recall you were chasing spies. Did you ever catch any?"

He did not reply, and she stole a look at his face, at a nerve in the muscle of his cheek that jumped, before his face tightened into a gaunt, rigid mask.

"I've been told that the Union Army uses female spies," she continued, her eyes widening, fascinated. "Is that true? It sounds terribly romantic. What would you do, Cole, if you caught a beautiful Yankee spy?"

"I'd turn her over my knee and give her a good spanking," he said curtly. They had stopped before Cousin Harry's house. She could not see his eyes in the darkness, but she could sense his glance searching her face. And suddenly she was aware of much more than that, how his presence so close to her sent a delicious weakness through her body, the knowledge that she could reach out and touch him, after all those nights of lying in bed, longing for him. All at once she could not bear to see him walk away.

"Won't you come inside for a nightcap?" she asked. "I'm sure Aunt Clare would like to see you."

He hesitated, then said slowly, "No, I think not. Some other time."

She lifted a mocking eyebrow. "Good heavens, Cole, don't tell me you still disapprove of me!"

She broke off abruptly. A rumbling, like thunder growling through the night, made her jump and step instinctively closer to Cole, her hand clutching at his arm.

His arm slipped around her waist, his voice calm. "It's just the shelling at Petersburg. The bluebellies must be trying a night attack."

"I know." She gave a shiver. "But I forget, and Petersburg is so close. Oh, Cole, do you think Lee's lines will hold?"

"They'll hold," he said grimly. "General Lee knows if Petersburg falls, Richmond will be next."

"I wish it were over," Lucy cried petulantly. "I'm so tired of the war. I hate seeing young men without arms and legs and doing without pretty new clothes and white biscuits and butter and real coffee." Tears clung like diamonds to her thick lashes and she said, meekly, "I suppose that sounds awful."

She was still standing within the circle of Cole's arms. He was conscious of the tininess of her waist, so small that his hands could span it easily. The lovely pale oval of her face was lifted to his in the shadowy moonlight.

Almost without meaning to, he found himself brushing those eyelids with his lips, tasting the saltiness of her tears, caressing the camellia softness of her skin as his lips moved slowly downward toward her waiting, parted mouth.

Then, so suddenly that he almost lost his balance, she pushed him violently away from her.

"What the hell?" he exploded. Catching her arm, he pulled her back to his side. "Don't play games with me, Lucy," he warned. "Or do you imagine that I'm one of your lovesick calves that you can twist around your little finger, the way you have half the men in Richmond? What are you holding out for, a general? Is that the way you prefer your men, gilt-edged and with stars?"

She twisted angrily in his grasp, trying to free herself, her eyes blazing. "Don't you dare lecture me, Cole Sinclair. I'm not one of your cheap little sluts that you can drag off to bed whenever you happen to feel like it."

The more she struggled, the tighter Cole's grip became on her arms. His voice was a soft drawl that still managed to flick like a whip across the pale oval face. "At least a slut delivers what she promises," he said, smiling coldly. "She doesn't jiggle her tits at a man and wiggle her little behind, then scream in outraged virtue when a man lays a hand on her." Slowly, still smiling that taunting smile, he drew her closer. "Maybe some-one should call your bluff, Lucy," he murmured. "Maybe it's time you paid for all those promises you made with that tempting little body and never kept."

Before his face lowered swiftly over hers, he saw the dark eyes widen, brilliant, enormous in her small face, not with anger this time—shock, fear, there wasn't time to tell which before his mouth took hers roughly, forcing her soft lips apart.

"No!" A voice screamed soundlessly in Lucinda's mind. She wouldn't let Cole use her again this way, taking her carelessly the way he had taken Sukey and the countess, and probably any number of attractive women who caught his roving eyes. But even as she thought this, she felt her treacherous body responding to Cole's searching mouth on hers. It was as if her senses, having once discovered the pleasurable path-ways of passion, reacted instinctively to Cole's touch, her mouth stirring hungrily beneath his, while her mind was witless, helpless to stop herself.

Cole himself was startled at the unresistant ardor of Lucy's response. He had expected her to continue fighting him off with properly indignant, maidenly modesty. Certainly he had no intention of actually se-ducing the girl. After all, she was Charles Appleton's sister. He had only planned to throw a scare into her, so that she would think twice before dangerously flaunting that softly flirtatious body before the next man. Instead she was matching his passion eagerly, her body straining upward against him, her mouth soft as silk under his. In another moment, he realized, shocked, he would be tumbling her on the grass.

Groaning softly, he thrust her away from him, held her at arm's length, scowling down at her darkly. "Who taught you to kiss like that?" he demanded angrily.

So he still hadn't recognized her, Lucy thought, dis-covering that it was desolation she felt rather than relief. Still, she realized she had been dangerously reckless. Suppose he had recognized her? Cole was much too clever at ferreting out the truth, and it was Matt's life that was at stake.

She glanced up at him with studied indifference and said coolly, "That's none of your business, is it, Cole?"

And felt a brief moment of sweet revenge when she saw the muscle beside Cole's mouth jerk and knew that at last she had hurt him as he had hurt her.

His hand tightened bruisingly on her arm. "I'm making it my business," he said tautly. "You're not some two-bit tart. You're Charles Appleton's sister. It's time you started acting like the lady you were taught to be."

A flush of anger rose in her pale face, her voice slashing furiously at him as she tried to pull free of his grip. "Let me go, damn you! What do you know of ladies anyway? Why don't you go back to that slut of a countess you were pawing this evening? I'm sure she'd be delighted to have any man crawl into her bed."

She was all at once released, so unexpectedly that she caught at the fence to keep from falling. Smiling a wickedly mocking smile, Cole bowed over her hand. "An excellent if a trifle unladylike suggestion, Miss Appleton. You will excuse me? No doubt Cousin Harry is panting just as eagerly, waiting for your return."

Then he had swung away and she could hear his footsteps, the slight limping sound they made on the pavement, as he disappeared into the darkness beyond the lamplight.

16

Her heart pounding so that she felt she would explode with rage, Lucinda picked up her skirt and ran up the steps and into the house, almost colliding with her aunt, who was crossing the front hall. Clare Appleton glanced, startled, at her niece's face and asked, "What is it, child? Is the party over already?"

"No, I..." Lucy took a ragged breath, forced the anger down deep inside her. "I had a headache, so I came home early."

"I'm sorry, dear. Can I get you anything, some peppermint tea, a cold cloth?"

"No. No, nothing. Is Cousin Harry home?"

"He came in about half an hour ago and went straight to bed. He's been so tired lately, working such late hours at the War Department." Aunt Clare started for the stairs, then stopped and turned, her face pinkening, embarrassed. "I wonder, dear...of course, it's silly of me, but you haven't seen my other wig, have you? I seem to have misplaced it."

Lucy felt a warmth rush into her cheeks, but she said, calmly enough, "Perhaps you left it at Black Oaks, Aunt Clare."

Her aunt nodded, but the round, ingenuous eyes surveyed her niece thoughtfully. "Yes, of course, that must be it."

After her aunt went upstairs, Lucinda went to the side door and unlocked it. Then she stepped into the kitchen and put a lighted lamp in the back window, her signal to Sam in the coachman's quarters above the stable that all had gone well—so far. How long, she wondered, before Arabella's party finished, the hostess retired and Jane was able to slip away from the Von Bruck house? Not very long, Lucy decided bitterly, not if Cole returned to Arabella's. The countess would see to that.

She wandered restlessly into the small front parlor and began to pace back and forth among Cousin Harry's tasteless, ornate black horsehair furniture. Over and over again she found herself reliving each second of those brief moments in Cole's arms. Relieved as she was that he hadn't recognized Sukey in Lucy Appleton, paradoxically she was resentful that he hadn't. How could he not have known it was Sukey he held in his arms? she thought, outraged. If she were deaf, dumb and blind and Cole made love to her, she was sure she would know at once it was Cole. Perhaps, though, it was different for a man. Perhaps to a man one woman's kisses were much the same as another's.

She stood staring, without seeing, through the open parlor window into the brick-walled, moonlit garden, the fragrance of flowering tobacco heavy in the night air. Just the same, she decided, she'd be wiser to stay away from Cole from now on. She didn't dare take any chances, not now, not with Matt lying in that prison hospital, wasting away before her very eyes, and she unable to help him. There must be some way she could get him out of that hellhole, she thought, before it was too late, before young Matt retreated so far into his own world that he could never be called back, or before the typhoid fever that had already killed dozens of the prisoners spread through the hospital wards. Once more Lucy began her restless pacing.

An hour passed before she heard a soft, timid knock, more like a scratching, at the side door. When she opened the door, Jane stepped quickly inside. She wore a worn shift and had a black kerchief tied around her head. Her eyes were wide with fear, and she was trembling, as if with a chill.

"Arabella doesn't know you're gone?" Lucy asked softly, pulling the girl into the kitchen.

Jane shook her head. "She's entertaining a gentleman."

A pulse in Lucinda's temple leaped. Then, putting

aside the thought of Cole and Arabella together, she went to the window and removed the lamp.

Turning back to Jane, she said, "There's nothing to worry about. Everything's been arranged. A woman here in town, Miss Elizabeth Van Lew, is going to hide you in her house tonight, then help you get out of the city to her farm in the morning."

Jane recoiled, her voice panicky. "Crazy Betsy! I can't stay in her house. I'd be too afraid."

"She's no more crazy than I am," Lucy said firmly. "And she'll see that you reach the Union lines. You'll be safe there until Troy can join you with the children."

Jane sat down at the table, her hands clasped tightly in her lap. "You told Troy about me ... about my face?" she asked.

"What about your face?" Sam had entered the kitchen so quietly that neither woman had heard him. Lucy saw that he was completely oblivious to her presence. His hawklike Indian's face was turned to Jane, who was seated with her back to him.

Slowly, her slim body braced, Jane rose to her feet and let the kerchief fall away from her hair. Then she turned to face her husband.

For the first time since she had met Sam, Lucy saw that blank, impassive expression vanish from his face. The naked look of adoration, of blinding joy, that took its place as he gazed at his wife brought tears to Lucy's eyes, and she looked quickly away. When she glanced back, Jane was enveloped in Sam's large muscular arms so tightly that her voice was muffled against his chest. "You don't mind ... I'm ugly now."

Sam's voice was an angry, frustrated growl from somewhere deep inside of him. "Don't ever let me hear you say that, you hear me, woman? Or I'll beat you black and blue myself!" Then, gently, he reached out his hand and caressed the scarred cheek. For a second a terrifying look of fury contorted his face, but when he spoke his voice was low and tender. "Ain't another woman I've ever seen beautiful as you," he murmured huskily. "Ain't ever going to be."

Then his arms crushed Jane to him again. Lucy slipped out of the room as if it were somehow indecent to intrude upon their happiness.

"Liebchen, you're not leaving already!"

Arabella lifted her arms to Cole, as if to pull him back into the bed, all her facial muscles lax, her lilac eyes drowsily content in the afterglow of lovemaking. When she stretched, she felt a pleasant pain in her thighs. She had been right, she thought smugly, there had been a terrible anger coiled inside Cole Sinclair which had made their lovemaking that much more exciting. Only too brief, she thought greedily. The night was still young.

Cole did not look toward the bed as he dressed rapidly, afraid the revulsion he felt would show on his face. Not at Arabella, about whom he had no illusions, but at himself. It was a mistake, his coming back here. Stupid of him to think he could forget the pain of losing Sukey by making love to another woman. No, not making love, he grimaced. Whatever emotions had possessed Arabella and him during their violent ravaging of each other's bodies, the emotion of love had not been present on either side. And after it was over, he had felt even more desolate and empty, except for the gnawing pain in his gut, which never seemed to leave him these days.

Damn Lucy Appleton anyway, he frowned, wincing as he pulled his trousers over his injured leg. For a moment, earlier, when he had held her in his arms, he had felt, to his own surprise, the sharp thrust of desire. Then, after arousing yearnings she had no intention of satisfying, she had deliberately withdrawn her teasing, virginal body in pretended outrage, practically driving him to Arabella's waiting arms. No, not Lucy's fault. His own, he thought, disgusted. He should have recognized at once in Lucy the behavior of the experienced coquette, always promising pleasures that were never meant to be delivered.

Arabella had left the bed, and, slipping up behind

Cole, she plastered her body against his back, her arms tightening around his waist, pulling him hard against her soft pillowy breasts. Standing on tiptoe, she blew into his ear, while her hands moved deftly, knowingly, downward over the hard, flat muscles of his abdomen. "Don't go, my love," she murmured.

Cole was saved the embarrassment of trying to think of a tactful way to make a strategic retreat by a light knocking at the bedroom door.

Arabella snatched at a filmy robe, scowling angrily as she jerked the door open. "What is it?"

The middle-aged black woman servant who stood in the doorway had a thin, ferretlike face, with eyes that darted in all directions, never directly resting on her mistress. "It's Jane, ma'am. You tol' me to keep an eye on her. Well, she's gone. I think she's run off."

"Run off? Where? Are you sure?"

"Yessum, I'm sure. And I recollect earlier this evening hearing Jane talking to a white woman, one of the guests at the party. It sounded to me like the woman was telling Jane to come to her house and she'd help her run off."

The darting eyes rested a moment, with a spark of malice, on Arabella's face. "It 'pears to me I heard the name Troy, too."

"What woman? What was her name?" Arabella's small plump hands dug into the servant's bony shoulders, shaking her furiously.

"Ah ain't sure ah heard a name," the servant said.

Arabella went to her dressing table, took some coins from her purse, pushed them into the woman's hands. "Now you'll remember," she snapped, "Or I'll see that you're sold south the first thing in the morning."

A sly smile curved the pinched lips of the woman. "Yes, ma'am, I remember now. It was that lady in the red dress who played the banjo."

Cole, who had been only half listening, now swung around, frowning. "It can't have been Lucy Appleton. She left early. I walked her home myself."

Arabella's eyes narrowed as she stared at Cole. "You didn't tell me you took Miss Appleton home."

Cole reached for his shirt, his voice a lazy drawl. "I wasn't aware that I had to account to you for my movements, Bella." Then he shrugged impatiently. "Anyway, you're making too much of the whole matter. Slaves are running away all over the South to their Northern deliverers." His mouth curved in grim amusement. "And causing no end of problems to the Yankees, I'm happy to say. The Union Army is finding out it's one thing to free the blacks and another thing to have to feed and clothe them."

"Not my slaves," Arabella cried, furious, pulling clothes from her wardrobe and tossing them on the bed. "Wake up Sampson," she ordered the servant. "Have him bring my carriage around at once. Then come back and help me dress."

Cole stared at Arabella as if he thought she'd gone out of her mind. "You don't actually plan to wake up the Appletons at this hour of the night."

"That's exactly what I plan to do," Arabella spat, her eyes glittering angrily. "If you don't believe me, come along and see!"

Sam turned at the door of the kitchen to give Jane one last hug while Lucinda listened anxiously for any sounds of movement overhead. Cousin Harry, she knew, slept like the dead, but Aunt Clare was a light sleeper. "You'll have to hurry, Sam," she whispered. "If you take the roan, you should make Maywood before daylight. Are you sure you know the way to the Van Lew farm afterwards?"

"Miss Van Lew drew me a good map," Sam said.

"You be careful," Jane urged, clinging to her husband with suddenly frantic arms. Lucy had to pull the girl free so that Sam could slip away. A few minutes later she heard hoofbeats, then quiet descended again over the night.

Lucy turned briskly to Jane. "Come along into the parlor. I have some different clothes for you to wear so you'll look more like one of Miss Van Lew's farm help. Then I'll take you to Miss Van Lew's for the night."

It was fifteen minutes later, after Jane had finished changing into a rough knit shirt and homespun blouse, that the knock came loudly at the Appleton front door.

Jane's hands flew to her mouth. She stared, frightened, at Lucy. "It's her," she whimpered. "It's the countess come to fetch me back."

Lucinda opened the front-parlor curtains a slit and saw the silver Von Bruck victoria stopped before the house. Then the knock came again at the door, louder, more insistent.

"She'll find me," Jane moaned. "She'll kill me this time, I know she will."

Lucy turned quickly away from the window, her skirt whirling around her like a great scarlet-belled flower. "Oh, no, she won't," she said, her dark eyes sparkling with a mischievous excitement.

A few moments later when a sleepy servant ushered the Countess Von Bruck and a sheepish-looking Cole Sinclair into the front parlor, they found Lucinda Appleton seated with her ankle propped on a footstool, a book in her hand.

Her face held a mixture of surprise and well-bred annoyance when she greeted them. "Countess ... Cole, what a pleasant surprise, but isn't it a little late to come calling? You'll excuse my not rising. I wrenched my ankle earlier."

"Where is she?" Arabella demanded, her glance scurrying around the room.

Lucy lifted a startled eyebrow. "Where is who?"

"You know perfectly well who! My maid, Jane. You were talking to her at my house this evening. Don't pretend you weren't."

"Of course I was," Lucy said calmly. "She helped mend a rip in my hem." She gave her guest a bewildered glance. "Why on earth should you think she'd be here at this time of night?"

Cole, who had taken a position by the door, saw the fury gathering in Arabella's face and said quickly, "One of the other servants said she overheard a conversation between you and the maid, Jane, offering her the shelter of your home."

Lucy's eyes widened innocently. "And she bothered you with an outlandish story like that?" A glint of spiteful amusement flashed in the dark eyes as she glanced from Arabella to Cole. "What a pity," she murmured. "I'm sure you two had much more pressing matters on your mind."

"What's going on here?"

Cousin Harry, unhappily aroused from his sleep by his mother to investigate the late-night callers, cast an irritated glance at Cole. Mrs. Appleton trailed anxiously behind her son in her nightrobe, her gray wig askew. Harry was wearing a nightshirt which showed quite a bit of his legs, and from the embarrassed flush that spread across his face, it was evident he hadn't expected to meet the Countess Von Bruck in his front parlor at this late hour and in his informal attire.

Before Arabella could speak, Lucy said with a smile, "Mrs. Von Bruck has some ridiculous notion that I'm hiding one of her servants here in the house."

"Two servants," Arabella corrected her sharply. "I have reason to believe a runaway slave of mine, named Troy, as well as my maid, Jane, are being hidden in this house."

"That's impossible," Harry said, bewildered. "The two women servants we have came with the house when I bought it. And our coachman, Sam, came with us from Black Oaks."

"How long have you owned Sam?" Arabella asked.

Lucy said quickly, "Why, Sam's been with us since I was a child." She turned and smiled sweetly at Cole. "Perhaps you remember Sam from when you visited Black Oaks?"

"I can't say that I do," Cole drawled, a flicker of amusement in his eyes as he studied Lucy and the propped ankle on the footstool. "But I seem to recall I did meet Sam once, at The Bower."

"If you're so sure your slave's not my man Troy, then you'll let me see him, of course," Arabella said shrewdly.

"You could, of course," Lucy said, her voice smoothly regretful. "Unfortunately we had to send Sam back to Black Oaks. He wasn't happy living here in the big city. Cousin Harry sent him back yesterday."

Arabella turned a distrustful glance upon Harry Appleton. "Is that true, Mr. Appleton?"

A desire to avoid an unpleasant confrontation with the countess struggled with greed and the loss of a valuable manservant. Greed won. "My cousin's right, countess. Sam is undoubtedly back at Black Oaks by now. Otherwise, I'd be only too happy to oblige you."

Aunt Clare, who had been gazing speculatively at her niece, now said quietly, "Perhaps Mrs. Von Bruck would care to search the house for her missing servants."

"That won't be necessary, Mrs. Appleton," Cole said, embarrassed. "Your word is—"

"I certainly shall search the house," Arabella interrupted, stalking indignantly from the parlor. Cousin Harry's house, though spacious, had few rooms and even fewer places where a runaway slave could be hidden. Within a half hour, Arabella returned to the parlor, her face frustrated, her lavender eyes glittering. "You haven't heard the last of this, I can assure you, Miss Appleton. I intend to speak to the provost marshal."

Cole, who had noticed how strained and pale-looking Clare Appleton's face had become, gripped Arabella's arm. His voice was low but firm. "I believe you've caused the Appletons enough inconvenience for one evening, Arabella. I'll take you home now." He made a hasty bow to Mrs. Appleton and then to Lucinda. His eyes lingered, amused, on the flaring scarlet crinoline skirt. "My apologies to both of you, and I hope you recover soon from your ... accident, Lucy."

Then he and Arabella were being ushered out the front door. When the door swung shut behind them,

Harry turned at once upon Lucinda. In his pale-yellow eyes, pinpoints of anger burned. "What is this all about?" he demanded. "Where is Sam?"

Lucy shrugged. "I sent him away from Richmond, just as I said. Or would you rather Mrs. Von Bruck had reclaimed her lost property?"

"You mean, you've known all along that Sam was the legal property of the countess?" Harry asked, shocked. "Do you realize the impossible position you put me into with—"

His mother stepped between Harry and Lucy. "You're tired, Harry, dear," she said softly. "Why don't you return to bed? I'll take care of straightening this matter out with Lucy."

Although ordinarily the most meek and amenable of women, there were times when Harry knew better than to cross his mother. And by the stubborn set of Clare Appleton's soft mouth, the touch of iron beneath the slurred, Virginia drawl, he recognized that this was one of those times.

Still grumbling to himself, Harry left the room. Sighing, Mrs. Appleton sank down into a chair across from Lucy. Once Harry was out of earshot, she said quietly, "Very well, Lucinda. Where are you hiding the girl?"

Lucy hesitated. Then with a swift movement, she stood up abruptly, lifting one corner of her crinoline skirt. Jane remained crouching for one second beneath the hoopskirt, then, straightening, came out of hiding and made a swift, frightened curtsy to Clare Appleton.

"You won't send her back to Mrs. Von Bruck, will you, Aunt Clare?" Lucy pleaded. "Just look at Jane's face. The countess had that done to her, and there are whip marks on her back."

Mrs. Appleton stifled a quick gasp of dismay when she saw the pale-brown face with the ugly brand mark splayed across the cheek.

"Sam and Jane are married, Aunt Clare," Lucy continued. "Sam's on his way now to the Von Bruck plantation to—"

"Don't tell me any more." Aunt Clare rose abruptly, casting a nervous glance toward the hall. "That way I won't have to lie to Harry." Walking over to Jane, she touched the girl's shoulder gently. "You have a fine husband, child. Sam's a good man. I wish you both a safe journey." She looked over at Lucinda. "If there's anything I can do . . ."

Lucy shook her head. "No, Aunt Clare. Everything's taken care of."

Clare Appleton gazed at her niece, her face troubled. "Be very careful of Mrs. Von Bruck, Lucy. I'm afraid she's not a very nice person. I can't imagine what Cole Sinclair sees in a woman like that"

Cole was wondering much the same thing himself, as he slumped irritably in a corner of the Von Bruck carriage. Seeing Clare Appleton again had brought back memories of his mother and Gray Meadows, a life of graciousness and dignity that he thought he had forced out of his mind forever. In addition, it was the first time he had been around Arabella when she was indulging in one of her temper tantrums. Her childish display of bad manners had only served to convince him all the more that starting up a relationship again with Bella had been a drastic mistake. As for that little minx Lucy . . . amusement pulled at the corners of Cole's mouth. It was lucky for her that Arabella had been too blinded with her rage to notice the tip of a third shoe sticking out from beneath Lucy's flounced skirt. Still, Cole thought regretfully, it would have been a stroke of delicious irony if that self-righteous prig Harry had been caught hiding an escaped slave in his own home.

Then the carriage turned a corner sharply, bringing his mind back to the present. He sat up quickly, casting a startled glance out the window. "We're going in the wrong direction, Bella. This isn't the way to your house."

"We're not going to my house. I told the coachman to drive us to Maywood."

273

"Maywood!" Cole said, annoyed. "That's a four-hour ride in the daylight. And I hardly think it likely that your maid is heading back to your plantation."

"Not Jane," Arabella said, fury still quivering in her voice. "Troy. Once he's sure Jane is safe, he'll try to reach Maywood and steal their two brats. If we hurry, we can get there before him."

"You didn't tell me that your maid and this . . . Sam or Troy, or whatever his name is, had offspring. Are they married?"

Arabella shrugged impatiently. "Don't be foolish, Cole. You know slaves can't marry. Unfortunately, my husband pampered both Troy and Jane outrageously, treating them almost like members of the family. You can't imagine the trouble I had with the two of them after he died."

"If they were so much trouble, why are you so anxious to get them back?" Cole asked curiously.

"Because Troy and Jane, they belong to me," Arabella said hotly. But Cole heard something else beneath her voice when she spoke Troy's name, an echo of the same ululating cry of passion with which Arabella had called out his name at the end of their coupling in her great lilac satin bed, her nails, like claws, ripping into his back as she clung insatiably to him, refusing to let him go.

Thoroughly irritated with himself and the whole impossible situation in which he found himself, Cole said icily, "You can go where you want, Bella. But leave me out of your vendetta."

She made a shocked mouth. "Surely you wouldn't let a woman drive alone through the night, Cole? And I don't have my pass with me. I'll need your help to get through the pickets between here and Maywood." She reached over and stroked his leg, her voice a coaxing, feline purr. "Please, darling, you can't desert me now."

All at once, Cole found himself remembering the face of Bella's maid, Jane, the few times he had glimpsed the girl at the Von Bruck home in Washington. A lovely pale-brown face with frightened hazel eyes, not much older than Sukey. If he went along with Arabella, he thought slowly, there might be a way he could help the girl and her lover. Perhaps, in some small measure, it would help make up for Sukey.

He leaned back in the carriage, his voice a bored drawl. "Oh, very well, Bella. But for God's sake, tell your coachman to slow down. This jouncing around is making my leg hurt like hell."

Dawn was just lighting the sky, an opalescent, misty glow drifting through the trees, when the Von Bruck victoria turned up the road that led to the Von Bruck plantation. Despite the earliness of the hour, it was evident the house was already astir. Glancing through the carriage window, Cole could see a bustle of activities in the slave quarters, a drab street lined with crude, ill-kept cabins, half shielded by lime trees from the big house.

When Arabella and Cole left the carriage, Cole limping stiffly, trying to ignore the rivulets of pain that ran down his calf, a short, grizzled, white-haired man came hurrying from the quarters to the carriage.

A startled look flashed across the overseer's wrinkled Gaelic face when he saw Arabella. "So it's yourself, countess, and how would you be knowing what happened, to come so quickly?" he asked, astonished.

"Jane's brats," she ordered, climbing quickly from the carriage. "Put a close watch on them. Troy is somewhere near."

"Sure and it's too late," the man blurted. "They're gone, and the big buck, too. I sent out a search party, but there's little hope they'll catch them. I only just discovered myself they were gone when I heard the terrible screams from Caesar's cabin, enough to curdle the blood."

"Caesar? What of Caesar?" Arabella asked sharply. She began to walk rapidly toward a small, more prosperous-appearing cabin set off to one end of the row of slave huts.

Her overseer rushed to overtake her. "Don't go in

275

there, countess," he pleaded, his voice panicky. "There's nothing you can do for the poor sod."

But Arabella was already at the doorway of the hut, and shoving open the door, she stepped across the threshold. Then she stopped so suddenly that Cole, close behind her, almost ran into her. The pale sunlight trickling into the dark hut fell upon a bundle of rags and blood on the floor. At first, Cole was sure the man was dead. God knows, he thought dispassionately, with all the knife slashes Troy had inflicted on the writhing body, the man should have been dead. Except Caesar wasn't dead, only wild with pain, spittle mixed with blood running from his mouth, his eyes crazed with agony while obscene gurgling noises came from a mouth that was little more than raw pulp.

Cole had seen men mangled and mutilated on the battlefield, blown to pieces before his eyes, but nothing to compare with the ripped and shattered remains of Caesar's body. Then he heard Arabella give a strangled cry, and he saw, as she had, the final revenge that Troy had taken with his knife upon the man who had been his wife's torturer. Using his knife as skillfully as a surgeon's scalpel, Troy had made very sure that Caesar would never be a whole man again.

17

The neighbors of Miss Elizabeth Van Lew were accustomed to keeping a close eye on the Van Lew mansion. Whispers of the strange goings-on in the gracious home, of secret passageways and hidden rooms, of escaped Yankee prisoners spirited in and out of the house at night, were rife up and down Church Hill Street. One bizarre story even told how Miss Elizabeth, to protect her last remaining horse from being confiscated by Confederate soldiers, had actually stabled the animal in the Van Lew library until the danger was past.

Miss Van Lew's more conservative neighbors discounted such stories, although, heaven knew, poor, eccentric Miss Lizzie was conspicuous enough with her odd behavior. Nevertheless, curtains twitched busily in nearby windows one morning late in June when a woman dressed all in black walked slowly up the front walk to the pillared veranda of the Van Lew home. Even from a distance, though, the woman appeared middle-aged and dumpy and eminently respectable, and disappointed curtains fell, after a moment, back into place.

Miss Elizabeth herself answered the door to her visitor. She took a second, sharp look before she recognized Lucinda Appleton behind the heavy makeup and padded black bombazine gown.

"I told you not to come here," she snapped, annoyed. Stepping back, she allowed Lucy into the front entryway, which was as large as most rooms. Rugs, if there had been any, had been taken up for the summer, and the hardwood floor was polished to the sheen of ice. From the hallway Lucy could see into neighboring rooms, where massive crystal chandeliers hung from rococo ceilings and walls were covered with brocaded silk.

"I have to talk to you," Lucy said desperately. "Please."

Reluctantly Miss Van Lew led the way into a back parlor with a vista across a row of terraces. A lovely little gazebo sat at the edge of the garden, overlooking the James River. She waited till Lucy sat down, then Miss Elizabeth perched rigidly on the edge of a straight-back chair.

"Was there some information you had to pass along that couldn't wait?" she asked hopefully.

"No." Lucy paused, then said, "That is, I do have some information, something my cousin let drop at dinner last night. There will be thirty thousand men with General Jubal Early when he starts up the Shenandoah Valley, which should be any day now. And Washington is their destination."

Miss Van Lew snorted inelegantly. "I already know that. I sent word to General Grant's headquarters last week."

"But how could you?" Lucy asked. "I mean, find out so quickly?"

Miss Elizabeth gave her an oblique glance, opened her mouth, then shut it again quickly. When she did speak, her voice was evasive. "You're not the only source of information I have in Richmond, you know." She jerked to her feet and with her nervous, angular stride walked to the window, then turned unhappily to face Lucinda. "Old Jubal is hoping his march on the capital will throw the country into a tizzy and President Lincoln will lose the election." Elizabeth's mouth narrowed bitterly. "Grant should have taken the valley long before now. He would have, too, if that old fool Sigel hadn't been stopped halfway down the valley at New Market, licked by a bunch of schoolboys. And that idiot General Hunter was no better, letting his supply lines be cut so his men dropped, starving, in the passes of West Virginia. Now the valley's wide open. With Grant's men tied down in the trenches at Petersburg, there's nothing to stand between Early and Washington."

Lucinda, caught up in her own private misery, hardly heard Miss Van Lew's furious tirade against the incompetence of the Union generals who had lost Grant the valuable Shenandoah Valley. Then she realized, belatedly, that her hostess had changed subjects and was staring at her, annoyed. "Well?" Miss Elizabeth demanded queruously. "After all the trouble I went to, aren't you even interested in hearing that your girl Jane reached the Federal lines safely?"

"Of course, I am," Lucy said hastily. "What of Sam and the children?"

"They're with Jane, of course." Miss Elizabeth nodded smugly. "Everything went smoothly as clockwork, if I must say so myself. Your Jane turned out to be quite a little actress. She shuffled past the guards posted outside Richmond, carrying her basket of vegetables on her head, looking so much like my Meg from the farm that she almost fooled me."

Miss Van Lew laughed, with a childlike titter of triumph at the memory. Lucinda, however, did not join in the laughter. Her face was fixed and pale beneath the makeup; her dark eyes shadowed with pain.

Miss Van Lew sighed and sat down across from the girl. "You might as well tell me, Miss Appleton. If it wasn't to bring me information about Jubal, then why did you come?"

"It's Matthew," Lucy blurted, her voice thin with misery. "I've just come from the prison hospital."

Miss Elizabeth's sharp glance softened as she gazed at the unhappy girl across from her. "Your brother's no better?"

"He's worse. If you could see him..." Her voice broke, and she had to struggle to regain her composure. "It isn't only that he doesn't recognize me. He's not eating, not even the soup I bring him. I have to coax him to take a few drops of water. He just lies there, staring into space. Already the patients on both side of him have died of typhoid fever. I'm so afraid that if I don't get him out of Libby..."

Tears streamed down the girl's face, streaking the

279

powdery makeup. "Dr. Madison says Matthew can't possibly last much longer." She lifted her tear-stained eyes to Miss Elizabeth, her voice imploring. "You've got to help me get Matt out of there."

"I wish I could help, child," Miss Elizabeth said sympathetically. "But I'm watched all the time. I can't even go on an errand without detectives following me on the street. And when I'm in Libby, I'm never allowed out of sight of the guards."

"He'll die! Don't you understand? My brother will die!" Lucy's voice rose, shrill with hysteria. "When I visited Matthew in the prison, there were holes between the slats in the floor by his bed. I could look through the boards and see the corpses of dead prisoners, stacked like so much cordwood in the 'dead house.' That's what they call the basement under the prison. The bodies just lie there until they're hauled away, no one knows where. I won't have that happen to Matthew," she said fiercely. "If he has to die, I want him to die decently at Black Oaks."

Miss Elizabeth had been listening intently. Now suddenly she leaned forward, bright-blue eyes glowing as they fastened upon Lucy's face. "You say that Dr. Madison has been treating your brother at the hospital?"

Lucy nodded, puzzled. "Yes. Do you know him?"

Miss Van Lew answered absently, "Before the war, he was the Van Lew family doctor. He's a good man."

"But he can't help Matthew. He says the Confederacy hasn't enough medicine to treat their own wounded."

Lucinda saw the excitement gathering in the plain spinsterish face across from her and asked eagerly, "What is it? Can you help Matthew?"

"I have an idea. I'm not promising anything, mind you," Miss Van Lew said quickly, warningly, at the look of happiness flooding Lucy's face. Then she smiled thoughtfully. "It will take all the acting ability you have, but it might just work...."

*　*　*

Earlier that same morning, Cole had left a meeting at the provost marshal's office and was riding past Libby Prison when he saw the gray-haired woman in widow's weeds leave the prison. It was unusual, Cole knew, for a woman to be allowed to visit the Union prisoners of war. No doubt she had bribed the guards to gain entrance. Cole shrugged indifferently. It was no longer any business of his. General Winder had spent the better part of an hour trying, in vain, to persuade Cole to join his command in Richmond. Cole, however, had received the promise of a cavalry command from General Early, and he had no desire to return to the shadowy, thankless world of the secret service agent. Nevertheless, he noticed automatically that the woman who had walked with the bent shoulders and slow, careful gait of the elderly as she walked away from the prison swung into her small trap with a surprisingly youthful agility and displayed for a moment a pair of very trim ankles.

His curiosity piqued, Cole followed the trap from a distance, watched the roan mare with the white stockings climb Church Hill Street and stop before the Van Lew mansion. There was, he thought, something vaguely familiar about the mare. Then the woman dismounted from her buggy with ease and again walked with painful stiffness up the front steps of the veranda, waiting a moment before she was ushered into the house. Cole dismounted, too, and settled down to wait out of sight of the house.

Naturally, he had heard of Miss Elizabeth Van Lew, her eccentric behavior and Union sympathies. He recalled sharing a bottle of claret with General Winder one evening and the general openly scoffing at stories of Miss Van Lew's spying activities. "The woman's a harmless lunatic," he assured Cole. "We've had her followed constantly, and we've searched the Van Lew home several times and found nothing. In my opinion," he assured Cole pompously, "no woman has the temperament or intelligence to be a successful spy."

Remembering Sukey, Cole decided grimly that if he were General Winder he'd arrest Miss Van Lew immediately, toss her in prison and throw away the key. Thinking of Sukey, though, brought a familiar stab of pain. His face gone oddly blank, Cole deliberately forced himself to push the memory from his mind. He had to accept the fact that Sukey was gone, he thought wearily. He couldn't forever live the life of a celibate because of one tawny-gold beauty who had somehow managed to get under his skin in a way that no other woman ever had.

There were plenty of women in Richmond, beautiful, charming creatures who had made it very plain that they would be willing to share Cole's bed, with or without a wedding ring attached. Not to mention Arabella, who besieged Cole constantly with invitations, and was half furious, half bewildered at his indifference to all her blandishments.

Yesterday evening at the lavish ball she had given to raise money for Richmond hospitals, when Cole had begged off from remaining after the party ended, she had demanded angrily, "It's Lucy Appleton, isn't it? That black-eyed little bitch has her claws in you, hasn't she?"

Her spiteful glance had sped across the room to where Lucy stood in a deceptively simple white-sprigged muslin gown, making her look all of sixteen with its sweetheart neckline and lacy puffed sleeves. Except, there was nothing youthful about the ripe curve of breast or the flirtatious invitation behind the demure smile. As usual Lucy was surrounded by a score of gallants, bestowing her smile apparently indiscriminately on the young or old, fit and maimed.

"I can't imagine that my relationship, if any, with Miss Appleton is any concern of yours, Bella," Cole said curtly, even more annoyed because he suspected that Arabella was right. Ironically, the only woman who had aroused Cole's interest these last weeks was Lucy

Appleton. And ever since their last encounter, it was obvious that Lucy went out of her way to avoid Cole. As if I had the plague, he thought wryly, not sure whether it was his vanity that was pricked by Lucy's indifference or his curiosity.

No, not indifference, Cole thought now, frowning. It hadn't been indifference he had glimpsed in Lucy's eyes the few times his glance had caught and held hers across a room. The emotion he had seen there had been closer to fear. And the young Lucy he had known, the headstrong, reckless tomboy who had tagged after him worshipfully, had never been afraid of anyone, certainly not of him.

Frowning, Cole swung back into his saddle, deciding to give up his surveillance of the mysterious widow. For all he knew she had a perfectly logical female reason for visiting the prison and Elizabeth Van Lew, and he was simply wasting his time. Damn women anyway, he thought irritably as he cantered away from the Van Lew house. What man could ever understand them? Even Sukey—what had he really known about her, except for the pleasure they had shared in bed, more profound and exciting than anything he had ever experienced before? A man was a fool to expect anything more than that from a woman, he decided grimly. As for Lucy Appleton, she could keep her seductive body unmolested as far as he was concerned.

He was halfway to Capitol Square when he pulled his horse up short, cursing softly at his own stupidity. For suddenly he remembered why the roan mare pulling the widow's trap had looked so familiar. It was the same roan mare with white stockings that Lucy Appleton had been riding at The Bower.

18

It was only a few minutes past sunrise when Lucinda arrived again at Libby Prison, two days later. The James River was at full tide, and if one looked past the ugly white-walled prison to the picturesque island in the middle of the river, the farmhouses and mills glowing in the early-morning sunlight on the far side of the river, the scene appeared peacefully pastoral. Lucinda, however, in her Aunt Clare's wig, her cheeks puffed out with cotton and her body encased in the uncomfortable padded gown, gave the scene no more than a passing glance.

The guard who let her into the prison accepted with an almost sleight-of-hand motion the coin she slipped into his palm and said dolefully, "The poor lad's better off, ma'am."

Lucy pressed her handkerchief to her face, careful not to smear the makeup applied expertly on her eyelids to give her eyes a raw-rimmed look of someone who had been crying for hours. "How...how did it happen?" she asked, her voice breaking pitifully.

"He must have passed on just before I came on duty, ma'am. It was the doctor who found him. Died peaceful in his sleep, Dr. Madison said."

"May I...see my son?"

The man cleared his throat unhappily. "Regulations say a dead prisoner's got to be removed right away, ma'am, in case whatever he had was catching, you understand. But Dr. Madison had your son placed in a nice pine box and even found a horse and wagon for you. If you follow me, ma'am, I'll show you where he is." Then, tactfully, "I wouldn't wait too long for the burying, though, ma'am."

A low moan escaped from the handkerchief pressed to Lucy's mouth, but she trotted obediently after the trooper as he led her through the blackened corridor of the prison to the rear courtyard. A farm wagon that had obviously seen better days and a spavined, ancient mare, head drooping, stood in the courtyard. On the back of the rough wagon was a six-foot-long pine box.

"Ain't much of a horse," the guard said. "Dr. Madison said to tell you it was all he could find. Ain't no fit horses left in Richmond for sale." Glancing around to make sure there was no one else present, he whispered, "If you like, ma'am, I'll prop open the lid and you can take one last quick look."

"No," the grieving mother said hastily, then, afraid that perhaps she had sounded too uncaring, gave a choked little sob. "You're very kind, but I have a long way to go."

The guard helped her up into the driver's seat, handing her the reins and giving a last word of warning. "If you're heading north, ma'am, watch out for patrols. Sentries are stopping everyone."

"I have a pass from General Winder," the widow said anxiously.

The guard shook his head. "That's only good within a mile of Richmond."

The widow smiled bravely at the sergeant. "I'll manage somehow. Thank you, and good day, sergeant." Afraid the man might delay her with more conversation, she urged the tired old horse forward, not taking a deep free breath until the walls of the prison were a good mile behind her.

As the sergeant had predicted, the wagon was stopped several times by sentries as Lucinda followed the Brook Road north of Richmond. Each time by sniffling discreetly into her handkerchief and gesturing helplessly back toward the pine coffin, she was waved forward with only a quick, embarrassed look at her pass.

Once beyond Yellow Tavern, where Brook Road branched off into Telegraph Road and Mountain Road, Lucy pulled the wagon to a halt. With all the fighting that had taken place lately in this area, she knew that neither road promised to be in good condition. She hoped, though, that Mountain Road, curving east toward Beaver Dam and cut across by numerous streams, would at least be passable. Just beyond the South Anna River, she remembered, the road branched off into little more than a wide footpath, winding through a wooded, seldom-traveled area.

It was past noon when she crossed the South Anna River and turned the creaking wagon onto a narrow side road. The wheels of the wagon bumped over the rock-strewn surface of the road, jolting Lucy unmercifully on the hard wooden driver's seat. Behind her, she could hear the coffin bouncing loudly against the bed of the wagon, while the blazing sun beating down through the overhanging tree branches added to her discomfort and worry. Closed inside the pine box, even with sufficient knotholes provided for air, how much more of this heat and jouncing could Matt endure?

At last, when she had driven far enough down the road to feel safe from passing patrols, she stopped the wagon beside a sparkling clear brook. Climbing quickly into the back of the wagon, she lifted the lid of the coffin.

For a moment, gazing down into young Matt's terribly still, gray face, she had the frightening feeling that her brother *was* dead. Then she felt, relieved, a slight but definite pulse beat in his neck.

"Matt," she couldn't resist saying softly, although she knew he couldn't possibly hear her. Thanks to the arrangements Miss Van Lew had made with Dr. Madison, her brother was deep in a drugged sleep—deep enough, at least, to fool the guards into thinking him dead. Gently she brushed a curly lock of hair, damp with perspiration, back from the young forehead. "It's going to be all right, Matt," she said softly. "Soon we'll be back at Black Oaks, and everything will be all right then."

Remembering the doctor's warning that she mustn't let Matt become dehydrated, she went to the brook and dipped her handkerchief into the water. After several attempts, she managed to squeeze several drops of water into Matt's mouth, watching until she was sure his throat muscles moved convulsively. Then she wiped his lips and face with the damp handkerchief, noticing as she did so how burning hot his skin felt to her touch.

Finally she knelt down by the creek and gratefully swallowed handfuls of the water herself, not even caring that the horse was also drinking greedily from the same brook. She had brought some hard bread and cheese hidden beneath her ample hoop skirt, but she ate only a small portion of it. The food would have to last at least another day, before they reached Black Oaks.

When she had finished her meal, she reluctantly closed the pine lid again and picked up the reins, urging the weary horse forward. She only hoped the horse would last another day, she thought, worried, studying the bony ribs, his slow, uncertain steps, slipping and sliding over the rocky road, as if at any moment he might drop in his tracks. Every hour she stopped and let the horse rest, while he nibbled at what graze he could find and she chafed impatiently. The countryside was more open now and the chance of running across mounted patrols much more likely.

Twice she thought she heard hoofbeats behind her on the road and quickly maneuvered the horse and wagon into the woods, hidden from sight from any passing patrols. But both times as she waited, heart pounding, the road remained empty and she decided her nerves were getting the better of her.

It was sunset when, half asleep, she was jerked to wakefulness by a man's voice from the road ahead of her. "Halt, who goes there?"

She pulled at the reins with fingers grown suddenly numb and adjusted her features to the proper look of grief as a young Confederate picket on horseback pulled out of the trees into the road in front of her.

"Do you have a pass, ma'am?" he asked, gazing curiously at the coffin, then back to the woman driver, swathed in black.

Fumbling in her skirt, Lucinda handed him the pass she had shown the other sentries. He studied the piece of paper for such a long time she began to wonder if he could read, then he said, almost triumphantly, "This pass ain't no good, ma'am. You see, it's only for Richmond." He jerked his thumb back to the coffin. "Who's in the box, ma'am?"

Lucinda began to sob delicately into her handkerchief. "My son, Matthew. I'm taking him home to bury him."

A second, older, gray-haired picket came out of the trees to join the first man. "What's going on, Johnson?" The older man had a lined, suspicious face and a sour look about his mouth.

"Wagon and driver without a pass, sir. The lady says it's her son in the coffin."

"You know the orders, Johnson," the second man snapped. "No wagon passes without being searched."

"Please, sir." The middle-aged matron's voice behind the heavy veil quivered piteously. "Must you?" How long, Lucy wondered, panic-stricken, would the drug last? Was Matt perhaps already stirring in the coffin, eyes open, staring blankly into space?

"Orders, ma'am," the corporal said, and then, sternly, "You shouldn't be wandering around the countryside without a proper pass. You could be arrested." He glanced back at the young trooper who had dismounted. "Look lively, Johnson. Get up on the wagon and take a look in the box."

Lucy's hand crept down the side of her skirt and fastened around the small derringer she had hidden in a pocket of the gown. With eyes that had gone an opaque, ebony black, she measured the distance between her and the corporal. There would be no difficulty in hitting him, she decided coldly, but the second man was another matter. The derringer held only one ball. There wouldn't be time for her to reload.

"Can't you get that blasted wagon out of the road, corporal?"

The question was asked in a lazy, annoyed drawl,

but there was the bite of command behind it. Lucy stiffened, but she forced herself not to turn around, to stare straight ahead.

The corporal snapped a smart salute to the officer on horseback who had come up the road behind them. "I'm sorry for the delay, colonel. But we have orders to search all vehicles coming through this area."

"Search a coffin?" Cole Sinclair lifted an amused eyebrow. "Isn't that taking your orders too literally, corporal?" He rode his horse forward beside the wagon so that he looked down into Lucinda's face. Even through the black veil covering her face, she could feel his penetrating gaze. Although the expression on Cole's face didn't change in the slightest, she was sure he had recognized her.

"Orders is orders, sir," the corporal said stubbornly.

Gallantly Cole swept off his plumed cavalry hat. "My apologies, ma'am, but I'm afraid the corporal is right. The coffin will have to be opened. If you'll allow me." He turned to the young sentry who had climbed up on the tailgate of the wagon. "Unless you prefer to do the honors, private?"

Hastily the young man climbed down from the wagon, an expression of vast relief crossing his face.

Cole returned his gaze politely to the woman. "I have your permission, ma'am?" he asked gravely.

Since there was nothing else Lucy could do, she nodded stiffly. What game was Cole playing now? she wondered, half terrified, half furious. She felt the back of the wagon bounce under Cole's weight as he swung from his horse into the wagon bed, then the creak of the hinges as the pine lid of the coffin was lifted.

Several seconds of silence followed in which Lucy could hear her heart beating so loudly beneath the severe black bombazine bodice that she was sure the corporal, standing next to her, must notice.

At last, Cole spoke in the same amused, lazy drawl. "There's a young man in the coffin all right, corporal. From the look of him, I'd say he died of the smallpox.

Is that right, ma'am?" he asked, his voice politely sympathetic.

Lucy covered her mouth with her handkerchief to stifle a sudden, almost hysterical giggle. Why hadn't she thought of that? Every soldier was terrified of the pox, which it was believed even the dead could spread among the living. When she spoke, though, her voice was grief-stricken. "Yes, colonel, it was the smallpox that killed my son."

Cole glanced deferentially at the corporal. "Would you care to take a look for yourself, corporal?"

An expression of fright on his face, the corporal stepped hastily away from the wagon. "No, sir," and then, frowning at Lucinda, added sharply, "You'd best get your boy underground as soon as possible, ma'am."

Lucy nodded her head meekly and reached for the reins, when to her dismay she saw that Cole had tied his horse to the rear of the wagon and was climbing into the driver's seat beside her.

"If you don't mind, I'll just ride along with you, ma'am," he said cheerfully.

"That isn't necessary," Lucy said coldly. "Please don't bother."

"No bother," he assured her, his blue-green eyes glittering, amused, as he took the reins firmly from her hands. "I wouldn't feel right letting a woman drive alone on these roads at night."

There was nothing Lucinda could do but simmer angrily as Cole reached across her to release the brake, slapping the reins to urge the weary horse forward.

They continued without speaking a quarter of a mile down the road, well out of earshot of the Confederate patrol, before Cole pulled the wagon to a stop. When he turned toward Lucy, his eyes were no longer amused, and his brows slashed angrily across his face. "All right, Lucy, start talking." He jerked his chin back toward the coffin. "Is that the real reason you came to Richmond, why you've acted as nervous as a cat on a hot tin roof every time I came near you, because you

290

were afraid I'd find out you were planning to rescue your lover from Libby Prison?"

She gazed at him, startled. "How ... how did you know?" she stammered. "How could you tell he was a prisoner?"

Cole shrugged. "Prison pallor isn't that difficult to recognize, even on a supposedly dead man. Anyway, I've been following you for several days, ever since I saw you leaving Libby Prison in that fetching widow's ensemble." He smiled mockingly. "Of course, I didn't take a close look into the coffin, but isn't he a little young for you, Lucy? Or do you prefer robbing the cradle for your men?"

"Oh, shut up!" she said, pushing him aside furiously as she climbed into the back of the wagon and flung open the coffin lid. The sun was sinking low enough so that the air felt cooler, and she lifted Matt's head gently in her arms so that the fresh air could reach his face. The boy's eyes were still closed, and when she touched his face, his skin felt alarmingly hot and dry. She had filled a canteen when they last stopped for water, and now she once more tried to force the liquid past Matt's lips.

Watching the girl minister tenderly to the young man she held in her arms, Cole was surprised at the anger he felt. After all, what did it matter to him if Lucy Appleton was not the innocent creature he had thought her, and that she had one or a dozen lovers? Or that she was apparently willing to risk her pretty little neck to rescue this particular one from Libby?

He wasn't even sure if it was anger he felt, he realized wryly. Wasn't it perhaps closer to jealousy, that tightness in his throat as he saw how tenderly Lucy cradled the young ash-blond head against her breast?

Irritably, he thrust that disturbing thought aside and, climbing into the back of the wagon, reached down and pulled Lucy to her feet. "I said I wanted to talk to you," he said harshly. "Or do we start back for Libby right now?"

Her face paled. "You wouldn't!" she gasped.

"Why not? He's an escaped prisoner, isn't he?"

"No." Lucy's hand moved swiftly, and the next second Cole found himself staring, startled, into a small but deadly-looking derringer pointed directly at his middle. For a second, he had a brief, confused feeling of *déjà vu*, and then Lucy said, her voice flat, "You know I can use a gun, Cole. You taught me, remember?"

He nodded ruefully. "I remember." Then, lifting a quizzical eyebrow, he added, "Now what happens? Or do you plan to kill me, Lucy?"

"Not if you do as I say. I want you to get out of this wagon and untie your horse. I'm afraid I'll have to borrow him for a while, Cole. And I want your word of honor as a gentleman that you won't report me for at least twelve hours. After that, you can do what you want."

Cole glanced thoughtfully at the gun, then at Lucy's coldly defiant face, the determined tilt of the chin. "Very well," he said slowly. "You have my word."

He started to turn away, then, so quickly that she only caught the flash of his arm flung out, at the same moment she felt a numbing pain in her arm as the side of Cole's hand slashed viciously against the wrist of the hand holding the gun. The derringer went flying out of her hand to land in the dust in the road.

Clutching her wrist and biting her lips against the throbbing pain, she stared with mute accusing eyes at Cole.

He shrugged grimly. "Sorry, Lucy, but I stopped being a gentleman the first day of the war." He smiled sardonically. "And I have the feeling you stopped being a lady much sooner than that. And now we'll have that talk, before we head back for Richmond."

She said nothing as he swung her out of the wagon. Then he pushed his handkerchief and the canteen of water into her hand. "Get rid of that ridiculous makeup and wig," he ordered irritably. It was disconcerting looking into Lucy's face and having a middle-aged woman stare back at him. "And that stuffing, or whatever you have beneath your gown. You must be stifling."

Obediently she did as he directed, scrubbing the makeup from her face and breathing a silent sigh of relief when she disposed of the padding beneath the gown. When she had finished and turned back to Cole, her creamy skin, smooth forehead and delicately arched brows no longer lined and disfigured by theatrical pencil and powder, Cole nodded approvingly. "That's better." His gaze wandered downward to the roundness of breasts thrust pertly upward by boned stays, the black bombazine gown falling loosely now, outlining the graceful curves of Lucy's slender figure.

Beneath lowered eyelids, Lucy recognized that look in Cole's blue-green gaze as it roamed with insufferable arrogance over her body, and she felt a faint stirring of hope. There might still be a chance. She took a half-step toward Cole, lifting her lovely face pleadingly to his. "Must we go back to Richmond, Cole?" Her voice was pitched low, huskily seductive, her dark eyes burning with a feverish brightness.

Just for an instant a black cloud of anger descended over Cole's face. Then it was gone, and he smiled lazily down at her. "Just what did you have in mind, Lucy?" His hands reached out and ran lightly over the softness of her breasts, then descended to rest on either side of her tiny waist. "Aren't you being a little melodramatic?" he drawled, amused. "Or do you really value yourself so highly that you think any man would jump at the chance for a roll in the hay with you?"

Her face flamed, her eyes no longer softly promising but filled with a hard, cold fury. Damn him, anyway! she thought furiously. He was laughing at her, making fun of her. She tried to twist away, but his hands had fastened like clamps around her waist, tightening slowly, taking her breath away.

There was no amusement in his eyes now, only a puzzled anger as he studied her face, then glanced back at the wagon. "Does he mean so much to you, then?"

he asked bitterly. "He doesn't look old enough to shave, much less take a woman to bed. What is the name of this paragon among men?"

"It's Matthew," she said quietly. "Matthew Michael Appleton."

Cole's hands loosened on her waist, like too-tight stays falling away, so she was able to take a deep, relieved breath.

"Matt? Young Matt?" Cole asked incredulously. "It can't be. He was just a child the last time I saw him at Black Oaks."

He returned to the wagon and studied the boy's face. Lucy saw that the drug had finally worn off. Matt's eyes were open. He turned his head slowly to stare blankly at Lucy.

"What's the matter with the boy?" Cole asked. "He acts as if he doesn't even know you."

"He doesn't," Lucy said, a helpless anguish filling her voice. "He's been that way ever since he was hurt. He doesn't remember anything. And he won't speak or eat or drink, unless he's coaxed like a baby. He was dying in Libby Prison. I have to get him back to Black Oaks, where I can nurse him and give him proper care. I lost Father and Charles. I won't lose Matt, too!"

Cole shook his head as if he couldn't believe what he was hearing. "You really thought you could get Matt back to Black Oaks in that broken-down horse and wagon? Early's troops have already taken over much of the area between here and Cold Brook. You'd never make it through their lines."

"I will make it," Lucy cried desperately. All the terrors she had lived with for the last weeks, the clandestine visits to the prison, the constant fear that she might be discovered, along with the tension of the last hours, had tightened her nerves to the breaking point. "No one is going to stop me. No one! I'm taking Matt back to Black Oaks. I'm taking him home!"

Without even consciously aware that it was Cole, she beat wildly at his chest with her fists, her eyes blinded by tears, her voice shrill with hysteria and nervous exhaustion.

She felt Cole's arms close around her again, but this time, he held her gently, his hands patting the luxuriant black curls that had tumbled out from beneath the gray, confining wig. "All right, Lucy, honey. It's all right," he said soothingly. "Don't cry. We'll get Matt home, somehow."

She nestled closer to his chest with a sigh. For the first time, in what seemed months, she felt warm and safe, the way she had in Cole's cabin at the camp, wrapped in his arms, the world far removed, as if nothing or no one could ever hurt her.

"I am curious," he asked, finally holding her away from him and gazing down at her, a quizzical amusement in his eyes. "How did you manage to convince your Aunt Clare and Cousin Harry to allow you to go on this wild escapade?"

"They don't know." She gestured toward the wagon. "I mean about Matt. I didn't dare tell them. I trust Aunt Clare, but not Harry."

Cole unharnessed the forlorn old horse, replacing him in the shafts with his own cavalry mount. "Won't they wonder where you've gone?"

"I picked a terrible argument on purpose with Cousin Harry last night. I called him all sorts of names and told him I wouldn't marry him if he were the last man on earth." The thought of the sweet satisfaction of telling Harry exactly what she thought of him brought an impish smile to Lucy's tired face. "Then this morning I left Aunt Clare a note, telling her I was going back to Black Oaks for a while, to think things over. Cousin Harry was probably glad to be rid of me." She climbed into the wagon, casting an anxious glance into Matt's face. His eyes were once again shut, his face an odd, mottled red.

Cole had climbed up on the driver's seat. Turning, he stared frowning at the young man in the pine box, his voice suddenly sharpening. "Sit up by me, Lucy."

She shook her head absently. "I'd better stay here with Matt."

Reaching back, Cole took her arm roughly. "I want you up here with me," he said.

She stared bewildered into his face, the muscles pulled taut. "What is it, Cole?" she asked, alarmed.

He dropped her arm, groaning softly. "For God's sake, Lucy, take a good look at Matt. It's typhoid fever. Can't you tell? I've seen enough of it to recognize the symptoms. I'll look after the boy. I don't want you infected."

"No," she said. Then before Cole could protest further, she said quietly, "Don't be foolish, Cole. If Matt has the fever, I've already been exposed to it by now. You haven't."

Still scowling, furious at her obstinacy, yet knowing she was right, Cole undid his blanket roll from his horse and tossed the blanket back to Lucy. "He'll be having chills soon. Keep him covered with this."

The rest of the night as the wagon bounced and jolted over the rutted road, Lucy forced herself to stay awake, every hour trying to coax water between Matt's dry, cracked lips. But by morning waves of weariness overtook her and she slipped into an exhausted sleep, curled up in the back of the wagon next to the pine box.

Several hours later she jerked awake. The sun, already high in the sky, beat painfully against her leaden eyelids. For a moment she couldn't remember where she was, and she stared around blankly. Then she saw the pine box and memory flooded back.

"Matt."

She clutched at the side of the wagon, bracing herself against the bumps as the wagon slipped between gullies. She grimaced as she moved, feeling as if every inch of her body were black and blue. Sometime during the night, she realized, they must have left the road, were striking across country. She recognized the Moreland house in the distance, deserted now, as so many of the big homes in the county were. If they were on Moreland land, though, that meant they weren't more

296

than a few miles from Black Oaks, she thought hopefully, looking down into her brother's dreadfully still face.

She reached for the canteen, then realized it was empty. "I gave him the last of the water an hour ago," Cole said. He was in shirtsleeves, and she saw it was his jacket he must have put under her head as a pillow when she fell asleep.

"You should have wakened me," she protested. "Matt might have needed me."

"You needed sleep more," Cole said, and then, without looking back at her, added, "I've been thinking, Lucy. This is crazy your taking Matt back to Black Oaks. Let me take you into Cold Brook. I have friends there. They won't turn Matt in, and they'll help you after—"

"After Matt dies," she finished coldly. "Isn't that what you mean?"

He shrugged helplessly. "You have to face the possibility, Lucy. And I can't leave you alone at Black Oaks with the county filled with stragglers and deserters from both armies."

"I won't be alone. Aunt Bessie and Uncle Joe are at Black Oaks." Her voice quivered, but her eyes were darkly defiant, staring at Cole's back. "And I'm not afraid of stragglers."

Cole groaned to himself. Heaven save him from stubborn women, he thought. If he'd had any sense he wouldn't have asked Lucy. He would have driven her into Cold Brook while she slept and left her there with his friends. There wasn't a snowball's chance in hell that the boy would pull through. He'd seen that deathlike pallor on mens' faces too often before.

He glanced back over his shoulder. Lucy was crouched beside her brother, holding her bonnet over his face to shield him from the sun. Even with her face drawn with worry and weariness, her black hair tangled loosely over her shoulders, there was still a beauty about her that stirred his senses, made him want to stop the wagon and take her in his arms, rip off that ugly black dress from her soft white body and lie beside her in the deep grass and cool shade of the trees.

Angrily, he flipped the reins across the back of his horse, urging him forward, his mouth setting grimly. Hadn't he promised himself that he wouldn't fall into that trap again as he had with Sukey? What did he have to offer a girl like Lucy Appleton, anyway? A burned-down plantation, land that would be worthless if the South lost the war. And in spite of the fact that General Early was sweeping forward through the valley, driving the Yankees before him, Cole had no illusions that that meant the tide of battle had turned in favor of the South. It was a delaying action only, like Lee's brave defenders at Petersburg, only holding off for a time the inevitable. Cole reflected coldly that his own chances of surviving the war were slim. He'd had his share of luck, of near misses, but luck could run out. And one thing he wouldn't do was leave a widow behind to mourn him, perhaps with a child to raise on her own. Lucy deserved better than that.

Nevertheless, as they finally drove down the long oak-shaded road, stopping at last before the front portico of Black Oaks, and he lifted Lucy from the wagon, his hands lingered longer than necessary around her waist.

It didn't help either to watch her thick-lashed eyes widen at his touch, see the desire gathering there deep in the darkness, and know that in spite of everything that had passed between them, she wanted him as much as he desired her.

He pulled her closer, his hands stroking the cool, silky flesh beneath the high-necked bombazine, tracing the delicate bones of her spine that he could feel through the stiff cloth, until he felt her trembling response through his finger tips, saw the quick rise and fall of her breasts, the peach-pink color rising in her cheeks.

And then, incredibly, without any warning, he saw the fear flood back into her eyes and felt her body stiffen in his arms, try to pull free. "Cole, no," she whispered.

He stared at her, his own face angry and bewildered. Why should she be afraid of him now? "You surely don't think I'd betray young Matt?" he demanded.

She shook her head helplessly. "It's not that."

"What then?" he demanded. His hand tightened ruthlessly on her chin, turned her face so that she had to look into his accusing, probing eyes. "I've had enough of lies between a man and a woman, Lucy. Let's have the truth between us, if nothing else."

Now, Lucy thought, trying to drive the desperation from her mind. Now she could tell Cole the truth about Sukey, before it was too late. But suppose he couldn't accept the truth? She gazed uncertainly up into those fierce eyes beneath the knotted black brows and realized uneasily how little she really knew about Cole. She was well aware of the streak of ruthlessness, of arrogance, he possessed, as well as the suddenly unaccountable gentleness that could disarm her, but she had no way of knowing if he would forgive her or despise her for tricking him, for breaking her word to him.

As she hesitated, struggling to find the right words and the courage to say them, she heard the front door of Black Oaks open. She looked up, surprised, to see her Aunt Clare standing in the sunshine on the veranda.

Her aunt's childishly round eyes pretended not to notice that Cole Sinclair's arms were holding her niece improperly close. Only her soft voice held the slightest note of disapproval as she said coolly, "Good morning, Colonel Sinclair... Lucinda..."

299

19

As if she were a child again, caught by her aunt in some act of mischief, Lucy felt her face flush guiltily, and she withdrew hastily from Cole's embrace.

"Aunt Clare! How . . . when did you get here?"

"By train, last night. I left Richmond yesterday morning, as soon as I read your note."

"Cousin Harry?" Lucy cast a quick glance behind her aunt as if she expected to see Harry suddenly materialize in the doorway behind her aunt. "Did he come with you?"

"His duties in Richmond made it impossible for him to leave. And I . . . we both agreed that it wouldn't do for you to stay here at Black Oaks alone," she said firmly. Her gaze moved past Lucy to fasten on the wagon, her eyes widening, shocked. "Good heavens, that isn't a coffin, is it?" she gasped.

Then before Lucy could stop her, she walked down the steps toward the wagon.

"Aunt Clare, wait!"

But it was too late. Her aunt had already swung as agilely as a young girl into the back of the wagon.

"It's Matt, Aunt Clare," Lucy said, and then quickly, "He's not dead, but he's very ill. He was in Libby Prison. I couldn't leave him there."

"Of course you couldn't," her aunt said, shocked. She knelt down beside the open pine box and studied her nephew's face happily. "He has your mother's coloring, Lucinda, and her chin." The smile faded as her fingers touched the burning skin. She gave Lucy a swift, questioning glance.

It was Cole who spoke. "It's the typhoid, Mrs. Appleton. I'm almost sure."

She nodded. "Yes." Then, caressing the fine light-brown hair one last time, she rose swiftly to her feet.

"Hurry and carry him inside, Cole," she ordered crisply. "The bedroom on the first floor—it's cooler. Lucy, fetch a bucket of water and some cloths and tell Aunt Bessie to stay away. She'll want to help, but she mustn't come near the room. She might catch the fever."

Cole frowned. "You shouldn't go near the boy either, Mrs. Appleton."

She glanced up impatiently. "For heaven's sake, Cole, what are you still standing there for? Didn't I tell you to hurry? This boy needs to be put to bed." She bustled ahead into the house. "I'll turn down the covers."

Cole shrugged and turned ruefully to Lucy. "Well, at least I don't have to worry about leaving you alone at Black Oaks."

Once he had carried Matt into the back bedroom, Mrs. Appleton ushered him politely but firmly out of the room. She tried to shut Lucy out of the sickroom, too, but Lucy refused to go. "You can't nurse Matt alone, Aunt Clare," she protested. "And I've been visiting Matt in prison for weeks now. If I were going to catch the fever, I would have by now."

Her aunt turned pleadingly to Cole. "Can't you talk some sense into her?"

Cole grinned wickedly at Lucy. "I doubt if anyone's talked any sense into Lucy since the age of three." His grin faded as he glanced uneasily at the two women. "I wish I could stay and help, Mrs. Appleton, but I received orders to join General Early just before I left Richmond. I still think all of you would be better off in Cold Brook."

Clare Appleton said placidly. "You mustn't concern yourself about us, Cole. We'll be quite all right here at Black Oaks. And thank you for helping bring Matt home. Lucy is inclined at times to be impulsive. I'm sure she never could have managed without you." She stood on tiptoe and placed a kiss on Cole's cheek before disappearing again into the sickroom.

Well, really, Lucy thought, annoyed. Aunt Clare didn't have to make her sound quite so feckless. After all, she had been doing very well before Cole came along.

She walked with Cole to the front door, where he stopped to pick up his slouch cavalry hat from the hall table, then turned to Lucy, his eyes holding a glint of amusement. "Doesn't the departing warrior get a farewell kiss, Lucy?"

"Of course, Cole," she said demurely, and reaching up, she dropped a light kiss on his brow.

Before she could move away, his arms tightened around her, pulling her hard against him so that the buttons on his tunic dug into her breast. "Not that sort of kiss, Lucy," he murmured. "One that will last much longer than that."

Then his mouth covered hers, at first brushing the soft lips teasingly until he felt her breath quicken and her own mouth moved searchingly, became as demanding as his own. Her soft white arms lifted to encircle him, pull him still closer, until the pounding of Cole's heart mingled with her own. Finally, shaken, her body burning as if consumed with Matt's fever, Lucy felt her body arch backward as Cole's lips traced a path down the silken skin and lingered in the warm hollow in her throat.

When at last, reluctantly, he started to pull away, she would not let him go, her arms clinging to him, her voice frantic. "Promise me, Cole. Promise me you'll come back."

She saw the hurt leap into his eyes, narrowing them as if against a glaring light. "I can't, Lucy," he said harshly. "I made that promise once to someone else. I couldn't keep it." Gently he put her away from him. "It's a mistake, making promises you can't keep."

She had forgotten, she thought. Weren't those the same words she had said to Cole when he left Sukey at his cabin that morning? "Did you love her, Cole?" she blurted, unable to stop herself. She had to know. "Did you love that other girl you made the promise to?"

His face was suddenly closed to her, all warmth

302

drained from his eyes as he turned away. "What does it matter now? She's dead."

She watched him walk out the door and unharness his horse from the wagon. Dead? She stared after Cole, bewildered. Why should he think Sukey was dead?

Then Cole was mounting his horse, a little awkwardly because of his bad leg. Turning, he took one last look at the house. As if a string had been cut, releasing her, she ran out onto the veranda. Suddenly she found she was filled with fury at Cole, at the war, at this terrible deception that was pulling them apart. "You come back to me, Cole Sinclair," she shouted fiercely. "You come back to me or I'll never forgive you for as long as I live!"

Cole threw back his head and laughed. "I'll try, Lucy. I'll try like hell!"

Then he was galloping down the road, the gravel flying beneath the horse's hooves. Lucy picked up her skirt and ran across the unkempt front lawn of Black Oaks to a rise where she could watch him ride away, watched until the very last minute, until his horse disappeared into the trees and she could see him no more.

For the next two weeks, Lucy and her aunt took turns nursing Matt, soaking cloths in cold water and gently sponging the boy's emaciated body, forcing water and gruel down his throat while their patient somehow miraculously clung to his fragile hold on life. As the days passed, though, it became painfully obvious that Matt was not the only gravely ill person at Black Oaks. Clare Appleton was growing noticeably thinner, her gowns hanging loosely on her once-plump body. Dark shadows were etched on the fine skin beneath the soft blue eyes, and she had so little strength in her matchstick-thin arms that she was of little use to Lucy when Matt went into convulsions and had to be physically held in bed.

Lucy was sure she never could have managed, but

then, unexpectedly, one steamy hot August evening, Sam returned to Black Oaks. Lucy had stepped out of the bedroom onto the front veranda for a moment, in an attempt to cool off, and suddenly there Sam was, standing at the foot of the steps, as if he had materialized out of the shadowy, purple dusk.

"Evening, Miss Lucy," he said softly, his dark eyes impassive as always, as he gazed up at her. "Hot night, ain't it?"

"Sam!" She ran down the steps, reached out almost hesitantly to touch the homespun shirt he wore, as if she couldn't really believe he was standing there. "What are you doing here?" Then, frightened, "Jane? Is Jane all right?"

"Jane's fine. That friend of yours, Mr. Jephthah, at General Sharpe's headquarters, he's taking good care of her and the children."

"How did you know I was here?" she asked, bewildered.

"Miss Van Lew sent word to Mr. Jephthah that you were coming back to Black Oaks with your brother, after you got him out of prison. Mr. Jephthah figured you might need some help, tending your brother."

"But you shouldn't have come back," Lucy protested. "You were safe in the Union lines."

"I owe you a debt," Sam said with simple dignity. "I ain't forgetting what you did for Jane and me." He glanced toward the bedroom window, the only room in the house that was lit. "I talked to your cook. She says your brother has the typhoid. I had the fever when I was a boy." He glanced back toward Lucy, his voice all at once wary. "Maybe, though, you ain't wantin' me to stay." She was reminded of that morning in front of the slave cabin where Harry had imprisoned Sam. His eyes held the same prickly pride then as they did now, waiting for her answer.

Lucy almost laughed with relief, except she was afraid if she did, she would burst into tears instead. Want him to stay! She had never been so glad to see anyone in her life.

"Of course I want you to stay," she said happily. "Come into the house, Sam. Aunt Bessie will fix you some supper."

After that, tending Matt became much easier. Sam took his turn nursing, his strong arms easily restraining the boy when convulsions seized him, yet gently sponging the fever-emaciated body as if Matt were a baby. Lucy was even able to talk her aunt into snatching some much-needed sleep.

Despite the lightening of the nursing load with Sam's return, there was still another worry plaguing Lucy. The first morning she had arrived at Black Oaks, she had gone back to the kitchen to ask Aunt Bessie to prepare breakfast for Matt and herself. "Eggs, I think, Aunt Bessie," she said. "And maybe we can get Matt to swallow some milk."

The old black woman stared blankly up at Lucy, then her lined face crumpled helplessly. "Uncle Joe and me, we ain't had eggs in months, chile, nor milk either. And not a bite of meat, not even chicken."

"What about the cow, the chickens?" Lucy demanded.

The old woman rocked back and forth, her voice quivering, childlike with despair. "They took 'em all, chile, all the chickens, the last piece of ham we had hid, and the cow. They found her, too."

"The Yankees?" Lucy asked, her stomach squeezing painfully, thinking of the breakfast she would not be getting.

"Not the Yankees, Gen'ral Mosby's soldiers. That's who they said they was. They was mighty polite, but they took everything, even the candles, our last bit of salt and my best skillets." Aunt Bessie's voice rose indignantly at this last transgression.

"What have you been eating?" Lucy asked.

"Uncle Joe goes fishing when he ain't feelin' poorly, and there's the root cellar behind the quarters the soldiers didn't find. We got dried apples, corn and turnips, sweet potatoes and field peas."

"Fix whatever you can, then," Lucy said, thinking
305

that if the Yankees didn't strip the valley clean, it looked as if Mosby's men would.

By late summer even the supplies hoarded from the slaves' root cellar were running dangerously low. Meals at Black Oaks consisted mainly of fried corn pone, yams and tea made from sassafras leaves, sweetened with sorghum. Eating a breakfast of fried yams one August morning, Lucy couldn't help thinking wistfully of other breakfasts she had known at Black Oaks, biscuits swimming in butter and honey, thick pink slices of fried ham, fresh strawberries in clotted cream, as many eggs as she could eat and real coffee, rich and aromatic.

Despite the breakfast's lack of appeal, she ate hungrily, then fixed a tray to take to her Aunt Clare in Matt's bedroom. When she came into the room, Aunt Clare, seated beside Matt's bed, turned to smile happily at her niece. "I think the worst is over, dear. His fever's gone, and he's breathing much better."

"You should have stayed in bed, Aunt Clare," Lucy said, worried, noticing how her aunt barely nibbled at the food on her tray. "Sam and I can take turns nursing Matt."

"It's the heat, dear," her aunt said absently. "I couldn't sleep." She studied her nephew's face anxiously, then turned to look at Lucy, her voice soft. "There's more to Matt's illness than the fever, isn't there, my dear?" When Lucy, numb with misery, could not speak, her aunt continued quietly, "Matt opened his eyes after the fever broke. He stared right through me. I thought at first it was the fever. It affects people that way sometimes. Only..." She shook her head sadly. "It was more than not recognizing me. It was as if Matt didn't even see me. Then I remembered that young boy they brought to the hospital after the Wilderness. The doctors couldn't find anything wrong with him, yet he never spoke, remember? He simply sat and stared, not eating or drinking, until finally he just..." Clare's voice broke, and she dabbed at her eyes with the edge of her sleeve.

Lucy clutched furiously at her aunt's hand. The

bones felt as fragile as if they were made of the finest, thinnest china. "Matt's not going to die, Aunt Clare! I won't let him."

Her aunt smiled faintly through her tears at her niece. "Of course not, dear. Your Grandfather Jacob always said that all the Appletons had constitutions like oxen. I'm sure Matt will get better, in time."

As the long, hot summer drew to a close, the days growing shorter, the air crisper, Matt did seem to grow better, at least in body. He was able to leave his bed, walk by himself, even feed himself. His young body began to fill out again, his skin taking on a healthy tanned glow. Only his eyes remained the same, like looking into the empty windows of a long-deserted house. He never spoke or smiled or cried. When Aunt Clare and Lucy spoke to him, he simply stared blankly through them, as if he didn't even hear their voices.

Ironically, it was Sam who was the only one able to stir any response at all from the boy. Not that Matt spoke to Sam, but like a small child, he tagged everywhere after the huge black man. He sulked childishly when Sam disappeared on one of his occasional foraging expeditions, leaving Matt behind. Always Sam returned from these trips with a chicken, a butt of ham, a dozen eggs or a pail of milk. Tactfully Lucy did not question the source of this largess, nor did she question Sam when one day he returned with a horse. A scrawny animal to be sure, long in the tooth, but a horse nevertheless.

Lucy was now able to take short trips away from Black Oaks herself. She rode through a countryside where the trees were as brightly colored as if a paisley shawl had been flung across them, and the blueness hovering over the mountains in the distance merged with the blue of the cloudless October sky.

She began to visit neighbors near Black Oaks, many of whom had returned to their homes now that the war news drifting slowly back into the valley was so encouraging. Lee's lines at Petersburg were holding firm, and General Jubal Early and his small army had cut a triumphant swath through the Shenandoah Valley. On July 5 he had crossed the Potomac and by the 11th was marching on Washington. With only convalescent soldiers, police and clerks to defend the city, Early defeated the ragtag army in one swift bloody battle. But within sight of the Capitol dome, General Early hesitated, and in that hesitation, lost the Confederacy's last chance to take Washington. Reinforcements arrived to defend the city, and Early began a strategic retreat. When he reached the town of Chambersburg, Pennsylvania, and the city fathers were unable to raise the $500,000 ransom the Confederate general demanded, the city was put to the torch.

"Jubal Early has frightened the Yankees out of their wits," old Mr. Colton chortled gleefully when Lucy stopped by their home one afternoon to pick up the latest war news. She hadn't received any word from Cole, and she pounced eagerly on any news of Early's movements.

"Were there . . . did General Early suffer many casualties?"

Mr. Colton, who had fought Indians in his youth and despite his age had somehow managed to get into the first battle of Manassas, brushed aside talk of casualties. "Bound to be some losses, but Early taught the Yankees they can't come into our valley, burning and looting, without fear of reprisal."

Listening, Lucy couldn't help wondering uneasily if General Early hadn't done more harm to the cause than good. Chambersburg had held no military significance. Burning the defenseless town to the ground, she suspected, would only incense the North further against the South. But guiltily, selfishly, she knew she no longer cared who won the war. All she wanted was for the war to be over and Cole to come home. For all she knew he could be lying wounded or a prisoner, in some dreaded Northern prison.

Mrs. Colton, looking up from her knitting, gave her young guest a sharp glance and said quickly, to change the subject from the war, "And how's your dear aunt?

She didn't look at all well the last time I saw her," she said, worried.

"She's not eating," Lucy said unhappily. "And I know she's in pain. I can hear her walking the floor of her bedroom at night."

"What she needs is a good tonic," the old woman said. "I'll give you some to take home with you. It'll perk her up. I expect she's missing Harry, too."

Lucy kept discreetly silent. Undoubtedly Aunt Clare did miss her son, but Lucy doubted if Harry spent much time thinking about his mother. From the few letters that had arrived at Black Oaks from friends in Richmond, Harry was apparently being seen more and more often in the company of the Countess Von Bruck. Although Lucy knew that her aunt wasn't happy at the news of her son's friendship, as far as Lucy was concerned, she couldn't have been more pleased. At least the countess was keeping Harry away from Black Oaks.

Riding back to Black Oaks from the Coltons, Lucy couldn't help thinking a little spitefully that Cousin Harry and the countess deserved each other. And it would certainly be a relief to her if Harry did take a wife, and stop pressuring Lucy with his proposals of marriage. Lucy frowned thoughtfully as she allowed Pegasus, the name she had given the horse Sam had brought home, to choose his own slow gait through the wooded path. The truth was she had always been mystified by Cousin Harry's insistence that they be married. She suspected that at the bottom, Harry cared for her as little as she did for him. Then she shrugged away further thought of her cousin. The idea of her marrying anyone but Cole was preposterous anyway.

She was thinking blissfully of Cole, her dark eyes soft and dreaming, when a man on horseback suddenly pulled out of the brush into the path before her. He was wearing a slouch hat, blue pants and a butternut jacket, which meant he could be either Yankee or rebel, or more dangerous, a deserter who would think he had found an easy prey in a woman riding alone.

Lucy sawed at the reins, attempting to turn Pegasus around and make a race back for the Coltons. Then, as her hands tightened on the reins, it occurred to her that there was something familiar about the rangy figure in the worn uniform.

Slipping from her saddle, she ran eagerly toward the man, hands outstretched. "Jephthah! How good to see you."

The scout dismounted and stood on the path, a boyish grin of pleasure splitting his long, bony face at sight of Lucy. "I was just passing by, ma'am, and thought I'd drop by to see how you were managing."

Lucy slid her arm through his, laughing up at him. "Isn't it amazing how you always seem to be just passing by, Jephthah? But this time I promise you the white rose won't be talked into returning to work for you."

He glanced down at her, smiling sheepishly. "I reckon you know me pretty well, ma'am. No, that's not why I stopped by."

They sat down on a log by the side of the path, their sudden presence disturbing a squirrel, who, chattering indignantly at the intrusion, dashed off into the woods.

"Must you call me ma'am?" Lucy asked. "Surely we know each other well enough by now for you to call me Lucy."

"Yes, ma'am," he said gravely, and then, hastily, "I mean, Lucy."

A flush rose beneath his fair skin as he looked at her, and just for a moment, she saw something slip into the gunmetal eyes watching her, a longing so intense that Lucy felt her breath catch in her throat. But she had never guessed, she thought, shocked. How could she have been so blind not have seen sooner how Jephthah felt about her?

All at once, embarrassed, she looked away. "You know it's strange, Jephthah. All we've gone through together and I don't even know your last name, much less anything about you."

"It's Green, ma'am, and there's not much to know. I grew up in Kentucky, did some trapping and hunting

310

for the railroad, then joined the 1st Cavalry as a scout in the Kansas Territory."

"You never married?"

"I had a wife. She and the baby she was carrying were killed in an Indian raid back in Kentucky."

His voice did not alter, but Lucy could hear the grief beneath the quietly spoken words. "I'm sorry," she said sympathetically. "Will you be returning to Kentucky after the war?"

Jephthah reached down and plucked a blade of grass, chewing at it thoughtfully. "Reckon not. I've been thinking of moving west, Texas, maybe. They say there's enough land there for a man to stretch out, build a life for himself without being hamstrung by the past. What about you, Lucy?" he asked suddenly. "Will you be leaving the valley after the war?"

"Leave the valley?" Lucy echoed, startled. The thought tightened her heart. Until she had returned to Black Oaks, she hadn't realized how much she had missed the valley, or how deep her roots went into the blue-tinted hills and lush, fertile fields. Of course, now that the plantation belonged to Cousin Harry, she couldn't stay on indefinitely. But there was still Gray Meadows, she thought. She and Cole could rebuild the house after the war, replant the barren fields, make a life together the way she had always dreamed of their doing as a child, ever since that long-ago day she had first fallen in love with Cole.

Jephthah watched the girl's mouth soften at the corners, a glow touching the lovely, oval face, and knew at once it was Cole Sinclair she was thinking about. Jephthah stared glumly at the grass at his feet. He'd been a fool to think that she might have forgotten Cole Sinclair, or that he'd ever have the chance to put that look of happiness into her eyes, feel her mouth, soft and trembling, beneath his.

He jerked to his feet and walked away from the girl. When he faced her again, his gray eyes were flint-hard, giving no hint of his thoughts. "I want you to leave the valley, not after the war, but now, as soon as possible," he said sharply.

Lucy stared at him, bewildered. "Why? I don't understand. Why should I leave?"

"Because in a few months, this valley will be a wasteland," Jephthah said. "There won't be a stalk of corn or field of grain that won't be burned to the ground. After General Sheridan and his Army of the Shenandoah finish with this valley, a crow flying across it will have to carry its own rations."

Lucy felt a chill of fear, like icewater trickling down her spine, even as she said lightly, "Other Union generals have tried to take the valley. They were all defeated. It'll be the same with General Sheridan."

"Not this time," Jephthah said flatly. "Not after what Early did to Chambersburg. The whole North is up in arms. President Lincoln himself ordered Grant to destroy the valley and follow Early to the death."

He didn't add the rest, the instructions General Grant had given Philip Sheridan in Washington—"It must be a pilgrimage of terror. We must ravage the Shenandoah from end to end." And Sheridan's quiet but terrible promise, in reply—"I will leave them nothing but their eyes to weep with."

"It won't be a war just against soldiers," Jephthah warned. "Civilians will be shown no quarter. Houses, barns, cribs, gristmills, anything that can help support the rebel troops will be put to the torch."

Lucy got slowly to her feet. "I can't leave, Jephthah. There's Matt."

"I thought by now . . . he's no better?"

Lucy shook her head. "And it's not only Matt. There's Aunt Clare. She hasn't been well. I don't think she could stand the trip to Richmond." At Jephthah's worried frown, she smiled affectionately up at the secret service agent. "Don't worry, Jephthah. We'll be safe enough. Black Oaks is far enough off the main road so that even if Sheridan's men do come into the valley, they'll never find us."

"Oh, Sheridan will come, all right," Jephthah said

gloomily, mounting his horse and staring almost angrily down at the girl standing in the road. "General Lee knows it, too. He's pulled Longstreet off the lines at Petersburg, sent him to support Early. Lee doesn't dare lose the valley or the war's lost. You keep your eyes open, and keep this handy."

He pulled a Smith & Wesson revolver from his haversack, along with caps and cartridge boxes, and thrust them into Lucy's hands. Then, before she could thank him, he lifted his hand in a farewell salute and spurred his horse down the path.

Lucy returned to her own horse and began to ride back toward Black Oaks. It wasn't possible, she thought, gazing around her at the peaceful woodland scene, the yellowing leaves turning to gold in the late-afternoon sunlight, the only sound that of a nut dropping from a careless squirrel, and a yellow-shafted woodpecker hammering against a hollow tree. When she broke out of the woods, there were the fields of sunburned grass, and in the distance the red brick walls of Black Oaks. The whole valley seemed to be sleeping. It was impossible to believe that anything could disturb such tranquility.

Yet, she had the sudden unpleasant feeling that a chill wind had risen at her back, and leaning forward in the saddle, she coaxed Pegasus to a faltering gallop, all at once anxious to reach the safety of Black Oaks.

20

Fall lingered in the valley that year. The days passed, crystal-clear and crisp, the air with a tang to it so that when Lucinda took a deep breath, it was like biting into a tart apple. At Black Oaks, life continued quietly, much as it always had. News trickling slowly back into the valley told of General Sheridan's arrival to take over command of the Army of the Shenandoah. He seemed, however, in no hurry to confront Early's battle-hardened veterans. Lucy began to wonder if Jephthah had been borrowing trouble; that Sheridan would prove no more successful against Early's troops in the valley than the other Union generals who had preceded him.

Nevertheless, she prudently removed the flat silver from the chest in the dining room and placed it in stone jars. After tying waxed cloths over the mouths of the jars, she buried them under the floor of the henhouse. Her mother's precious china she packed away in boxes and hid the boxes under the landing of the staircase leading to the attic. The embossed silver candelabra and the gold-handled sword her great-grandfather had worn at the surrender at Yorktown in the Revolutionary War she wrapped in an old buggy robe and stored deep in a hollow tree.

Since her aunt seldom left her bed these days, Lucy hoped she wouldn't notice the missing items. Then one afternoon she found Aunt Clare in her nightgown and robe in the dining room, staring, puzzled, around her.

"I put the silver and china away, Aunt Clare," Lucy said quickly. "They were only catching dust and making work for Aunt Bessie."

Her aunt nodded vaguely, running her hand caressingly over the satiny surface of the mahogany dining-room table. "As you wish, dear," she murmured. Then, glancing around the room, she said wistfully, "We had such lovely times here, the family all gathered around the table, your uncle and your father, your grandfather, all you children, such happy times."

Lucy slipped an arm around her aunt's waist. "We'll have good times again, Aunt Clare. The war can't last forever."

Her aunt's shoulders slumped wearily. "No. No, even when this dreadful war is over, nothing will be the same. It'll be a different world." She looked up at Lucy, her face suddenly childishly frightened. "I'll be lost in that world, Lucy. I won't belong."

"You're tired, Aunt Clare," Lucy said reassuringly. "Let me help you back to bed and I'll make you some nice hot sassafras tea."

But if her aunt didn't guess why more and more of the Appleton valuables were mysteriously disappearing from the house, Sam did. He had been gone for several days on one of his foraging trips, without which the larder at Black Oaks would have been very lean. This time he returned with two smoked hams slung over the saddle of his horse.

He found Lucy back in the deserted slave cabins. She had torn up the rotten planks of one of the floors and was preparing to hide a set of almost new harness which had somehow managed to miss the eyes of Mosby's men.

"You'd best put some of this meat in that box instead," Sam said gruffly, his huge body filling the doorway, blotting out the sunlight. "You can't eat harness, and the Yankees ain't leavin' any food behind, nor much else for that matter."

"Is it Sheridan?" Lucy asked, getting quickly to her feet. Wiping her hands on her skirt, she followed Sam out into the sunlight. "Has there been a battle?"

"A big one." Sam nodded soberly. "At Opequon Creek. Sheridan licked Early's troops, chased them clear through Winchester. Then they finished the job at Cedar Creek." A grudging respect crept into the black man's stolid face. "They say Early's men put up a good fight, had Sheridan's men on the run, when
315

Sheridan himself turned his men around, and threw them back into the fight."

It wasn't possible, Lucy thought, dismayed. Old Jubal defeated! Then, glancing into Sam's face, his eyes not quite meeting hers, she asked quietly, "There's more, isn't there?"

"The whole valley's been put to the torch," Sam said slowly. "Houses, fields, barns, anything that can burn. I seen the sky so black with smoke, it's like day turned into night. And what the Yankees can't burn or destroy, they carry off with them." His dark eyes rested gravely on Lucy. "You'd be better off in Richmond. Won't be long before the Yankees reach here. They're already at Staunton."

"No!" Lucy heard the fear in her voice and stiffened her spine. As terrified as she was of Sheridan's men, the thought of leaving Black Oaks deserted, open to the desecration of any passing band of soldiers, terrified her even more. Anyway, how could she leave? she thought in despair. Aunt Clare was hardly strong enough to get out of bed, much less stand the trip to Richmond. And what of young Matt? Just that morning she thought for a moment she had caught a flicker of awareness in his eyes, *something* stirring within the boy, coming fitfully back to life. She couldn't take the chance of Matt's being recaptured in Richmond, thrown back into Libby Prison to sink once more into that deathlike stupor. "Maybe," she said hopefully, "the Yankees won't come as far as Black Oaks."

"Maybe," Sam said, but his voice was dubious.

Lucy started to turn away, then stopped. "I don't suppose . . ." Her throat felt dry. "I don't suppose you heard anything of Colonel Sinclair?"

She glimpsed for a second a flash of sympathy in the depths of the sable-black eyes watching her. Then Sam shook his head. "No, ma'am, but men like the colonel, they don't die easy."

Yes, Lucy thought, clinging eagerly to the thought. She had to believe that. How else could she go on otherwise? She forced her voice to calmness, made her face as carefully impassive as Sam's. "We'll hide as much food as we can, and first thing tomorrow I'll ride over to warn the Coltons. They may not have heard the news."

The next morning, though, as she rode through the woods and out into the open fields that sloped gently down to the Coltons' place, she smelled, before she saw, the columns of black smoke staining the lovely azure sky. Mr. Colton had managed to plant behind the house several acres in corn, and flames raced across the dry stalks, while a thick black oily smoke hung over the smoldering ruins of house and barn and stable. Lucy could see no sign of soldiers, except for the lawn around the house, which had been cut up by dozens of horses' hooves. She urged her own horse forward, hoping that the elderly Coltons had heard the news of Sheridan's victories and left their home before the Yankee soldiers arrived.

Then, as she approached the house, she heard an odd, keening cry which lifted the hairs on her arms. Sliding off her horse and hooking the reins over her arm, she walked slowly around to the back of the charred remains of what had once been the Colton home. Mrs. Colton sat on the grass under a gnarled apple tree, her husband's bloody head pillowed in her aproned lap.

The woman fell silent at Lucy's approach, staring dazed at the girl. Her wrinkled skin was coated with soot. Her neat gray hair, slipped from its bun, hung in wisps around her grief-stricken face. Lucinda glanced down at Mr. Colton, then quickly averted her eyes from the thick wiry gray hair soaked with blood. There was no doubt the old man was dead.

Reaching down, she touched Mrs. Colton's shoulder gently. "Are you hurt? Can you tell me what happened?"

"They came early this morning," the woman said dully. "Just before daybreak, Mr. Colton saw the Yankee soldiers coming down the road. He got that old musket of his, the one he used fighting the Indians back in '46. Then he went out on the veranda, shouting at the soldiers to get off his land. The old fool, trying to scare off a passel of Yankees with a gun that wouldn't even shoot. I ran out on the porch and tried to stop him, but it all happened so quick. Three of the soldiers lifted and fired their rifles, like it was a turkey shoot, with no more expression on their faces than that, and Mr. Colton, he fell dead at my feet. Then their officer ordered them to burn the barn and the fields and the house. They were going to leave Mr. Colton lying there, on the veranda, but I dragged him away from the fire." She looked almost accusingly up at Lucy. "I couldn't let him burn, now could I?"

"Of course not." Lucy knelt down beside the woman, feeling pity like a rock in her throat. "Only you can't stay here. I'll fetch Sam. After . . . after the burying, you'll come back to Black Oaks with Aunt Clare and me."

But after Sam had dug the grave and Mr. Colton had been buried just a few feet from the back stoop of his home, Mrs. Colton refused to return to Black Oaks with Lucy. "You've got enough on your hands," she told Lucy with a stiff dignity that defied any attempts at sympathy. "You don't need another mouth to feed. I've got kinfolk at Orange Church. If you'll lend me your horse and wagon, I'll see that you get them back."

Lucy did not tell her aunt about the Coltons. After what had happened, though, she and Sam began to take turns watching the road leading to Black Oaks. It was while she was half dozing seated at the second-floor hall window one late November afternoon that she saw a glimpse of blue through the alley of oak trees winding up to Black Oaks. Then she saw them cantering two abreast, about twenty troopers, the sunlight glinting off their stirrups and their gleaming rifle muzzles. At first, all Lucy felt was a cold, hard knot of fear in the pit of her stomach, then, surprisingly, almost a sense of relief as if the unknown fear was worse than the danger that was actually at hand.

When she found Sam at the stable, she discovered

he had already seen the Yankee troop. He was gathering food into a sack and had young Matt already mounted on Pegasus. Sam and Lucy had agreed that at the first sign of the approach of Union troops, he would take young Matt and the horse and as much food as he could carry to a cave deep in the woods behind Black Oaks.

He hesitated now, scowling unhappily at Lucy. "It don't seem right, my running off, leaving you this way."

"Don't be foolish," Lucy said impatiently. "What could you do against a troop of armed men? They'd kill you the same way they did Mr. Colton. And how could I prove that Matt was in the Union Army? They'd think he was a Confederate deserter and kill him, too, or take him prisoner. He'll be safer with you."

"At least keep the revolver," Sam said, glowering, unmoving.

She handed him the reins of Pegasus. "The Yankees will just steal it. For heaven's sake, hurry! They'll be here any minute. You needn't worry about Aunt Clare and me. Even Yankee soldiers won't hurt two unarmed women. As soon as they've gone, I'll ring the old slave bell behind the quarters and you can come back."

Reluctantly, Sam swung into the saddle behind Matt while Lucy hurried into the house. She didn't have to tell Aunt Bessie and old Uncle Joe what was happening. They had quickly and prudently disappeared. Upstairs she found Aunt Clare in her nightgown, coming out of her bedroom, her wig settled askew on her head.

"What is it, Lucy?" she asked, clinging weakly to the door knob. "I heard horses."

"It's just some soldiers, probably lost their way," Lucy said lightly. "You go back to bed, Aunt Clare. I'll take care of them."

Clare Appleton gave her niece a measuring glance, then said, "It's the Yankees, isn't it?"

Lucy saw the panic gathering in her aunt's drawn face, but before she could reassure her further, Aunt Clare disappeared into the bedroom and returned immediately with a string of matched pearls and a gold necklace set with rosettes of diamonds and emeralds dangling from her hand. "Your uncle gave these to me on our wedding day, but they should by rights be yours, Lucy. They belonged to your grandmother. I had hoped to give them to you when you and Harry, married, but..." She thrust the jewelry into Lucy's hands. "Hide them somewhere where the Yankees won't find them," she said urgently.

Lucy could hear the sound of horses on the front lawn of Black Oaks, the jangle of bridle, heavy footsteps mounting the veranda steps. She pushed the jewelry into her skirt pocket. "Don't worry. I'll hide them, Aunt Clare. Only stay in your room. Promise me."

Her aunt nodded weakly. "Matt?"

"Sam is taking care of him. He'll be all right."

The pounding at the front door made the window on the second-floor landing clatter as Lucy ran down the steps. In the hallway, she paused, feeling the weight of the jewelry in her skirt pocket. She didn't suppose the Yankees would search her, but still, how could she be sure? Her glance darted around the hall, seeking a hiding place for the jewelry. Then, acting on impulse, she stepped into her grandfather's study. She remembered once years ago, when she had been playing near the fireplace in that study, her grandfather had shown her how the brass balls that ornamented the tops of the andirons lifted off. She pulled off one of the balls now and quickly pushed the pearls and gold necklace down inside the hollow andiron. As she did so, she felt an obstruction, like a wad of paper. There was barely space left for the jewelry.

The knocking at the front door was louder now. There was no more time to find another hiding place. She shoved the jewelry downward as far as she could, then replaced the brass ball quickly. As she returned to the hall, she passed the tall pier glass in the entrance hall and caught a glimpse of her face, a pale frightened oval between the dark sweep of her hair. Deliberately she stopped and pinched her cheeks to bring a rosy color into them, then tugged at the oval neckline of her faded pink muslin dress to show more of her creamy smooth shoulders.

The Yankees were men, after all, she thought grimly. It wouldn't help for her to greet them looking like a scared rabbit.

When she pulled open the heavy oak front door, it was to confront a lieutenant with two troopers standing behind him. Other soldiers were already fanning out through the yard, heading toward the barn and the stable.

Both the troopers were bearded, one short and burly, the other slender and swarthy-looking, but the lieutenant was beardless and blond, and looked only a few years older than Matt. At sight of Lucinda, a startled look crossed his face and he hastily removed his hat with an awkward flourish. "Good afternoon, ma'am. My apologies for disturbing you, but I have orders to search this house and grounds and seize any contraband that's found on the premises."

Lucy batted her eyelashes, smiling helplessly up at the young lieutenant. "I don't understand," she murmured. "We have no contraband. There's just my aunt and myself in the house, and my aunt isn't well."

Unwillingness to offend the beautiful young creature who stood before him warred with duty in the lieutenant's face. Behind him one of the troopers growled, "This is the house that fed and sheltered Mosby's cutthroats, lieutenant."

"Do you think we had a choice?" Lucy asked, giving the man a scornful glance. "You don't suppose Mosby's men asked our permission any more than you're doing."

The lieutenant shuffled his feet, embarrassed. "I'm sorry, but I am acting under orders. This is as disagreeable to me as it is to you, but if you'll give the corporal here your keys, he'll finish the job that much more quickly."

Over the officer's shoulder, Lucy could see a thin spiral of smoke rising skyward from the vicinity of the stable.

"Is that part of your orders, too, lieutenant?" she asked, icily.

The lieutenant's face burned a deep red at the disdain in the lustrous black eyes staring at him. "Sorry, ma'am," he mumbled. "But all farm buildings that can give sustenance to the enemy are considered contraband and must be destroyed." He turned to the corporal. "I'll keep an eye on the men. You finish what you have to do here, and be quick about it."

"Yes, sir. Right away, sir," the corporal said loudly, but Lucy caught the undertone of contempt in the trooper's voice, even as he saluted the lieutenant smartly.

Silently, she handed over the keys to the corporal, who, followed by the second man, moved with a skill born of practice through the first floor of the house, tossing anything that looked the least bit valuable into a burlap sack. Precious candles, the last ones at Black Oaks, disappeared into the bag, along with all the food left in the larder that Lucy hadn't had time to hide. Rummaging through chests, closets and trunks, what the two men didn't take, they threw to the floor or smashed to pieces beneath their boot heels. The brocade chair and sofa covers were cut to pieces by their sabers in their search for hidden valuables, cotton batting flying like a snowstorm around the men as they attacked the fragile pieces of furniture.

In the front parlor, the corporal looked regretfully at the rosewood spinet Lucy's mother had brought with her from New Orleans. "Too bad we can't take that with us," he grumbled.

The second man gave the sergeant a wink, and reaching into the sack, he pulled out a jug of sorghum they had taken from the kitchen. Grinning, he poured the molasses over the piano keys. "Reckon they won't be playing 'Dixie' on that piano for a while," he chortled happily.

Lucy bit her tongue to keep back the cry of outrage that rose in her throat. "Are you finished now?" she asked coldly.

322

"We ain't searched the upstairs yet," the corporal said.

"There's nothing upstairs but bedrooms. There's no contraband there!"

"We got to check just the same," the second man said, and there was an unpleasant leer behind the bearded smile that made Lucy wish that she hadn't bothered to make herself more attractive. Still, the lieutenant had seemed a gentleman. Reluctantly, she led the way up the stairs, very conscious of the eyes of the two men following her, watching every movement of her slender hips beneath her hoopless skirt.

In the upper hall, the men stopped in front of the family portraits. "You 'spose those frames are real gold?" the dark trooper asked, awestruck.

"Sure as hell one way to find out," the corporal commented. As if it were made of papier-mâché, he lifted the portrait of Lucy's grandmother from the wall and flung it to the floor. Then, taking his saber, he slashed the portrait until it fell in shreds from the smashed frame. "Just gold-painted wood," he said, disgusted. Then, almost indifferently, he slashed the other portraits to ribbons while Lucy watched, white-faced, her hands bunching into helpless fists at her side. She wished now she had kept the revolver, except common sense told her that shots would have only brought the other soldiers and swift retribution to Black Oaks.

With a supreme effort she was able to keep the anger from her face when the sergeant at last turned to her, to see her reaction to his pointless vandalism. She returned his glance, her face carefully expressionless. At least, she thought coldly, she wouldn't give him that satisfaction.

In her bedroom, the two men pulled her dresses from the wardrobe. The few lace and silk ball gowns she had left they added to their collection in the sack, while her simple cotton housedresses the corporal simply ripped apart and tossed aside.

"A pretty lady like you looks better without a dress anyway," the young, swarthy-faced trooper said, running his eyes appreciatively over Lucy's slim figure, lingering on the swell of the young breasts beneath the tightly buttoned bodice.

The corporal frowned at his companion. "We ain't got time for that, Tom," he said sharply.

The black-bearded man ran the tip of his tongue over his moist, full lower lip, his eyes glistening, as he stared insolently at Lucy. "Hell, it don't take me no time," he bragged. "I ain't an old man like you. And she's contraband, ain't she?"

Then at the steely look in the corporal's eyes, he shrugged, resigned, and followed the corporal and Lucy out of the bedroom. At Aunt Clare's door, the corporal stopped and asked, "What's in here, lady?"

Lucy stopped short, fear pulling her voice thin. "That's my aunt's bedroom. She's sick. Please don't disturb her."

The corporal glared at her distrustfully. Without a word he put his shoulder to the door and with one powerful thrust broke it open.

Aunt Clare sat bolt upright in her bed, her voice soft and confused as she glanced, frightened, at Lucy. "Who are these men, Lucy?"

Lucy hurried forward. "It's all right, Aunt Clare," she said hastily. "They're searching the house."

"We'll just take that quilt, ma'am." The corporal jerked the coverlet from the bed, tumbling Clare Appleton unceremoniously to the floor. "Come in handy this winter. Look under that mattress, Tom. Ladies like to hide their valuables there."

The trooper stepped forward, but Lucy was there before him. All the fury she had managed to keep pent up inside her as she had watched the two men pillage and ravage her home suddenly exploded into a violent rage. How dare they lay a finger on Aunt Clare? She sprang at the younger man, her fingers outstretched, clawing at his face, feeling a gloating satisfaction as her nails dug into the fleshy cheeks, at the scream of pain that came from the man's startled lips.

For a few seconds the element of surprise was with

er, and the younger man retreated before her tigerlike fury, her flailing arms and kicking legs. Then she felt a hand dig into her shoulder, pulling her away so roughly that the soft muslin sleeve ripped, while a second hand reached around her and fastened over her mouth.

"You hold her, Jim," the other man cried, his voice shrill with anger as he gingerly touched his torn, bleeding face. He glared at Lucy. "I'll teach that secesh gal a lesson she won't forget."

Lucy bit down hard on the hand over her mouth. The corporal swore and dropped his hand away. The minute the hand fell away, Lucy remembered screaming, not at the sergeant but at the sight of Aunt Clare, who had somehow scrambled to her feet, her gentle face contorted with rage, watching the soldier manhandling her niece. She was poised, the iron prod from the fireplace brandished over the corporal's head. The corporal whirled around, and without a second glance his thick arm snapped out in a backswing, tossing Clare Appleton as if she were a rag doll across the room. Her head struck the brick edge of the fireplace, and she ended up in a crumpled heap on the floor.

After that, Lucy remembered screaming again, but then there was a gap in her memory. The next thing she remembered was the lieutenant's young, shocked face in the doorway. The rough hands holding her released her, and she was kneeling beside the tiny, still figure on the floor, crying helplessly, "Aunt Clare. Please, Aunt Clare."

Then the two men were gone and there was only the officer left in the room. He lifted her aunt in his arms and carried her gently to the bed. Lucy stumbled to her feet and wet a cloth at the Delft water pitcher on the washstand. When she turned back to the bed, the lieutenant, his boyish face looking stunned, shook his head and stepped away from the bed. "I'm . . . I'm sorry," he stammered, swallowing convulsively. "I'm afraid she's . . . she's gone."

"No!" Lucy pushed the lieutenant aside and knelt

down beside the bed, rubbing frantically at her aunt's hands. She needed only one look, though, into her aunt's still face to know that the lieutenant was right. Aunt Clare would no longer have to be frightened of the world that would await her after the war. Her aunt was dead.

"I'm sorry," the lieutenant said again, gazing unhappily at the grieving girl beside the bed, the small, still figure beneath the coverlet. He'd been in the army only six months. He had prepared himself to see death in battle, but he hadn't expected that the first death he would see would be an elderly lady who reminded him of his grandmother. "You must know... I would never have had this happen... it was... it was an accident."

Lucy tucked the coverlet carefully around her aunt. Then she pulled a chair up to the bed and sat down, not even looking at the officer as she asked stonily, "Was there anything else you wanted from us, lieutenant?"

"You can't stay here," the young man said, dismayed. "I have orders to burn this house."

"I'm not leaving." Lucy gave the lieutenant an indifferent glance. "Your men have already murdered one defenseless woman. Why should it bother you if they kill two?"

"Please, ma'am..." The lieutenant gestured nervously toward the window. "Even if I don't put a torch to the house, a spark from the barn or the stable could set the roof on fire. It's not safe for you to stay here."

He realized that the young woman was no longer listening to him. It was as if her whole being was centered on the woman on the bed, as if she had already forgotten him.

He withdrew reluctantly to the door. "There'll be others coming after me," he warned. "You shouldn't stay here alone." Then, as the girl didn't even turn her head, he gave a shrug of despair and left the room.

Vaguely, Lucy heard the lieutenant's footsteps going down the hall. There were orders being shouted outside the house, and once again the clatter of bridle, the creak of saddles, a few random pistol shots. She heard the downstairs windows shattering. Then quiet once again descended over Black Oaks.

She didn't know how long she sat, dry-eyed, beside her aunt's bed, consumed by a mingled grief and guilt too deep for tears. It was her fault Aunt Clare had left the safety of Richmond and come to Black Oaks. And if it hadn't been for her aunt's valiantly trying to protect her from the soldiers, she might still be alive.

Dusk had crept into the bedroom, purple-black shadows filling the corners of the room, when she heard the door to the room open quietly behind her, heard Sam's voice speaking softly. "Miss Lucy?"

She turned stiffly, saw his glance move to the bed. If Sam felt any grief, it did not show in his face as he joined her beside the bed. Only his hand reached down and very gently pulled the coverlet over Clare Appleton's face, and he stood very still for a moment before turning to Lucy.

"I shouldn't have left you," he said quietly.

Lucy shook her head. "No, it's my fault, Sam." Her face was filled with childish despair. In a rush, as if telling everything that had happened somehow made it easier to bear, she told of the senseless destruction of the two men, culminating in the final, almost indifferent act of violence that had killed her aunt. And suddenly the tears that she hadn't been able to cry ran burning down her cheeks. "If it weren't for me, Aunt Clare would still be safe in Richmond."

"That's foolish talk," Sam said, disapprovingly. He was quiet again for a moment, then spoke slowly, as if choosing each word with care. "Maybe if Mrs. Appleton hadn't died the way she did, that Yankee officer would have burned down the house. Did you think on that? Mrs. Appleton saved Black Oaks. I think she would have wanted it that way."

Lucy took what comfort she could from Sam's words the next afternoon as she stood by young Matt in the Appleton burying ground. The small family cemetery was on the crest of a hill near a grove of blazing maple trees. The leaves drifted slowly downward as the Reverend Mr. Simpson, fetched from Cold Brook that morning by Sam, read from his Bible over the grave of Clare Appleton. Lucy held tightly to Matt's hand during the service, but if he understood anything at all of what was happening, the boy gave no sign. Lucy wondered wearily if the frightening hours hiding in the cave had once again driven Matt deeper into himself.

There had been no time to notify Cousin Harry of Aunt Clare's death but before the minister left, he promised he'd send word to Richmond. "The Yankees cut the telegraph wires, of course," he said, gazing sadly out over the fields around Black Oaks, blackened as if with a plague, his eyes wandering to the charred beams where once a stable and barn had stood. His arthritic fingers tightened on the Bible as he murmured half to himself, "General Early has sown the wind in Pennsylvania, but it's our valley that has reaped the whirlwind."

"Is there any news from Richmond?" Lucy asked absently, her thoughts still back on that small mound of newly turned earth, being gently covered with scarlet and gold leaves.

"With the good Lord's help, our lines are still holding firm at Petersburg," the minister said, brightening a little. "But the latest news from the North is that President Lincoln has won his bid for reelection. That means there'll be no peace party in the White House and the destruction in the valley will continue." He sighed unhappily, turning his gaze back to Lucy. "You can't stay on here by yourself, Miss Appleton. My wife and I will be happy to take you and your brother into our home."

But the Reverend Mr. Simpson was unable to persuade Lucy to leave Black Oaks, any more than Cousin Harry's letter which arrived two weeks later. He expressed his grief at his mother's death and his disappointment that pressing War Office matters kept him from coming immediately to Black Oaks. He ended by insisting that Lucinda return at once to Richmond, "where arrangements can be made for our marriage as soon as the proper mourning period for Mother has passed."

Lucy tossed the letter aside without giving it a second thought. She had little time to wonder these days about Cousin Harry's apparently unending obsession that they should be married. Trying to keep her mind off her worry about not having heard from Cole, and her grief at Aunt Clare's death, she threw herself into repairing as much of the damage as she could from the Yankee soldiers' assult on the house. And what with Aunt Bessie becoming more and more feeble, she also took over the housekeeping and cooking chores. Not that there was a great deal of food to be cooked. The soldiers had depleted almost all the supply of food left at Black Oaks, and with bands of soldiers still roaming the valley, looting and burning, Sam was reluctant to roam too far from Black Oaks in search of food.

The days passed somehow, but it was the nights that Lucy found endless. She was sleeping restlessly, partly because of hunger pangs, and partly from lying awake, worrying, nerves tensed, listening for the sound of Yankee raiders coming down the road again to Black Oaks.

While there was still daylight, she would take a book from her grandfather's study, usually one of Sir Walter Scott's novels, and read to Matt. She had no idea if he heard her or not; his eyes never completely lost their vacant, empty look, but she kept hoping that one day, one night, her words would break through, reach the speechless, frightened boy hidden inside of Matt.

It was one evening after she left Matt's room, a book under one arm, holding a woolen rag stuck into a pan of grease for light, in the other hand, that she heard the scrabbling, furtive sound on the front veranda. She hurried down the stairs to the front hall, then stood quietly, her heart jerking wildly in her chest. At first, she hoped she was imagining things. Her head, cocked, listened toward the door. In her hand she clutched the plate holding the grease. A by now familiar knot of fear was gathering in her stomach. Then she knew she wasn't imagining the sound. Footsteps were moving quietly, stealthily, across the wooden floor of the veranda.

21

Holding the palm of her hand before the small flame, Lucy moved quietly toward the boarded-up front hall window. It was a chill, clear night, and through the cracks between the boards, she could see the outlines of trees, leafless now, twisted, black branches flung up against the sky. As her eyes grew accustomed to the darkness, she could glimpse the shadows of horses and men, oilskin capes flung over their shoulders turning them into shapeless mounds in the saddles.

Then, moving so softly that she hadn't even heard his footsteps, Sam was standing beside her. "Take this," he said, and she felt the cold steel of the revolver in her hand. "I figure there's only four or five of them, probably stragglers or deserters," Sam continued, in the same low voice. "Any of them try to get into the house, use the gun."

"What about you?"

"I've got my knife." For a moment Sam's teeth flashed whitely in the darkness of the hall, his eyes glittering in the smoking grease candlelight. Then he was gone.

Lucy ran her tongue over suddenly dry lips, but the knot of fear in her stomach had become a hard core of anger. She had no idea if the men were Confederates or Yankees, and she no longer cared. All she knew was that Black Oaks had been plundered and looted for the last time. She would put a bullet into the head of the next man who invaded Black Oaks.

This time, the marauders did not bother to knock. She heard the front-door knob being twisted, but she had locked the door securely, as she did every night before retiring. Now the man had left the door and was pulling at the boards nailed over the smashed windows. She could hear him grunting with the effort. She backed away into the front hall, put down the candle, and held the gun braced in both hands, facing the windows.

She could see the candle reflecting itself over and over again in the pier mirror, and stepped farther away so that she was standing in the shadows and the man breaking in would make a well-lit target. She heard the boards give a final piercing scream as the nails pulled free, then a blue-trousered leg was flung over the window sill. Coldly, steadily, she lifted the revolver and cocked the trigger. Then the man's torso and head followed the leg. For a moment, she stood, frozen. Only a split-second reflex action on her part kept her finger from squeezing the trigger.

The flickering light of the candle danced across Cole Sinclair's face. He glanced at the revolver clutched in Lucy's hand, then drawled uneasily, "I'd appreciate your pointing that in some other direction, Lucy."

Almost, the gun dropped from her suddenly nerveless hand. Her voice was weak with dismay. "Oh, my God, Cole, I might have killed you!"

"The thought crossed my mind, too," he admitted. He shook his head, bewildered. "I never dreamed you'd still be at Black Oaks. I thought the house was deserted, that naturally you had gone to Richmond after Sheridan moved into the valley."

A sudden scuffling noise on the front veranda pulled him quickly back to the window. Lucy, all at once remembering Sam, put down the gun and rushed to the window, calling loudly, "It's all right, Sam. They're friends!"

"Yessum." Sam's voice, drifting into the hall from the veranda, sounded a little disappointed, Cole thought. He lifted a quizzical eyebrow. "Sam, your ex-coachman? I thought he headed north along with Bella's maid. What is he doing back here?"

"I'll explain it all to you later," Lucy said, happily flinging her arms around Cole. "It's so good to see you. I've been worried sick, thinking that I'd lost you, too."

Cole's arms wrapped in a bear hug around her that

332

left her delightfully breathless, then he frowned down at her, his voice anxious. "What do you mean, 'too'? Did Matt..."

"No," Lucy broke in hastily. "Not Matt. Aunt Clare." Quickly she told Cole of Aunt Clare's death. She did not have to furnish the details. Cole could guess what had happened. He had come across too many hollow shells of houses in the valley, had seen at first hand the vicious destruction accomplished by General Hunter's men at Sheridan's orders. He had listened to the terror-filled stories told by grief-stricken women and children, left homeless, shivering in their open fields, after a Yankee raiding party had swept through their farm.

"You stayed on here afterwards?" he demanded fiercely. "You and a sick boy with the Yankees stripping the valley like a scourge of locusts. How did you get food?"

"We managed," Lucy said shortly.

Cole lifted the candle so that the light shone down upon Lucinda's face. He remembered how slight her body had felt in his arms. Now he saw the disturbing change in her face. Not that Lucy Appleton wasn't still beautiful, but it was a delicately chiseled beauty now. The softly rounded face had disappeared. The fragile high-arched cheekbones seemed to lie just beneath the surface of the flesh, and there were faint dark shadows beneath the enormous black eyes, like bruises against the pale skin. He had seen hunger too often in his own men's faces not to recognize it when he saw it staring at him from Lucy's features.

A cold rage swept over Cole. He remembered those soldiers in his troop who had received painfully scribbled letters from home, wives writing, worried, to their husbands—"The children are growing thinner and thinner each day.... If you could hear their cries for food.... We have no one to put in a crop.... Unless you come home soon, we must die...."

Looking at Lucy, Cole could sympathize now with their torment, understand why a steady flood of desertions was crippling Lee's tiny army as soldiers melted away in the night, not through cowardice, but only desperate to return home and care for their starving families.

Well, at least no one at Black Oaks would go to bed hungry tonight, he thought savagely and yelled out to his men clustered quietly, waiting on the veranda. "Sullivan, bring your saddle bags around to the kitchen."

While Lucy watched, wide-eyed with anticipation, he removed from the leather bag biscuits and cheese, a jar of strawberry jelly, cold ham and tongue, and finally, triumphantly, a bottle of white wine. "We ran into a couple of Yankee officers earlier this evening on the Cold Brook road. I suspect they were on their way to a midnight supper with some lady friends. They made the mistake of putting up a fight. We sent them on their way, minus their uniforms and horses—and their midnight supper neatly packed in picnic baskets." Cole grinned wickedly. "I only hope their young ladies weren't too disappointed."

It was one of the happiest evenings Black Oaks had ever known, Lucy thought blissfully, several hours later. All had stuffed themselves with the food from the Yankee officers. Afterward, one of the soldiers had brought out a harmonica and played one rollicking tune after another, until even Sam's face held the glimmer of a smile, and she could have sworn that for a few seconds Matt's foot had tapped time to the music.

Then the party had broken up and she and Cole shared the last of the wine by themselves before the fireplace in the small sitting room off the front hall. Replete with food and a drowsy feeling of contentment, she watched the firelight play across Cole's features, softening the hard lines of his lean face, bringing a deep warmth to the blue-green eyes, beneath the slashing black brows.

"You haven't told me yet, Cole," she murmured. "How did you happen to be near Black Oaks this evening? Are you on your way to Petersburg?"

He shook his head, staring soberly into the fire. "No,

not Petersburg. We're on our way to Cold Brook. There's a Union supply train passing near the town tomorrow morning, on its way to supply Grant's troops at Petersburg. I have orders from Richmond to stop the train from reaching the Federal lines."

"With so few men?" Lucy asked, appalled.

Cole grinned wryly. "They were all General Early could spare. And at least the element of surprise is on our side. With Early's forces so scattered, the train won't be expecting an attack."

To her chagrin, Lucy suddenly found herself yawning and covered her mouth, embarrassed. "I'm sorry, Cole. It's not the company. It's the food and wine and not having slept well for so many nights."

He laughed softly and, taking the wineglass from her hand, pulled her to her feet. "You'll sleep well tonight," he promised. One arm slipped around her waist and the other hand carried the candle as they mounted the darkened staircase together. Like an old married couple, Lucy thought, not sure whether it was the wine or happiness that made her feel so heated and delightfully giddy.

Once within the bedroom though, facing Cole, the door shut behind them, the fear she thought she had all but forgotten swept back over her. "Put out the candle, please, Cole," she whispered.

His eyes narrowed, searching her face, his voice quiet. "You're not still afraid of me, Lucy?"

For a fleeting moment she thought of Sukey. But Sukey was dead, she told herself firmly. Cole believed that, and during these last weeks, she had come to believe it, too. What did she have to fear from a dead girl? Looking into Cole's face, she could feel her love, her need for him, welling up inside of her with such force that she felt as if she would suffocate. All other emotions, fear, shyness, uncertainty, swept away, leaving only the aching yearning for his touch.

"No," she said softly. "No, I'm not afraid."

He nodded, satisfied, and extinguished the candle. Even without the small flame, though, the room was not completely dark. The curtains had been drawn, but a pale silvery moonlight filtered like mist through the sheer curtains. Quickly Cole removed his clothes, and when he turned back to Lucy, he drew in his breath with a sharp stab of pleasure. She had slipped out of her gown and shift and stood by the bed, her pale, slender body like a lovely white flame in the moonlight, her black hair tumbling over her shoulders covering her proud, high breasts. Her dark eyes were shining, as if lit by a golden flame from within, as he crossed the room in two strides.

Impatiently he swept aside the silken coils of hair so that his hands could stroke the silken-soft breasts, while his mouth found hers, at first brushing her lips lightly, then her eyelids, tracing a path to the hollow nestled in her throat, finally possessing a pink, velvet-tipped breast, until he heard her give a soft cry of pleasure. Even as he lifted her into the bed, his hands and mouth never stopped their gentle exploration of her body, moving slowly, carefully, so as not to frighten her.

For all Lucy's bravado talk the evening in front of the house on Franklin Street, he was half convinced she was still a virgin, and he was startled, at first, when he felt her body responding swiftly to his embrace. Her ardor rose eagerly to match his, her body moving with a sensuous, provocative grace beneath him while her mouth sought and held his, her tongue darting between his lips, her arms pulling him closer, and still closer, exciting him past endurance. All thought of wooing her slowly, gently, fled. Within a matter of seconds, he had possessed her completely, and in that moment of possession, knew at once he was not the first. But then it no longer mattered.

All that mattered was the waves of pleasure that swept over them both, carrying them swiftly into a maelstrom, an explosion of pure sensation without thought or reason that left them finally spent and exhausted, their arms still twined around each other, but their bodies completely still.

336

When at last Cole rolled away from her, Lucy asked, hesitantly, "Do you mind, darling, very much?"

He did not have to ask what she meant. He scowled into the darkness. Of course he minded. He minded like hell. He wanted to be her first lover. The thought of other men holding her slim, fiery beauty in their arms made him feel as if someone had stuck a knife between his ribs.

Then he propped himself up on his elbow and gazed down into Lucy's face, the moonlight lying like a veil across the blurred beauty of her features. He sensed rather than saw the fear shadowing the dark eyes, the wary stiffness of her body half turned to him, as if waiting for a blow to fall.

"I mind." Reaching down, he traced with his thumbs the lovely arch of her cheekbones, burying his hands finally in the dark mass of her hair on either side of her face. He smiled lazily down at her. "Only maybe it's not the first man that's important, but the last. And make no mistake about it, Lucy, my love," he said, his voice suddenly harsh. "I intend to be the last."

"Of course," she said, smiling drowsily now, as she snuggled closer to him, her head fitting neatly into the hollow beneath his shoulder, her arm flung lightly across his chest.

For a few moments Cole lay quietly, savoring her nearness, the delicious warmth of her soft body curled up so closely to his, as innocent and vulnerable as a child's. His mouth twisted in a wry smile. But not a child, he thought, remembering the excitement of their lovemaking. A woman, a desirable, passionate woman. Tentatively he cupped one soft breast in his hand, caressing the silken flesh gently. Lucy gave a contented sigh, but her eyelids remained shut, and Cole realized, half amused, half frustrated, that she was sound asleep.

He was sure he was too wound up to sleep himself, but like Lucy, he'd had little rest these last weeks and within a matter of minutes he had also slipped into a deep slumber.

It was the sound of the bedroom door opening and

337

shutting that brought him instantly awake. Almost automatically his hand reached for his pistol, which he had placed on the table beside the bed. Then he saw that it was Lucy, a robe thrown around her against the chill.

"Is something wrong?" he asked, half raising himself as she came toward the bed.

She spoke in a whisper. "No, it was just Matt. He has bad dreams sometimes at night and calls out. If I sit with him for a few moments, he goes back to sleep."

Cole saw that she wasn't wearing any slippers and that she was shivering beneath the thin robe she wore. It had been more than a few minutes she had sat beside her brother's bed, he thought, worry for her turning his voice sharp as he lifted the cover beside him and ordered, "Get back into bed before you catch your death."

"Yes, sir," she said meekly. Letting the robe fall to the floor, she slid into the bed beside him. He was shocked at how chill her skin was to his touch, her small hands like ice, as he rubbed them swiftly between his own. Then his hands moved up her arms and down her back, chafing her whole body until the silken skin was glowing, burning like fire beneath his fingers.

Lucy gave a blissful sigh, then giggled teasingly as she squirmed closer to him. "You're much better than a hot-water bottle in bed, Cole."

"Oh, am I?" he growled in mock ferocity, suddenly pulling her body beneath his. She gave a little gasp of pleased surprise as she felt a hardness between her thighs, pressing gently, coaxingly, until he felt her opening to him, petal-soft. This time they made love without their earlier tumultuous haste, giving and taking pleasure, slowly, languorously, deliciously prolonging the sensation that teetered on the fine line between ecstasy and pain, until there was no more giving or taking, only a sharing of the same joy, as they gave themselves completely, losing themselves in each other.

It was dawn when Cole reluctantly left the warmth

of Lucy's arms and began to dress quickly in the gray early-morning light suffusing the room. Lucy sat up in bed, pulling the covers up around her as she watched Cole dress, her eyes bleak. "Must you go, darling?" she asked wistfully. "So soon?"

For a moment something in Lucy's voice, a sweet, almost forgotten echo of another woman's plaintive cry, whirled Cole around, startled. He realized, almost guiltily, that he had forgotten Sukey completely. Not that Sukey's and Lucy's voices for all their disturbing similarity in features, were even remotely the same, he realized. Sukey's voice had held a Negroid slurred softness, while Lucy, for all her Southern upbringing, had picked up a trace of New England beneath her soft, lilting drawl. Then Cole thrust the memory of Sukey from his mind as he saw Lucy swing her legs out of the bed and reach for her robe.

Quickly he returned to her side. With his hands on her shoulders, he pushed her back against the pillow. "I've started a fire in the fireplace. Stay in bed until the room's warm." Reaching down, he kissed her, his mouth hard and bruising until her face grew flushed and pink, and the coverlet fell away and he could see the color running down between her breasts. When he pulled away, her mouth was still lifted, half parted, to his. He smiled teasingly down at her. "That's the way I want to remember you, sweetheart, naked in bed waiting for me, warm and willing, not shivering and freezing on the veranda, watching me ride away."

"Cole, wait!" she cried, a sudden premonition of impending disaster seizing her. She reached out for him, but he had already turned and was walking out the door. Wrapping herself in the covers, she ran out into the hall so that she could stand at the front hall window and watch Cole and his men ride away until a curve in the road hid them from view and she could see them no more.

Even after she dressed and made breakfast, the feeling of foreboding, like an icy hand gripping at her, remained. All day as she went about her tasks, the feeling stayed with her, pulling her nerves taut, so that the slightest sound made her jump. She found herself snapping at Aunt Bessie for no reason, even speaking crossly to young Matt. By evening her anxiety had reached such a pitch that she could not sit still but roamed restlessly through the rooms of Black Oaks.

Finally, unable to endure the suspense any longer, she decided to send Sam into Cold Brook. Perhaps he could pick up some news of the wagon raid. She hurriedly lit the taper of cloth and stuck it into the pan of grease. The December days were short, and the hall was already dark as she started for the back door. Then she stopped as she heard an odd stumbling noise in the front hall. Sam? she thought, puzzled. But Sam never used the front door. And Matt was in the kitchen with Aunt Bessie.

She returned down the passageway to the entry hall, then gave a cry of joy. "Oh, Cole, thank God!" Then, taking a closer, shocked look at his smoke-grimed, bloody face, she gasped.

Cole's uniform was torn and bloodstained, and he swayed drunkenly, bracing himself against the wall, leaving a bloody handprint on the creamy paint. Lucy rushed to his side, slipping an arm around his waist. "Lean on me, darling. Come into the sitting room. There's a fire lit there."

Once in the small room, though, she was startled when Cole pushed her away from him so abruptly that she almost dropped the candle. The grease slipping over the side of the dish spilled on her hand, and she cried out with the pain.

She placed the candle on the mantelpiece and turned, bewildered, to look at Cole. Then flinched and instinctively stepped back, away from the wild anger glittering in his narrowed eyes. She had seen that same glacial look of fury before in his eyes, the day she had shot him, those first hours in the cabin at the winter quarters, but never like this, as if he despised everything about her.

He spoke in the familiar lazy drawl, but each word

cut savagely at her, drawing blood. "Bitch! Lying, worthless bitch!"

She caught at the mantel, the color draining from her face. "What is it, Cole? What's happened?"

"They're dead. All my men are dead. They never had a chance to draw their guns." Cole's mouth twisted bitterly, pain gouging deeper the gashes that ran from his nose to his chin. "But you know that, don't you? After all, you set up the ambush, didn't you . . . Sukey!"

Lucy felt her throat close as if a hand had suddenly tightened around her windpipe. "I . . . I don't understand," she stammered.

Cole smiled mirthlessly, but she sensed the deadly menace behind that smile. "I didn't understand either, not at first. The Yankees thought I was dead, too, or they would never have left me behind. It was while I was lying there, my face buried in the dirt, and later, hiding in the woods, that I started putting the pieces together. No one knew about the raid, except my men, General Early . . . and you . . . sweet little treacherous Sukey." His eyes narrowed sardonically. "Or should I call you the white rose?"

Lucy felt as if she had stepped into a nightmare. The room spun crazily around her. The candlelight flickering across Cole's face highlighted the slashing eyebrows, the trickle of dried blood on his forehead, the cruel set of his mouth. It was like staring into the face of her own private demon.

"Sukey's dead," she whispered. "You told me she was dead."

"Stop lying," he said harshly. "It's been a lie from the beginning, hasn't it? From the very first day you went to work as a spy for Lafayette Baker in Washington, pretending to be a black girl so you could get into the Von Bruck home, and then Lucy Appleton, the belle of The Bower and Richmond, and all the time lying, betraying your family and friends. That morning in my quarters when you promised me you'd stop spying, that was a lie, too, wasn't it? The next time I

341

saw you, you were acting as an agent in Richmond. Isn't that what you were really doing there?"

"No, it was Matt. I was in Richmond to help Matt escape," she protested.

"And how did you manage to whisk Matt out of Libby except with the help of your Union agent friends?"

"I had to get him out of Libby," she said desperately. "I had to break my promise. I couldn't let Matt die."

As if he didn't even hear her, he continued in that same lazy, deadly drawl, "All the time I was lying there in the dirt, I kept thinking, wondering, when you could have passed the word to your friends about the raid. Then I remembered that sisterly visit to Matt in the middle of the night, to sit by his bedside, isn't that what you said? Or was it to find your black buck, Sam, send him into Cold Brook to warn the wagonmaster, to prepare the ambush?"

"No!" Lucy gasped. "You can't believe that. It's not true."

She saw that the wound on Cole's forehead had begun to bleed again—it looked like the slash from a saber—and she hurried to him. "You're hurt, darling. Please let me help you."

"Stay away from me!" His voice stopped her like a hand thrust hard against her chest. And suddenly for the first time, staring into Cole's pain-glazed eyes, she was afraid, afraid of what he might do, afraid for her own life.

"Cole ... please ..."

He laughed, enjoying the fear he saw leap into her wide, dark eyes. He walked, swaying, toward her, still smiling that deadly smile. "Are you afraid now, little Sukey? You should be. Do you know what kept me alive after I saw my men shot down around me? Why I would have crawled here on my hands and knees if I had to. It was thinking about you, remembering how my hands had felt around that slim, beautiful neck back at the cabin. I should have killed you then."

She forced herself to stand still while his hands circled, almost gently, her neck. "Remember, Sukey?" His thumbs rested in the hollow of her throat. "Aren't you curious how I knew, how I finally guessed? You're a good little actress, Lucy, but there was always something about you that bothered me, that reminded me of Sukey. I even thought that perhaps your father, that you and Sukey . . ." He shrugged impatiently. "Well, no matter what I thought. You played your role very well. And then I never did see Sukey in a good light, did I? Until this morning, until I left you this morning in the daylight. And lying there in the woods, I remembered . . . this!"

His hands caught at the neck of her gown and ripped the material, exposing the upthrust breasts, pearl-white against the darkness of her gown. His eyes raked her face, moved downward, to the heart-shaped mole nestled beneath her left breast. "That was just too much of a coincidence," he said softly, "even for me. Two girls with the same heart-shaped mole in exactly the same place."

She said nothing, at first too terrified to speak, and then knowing it was useless; Cole was past listening or hearing anything she might say. Pain and outrage at her duplicity, perhaps even guilt that he was alive and his men were dead, had pushed Cole to the razor's edge of sanity.

She said quietly. "Why don't you kill me then, Cole, and get it over with?"

He shook his head, smiling lazily down at her, but the violence was there, simmering beneath the surface. "Not that fast, my love. Remember Dick, the boy who played the harmonica last night? After they shot him, it took him a half hour to die. I could hear him screaming while I lay there, playing possum. And there was nothing I could do. Why should you die easily after all the men you've sent to their death?"

From somewhere she drew on the reckless courage that had always been hers when faced with danger. "I won't beg, Cole," she said coldly. "If that's what you expect."

He laughed, almost lovingly, as his hands moved

suddenly to cup and squeeze a soft breast in his hand. "Oh, you'll beg before I'm through with you, my sweet." She bit back a cry of pain, remembering last night, the tenderness of Cole's hands on her body, and stared in disbelieving anguish into the face of an icy-eyed stranger who meant to kill her, would kill her. She took a deep breath, closed her eyes and waited.

"Stand away, colonel."

Her eyes flew open and she stared, dazed, at Sam in the doorway, holding Jephthah's revolver in his hand, pointed at Cole. A rage flooded Cole's face when he saw the black man. His whip-slender body grew taut. Two pinpoints of fury burned in his eyes, the muscles in his shoulders gathering, like a panther ready to spring.

Sam didn't move. He stared stolidly across the room at Cole. "Ah don' want to kill you, suh," he said softly. "But I will."

Cole hesitated, then his face went dead. Only his eyes were alive as he shrugged contemptuously, turning back to Lucy. "You're not worth dying for. And you won't always have your watchdog around. Keep looking behind you, Sukey. One of these days, I'll be there. You can count on that!"

He thrust Sam aside and stalked out the door. Lucy heard his footsteps in the hall and the front door slamming shut. The sudden draft from the hall extinguished the tiny flame in the fireplace. A current of icy air slipped around her ankles, a bitter chill creeping unseen into the small sitting room. Lucy felt as if her blood had turned to ice, and she began to shiver helplessly and couldn't stop.

22

The next few weeks Lucy moved numbly about her chores at Black Oaks. Her hands automatically prepared meals, dusted and cleaned and tended Aunt Bessie and young Matt. All her movements, though, were stiff, her eyes dazed, as if she were sleepwalking.

Sam watched her closely. Lucy ate little and, he guessed, slept less. One cold, rainy day with the rain fast turning to sleet that rattled at the remaining windowpanes, he found the girl mending a rip in Matt's shirt by the light of the small fireplace in the sitting room. Except the shirt had dropped into her lap and her dark eyes, lusterless now, had a blank look, much like her young brother's, as she stared into the fireplace.

Sam stared, frowning, at the young girl. His own sense of privacy was so intense that it was difficult for him to intrude on another person, and particularly to meddle into the affairs of a white woman. Yet beyond the debt he owed Lucy Appleton, he respected the girl's courage and spirit. There were even times when he had found her beauty disturbing. Always before the flesh of a white woman had been repulsive to him, reminding him of the underbody of a fish, without the warmth and rich color of a black woman's skin. Yet when he had held the girl in his arms in the cave to keep her warm, he had felt an unmistakable stirring within him. Only the girl's illness had stopped him from taking her there and then.

Afterward, in the months he had helped Lucy Appleton with her spying activities in the valley, there had been the memory of Jane, the news Lucy had brought him that his wife and children were alive and might still be rescued, that had prevented him from taking another woman. If occasionally, when he watched

Lucy walk by with that graceful swing of hip and buttocks, her young breasts as proudly upthrust as those of any Ashanti woman, he had thought with pleasure how it would be to hold her in his arms, he had felt no sense of guilt. After all, he was a man. How could it be otherwise?

The evening when he had come into the sitting room and had seen the murderous rage in Colonel Sinclair's face, the fear in Lucy's eyes, he had guessed at once what had happened. He could almost feel sympathy for the colonel. No man liked to be made a fool of, to be deceived by a woman.

Now he stared, annoyed, at Lucy's grief-shadowed face, his voice blunt. "It was right that your man should feel anger at your deceiving him. He should have taken a stick and beaten you. That would have made him feel better and settled the matter once and for all."

Lucy smiled wanly and returned to her sewing. Perhaps Sam's solution would have been better. Anything would be better than living the rest of her life with the knowledge that Cole despised her.

It was shortly after the first of the year that Cousin Harry returned to Black Oaks. He rode up with four men. Although the four were riding cavalry mounts, Lucy knew at once they weren't regular cavalry troopers. They had the hard-bitten faces of men who lived lives of constant danger and relished every minute of it.

Cousin Harry introduced his escort as he swung off his horse and walked up the veranda steps to Lucy. "General Mosby was kind enough to lend me a few of his men in case I ran into trouble coming through the Federal lines." If he was startled to see how thin and worn Lucy looked, he gave no sign, only bowing his head gravely. "I've come, of course, to visit Mother's grave. As you can imagine, her death was a great blow to me. I would have come sooner, but matters at the War Office were too pressing. Perhaps you've heard that Secretary of War Seddon has resigned and General Breckinridge has taken his place."

Lucy shook her head. Little news of the outside world reached Black Oaks these days. In any case, she doubted if filial grief alone had brought Cousin Harry back to Black Oaks. Nevertheless, she found her shawl and walked with her cousin to Aunt Clare's grave, where he bowed his head and they both stood quietly for several minutes. Lucy was relieved, though, when they left the burying ground and walked back to the house. She still had a nagging sense of guilt whenever she thought of her aunt's death, as if she could not rid herself of the feeling that she was partly to blame.

It wasn't until later, after dinner that evening in the small sitting room, that Cousin Harry met young Matt. There hadn't been time to hide her brother; Cousin Harry had appeared too unexpectedly. In any case it was much too cold to keep Matt hidden in the cave in the woods.

"So this is young Cousin Matt," Cousin Harry said jovially, holding out his hand. "It seems to me I heard you were in the Union Army, young man."

When Matt simply stared blankly at the proffered hand, then turned and walked away, Harry turned, frowning, to Lucy. "What's the matter with the boy? He acts as if he doesn't even know me."

"He doesn't. He doesn't recognize anyone," Lucy said stiffly. "He was hurt . . . in the Wilderness, and lost his memory."

"Then how did he happen to come here, to Black Oaks?" Harry asked. When Lucy didn't answer, he gazed at her speculatively. "It's odd, but I heard of a case like young Matt's only recently. I was having dinner with Dr. Madison at the hotel the other evening. The doctor had had too much to drink, I'm afraid, and he told me about a young soldier in Libby Prison who'd had a complete loss of memory. It seems there was also a woman involved. An elderly gray-haired widow claimed to be the young man's mother, and somehow managed to spirit the young man out of prison in a pine coffin."

Cousin Harry sipped the brandy he had brought with

347

him from Richmond and studied Lucy's face, his pale-yellow eyes amused. "Is that what happened to mother's wig, Cousin Lucy, the one she was constantly complaining about missing?"

Cousin Harry's unexpected shrewdness always startled Lucy. He gave the impression of being so dull and stodgy that she forgot how clever he was when he wanted to be. She had changed for dinner into the one other good dress she still possessed. The bodice of wine-red wool was laced with black soutache braid, and as she leaned forward to refill Harry's brandy glass, she could feel his eyes, like questing fingers, slipping down between her breasts.

She drew back coolly. "Will you be staying long at Black Oaks, Harry?"

The corners of Harry's mouth twitched in sudden annoyance. "You make it sound as if I'm a guest in your home, Cousin Lucy. You haven't forgotten that Black Oaks belongs to me?"

"How could I forget?" Lucy asked bitterly.

The flash of ill humor disappeared from Harry's face, and he smiled ingratiatingly, leaning forward to pat Lucy's knee. "I'm sorry, my dear. I shouldn't have said that. Black Oaks belongs to both of us. Once we're married, as my wife, you'll take your rightful place as hostess here, and a most charming one you'll be."

Lucy sighed. "I thought we'd settled that, Harry. I have no intention of marrying you."

Her cousin continued as if she hadn't spoken. "That's really why I'm here at Black Oaks, to take you back with me to Richmond. Ordinarily, of course, with Mother's death, we'd observe a year's mourning period before our wedding, but what with the war and all ..." He shrugged. "I'm sure no one will think the worse of us if we forgo a long engagement. I've arranged for our wedding in March at St. Paul's."

The lethargy that had gripped Lucy these last weeks slipped away and she felt a spurt of familiar anger, bringing a glow of color to her pale face. "I told you,

Harry," she said, rising to her feet. "There will be no marriage."

Her cousin glanced around the small room, once so elegant, now threadbare and sad-looking with the slashed chairs and boarded windows. "Don't be childish, Cousin Lucy. You certainly can't stay on here alone with a crazed brother. And from what passed for a dinner you served me this evening, your food supply must be deplorably low. You'd never make it through the winter."

"We'll manage," Lucy said. "And Matt isn't crazed!"

Cousin Harry yawned sleepily, stretched and pulled himself to his feet. "Well, I won't argue with you on that point. It's been a long day, and I'm sure you're as tired as I am, Cousin Lucy. We'll talk about it in the morning. Your head will be clearer, after a good night's sleep."

He walked to the door, then turned, arching a disapproving brow at Lucy. "If I may say so, cousin, you look quite peaked. You haven't been worrying about your friend Sinclair, and that sorry debacle of his with the wagon train?"

"It was an ambush," Lucy said indignantly.

Cousin Harry smiled skeptically. "So Colonel Sinclair says. Most people in the War Office, though, believe he simply handled the whole affair badly. Did you know Sinclair's been transferred to Longstreet's battalion on the Petersburg line?" He paused, then said with deliberate malice, "Longstreet's been receiving the worse of Grant's pounding for several days now, I understand."

Lucy did not answer, but as she knelt and banked the fire for the night, she couldn't help remembering how as a child, Cousin Harry would make her watch while he pulled the wings off butterflies.

She spent another restless night so that when she finally fell asleep, she overslept and awoke with a start. After dressing quickly, she hurried down the hall, then stopped, alarmed, at the window when she heard the unmistakable sounds of horses and men. One glance at the scene on the front lawn of Black Oaks sent her flying down the stairs, almost colliding with Cousin Harry, who had just started up the stairs. He put out a hand to keep her at his side.

"Oh, there you are, my dear. So you're awake at last. I'm afraid you'll have no time for breakfast. I've decided we should get an early start to Richmond."

Lucy pulled herself free, her voice raging. "Those men who came with you—they have young Matt and Sam with them, tied to their saddles!"

"They're just following my orders," Harry said placidly. "I don't suppose Cousin Matt would try to run away, but after all, he is an escaped prisoner of war. As for Sam, naturally he has to be tied. It took all four of the men to overpower him." Cousin Harry nodded smugly. "I'm sure the countess will be most gratified when I return her manservant to her."

A weakness swept through Lucy. She grabbed at the sharply carved edge of the wooden pineapple which graced the pedestal at the base of the staircase. "I won't let you," she cried furiously. "You can't do this."

"My dear girl, of course I can. I am a sworn officer of the government of the Confederate States of America. I have taken into temporary custody an escaped prisoner of war and an escaped slave." The yellow eyes suddenly grew hard as agates, watching her. "However, perhaps if you'd reverse your, I'm sure, hasty decision of last night, some other arrangement might be made."

Lucy understood then. She stared at her cousin incredulously. "You'd do all this, just to marry me."

Harry rested his hand lightly but firmly over Lucy's. He felt the almost instinctive shudder of revulsion, saw the immediate defiance in her dark eyes and smiled, pleased, to himself. He had no wish for a compliant, submissive bride. "You mustn't underestimate yourself, Cousin Lucy," he said. "At the moment I admit you're not at your most attractive, but after a few weeks of good food and rest in Richmond, I've no doubt you'll make a stunning bride." His face took on an expression

350

of solemn devotion. "And you know it's what Mother always wanted, that we should be married."

"Yes," Lucy said dully. She remembered it was almost the last words her aunt had said to her, her wish that her son and Lucy be married. She pulled away from Harry and walked to the open front door. She could see young Matt on horseback, his face frightened, bewildered. He was pulling at his tied wrists, confused moans of fear coming from his lips. Sam sat like a statue, staring straight ahead, as if his face were a dark-brown mask. She could not bear it, she thought suddenly, wearily. Matt back in prison, Sam again a slave to that horrible Von Bruck creature. And after all, what did it matter what happened to her? If she couldn't have Cole, why should she care whose bed she shared? All her emotions and feelings felt curiously atrophied, so that she felt nothing, cared about nothing, except keeping Matt and Sam alive.

She turned back to Cousin Harry, her face pale but determined. "I'll agree to the marriage only on two conditions. Matt won't be returned to prison and Sam will be set free."

Cousin Harry frowned. "Well, of course, your first condition is no problem. I have no wish for my friends in Richmond to know I have a brother-in-law in Libby. However, the matter of Sam . . ." He pulled at his lower lip, annoyed. "That's a different kettle of fish."

"Sam, too," Lucy said stubbornly. "Or there'll be no marriage."

A spark of anger at her obstinacy leaped in Harry's small yellow eyes, then he shrugged with ill grace. "Very well. Sam, too. You can consider it my wedding present to you, my dear." He shouted orders to the men, then turned back to Lucy. "We've no time for packing. If you'll fetch your shawl, you can buy any clothes you'll need in Richmond."

When Lucy came out of the house, Sam had been released and was standing at one end of the veranda. Lucy walked quickly to him. "You're free, Sam. Only

I'd leave here as soon as I could." Her mouth twisted scornfully. "I don't trust my cousin to keep his word."

Sam jerked his chin toward the men on horseback. "I heard them talking, something about your marrying Mr. Appleton. You ain't doing it on account of me? I can look after myself."

Lucy shook her head, forcing her voice to steadiness. "Not just because of you. There's young Matt, too. And in a way Cousin Harry's right. We couldn't have lasted here through the winter, and you couldn't take care of us forever, Sam. You have your own family to think about." She blinked back sudden tears. "I'll miss you, Sam. Perhaps after the war, you and Jane and the children can come back for a visit."

Impulsively she reached out her hand, laid it gently in Sam's large, dark palm, except she realized, without consciously thinking about it, that it wasn't a black hand she saw, or a white hand. It was simply the hand of a friend, to whom she would be forever in debt.

Then she turned quickly away. She had no wish for Cousin Harry to see that he had reduced her to tears. Just before she mounted her horse, though, she paused. "I forgot about Aunt Bessie and Uncle Joe. I can't leave them here alone. They're too old and feeble to take care of themselves."

Cousin Harry scowled, his lower lip sticking out sullenly. "You're being ridiculous. I certainly don't intend to take two worn-out slaves all the way to Richmond."

"That won't be necessary. The minister, Mr. Simpson, and his wife will look after them." She smiled coaxingly at Cousin Harry, and for a moment the smile lit her face with its former provocative beauty. "You can leave money with the minister to pay for their food. Please, Harry."

Harry hesitated, then shrugged impatiently. "Oh, very well. Now let's get moving, or we'll never make Richmond by dark."

23

After Sheridan's destruction in the valley, Grant's merciless battering at Petersburg, and the latest disastrous news on Christmas day that Sherman had captured Savannah, the Confederacy's last seaport, Lucy expected Richmond to be plunged into gloom. Instead she found the city much as she had left it, overcrowded with refugees, yet optimistically certain that Lee's Army of Northern Virginia would somehow still triumph, even with the thunder of Grant's siege guns at Petersburg shaking Richmond on a clear day.

Extravagant rumors circulated throughout the capital. General Johnson was joining forces with General Lee . . . a new Confederate offensive would be underway in the spring . . . Emperor Napoleon would soon be recognizing the Confederacy . . . a negotiated peace with the North, declaring the Confederacy's independence, was only days away . . .

Even the most optimistic of rumors, though, couldn't evade the reality that with the fertile Shenandoah Valley captured, the food supply in Richmond was dangerously low. What food there was for sale was so outrageously expensive that few could afford to buy. Once-wealthy aristocratic Southern families were reduced to living in genteel poverty, selling precious family heirlooms in order to survive for one more day.

Despite the uncertainties of the day-by-day existence, the rebel capital was still a merry place. "Starvation" parties, lasting well into the morning, were all the rage. Romances blossomed quickly, and gossip, as always, swirled through the town about which belle was having an affair with which officer. Whereas in the past courting would stretch out six months to several years, now within a matter of weeks there was a hasty rush to the altar. Of all the numerous weddings celebrated at St. Paul's Church that winter, none was more fashionable than the marriage of the beautiful auburn-haired Hetty Cary, queen of Richmond society, to handsome young Major General John Pegram.

Lucy and her cousin Harry were invited to the Cary-Pegram wedding. Watching the young couple at the altar, seeing the adoration in the groom's eyes as he gazed down into his bride's veiled face, Lucy felt a surge of pain, so unexpected that she almost cried aloud. It was Cole's face she saw, the love and longing in his eyes when he had left her in bed that last morning at Black Oaks. The anguish of remembering was as painful as feeling returning to frostbitten flesh, and she ducked her head and dabbed at the sudden tears that stung her eyes.

As they left the church, Harry gave Lucy's tear-stained face a sharply amused glance. "I had no idea you were so sentimental about weddings, Cousin Lucy. I hope you won't be crying tears of joy all through our wedding."

"I'll try to restrain myself," she said tartly.

When they reached Franklin Street, she hurried into the house, grateful for the warmth after the chill of the carriage. Coal and wood were as expensive and scarce as food in Richmond, but Harry always managed to keep his home heated, just as ham and terrapin and brandied peaches somehow mysteriously managed to appear on his table. Although Lucy felt guilty about the comforts Harry was able to secure while other families in Richmond went to bed cold and hungry, yet she was selfishly glad for Matt's sake that he had a warm room and plenty of food.

Now, as she started up the stairs to check on Matt, Harry caught at her arm. "You haven't forgotten that we're to attend the reception for Colonel Mosby at the Von Bruck home this evening?"

Lucy hadn't forgotten. The whole city was agog with the news that the legendary rebel hero was visiting in Richmond. Although Sheridan controlled the valley, General Mosby's partisans still managed to evade capture and harass the Federal troops like particularly nasty gadflies.

Lucy was curious to meet the guerrilla leader, but she always felt uncomfortable in the presence of Arabella Von Bruck. The countess was always outwardly gracious toward Lucy, but there were times when Lucy caught the lavender eyes watching her with a reptilian chill, as if just waiting for the proper moment to strike.

"It's been a tiring day, Harry. Why don't you go to the reception without me?"

"Because I choose to have my fiancée accompany me," Harry said. A silly, almost facetious smile touched his thin mouth as he murmured, "It couldn't be that you're jealous of Arabella, my dear."

Lucy repressed a desire to giggle at Harry's stupidity. Did he really think she cared that when he left the house in the evenings, supposedly to return to work at the War Office, it was Arabella's charming townhouse he visited till early in the morning? Still, it wouldn't do to let Harry suspect that she was well aware it was Arabella's bed Harry was keeping warm these cold winter nights, and she widened her eyes innocently. "Jealous of Mrs. Von Bruck? Why should I be?"

"No reason, of course," Harry said smoothly. "So let's not have any more discussion about not attending the reception this evening." He studied Lucy, frowning. "And I want you to wear that new green gown I bought you last week from Captain Marshall. Since I have to pay a mint to buy the latest gowns for you from a blockade runner, the least you can do is wear them!"

Lucy stared at her cousin, disgusted by his insensitivity. Didn't he realize how ill at ease she felt, wearing the new fashionable gowns he bought her when the other women in Richmond proudly wore calico and twice-turned ball gowns? Then, seeing Harry's face harden and a petulent flush rising in his cheeks, she decided it wasn't worth another argument.

As it turned out, she wasn't the only guest at the Von Bruck reception that evening wearing the latest fashion from Paris, slipped through the blockade. Her hostess' gown of lavender satin and Valenciennes lace, caught up at the shoulders with silver-gilt roses, was also obviously very new.

When Arabella saw Lucy's gown, the spring-green velvet setting off Lucy's blue-black hair and tiny waist to perfection, her smile became brittle as she murmured spitefully, "Your cousin Harry has excellent taste, don't you agree, Miss Appleton?"

So Harry had bought Arabella her gown, Lucy thought, not particularly caring, only vaguely curious. Harry's personal fortune must have fared very well these last years, she decided. The two gowns would have had to be paid for in gold or Yankee specie. Blockade runners like Captain Marshall had for some time refused to accept Confederate currency for their shipments.

Then she put Araballa out of her mind as she was introduced to General Mosby. The guerrilla leader had arrived at the reception wearing his old gray felt hat with a curling ostrich plume, his cape turned back to show a flow of scarlet. Without the hat and cloak, though, Lucy saw that the general was of medium height, with a slight frame, sandy hair and an elderly stoop to his shoulders. Only when his glance met hers, his eyes deep-blue and piercing, did she recognize the power in the man that would compel other men to follow him, blindly, if necessary, to their deaths.

He nodded pleasantly at Lucy when she curtsied before him. "I've heard of your charming singing voice, Miss Appleton. Perhaps you'll favor us with a song this evening."

She was about to refuse—she hadn't sung in public since her return to Richmond—but then she saw the annoyance gathering in Arabella's face at Lucy's becoming the center of attention, and she smiled sweetly. "I'd be happy to, general."

Someone handed her a banjo. At first, she wasn't sure what to sing. The popular songs were all so melancholy, sad songs like "Lorena," and "When This Cruel War Is Over." Then suddenly she remembered

356

the songs she had heard the slaves singing at Black
Oaks, as a child. Flinging the ribbons of the banjo over
her shoulder, she began to strum and sing:

> *"I had a honey,*
> *She wouldn't stay,*
> *Ac' kinda funny,*
> *Cry all day,*
> *Tuk all my money,*
> *Done run away,*
> *Runaway Ann am de*
> *debbil tuh pay!"*

She mimicked so exactly the rich slurred voice and
catchy rhythm of a black singer that when she finished,
a startled burst of applause broke loose throughout the
room. Only Arabella, she noticed, did not clap. The
countess gazed at Lucy, her lavender eyes narrowed to
slits, a look of concentration on her white face that all
at once made Lucy feel uneasy.

Then, glancing up, she saw that a late-arriving guest
had just appeared at the doorway of the Von Bruck
parlor. Cole's face was worn even thinner than she
remembered, and there was a narrow scar at his temple, white against the bronze skin. But the arrogant
way he held his head, the slashing black brows giving
him a faintly piratical look, were the same. For a second
his glance met Lucy's, and she felt the blood drain from
her face at the hatred she saw glittering in the blue-
green eyes.

Lucy discovered she was trembling, her hands ice-
cold. Harry pushed his way to her side. He was pleased
at the flattering applause she had received, but he
wasn't sure it was proper, Lucy singing Negro songs.
"Why not sing 'The Bonny Blue Flag' next?" he suggested.

"I don't want to sing any more," she said abruptly,
pushing the banjo into his startled hands. "I have a
headache. I'm going home."

Harry glared at her, outraged, but without making a scene there was no way he could stop her. She didn't wait for him to accompany her, could still hear him making nervous apologies for her as she snatched her wrap from a servant's hands and rushed out the door. She walked quickly, almost running, back to Franklin Street, as if she were being pursued by threatening footsteps stalking her.

Even after she reached the house and undressed, slipping into her nightgown, brushing her hair down over her shoulders in a silken cloud, the fear stayed with her. She began to pace, frightened, back and forth in her bedroom. Surely there was no way Cole could reach her, here in Cousin Harry's house. Or was there? She remembered the icy menace in Cole's voice in those last moments at Black Oaks—"Keep looking behind you, Sukey. One of these days, I'll be there!" Would anything stop Cole, if he was bent on vengeance?

The walls of the bedroom seemed to be closing in on her. She roamed downstairs to the front parlor and saw the crystal decanter of brandy on a silver tray that Harry always had sitting there. On an impulse, to restore her suddenly flagging courage, she poured herself a small glass of brandy, swallowing it so quickly that she began to choke and cough as the liquid seemed to explode inside her.

"I assume your headache is better, Cousin Lucy."

She whirled. Cousin Harry stood, legs akimbo, in the doorway, watching her. His yellowish eyes flicking over her body made her wish that she had thought to put a robe over her nightgown before she had come downstairs. Although the white muslin nightgown covered her modestly from high, lacy neck to ankle, the gown had been washed so often that it was practically sheer, clinging to her hips and breasts.

"Yes, thank you." She returned the glass to the tray, preparing to make a hasty departure. "I'm sorry if I ruined your evening."

As she passed her cousin in the doorway, he put out his good arm and barred her way. "Why the hurry,

358

Cousin Lucy?" he asked softly. "And you didn't ruin my evening. It was a dull party." His eyes, gleaming in the lamplight, ran slowly, with pleasure, over the demure white gown. "I'm sure I can have a much more interesting time here at home with you."

His arm moved to encircle her waist. Lucy forced herself to stand perfectly still within his grasp, sensing that any struggle to escape would only incite Harry further.

"It's late, Harry," she said. "And you don't want to wake Mrs. Emerson."

Harry had installed one of Richmond's most respectable and poverty-stricken widows in his home so there could be no gossip about his sharing his home with his future bride, unchaperoned. The only problem, Lucy thought wryly, was that Mrs. Emerson was almost eighty and slept like a rock.

Harry smiled fatuously at Lucy. "I'd forgotten, you know, how beautiful you are, my dear."

He had forgotten, he thought, his gaze dwelling on the peach flush rising beneath Lucy's fair skin, the lustrous sheen of her dark hair falling softly around her face. And somehow the modest nightgown covering every inch of her body, even as it revealed the tempting curves beneath, made the thought of possessing her even more tantalizing. If only more women realized that a clothed body was often more sexually alluring than the naked flesh, Harry thought reflectively, remembering Arabella, and how she loved to parade nude around her bedroom. It wasn't that Harry didn't appreciate Arabella's particular talents in bed—she had taught him some variations that even he hadn't known—but the truth was, he was becoming jaded with the countess. She was, if anything, almost too willing, too eager. A man appreciated some restraint, a little resistance. Now Lucy, he thought, caressing the small waist, feeling the stiffening of that soft body at his touch, would never give herself willingly to him, he was sure.

His arm tightened, drawing her closer. "I'm afraid

359

I've been neglecting you shamefully. I don't blame you for being annoyed with me."

There was only the slightest touch of sarcasm in her voice as she replied, "I'm not annoyed with you, Harry. I know you have many important concerns."

"From now on, none more important than you," he promised, his mouth finding the fragrant hollow in her throat, then nibbling playfully at her earlobe before he crushed her soft mouth beneath his dry, cold lips.

Although she made no move to resist him, her body was stiff, unresponsive in his arms, her mouth unyielding, closed tightly against his. As if he were embracing a statue, Harry thought, all at once furious, as he thrust her away from him. "I don't plan to suffer frostbite on my wedding night, Cousin Lucy," he said coldly. "Or was that what you had in mind?"

She shrugged indifferently. "I said I'd marry you. I don't recall any mention of enjoying the prospect." She started to turn away. "Now if you'll excuse me, I want to look in on Matt."

"How is Matt?"

Something in Harry's voice rang a warning bell in Lucy. She turned to stare warily at her cousin. "He's much the same," she said. And then, not bothering to hide the scorn in her voice, she added, "Surely the guard you keep posted in his room has already told you that."

Harry ignored the insolence, as he murmured with mock concern, watching Lucy's face closely, "I've been thinking, my dear, that your brother needs more care than you can give him. There are places, you know, asylums for insane people like Matt."

"No!" Lucy's hands clenched into fists at her side in an effort to hold her temper. "I won't allow it! Matt stays with me!"

Harry lifted an amused eyebrow. "You forget, when I am your husband, legally Matt will be my responsibility." He reached out a hand, ran his fingers lightly up Lucy's arm, smiling unctuously. "Of course, we both know a clever wife has ways of twisting a husband around her little finger." He saw understanding fill Lucy's dark, luminous eyes, then the helpless angry flush mounting in her face, as he once again pulled her into his embrace. This time when he kissed her, there was only a moment's instinctive stiffening of her body, before her mouth opened, soft and pliant, beneath his. Even when his hand fondled her breast roughly, then began to explore slowly, calculatingly, the delicious curves and hollows of her body, she did not pull away.

It was Harry who finally, reluctantly, stepped back, his voice regretful. "As much as I'd like to continue, my dear, I'm afraid we'll have to postpone our own pleasures for the moment. There are some people dropping by in a few minutes." He paused. "Some government matters that must be discussed, privately. I'm sure you understand."

For a moment Lucy couldn't speak. She felt as if she could still feel Harry's hand on her body, the leaf-dry mouth against her lips, the almost detached way his fingers had stroked, exploited her body, as if she were not a person at all, only a receptacle for his passion, her responses needful only as they satisfied his cravings.

"Of course, I understand," she said, fighting back a feeling of nausea. As a matter of fact, as she walked slowly up the stairs, it occurred to her that Harry had entertained government officials several times at home lately and asked pointedly not to be disturbed.

Before going to her bedroom, she stopped at Matt's room. The guard Harry had installed looked up when she entered. He was a small, wiry man with two outsized pistols in holsters at his waist. He looked up when Lucy entered but didn't rise to his feet, leaning precariously against the wall on the two back legs of his chair.

"I want to be alone with my brother," Lucy said.

The man grinned and shook his head. "No, ma'am. Mr. Appleton's orders. I'm to stay with the pris—" He amended himself hastily. "... with the young man at all times."

Lucy was in no mood for cajoling. She kicked her foot out, and the chair and the guard tumbled ignominiously to the floor. As the man scrambled to his feet, clawing for his gun, Lucy smiled coldly. "Do you have orders to shoot me, too? I can tell Mr. Appleton how I almost overpowered you, or you can wait out in the hall by the door. It's your choice."

His face an angry red, the guard withdrew from the room, and Lucy went to sit beside Matt's bed. She was afraid the noise of the guard's fall might have awakened him, but he was still asleep. With his eyes closed, that frightening, vacant look gone from his face, he looked young and handsome and boyishly vulnerable, a faint scattering of freckles across the bridge of his nose.

Lucy deliberately drove out of her mind what had happened between Harry and her. What was it Aunt Clare had been fond of saying? What cannot be changed must be endured. Somehow, for Matt's sake, she would learn to endure living with Harry. After all, she wouldn't be the first woman to marry a man she didn't love.

After a while, she realized the room had grown cold. She rose stiffly, going to the small wood-burning stove in a corner of the room. When she opened the stove door, she saw the fire had gone out. She was reaching for wood to place in the grate when she heard snatches of voices, sounding strangely disembodied, coming from the stove. "That fool Vallandigham ... knew the plan wouldn't work ... waste of time and money ..."

Lucy had closed the stove door before she realized what she had overheard. Cousin Harry must be holding his meeting in the back parlor, directly beneath Matt's bedroom. With the two rooms sharing a common flue, the conversation in the room below could be heard whenever the occupants of the room opened the door to the stove as she had just done.

She remembered there had been a story in the Richmond *Examiner* several weeks before about Clement Vallandigham and the Sons of Liberty plot to burn the cities of the North, with the help of freed Confederate prisoners of war. The Sons of Liberty had evidently been rounded up before the fires could do any great harm, and the leading conspirators had fled to England or been thrown into prisons in the North. She couldn't help wondering if the information she had overheard at Black Oaks, and passed along to Jephthah and General Sharpe, had been of some help in destroying the conspiracy.

She frowned, gazing at the stove. What, she wondered, were Harry and his friends up to now? One of the voices she had overheard she could have sworn was a woman's. Arabella's?

She opened the stove door again. The visitors in the room below must have had their stove door closed, because she could hear only a faint murmur of voices. Frustrated, she went out into the hall, waited till Matt's guard returned to the room, then crept quietly down the stairs, her footsteps muffled by the deep-piled turkey-red carpeting.

The front hall was drafty, and she remembered that the back-parlor door never latched securely. If she could get close enough, and the door was open only a little, she might be able to hear something. As she approached the parlor door, she saw a sliver of light falling out into the darkened hall. She moved stealthily forward. She could hear voices clearly now.

"There's no use in pointing the finger of blame," a man was saying. "We all knew it was a gamble, but desperate times call for desperate remedies. The peace negotiations have fallen through. President Lincoln refuses to listen to any condition for ending the war except complete restoration of the Union."

"Lincoln, that ape of a man!"

It was Arabella, Lucy decided, recognizing that throaty voice that now held an undercurrent of contempt as Arabella said furiously, "To destroy an enemy one must do more than cut off his legs. One must cut off his head. In Europe, such a tyrant would have been disposed of long before this."

"You are speaking, madam, of assassination?" the man asked, shocked.

"Why not?" Arabella asked. Lucy could imagine the slight Gallic shrug to her shoulders. "Are you saying that such a thought has not occurred to you gentlemen before this?"

A second man's voice began to sputter indignantly. "I can assure you, countess, that no official of the Confederate government would be party to such a dishonorable action."

Lucy, who had recklessly advanced farther down the hall in order to hear better, became aware suddenly of footsteps approaching the parlor door, and Arabella's voice interrupting. "Would you mind if I close the door, Mr. Appleton? There's a bitter draft coming in from the hall."

Lucy had fled back to the stairs by the time Arabella reached the door. She caught a glimpse of a pale-lilac dress, and shrank back against the staircase wall, wondering if her white gown could be seen through the darkness. Then as she stood paralyzed with fear, she saw the parlor door close, and her body went limp with relief.

As she withdrew to the upper hallway, slipping quietly into her bedroom, she was still unnerved by what she had overheard. She was sure there were many honorable men in the Confederate government who would never stoop to assassination as a weapon. But Cousin Harry, and Arabella? She wondered uneasily how far they would go to protect their wealthy estates from a Yankee victory.

It was early the next morning when Miss Elizabeth Van Lew hurried out into her kitchen, a frown of annoyance on her face as she surveyed the young colored girl waiting to see her.

"What is it?" she demanded. "I understand you insisted upon talking to me personally."

"Yessum." The girl ducked her head, too frightened to continue.

"Well, speak up, girl," Miss Van Lew said sharply. "Are you running away?"

"No, ma'am." Lifting her head, the young girl stared full into Miss Van Lew's face, a flash of mischief in her black eyes as she asked softly, "Ain't you knowin' me, ma'am?"

"Miss Appleton!" Miss Van Lew cocked her head and commented drily, "I assumed the white rose had retired from the secret service."

"You might call this my farewell appearance," Lucy said, smiling faintly. "I overheard something last night that I think you should pass along to General Sharpe."

Quickly she repeated the snatches of conversation she had overheard in the back parlor. When she finished, Miss Van Lew's face had grown thoughtful, her bright-blue eyes alert. "I'll send the information along, of course, but I doubt if it'll do much good. It's not the first time the President's life has been threatened. His aides have warned him time and time again that he needs more protection against assassins, but the President refuses to listen." She gave Lucy a troubled glance. "You heard nothing else?"

Lucy shook her head. "The countess came to the door. I had to leave before she saw me."

"That jezebel!" Miss Van Lew's face darkened. "I wouldn't put any wickedness past her."

"If I hear anything more, I'll let you know," Lucy promised.

Except, she remembered, with her wedding only three weeks away, she'd have precious little time for spying.

Miss Van Lew said curiously, "It's true, then? You're going to marry Harry Appleton?"

Lucy nodded, proudly unwilling to go into details of the reasons behind her engagement, even with Miss Van Lew.

When the girl said nothing further, Elizabeth Van Lew shrugged. "It's none of my business, of course. I can't say I've ever been interested in the marital state, myself. I prefer my independence. Still, I suppose there are worse fates for a woman." The shrewd gaze penetrated Lucy's smooth facade, saw the misery in the girl's dark eyes. She made a touchingly awkward gesture toward Lucy, then her hands fell to her side. "If there's anything I can do ..."

"There's nothing, Miss Van Lew," Lucy said quietly. "But thank you."

As she left the Van Lew home, slipping out the kitchen door and circling back to Church Hill Street, she saw a black man slouching against a tree across the street from the Van Lew home. Something about the man, the massive head, the slope of the shoulders, reminded her all at once of Caesar, and her heart lurched, then began to race. She fled down the street, stopping at the corner to gaze back uncertainly. The man was shuffling away from her up Church Hill Street. Lucy frowned, annoyed. It was her overwrought imagination, that's all. If Caesar were still alive, he was back at the Von Bruck plantation. What she should be worrying about was hurrying back to Franklin Street and washing the black stain off her face before anyone saw her.

During the weeks before her wedding, Cousin Harry held no more unofficial late-night meetings in the parlor. He even made a halfhearted apology for his behavior toward her the night of the Von Bruck party. "I'd had too much to drink, my dear, and your charming appearance in that nightgown ..." he smiled penitently. "I'm afraid I was carried away."

Almost, Lucy believed him. Except every now and then she caught an anticipatory gleam in Harry's amber eyes watching her, like a cat crouching patiently outside a mouse hole, waiting.

The night before her wedding day, her seamstress, Mrs. Caspar, came by the house for a last fitting on Lucy's wedding gown. Lucy was grateful that Cousin Harry had gone off to a bachelor's party. At least she could spend one last night alone.

After adjusting the white mousseline de soie gown

and tulle veil, the seamstress stepped back, sighing happily. "What a beautiful bride you'll make, Miss Appleton—just as lovely as Miss Hetty Cary." She flung her hand up to her mouth. "Oh, dear, I hope you're not superstitious, my mentioning Mrs. Pegram."

"Of course not," Lucy said. All Richmond had been shocked at the news of General Pegram's death in battle. Exactly three weeks after her wedding day, the grief-stricken bride, now swathed in crepe, had knelt beside her husband's coffin at the altar where she had been married.

Lucy gazed absently at her reflection in the mirror. How odd, she thought. It was as if the young woman in the embroidered flounced gown and long, trailing satin train staring calmly back at her were a complete and total stranger. The woman in the mirror would walk down the nave of St. Paul's, repeat the wedding vows, share Cousin Harry's bed, and yet she had nothing to do with the real Lucy Appleton at all. It was as if that other Lucy had vanished somewhere deep inside the stranger in the mirror where no one, not even Cousin Harry, could reach her.

With an effort, she pulled her gaze away from the mirror, and that other unknown woman who was taking over her life, and listened to Mrs. Caspar. "If you'd like me to help you out of your gown before I leave, Miss Appleton, there's nothing more that needs to be done. My husband worries so when I'm not home by dark."

"You needn't bother staying," Lucy said. "I can manage by myself. You run along."

It wasn't until after Mrs. Caspar had left that Lucy remembered she had given her maid the evening off. She also quickly realized that no matter how she tried, there was no way she could reach the long row of tiny pearl buttons that marched down the back of her gown.

She'd have to call Mrs. Emerson, Lucy decided. The old lady liked to have a cup of tea in the parlor before retiring. She went to the head of the stairs and called,

"Mrs. Emerson, I need your help. Could you come upstairs for a moment?"

When she had called several times and there was no answer, she sighed and started down the narrow staircase. Then she stopped abruptly. Arabella Von Bruck came out of the front parlor, closing the sliding doors behind her. She walked to the foot of the stairs, gazing up at Lucy. "I'm afraid Mrs. Emerson is indisposed. Perhaps I can help you."

Then, smiling lightly, her lilac eyes glittering, she daintily lifted her skirt in one hand and started up the stairs toward Lucy.

24

For a moment, watching Arabella climb the steps toward her, Lucy felt her heart slam against her ribs in sudden, unaccountable terror. Then Arabella's words cut through the fear and she asked anxiously, "Is Mrs. Emerson ill?"

The countess shook her head. "We were having tea and she just . . . nodded off. Is something wrong? I heard you call."

Lucy gestured helplessly. "It's this gown. I can't unbutton it."

"Let me help you," Arabella offered, following Lucy into her bedroom.

Lucy, turning to face her uninvited guest, saw by the flickering candlelight Arabella reflected in the wall mirror, as if, disconcertingly, there were two Arabellas in the room, both watching her with that look of hidden, malicious amusement in their lavender-shaded eyes. The countess was dressed as if she were on her way to a party. Her gown of gauzy pale-lilac material was striped with velvet ribbons matching the tightly fitted velvet bodice. Diamonds and amethysts glittered at her white throat and in her earlobes. All at once Lucy was reminded of another evening when Arabella had been dressed in much the same fashion. Only that evening Arabella had been standing amid the squalor of a cellar room, watching, with a gloating, sensual pleasure on her face, as Caesar's skilled hands had brought screams of pain from a luckless colored girl named Sukey.

Remembering that evening, Lucy felt again that same sense of sickening fear, even as she told herself she was being foolish. She wasn't some helpless colored servant that Mrs. Von Bruck could mistreat as she pleased. She was Lucinda Appleton. What could possibly happen to her in her own home, especially with

Matt's guard not more than a few feet away if she should call out?

"Turn around, dear," Arabella said sweetly. "You can undo the lower buttons, can't you? I'll start at the top."

Reluctantly, Lucy turned her back on Arabella, and reaching behind herself, started to fumble for the tiny pearl buttons. So suddenly there was no time even to cry out, she felt a sharp jerk at her arms, as a thin rope was snaked around them, then twisted cruelly, biting into the soft flesh of her wrists.

At first, she was more startled than frightened as she felt herself whirled around and stared into Arabella's angelic face. The gloating look of malice was no longer hidden behind the sweeping dark lashes. Arabella's violet eyes were glassy with rage, her small mouth contorted and ugly, as she cried furiously, "Did you really think I'd let you steal Harry away from me, the way you took Cole? Or that I don't know what you and that crazy old Van Lew woman have been up to here in Richmond? You're Union spies, the both of you. I began to suspect you the night you sang that nigger's song in my house. There's always been something about your face—I knew I'd seen you somewhere before. Then when I saw you hiding on the stairs, eavesdropping on our little group, I had Caesar start following you. He saw you go to the Van Lew home the next morning, dressed as a colored girl, as Sukey."

"It was Caesar!" Lucy blurted, without thinking.

"Oh, yes," Arabella said, reaching for the door. "Would you like to see what's left of him?"

She opened the door. Lucy shrank back as Caesar stepped into the room. At first glance, she would not have recognized him. His nose was crushed flat, and a scar from his mouth to his ear pulled his thick lips into a perpetual foolish, lopsided grin. But the slope of the broad shoulders and the malevolence in the black, opaque eyes staring at Lucy were the same.

Arabella ran her hand lightly up the man's arm, her voice purring spitefully, "Poor Caesar. He's not much to look at any more, is he? I would have sold him, but who would buy him now? And, occasionally, he still has his uses, haven't you, Caesar?"

The man made a disagreeable grunting sound deep in his throat; the eyes turned to his mistress were like those of a beaten, cringing animal.

"He can't speak, you see," Arabella said, her nose wrinkling distastefully at the guttural sound. "Troy took care of that, too. He split Caesar's tongue." She turned back to Lucy, her eyes narrowing to angry slits. "That's something else you'll pay for—stealing Troy from me. I've always known it was you no matter how often Harry denies it. Did you let Troy crawl into your bed, too?" she demanded furiously. "How shocked Cole and dear Harry would be if they knew the truth about their precious Lucinda Appleton, traitor, spy . . . nigger's whore."

When Lucy said nothing, straining frantically and in vain at the rope binding her wrists, Arabella laughed shrilly. "You can't imagine the pleasure it's given me these last weeks, deciding exactly how I would make you pay for all the trouble you've caused me." She smiled slowly, running her tongue over her moist pink lips. "Your death had to be painful, of course, and naturally no one must suspect that I had any part in it."

Lucy stopped struggling and gazed incredulously at Arabella. "There's a guard down the hall. If I scream, he'll be here in a moment."

Arabella shrugged indifferently. "Oh, Caesar took care of him, didn't you?"

The black man nodded, the foolish grin growing wider at the memory.

"As for Mrs. Emerson, she'll sleep very soundly. I put a little something in her tea. I doubt if she'll even remember I was in the house when she wakes up. Old people have such dreadful memories, don't they? Of course, I could have Caesar gag you," she continued, smiling thoughtfully. "But then I wouldn't have the pleasure of hearing you scream, would I?"

As Lucy watched, frozen, a terrifying knowledge filling her eyes, the countess went to the dressing table and picked up one of the tallow candles which Cousin Harry somehow still managed to buy for his home.

"Your tragic death won't be so unusual, you know," Arabella said, still smiling as she walked slowly toward Lucy, the candle flame fluttering. "It's common knowledge that our crinoline skirts are a death trap when they're accidentally ignited. A dear friend of mine in Charleston died a horrible death in exactly the same fashion when she clumsily dropped a lighted candle near the hem of her hoopskirt. Of course, I couldn't have known that you'd be wearing your wedding gown, but it adds a nice touch, doesn't it? Poor Harry will be desolate for a few weeks, but I'm sure he'll recover quickly from your loss." A puzzled, almost petulant look crept into the violet eyes. "Frankly, I've never understood why Harry was so insistent upon marrying you anyway."

"I don't want to marry Harry," Lucy protested. "He's forcing me into the marriage by holding my brother as hostage."

"Well, it doesn't really matter," Arabella said smugly. "Once you're out of the way, he'll come back to me." She was standing very close to Lucy now, so close that Lucy caught the scent of the lavender perfume, could see the pale-gold ring around the violet corneas of Arabella's eyes.

Deliberately the candle tilted so that a drop of hot wax dropped on the bodice of Lucy's gown, searing quickly through the sheer material to burn the soft flesh beneath. A cry of pain leaped to Lucy's lips, and she bit it back savagely, glaring angrily, helplessly, at her tormentor.

The corners of Arabella's mouth curved upward when she saw Lucy flinch and bite her lips against the pain. "Oh, you'll scream, my dear," she murmured sweetly. "You'll scream louder than when Caesar had his way with you in Washington. When you feel the flames licking at your legs, reaching for your face..."

Behind her, Caesar made that odd, guttural sound

372

in his throat, and Arabella nodded regretfully. "Caesar's right. I'm wasting time. And I'm expected at the Benjamins' for dinner this evening. That way I'll be with people when the shocking news is received of the tragic accidental death of Harry Appleton's fiancée."

Arabella lifted the candle higher, closer to Lucy's face. Lucy could see the tiny golden flame reflected, dancing in Arabella's glossy violet eyes, before the candle tilted again. Another fat drop of wax dropped, this time on Lucy's uncovered shoulder. "How long do you imagine Cole will grieve for you?" Arabella asked tauntingly. "I notice he didn't seem too pleased to see you at my party the other evening. I wonder, now, what happened between you two lovebirds?" She giggled softly. "I have the feeling that Harry's fine hand was in there somewhere. A very devious man, your Cousin Harry," she added approvingly.

"Cole!" Despair filled Lucy so that for a moment even her terror was forgotten. If only she could see him for one last time, feel his arms hard around her, she would do anything. She would get down on her knees to Arabella, beg, plead, grovel. But gazing into those translucent violet eyes watching her without a spark of warmth or compassion in them, she knew any pleas would be useless. Her begging would only serve to excite Arabella further, bring the woman an extra perverted pleasure to have her victim grovel and plead for her life, before she finally allowed the candle's flame to ignite the lacy flounces of Lucy's crinoline skirt.

After that, the countess had only to stand back and watch the fire do its deadly work, turning the wedding gown into a fiery shroud. Even the ropes cutting into her wrists—would anybody afterward notice the bruises on the charred flesh?

As if guessing what Lucy was thinking, a smugly triumphant look spread across Arabella's lovely, angelic features. "It's too bad you didn't stay on the stage, my dear. I must admit you played the role of Sukey to perfection. You really are quite a good little actress."

Lucy strained at the bonds on her wrist, her heart

pounding. If only she could free herself, she thought furiously, she would claw that gloating smile off Arabella's face. The fear that had paralyzed her muscles, turned her blood to ice, loosened its hold. A fierce, burning anger took its place. She was an actress, she reminded herself angrily, and no matter what Arabella thought, she had no intention of dying easily. If nothing else, she decided, she wouldn't die alone.

She moaned deep in her throat, then whimpered, "Please! No, please! I'll do anything you want, pay you anything. I don't want to die." It wasn't difficult to feign fear, to put a cringing horror into her voice. What was more difficult was retreating slowly backward away from Arabella and the flickering candleflame. But not too far away, although every instinct in her body screamed for her to turn and run.

Arabella didn't even bother to pursue her. She was still close enough so there wasn't more than two feet between her and her victim. Still smiling, savoring the sound of Lucy's pleading, the terror in the girl's face, she lowered the candle slowly, its gold flame flickering, casting shadows through the darkened room, as the flame reached for the white lace crinoline skirt.

Arabella was still smiling when with a lightning movement, Lucy kicked her right leg forward. The pointed toe of her white kid leather boot struck Arabella's shinbone with such force that Lucy felt the painful shock of it clear up her spine, even as she twisted sideways and flung herself to the floor, rolling out of harm's way.

She watched Arabella lurch backward. The candle was jerked free of her hand at the sudden, painful impact, and dropped to the carpeted floor. Lucy saw the tiny flame nibble teasingly at the wide hem of Arabella's flimsy gauze skirt, then flash upward so rapidly that it seemed only seconds before the crinoline was a torch billowing around the woman.

For a brief moment, as if time stood still, Lucy saw the look of horror transfiguring Arabella's face as she tried to scramble away from the candle. Then she heard the woman scream in agony as the flame, like the golden petals of a flower, encircled her. As long as Lucy lived, she would never forget the blood-chilling horror of that scream. Arms outstretched, Arabella ran toward Caesar, moaning, "Help me! Caesar, help me!"

Lying huddled on the floor, Lucy watched, horrified, as if she were taking part in a nightmare over which she had no control. Caesar stood staring with that vacant simpleton's grin at his mistress. The grin suddenly grew wider, split the black shining face. As Arabella clutched desperately at his arm, Caesar shoved her violently away. Then, turning, he plunged out of the room.

Arabella's back was a sheet of flame now. Her agonizing screams dragged Lucy to her feet. No one, not even Arabella, deserved to die that way, she thought, sickened. But with her hands tied behind her, there was nothing Lucy could do except stare helplessly as Arabella ran out of the bedroom, her frantic movement only fanning the flames engulfing her.

Then Lucy saw that the woman's mad dash through the bedroom, trailing flame, had ignited the muslin-and-lace skirt of her dressing table. The flame reached upward eagerly, flared toward the curtains. In seconds, flame and smoke filled the bedroom, licking at the wallpaper. Tiny ribbons of fire raced across the carpet toward Lucy.

She retreated quickly to the hall, coughing and choking as the smoke followed her, cut like a razor into her lungs. She could no longer see Arabella through the haze of the smoke. The woman's terrible screams had stopped, but the crackling of the fire was louder now. A draft from the open bedroom door drew the flames out into the hallway. The whole house would go, Lucy thought, terror-stricken. She had to rouse Matt!

She remembered starting down the hall toward Matt's room, then felt an excruciating pain, like a red-hot poker, laid against her leg. Glancing behind her, she saw that the edge of her long trailing satin train had caught fire. The satin smoldered slowly but relentlessly, turning the satin an ugly black. How long, Lucy wondered helplessly, would it be before the flame reached the flammable sheer crinoline skirt attached to the train? She remembered hearing screaming, not knowing it was herself, trying frantically to reach around her, to stamp out the flame with her feet. The smoke in the hall pressed thickly into her lungs. She could no longer breathe. The hall spun dizzily around her.

For one last second, before a merciful darkness descended over her, she thought she saw Matt, standing wide-eyed and stunned in the doorway of his bedroom. Then the pain became intolerable and there was only blackness and oblivion.

25

When Lucy awoke again, she was in an unfamiliar bed in a room she had never seen before. The pain was still there in her legs, and it hurt to breathe, but she could move her neck, she discovered, turning her head cautiously to discover Mrs. Emerson seated beside the bed, prosaically mending a tear in a petticoat.

Seeing the girl's movement, Mrs. Emerson put down her mending and got quickly to her feet. "You should lie still, Miss Appleton," she said. "And you mustn't try to talk. The doctor said the burns on your leg will heal, but he's worried that the smoke you inhaled might have affected your lungs."

At the girl's questioning glance, she added, "You're at the Spottswood Hotel. Mr. Appleton secured rooms for us here after the fire. I'm afraid it will be months before his home will be fit to live in again. Fortunately only the second floor of the house was destroyed."

"Matt?" Lucy dragged the name past the aching rawness in her throat.

"Your brother is fine," Mrs. Emerson assured her. "There are some burns on his hands from when he carried you out of the house and then came back and got me." Mrs. Emerson's voice was puzzled. "I can't imagine how I could have slept so soundly through it all. I shudder to think what might have happened to both of us if your brother hadn't acted so promptly." She hesitated tactfully, then murmured, "Mr. Appleton's behavior is especially praiseworthy when I gather he has been ill for some time."

Living in the same house, naturally Mrs. Emerson had been curious about the Appleton brother who never left his room, and the rather uncouth man who evidently served as Matthew Appleton's nurse. Still, good manners forbade her asking too many questions, especially when she was receiving a handsome wage from Mr. Harry Appleton to act as chaperon in his home.

Lucy was digesting the remarkable information that it was Matt who had saved her life. Was it possible? she wondered hopefully. Had the shock of seeing his sister, her gown in flames, jolted Matt out of the shadowy lost world he had been inhabiting these last months?

Engrossed in her own thoughts, she wasn't listening to what Mrs. Emerson was saying until the name Arabella caught her attention. "... such a pity, a beautiful woman like the Countess Von Bruck. They say she lingered only a few hours ... a blessing, really, her face and body were so badly burned."

Memory returned then to Lucy—Arabella's angelic face and golden hair, wreathed in flames, violet eyes wide with disbelief and horror, the inhuman screams coming from the round pink mouth. Waves of nausea swept over Lucy.

Mrs. Emerson quickly brought a basin and a cold cloth for Lucy's forehead. "There, there," she said soothingly. "It must have been a frightful experience for you. Such a tragic accident." She cast Lucy a quick sideways glance. "I suppose it was a candle," she murmured. "An open flame in a bedroom is so dangerous, I always say. Try not to think about it, child." She brought a glass of water and put some drops from a green bottle into the water. "Drink this, child. The doctor said it will help you sleep."

An accident, Lucy thought. Well, why not? What was the good now of accusing a dead woman of attempted murder? Perhaps in time, if she was lucky, that was how she could make herself think about it. As she lifted her arm to take the glass from Mrs. Emerson, the ruffle at the wrist of her nightgown fell away and she saw the ugly red raw marks the rope had left.

If Mrs. Emerson noticed, she tactfully averted her gaze. She, as well as others in Richmond, had their own unanswered questions about what had happened at the Appleton home between the countess and Lucinda Appleton. Whatever the suspicions, though, they would only be gossiped about behind closed doors in hushed whispers. After all, Lucy was an Appleton, while the countess, for all her Southern sympathies, had always been an outsider, married to a displaced Yankee.

The medicine Mrs. Emerson gave her was strong enough so that Lucy fell into a deep sleep almost immediately. When she awoke again, it was evening and Matt was sitting beside her bed.

She blinked her eyes drowsily, at first thinking she must still be asleep, then Matt smiled shyly, a boyish, half-embarrassed grin, and reached out awkwardly to cover her hand with his. "Hi, sis," he said. "How are you feeling?"

Tears of happiness stung Lucy's eyes. There were so many things she wanted to say, but her throat pained her too much to speak. She contented herself with smiling blissfully up at her brother, discovering that, after all, there was a happiness that didn't need words.

It was Sunday morning, almost a week later, before Cousin Harry came by to see her. Matt had taken Mrs. Emerson to church, and Lucy was alone in the hotel room. Harry's face was strained and tired, and Lucy wondered if the war news was bad, although according to the Richmond *Examiner*, Lee had crushed Grant's whole front in a surprise attack the night before.

"I'm pleased to see you looking so well, Lucy," Harry said, although his glance barely touched her face before moving nervously to the window. In the distance through the open window could be heard the constant, faint rumbling of siege guns. Then abruptly he announced, "I've decided that after everything that's happened, it would be best if we were married at once. I've arranged for the Reverend Mr. Adams to come by after services this morning. It'll be a quiet wedding here at the hotel."

Lucy straightened in her chair, her voice very quiet. "No, Harry, there'll be no wedding, not today, not ever."

His head snapped back toward her, his face at first shocked, then darkening angrily. "You gave me your word, Cousin Lucy. I intend to hold you to it." His thin mouth twisted in a disagreeable sneer. "If nothing else, you might think of your brother's welfare. There's still a possible murder charge hanging over his head."

"Murder! What murder?"

"The man guarding Matt the night of the fire," Harry said. "He was found in the house after the fire, his body badly burned. However, it was plain his throat had been cut. So far I've persuaded the authorities not to arrest your brother, to keep the circumstances around the man's death quiet, but—"

"Caesar killed that man," Lucy interrupted hotly, "so he wouldn't interfere with Arabella's plans for murdering me."

"Nonsense!" Harry said coldly. "The fire was an accident, or your brother set it. In his crazed condition, I wouldn't put it past him. It was just bad luck that the countess happened to be in the house, visiting you at the time."

Lucy sprang to her feet. "That's not what happened. Arabella came to the house deliberately to kill me. She was going to set my gown on fire, make my death seem an accident."

Harry smiled complacently. "Come now, my dear, do you really think anyone would believe such an outlandish story?" The smile thinned as he walked slowly toward her, his glance raking her tense figure as she braced herself against him. His voice dropped threateningly. "And I can assure you I have no intention of having our wedding plans disrupted by any hysterical lies on your part."

Watching him walk toward her, Lucy was suddenly reminded of Arabella. The same violent, murderous rage was in Harry's yellow eyes. She had always known that Harry didn't love her. Now she realized, frightened, that whatever feeling he did have for her was closer to hate than love.

She tried to put the chair between them, but she didn't move quickly enough. His arm reached out and fastened around her like a steel band, cruelly tightening, as he drew her toward him. Her body was bent in a painful arch as his mouth found hers and bruised her lips savagely. The more she struggled against him, the tighter his arm pinched her waist, his mouth fastening over hers so completely that she couldn't breathe. Her lungs felt as if they were bursting, her head pounding. She felt darkness crowding in on her, a bewildered terror filling her mind. My God, she thought, he's going to kill me, right now, right here . . .

Then just as she felt her body grow limp, he released her abruptly. She sank into the chair, staring at Harry in disbelief.

The amber eyes stared coldly down into her pale, dazed face. "Just so we understand each other, my dear. Whether your brother returns to Libby as an escaped prisoner or as a murderer makes no difference to me. But we will be married. Make no mistake about that."

After he left the room, Lucy stared at the closed door, her eyes dilated with fear. Then, as if a spring had been released inside her, she flew to the wardrobe, pulled out a carpetbag and began throwing clothes into the bag. She and Matt had to leave Richmond right away, before Harry returned with the minister. It was only after she had finished packing that she remembered that she had no money. She dug feverishly through her purse, but all she found was a few coins, not enough for a train ticket, much less to buy a horse.

"My dear, have you heard the news?"

Mrs. Emerson burst into the hotel room. Her black silk bonnet was trembling with agitation, her face drained gray with fright. "It's the Yankees! A messenger came and fetched President Davis during the church services. The Yankees broke through General Lee's lines at sunrise this morning. Lee is evacuating

Petersburg. They say the Federal troops will be in Richmond by this evening. We'll all be murdered!"

Matthew had come into the room more quietly. "It's true enough, sis," he said soberly. "There's nothing to stop the Union troops from taking Richmond now. President Davis and the rest of the government officials are already packing, preparing to leave before the Federal troops arrive."

This was their chance, Lucy thought eagerly. With the city in a state of confusion, Matt and she could slip away before Cousin Harry returned looking for them. She wasn't sure if Harry could make his murder charge against Matt stick, if the Yankees took over the city, but she couldn't take the risk. Not after what she had seen in Harry's eyes, the murderous rage burning there. She didn't dare face Harry again.

"Mrs. Emerson, do you have any money you can lend me?" she asked urgently. "Matt and I have to leave Richmond at once."

Mrs. Emerson looked flustered. "Why, no, dear, I'm sorry. Mr. Appleton was to pay me the end of last month, but I'm afraid, in all the excitement, he forgot."

Matt frowned with brotherly annoyance at his sister, as if he were the older brother and she the child. "There's no need to panic, sis. We'll be perfectly safe in Richmond. The Yankees won't kill us."

No, but Cousin Harry might, Lucy thought grimly. Every instinct within her screamed for Matt and her to get as far away from Harry as they could. She picked up the carpetbag, and bidding Mrs. Emerson a hasty goodbye, she dragged her brother downstairs to the hotel parlor. Ordinarily the room was crowded with guests, but it was completely deserted this morning. At the door Matt grabbed her arm. "This is crazy, Lucy," he protested. "How are we going to get out of Richmond? We don't have any money. And I doubt if there's a horse to be had, even if we had the money to buy one."

"We'll steal one, then," Lucy said fiercely. "I still have friends in Richmond. Someone will help us."

When she and Matt walked out of the hotel, she stared around her, dismayed. Wagons piled high with the archives of the government were being driven furiously through the streets to the Danville depot. More wagons rumbled by, overflowing with personal possessions, furniture, trunks, portraits, while the sidewalks were filled with men, women and children who owned no vehicles for escape. They jostled Matt and Lucy aside as they rushed by, carrying their possessions on their backs, heading for the railroad terminal or the towpaths that led to the canal packets. It was as if the whole city were trying to flee with the government before the Union soldiers arrived.

An elderly man that Lucy recognized passed her, and she grabbed at his arm. "Judge Copley, please. I have to talk to you."

The judge stared at her blankly, then muttered, "There's no time. I have to get to the bank. Everything I have is there."

He pulled his arm free and hurried off across the street, where crowds had already gathered before the bank, frantic to withdraw their deposits before the Yankees arrived.

Shoving and elbowing their way, she and Matt finally reached the section of Franklin Street where there were no homes, only shops and factories. Here the crowds were even thicker, but they were not bent on fleeing the city but on looting and ransacking the deserted stores.

Hogsheads of liquor had been dragged from the shops. City officials were knocking in the heads and pouring the spirits into the gutters. The smell of brandy, whiskey and rum filled the air, and men and women rushed into the streets with any containers they could find, buckets, pails, hats and boots, to scoop up the liquor. Drunken men and women were already reeling down the street, shouting raucously. One brawny man would have knocked Lucy down without even seeing her if Matt hadn't grabbed her and pulled her into the safety of a doorway.

Lucy watched, appalled, as the frenzied crowds broke into the stores, carrying off food, clothes, tobacco, screaming and shoving, some laughing, as if it were a holiday. Lucy recognized some of the women among the looters, delicately reared matrons who graced the finest parlors in Richmond, carrying sheets and shawls filled with whatever they could seize and carry off.

Then an explosion suddenly split the air, and the sidewalks shook beneath her, the glass in the shop window shattering around her. Once again Matt dragged her to safety, down a side street.

"What is it?" Lucy gasped. "Are the Yankees here already?"

"The rebels must be blowing up the gunboats and arsenals before they evacuate the city," Matt said, frowning. "They'll set the whole town on fire if they're not careful."

Already Lucy could see black columns of smoke rising from a factory on Cary Street. Another bursting shell rent the air and a second tobacco factory went up in flames, spreading quickly to the small shops next to it.

"We've got to get out of here," Matt said, tugging at Lucy's arm. "This whole street will be an inferno soon."

"The railroad," Lucy said desperately. "We might still be able to get out on the railroad."

Matt looked as if he were about to protest again, but at the wild determination in Lucy's face, he nodded, resigned. "All right. We can try."

It took an hour for them to fight their way through the streets to the station, and then reached there just in time to hear the departing whistle of the last train to leave Richmond. Once the train, crowded with government officials, passed over the James River bridge, soldiers rushed forward. Several minutes later the bridge exploded into flames. Other bridges over the river one by one went up in flames in a last futile attempt to keep the enemy from entering the city.

Was Cousin Harry on the train? Lucy wondered. Somehow she doubted it. Harry was not one to go down with a lost cause. She suspected he was right here in Richmond, looking for Matt and her.

"What now?" Matt asked wearily. His face was streaked with perspiration and soot, and his hair clung damply to his forehead. Lucy felt a pang of guilt. She knew noise and confusion still bothered Matt. Surely the frenzy all around must be upsetting for him.

Her mind raced, seeking a way out, then she grasped Matt's arm. "There's Miss Van Lew. She'll help us."

Matt gazed at her, baffled. "Who's Miss Van Lew?"

"Don't you remember? She used to visit you in prison."

An uneasy look crept into Matt's face. "I don't remember the prison," he confessed. "I don't remember anything after the Wilderness. One day I was lying wounded in the underbrush, watching the brush and trees burning around me, knowing that I was going to die, and the next thing I heard screaming and woke up in a strange bedroom with a man whose throat was slit. Then I went to the door and saw you in the hall with your dress on fire." His eyes clouded. She could almost see him straining, trying to recall time that was lost in his mind.

"Don't try to remember, Matt, honey," she said quickly. "Take my word for it. Miss Van Lew is a dear friend to both of us."

"Where does she live?"

"Church Hill Street."

Matt stared at his sister, aghast. "Why, that's clear across town. Lucy, why are we running? Why don't we just stay here?" he asked plaintively. "The Yankees aren't barbarians. They won't harm us."

Lucy took a deep breath. "We can't stay here, Matt. Cousin Harry is here." When Matt stared at her, bewildered, she continued quickly, "Cousin Harry claims that you killed that man in your room and set fire to his house. If I don't agree to marry him, he's threatened to go to the authorities with his story."

"That's not true," Matt said indignantly. "The man was already dead when I woke up. I never saw him

385

before." He gazed, worried, at his sister. "You believe me, don't you?"

"Of course. Only I think it's better if we go north for a while, stay out of Cousin Harry's way. First, though, we have to get to Black Oaks."

"Black Oaks?" Matt hurried to keep up with her. "Won't that be going out of our way?"

"It can't be helped," Lucy said. "We'll need money to live on, and before Aunt Clare died, she gave me some valuable jewelry. It's still hidden in the study at Black Oaks. The money I can get from selling the jewelry will give us a start until I can find work."

Plodding wearily on foot, it was another hour before they finally managed to reach Church Hill Street. Explosions still rocked the ground underfoot from bursting shells in the armory, and a thick haze of smoke from the burning factories and stores had drifted into the residential area of the city. Lucy held her handkerchief tight against her mouth to keep out the gritty soot that fell like a black rain around her.

Once she and Matt had to stop for several hundred prisoners, ragged as scarecrows, being herded from Libby Prison out of the city. Some of the prisoners were so weak they fell in their tracks, and the other prisoners and guards simply walked around them. Matt stared at the gaunt men with compassionate curiosity but no recognition in his eyes. Perhaps it was just as well that part of his life was a blank now, the horror of his months in Libby forgotten, Lucy thought.

It was early afternoon when they arrived at the Van Lew home and discovered they were not the only visitors Elizabeth Van Lew had that day. The neatly trimmed rose garden before the white-pillared mansion was filled with a mob of men, waving torches and brandishing their fists angrily at an American flag flying over the veranda of the house.

Lucy could hear their furious shouts—"Hang the Yankee spy! Burn the house!"

Lucy pulled at Matt's arm, and he followed her around to the rear of the house. They slipped into the deserted kitchen; the whole house seemed deserted, Lucy realized uneasily. Had Miss Van Lew fled with the servants? she wondered. An explosion shook the golden chandelier in the front hall, setting the crystal pendants to chiming, while a fine white dust fell from the rococo ceiling.

Then Lucy saw the mistress of the house standing by the front door. She smiled happily when she turned and saw Lucy. "It's a splendid day, isn't it, Miss Appleton? Did you see my flag? General Butler had it smuggled into my house just last week. I always promised myself I'd have the first American flag flying in Richmond to greet General Grant when he arrives."

Lucy wasn't sure whether to applaud the woman's courage or marvel at her foolhardiness. Then the sounds of the mob, growing louder, drifted into the hallway, and she grasped impatiently at the elderly woman's arm. "You've got to get out of here. Those men mean to hang you."

"Don't be foolish," Miss Van Lew said briskly. "This is my home. I'll do as I please."

She pulled free of Lucy's restraining arm and walked, stiff-necked, out onto the veranda, a slight, ungainly figure in an ugly shapeless gown. Nevertheless the mob fell silent when she stepped to the edge of the stairs. Her disdainful glance swept the men scornfully. "I know you, Tom ... and you, William ... and you, Jeremy," she cried loudly, pointing her finger at each man in turn as she called out his name. "General Grant will be here in the city in a few hours. If my house is burned, I promise you your homes will be burned an hour later."

Lucy, who stood in the doorway with Matt, saw the look of hesitation cross the faces of the angry men. She had no doubt that "Crazy Betsy" would keep her promise. Apparently the men realized it, too, and one by one, they began to move away, muttering to themselves, trailing out of the garden into the street.

When the last man had gone, Miss Van Lew turned and looked proudly up at the Stars and Stripes, fluttering in the breeze. Tears of happiness sparkled in her eyes as she turned to Lucy. "The war will end now, Miss Appleton. Many young men's lives will be saved." Then her sharp glance traveled swiftly from Lucy's troubled face to that of her brother, who was staring at the woman as if he had never seen her before.

"What is it, child?" she demanded brusquely. "I haven't much time, you know. Many of the prisoners they're transferring from Libby have managed to escape and have come to the house for shelter. And I'm sure General Grant will drop by for tea as soon as he arrives in Richmond. I have a thousand things to take care of."

Lucy stepped forward, trying to keep her voice calm, to push the terrifying memory of Harry's face, those cold, murderous eyes, from her mind. "We need your help, Miss Van Lew," she said. "Matt and I, we must have a horse. We have to leave Richmond. . . ."

26

On Monday morning, April 3, with a tremendous shout of bugles, the victorious Army of the James marched into Richmond. An unbroken, seemingly endless sea of blue uniforms flowed through the town. Cavalry horses pranced to the tune of "Garry Owen"; artillery dashed up Broad Street, and at the head of the infantry, a regiment of black troops marched proudly, their sabers flashing in the sunlight. While Richmond's black servants went wild with joy, the white citizens who had not fled the captured city watched sullenly from the sidelines, or wept silently behind closed curtains, as the Confederate flag was lowered and the Stars and Stripes raised above the Southern Capitol.

At the rear of the procession rode Jephthah on his lanky hunter. He wore his old slouch hat and worn blue jacket and trousers. Unlike the other officers he had not bothered to put on a new uniform for the victory parade through Richmond, and the expression on his face was somber. Although he had no doubt that General Lee might make a gallant last stand, Jephthah knew that with the fall of Richmond, the long, bloody civil war was finally ending. Yet, looking into the grim faces of the spectators lining the street, remembering the ruin and desolation of the Southern countryside, he couldn't help wondering if the aftermath of war might not be more cruel than the war itself.

As the parade wound its way past the Exchange Hotel, explosions still rocked the city and a black mantle of smoke hung low in the sky. Drunken men staggered through the streets, and looters could be seen roaming in and out of stores, carrying away whatever they could.

Jephthah frowned as he looked around him. Martial law, he knew, would soon be put into effect, but he was still troubled by what he saw. President Lincoln planned to visit Richmond the next day, and uneasily Jephthah remembered the information General Sharpe had received several weeks before about the possibility of an assassination attempt on the President. Ordinarily Jephthah would have been skeptical of such a report, except for the fact that it was the white rose who had forwarded the information and Countess Von Bruck was the woman who had made the threat.

Providing security for the President was not Jephthah's job. Nevertheless he decided to make a side trip to Church Hill Street. If anyone in Richmond would know what was going on, it would be Grant's favorite spy, Elizabeth Van Lew. Jephthah grinned sheepishly to himself. The truth was he wasn't going to visit Miss Van Lew just to question her about the countess. He wanted to find out if Lucy Appleton was still in Richmond.

He had almost reached the Van Lew home when he passed a group of guarded rebel prisoners halted in the shade alongside the road. Some of Longstreet's men, Jephthah thought, giving them only a cursory glance, probably captured when Sheridan broke through their lines. He saw that Miss Van Lew was walking among them, handing out water and pieces of bread and butter. He wondered if the poor devils would ironically end up in the infamous Libby Prison where so many Union prisoners had died.

Most of the Johnny Rebs already looked half dead, their bodies emaciated, the wounded leaning on makeshift crutches, others slumped wearily on the ground. Except one man, Jephthah noticed, picking the officer quickly out from the rest of the prisoners. The man stood by himself, and although there were lines of exhaustion carved in his face, he held his whip-thin body proudly erect.

Spurring his horse forward, Jephthah dismounted near the man. "Morning, Colonel Sinclair," he said, his voice a soft, mocking drawl. "I always figured we'd meet

390

again. Sorry it couldn't be under pleasanter circumstances."

Cole's face stiffened for a moment, then he grinned and asked, "You mean with me dangling at the end of a rope?"

"I'll admit the silver fox led us a merry chase until he retired," Jephthah said. He gave the man a curious glance. "I never could figure why you left the spy business. You were mighty good at it."

Cole shrugged impassively. "I decided I preferred killing a man face to face."

"I got that feeling at times, myself," Jephthah admitted. "At least, thank God, it's over. And no one can say you graybacks didn't put up a good fight, while it lasted."

"It's not finished yet," Cole said harshly. Then, smiling tightly, "Prisoners have escaped from Libby before."

"You don't have to go to prison, you know," Jephthah said quietly. "You can give me your parole."

Cole's smile did not alter, but his voice became dangerously soft. "You can go to hell," he said equably.

Jephthah nodded again, a look of bland innocence creeping over his open features. "I kind of thought you'd say that. You know, it's funny," he drawled, chewing contemplatively on his cud of tobacco. "I always thought your leaving the secret service had something to do with Miss Lucy Appleton."

Jephthah had deliberately attempted to strike a nerve, but he was startled himself at the raw anger that flashed for just a second in the narrowed blue-green eyes.

"Are you gentlemen friends of Miss Lucinda Appleton's?"

Miss Van Lew had come up behind them, unobserved. Now she cocked her head and stared from one man to the other, pretending not to recognize Jephthah.

"It's all right, Miss Van Lew," Jephthah said, sweeping off his hat. "Colonel Sinclair and I were in the same business at one time, back in Washington City at the Countess Von Bruck's home."

Elizabeth Van Lew sniffed. "That woman! I try to be a good Christian, but I can't say I'm sorry she's dead."

"Arabella dead?" Cole asked, startled. "How did it happen?"

"There was a fire at the Appleton home. Mrs. Von Bruck was visiting Miss Appleton at the time. The countess didn't survive the fire."

"Lucy . . . Miss Appleton," Jephthah said quickly. "Is she all right?"

Cole caught the alarm in the man's voice and, turning, gave Jephthah a speculative glance.

Miss Van Lew nodded. "Oh, yes. She suffered some minor burns, but her brother managed to get her out of the house in time. And at least some good came out of the tragedy. The shock of the fire apparently restored the young man's memory."

So he no longer had to worry about Arabella Von Bruck's being involved in any assassination attempt on the President, Jephthah thought, relieved. Yet he could see that something was still bothering Miss Van Lew. The woman was fidgeting unhappily with the high-necked collar of her dress.

"How did the fire start?" he asked.

"I understand it was a dropped candle," Miss Van Lew said, frowning thoughtfully. "But there are rumors that a man was found dead in the house after the fire, with his throat cut."

"Good lord," Cole said softly.

"That's not all." Miss Van Lew gave Jephthah a worried, birdlike glance. "I suppose it's none of my business, but I couldn't help noticing how upset Miss Appleton was when she came by to see me yesterday afternoon. She said she had to have a horse; that she and her brother had to leave Richmond immediately. Naturally, I was surprised. It was my understanding she and Mr. Appleton were to be wed. I had only one horse left in the stable, a broken-down old nag, I'm afraid, but of course I told her she could borrow it. It was plain the poor child was terrified."

"Did she say where she was going?" Jephthah asked.

"First, to the Appleton home at Black Oaks, and afterwards to Boston, I believe. Then this morning Mr. Harry Appleton appeared at my door. He demanded to know if I knew the whereabouts of Miss Appleton. He even had the nerve to threaten me if I didn't tell him. Naturally, I told him nothing." The spinsterish mouth tightened in a scornful smile. "The ridiculous man seemed to feel I owed him the information because of his services to the Union. As if he hadn't been paid more than enough in gold for the information he provided us."

Cole stared at Miss Van Lew. "Harry Appleton ... a Union spy?"

Jephthah grinned mirthlessly. "Harry Appleton is a man who likes to hedge his bets. The last year of the war he played both sides of the fence, so no matter who lost the war, he'd win. Even Lucy didn't know that we had two agents in the Appleton home." He turned back to Miss Van Lew. "I'm grateful to you, ma'am, for not letting Mr. Appleton know where Lucy had gone."

"But he does know!" she blurted. "My stable boy told Mr. Appleton. I just found out myself an hour ago." Her face clouded anxiously. "Of course, I may be worrying unduly, but Harry Appleton was like a man possessed."

Before she had finished speaking, Jephthah had thrown one leg over the saddle. Cole Sinclair caught at the hunter's bridle. "You're riding to Black Oaks?"

Jephthah nodded impatiently.

"A few minutes ago you said I could give you my parole," Cole said. "I want to give it to you now. I want to ride with you to Black Oaks.

Jephthah eyed the colonel warily. Something was stuck in the man's craw. He'd seen more warmth in the eyes of a man behind a dueling pistol. The glances of the two men met and locked. Jephthah shrugged.

He owed Lucy that much. "I figured you'd want to come along. We'll need another horse."

"Matt, what are you doing out of bed?"

Lucy glanced up from the fireplace in the kitchen at Black Oaks, where she was trying to concoct a breakfast out of what little food she could find in the larder. They had arrived at Black Oaks the night before, after a two-day ride from Richmond, stopping at least a dozen times and hiding when they heard voices or hoofbeats anywhere near. With the war in its last convulsive days, the area between Richmond and Black Oaks was a hunting ground for dregs from both armies. Even the bony nag Miss Van Lew had lent them, Lucy knew, was a prize worth taking, murdering for. Both she and Matt had been exhausted when they reached Black Oaks, Matt half asleep on the horse, which had stumbled its way up the road with Lucy trudging wearily along beside it. She was afraid the house might not even be there. Her eyes strained through the night, remembering Gray Meadows and wondering if there would only be chimneys and burned timbers to greet them. Then a sob of joy caught in her throat as she saw the sturdy red brick walls of Black Oaks rising before her, a darker shadow in the darkness.

Both she and Matt had fallen into bed without bothering to look for food, although it had been a day since they had eaten last. Now Lucy was trying to stir up a flame in the kitchen fireplace and bake some hard little potatoes she'd found in a corner of the root cellar.

She studied her brother, worried. Despite the night's rest, his young face was gray with fatigue. "I told you to stay in bed," she scolded.

"Stop fussing like a mother hen, sis," Matt said petulantly. "I'm not a baby any more, you know. Let me help you with the breakfast." He grinned at her, something of the old exuberance she remembered returning to his face. "You'd be surprised how much I learned about cooking in the army."

After they finished their breakfast, he trailed after

Lucy into the study and glanced around curiously. "It's funny how much I remember about this house. I even remember how I used to make a nuisance of myself, tagging after Charles and his friend Cole Sinclair. And how sometimes Cole would let me ride on his horse in front of him." He gave his sister a teasing glance. "If I remember correctly, you had a terrible crush on Cole. Your face used to get beet-red if anyone mentioned his name. Or have you forgotten?"

Lucy felt the pain twist through her body, but when she spoke, her voice was carefully neutral. "No, I haven't forgotten, but we're not likely to run into Mr. Sinclair, not in Boston," she added briskly. She forced all thought of Cole from her mind, telling herself all that mattered now was finding Aunt Clare's jewels and leaving Black Oaks for the north as soon as possible, before Cousin Harry somehow got on their trail.

She wrenched the brass ball off the top of the rod and gave a sigh of relief. The jewelry was still there, the diamonds and emeralds gleaming softly in her palm when she drew them out, before she dropped them into her skirt pocket.

"I didn't know that top came off," Matt said, coming over to stand beside her and staring down into the empty tube. Then he said eagerly, "Hey, look, sis, there's something else inside there . . . some paper."

He reached his hand into the tube and withdrew two sheets of thick, legal-size parchment paper, spreading the crumpled sheets out carefully on their grandfather's desk. He turned a puzzled gaze to Lucy. "It looks almost like a will, Lucy. Come here and see for yourself. It's signed by Grandfather Jacob."

"It can't be Grandfather's will," Lucy said. "That was kept in the bank in town. The bank president was executor for Grandfather's estate."

"But it is Grandfather's will," Matt said eagerly. "Here's his signature, and it's dated only two days before he died."

Lucy had joined him at the desk and was reading over her brother's shoulder. When she had finished, she spoke slowly, her face baffled. "This isn't the same will Mr. Curtis had. This will has an extra clause. At Uncle Joseph's death, all Black Oak property is bequeathed to Father or to Father's heirs." She shook her head, frowning. "I don't understand. That clause wasn't in the other will."

She could still remember how apologetic Mr. Curtis had been when he had told her father about the contents of her grandfather's will, disinheriting his eldest son and leaving everything to his younger son, Joseph.

"Well, then, Grandfather must have rewritten his will, just before he died," Matt said practically.

"You're right, Cousin Matthew. He did."

Lucy whirled to face Harry in the doorway. He was smiling as if in secret amusement, but the smile didn't touch the cold yellow eyes.

Lucy had the odd sensation that something had slammed hard against her chest. When she spoke, her voice was faint, "How long have you been here, Harry?"

"Since yesterday morning. I've been staying in my old bedroom. I was beginning to think you and Matt would never arrive."

He walked toward the desk, watching Lucy closely, only for a second glancing at the will, then swiftly, warily, back to Lucy. "I can't imagine how you found that will," he said irritably. "I searched everywhere for it."

"You knew about this second will?" Lucy was unable to conceal her surprise.

"Of course," Harry said impatiently. "Why else do you suppose I was so insistent that we be married? Not that you don't have considerable charms, my dear, but the truth is, I was always afraid this will would turn up one day. Once we were married, however, as your husband I'd still own Black Oak and its estates."

"If you never saw the will, how did you know it existed?" Matt asked, staring curiously at the cousin he only dimly remembered from his childhood at Black Oaks.

"Your grandfather told me about it. As a matter of

fact, he told me about it right here in this room. It seems he had second thoughts about someone not of Appleton blood inheriting Appleton land." Harry's mouth twisted bitterly in memory. "He called me in and told me he was adding a codicil to his will which would effectively keep me from inheriting any part of Black Oaks, even if Uncle Joseph should die. He said it was only honorable that he tell me of the new will so that I could make other plans for my future. As you might expect, I wasn't too happy about his decision. We quarreled, and I'm afraid we both lost our tempers. He came at me with that heavy oak cane he always carried. I took it from him and . . ." He shrugged and fell silent.

"You killed him!"

At the outrage in Lucy's voice, Cousin Harry frowned. "It was self-defense. I never meant to kill the old fool. But when I saw he was dead, there seemed no point in causing a family scandal. I arranged his body so that it looked as if he'd had a heart attack and hit his head when he fell. Everyone in the family knew his heart was bad. I thought, naturally, he had the new will in his desk. He'd told me he was planning to take it to Mr. Curtis at the bank that afternoon. I looked through the desk, but I couldn't find it, and I didn't dare hang around the study much longer. Someone might see me. As it turned out, only one person had seen me go into the study that morning—your little friend Dora Lee."

Harry smiled smugly at Lucy. "Of course, I didn't have to worry about Dora's saying anything. Dora and I had come to an understanding much earlier. She had learned to do as I told her. Not that any court would have taken a slave's word anyway."

"It was your baby Dora was carrying," Lucy said slowly. She gave her cousin a look of loathing. "And you let Uncle Joseph sell Dora Lee south."

"Well, I could hardly let her have the baby here at Black Oaks," Harry said, aggrieved, glancing at his withered left arm. "My . . . affliction . . . is hereditary, you know. My real father had the same problem. If Dora's baby was born with a bad arm, it wouldn't have taken Uncle Joseph long to pin the blame on me, and you know how straitlaced he was." A flash of malicious delight touched for a moment the lambent amber eyes. "And I must confess, Cole struck me as a most likely suspect for a father."

Then his gaze slipped past Lucy to Matt, and he ordered, still smiling, "Now, if you'll just hand me that will, Matt."

Matt's face flushed indignantly. "Why should I? It doesn't belong to you."

Lucy saw, before Matt did, the revolver which suddenly appeared in Harry's hand, pointed at Matt and her, the controlled but deadly menace in Harry's face. "Let him have the will, Matt," she said sharply.

Not, she thought desperately, that giving Cousin Harry the will would make the least bit of difference. Harry would never have told them about killing Jacob Appleton if he had had the slightest intention of leaving them alive. She stepped closer to Matt, shielding his body with her own, trying to keep the fear from her voice. "We can still be married, Harry. In Cold Brook, this afternoon, anytime you want."

"You can't be serious, sis," Matt said, outraged. "You can't marry him!"

Harry's smile thinned, his glance roving regretfully over Lucy as he murmured, "It's a flattering offer, my dear, but I'm afraid marriage to you is a luxury I can't afford. Even if you wouldn't betray me, there's always young Matt here to talk to the authorities. I can't take the chance. I'm sure you can understand my situation."

"You'll never get away with murdering us," Lucy said, fear tightening her voice. "Someone is sure to find out."

"Oh, I doubt that," Harry said, almost thoughtfully. "After all, the countryside is filled with deserters, murderers and cutthroats. No one is safe on the road these days. If you and your brother are found unhappily murdered, on your way back to Black Oaks from Richmond, who's to connect your deaths with me?"

Behind her, Lucy sensed, rather than heard, her

brother's feet sliding over the floor. She could imagine the reckless anger charging his young face, and she said quickly, "No, Matt!"

Harry leveled his gun at Lucy, his voice cold. "Before you get any foolish ideas about playing the hero, Cousin Matthew, you might remember it's your sister I'll shoot first."

He edged to the heavy brocade drapes at the window, ragged with saber tears, and yanking the cord loose, handed it to Lucy. "Tie Matt's wrists, tight, behind his back."

When Lucy hesitated, he scowled. "I can tie them just as easily after he's dead, if you prefer."

Reluctantly, Lucy took the cord and tied Matt's wrists behind him while Harry continued, more cheerfully, "You're an actress, Cousin Lucy. You understand how this all has to be staged properly, so that when you and Matt are found, it will be believed at once that you were set upon by brigands. I'm sure they'd tie your brother's hands, just to be on the safe side."

He's enjoying himself, Lucy thought, and somehow the sickening horror of that thought made her forget for a moment that other horror, the knowledge that death was waiting only a few minutes in the future.

Harry tested the knot she had made and smiled, pleased. Then the smile widened as the yellow-shaded eyes studied Lucy. "As for you, Cousin Lucy," he murmured, "I have no doubt that with your beauty, the miscreants wouldn't be content with just shooting you. Not at first, anyway. I'm sure they'd find other uses for that tempting little body first."

Swiftly Harry tucked the pistol into his belt, and with his hand now freed, caught at the neck of Lucy's gown and ripped downward. The material gave way easily. Instantly Lucy sprang furiously at Harry, clawing at his eyes. His hand, palm open, shot out and slammed against her face so that she went sprawling to the ground.

When she scrambled again to her feet, the revolver was back again in Harry's hand, pointing at Matt, who was straining at the bonds on his wrists, his face pale with rage. "A few bruises will add a nice touch, don't you think?" And then lightly, jeeringly, "After all, you wouldn't want people to think you didn't do battle for your virtue, now would you, Cousin Lucy?"

She said nothing, clutching the pieces of her torn gown over her breasts and moving closer to Matt, as if still determined to shield her brother's body with her own. Although her emotions felt numbed, her thoughts were still darting rapidly in all directions, still seeking a means of escape. Then, looking into Harry's face, his tongue running over his lips, the greedy hunger in his eyes as they fastened upon her breasts, she deliberately dropped her hands away from her body. Her head lifted proudly so that the full, pale breasts were pulled high and taut, the rosy tips visible through the torn gown. She gave Cousin Harry her most ravishing smile as she walked slowly toward him, her voice low and enticing as she asked, "Why should we have to pretend I've been ravished, Harry?"

She saw her cousin's eyes savor the sight of those silken breasts, the almost oily pleasure filling his eyes as he thought of how it would be, what enjoyment it would bring him to make Lucy pay in full for the humiliations and rejections he had suffered at her hands. Not just Lucy, but all the Appletons, who had given him their name but never really accepted him into the family, always the outsider, always the stranger. To save her own life, he was sure Lucy would never submit to him, but what indignities, what degradation wouldn't she endure to save her precious brother's life! The idea, Harry thought, had delightful possibilities.

Then Harry's glance lifted from the satin sheen of those breasts to Lucy's lustrous dark eyes, watching him, and glimpsed for just a moment what lay behind that radiance, behind those thick-fringed lashes, a look that was deadly as a drawn blade.

He shook his head warily. "You'll have to forgive me, Cousin Lucy, but I have an aversion to making love to a woman while wondering just how she plans to kill me, the first chance she gets. Now, stand away from your brother!" His voice sharpened, the gun lifting.

"A lover's quarrel already, Harry?"

The familiar amused drawl behind Harry jerked his head around. He stared, shocked, at Cole Sinclair standing in the doorway to the hall, a gun held almost negligently in his hand.

"What the devil..." he sputtered, then snapped angrily, "This is none of your business, Sinclair."

Cole smiled lazily. "But it is, Harry. I've come to settle a score." He flicked a glance in Lucy's direction. "With her." His face hardened, his voice all at once harsh. "She killed four of my men at Cold Brook, and God knows how many more. So if you have any designs on the lady, I'm afraid you'll have to wait until I'm through with her."

Confusion struggled with uncertainty in Harry's face, then he blurted, "I don't believe you."

Cole shrugged indifferently. "I don't give a damn what you believe," he said. "After I've finished, you can do what you please. Only you'll have to wait your turn, Harry."

The faint glimmer of hope Lucy had felt when Cole had miraculously appeared died a swift, painful death when she looked into Cole's face. His mouth was a cruel slash mark, and a lust for vengeance glittered in the narrowed blue-green eyes.

Harry laughed nervously. "Aren't you forgetting something?" Before Lucy could move, he had stepped behind her, and she felt the muzzle of Harry's gun cold against the nape of her neck. "I have the lady. You haven't. I'd say that gave me a prior claim, wouldn't you?"

She could not see Harry's face, but she could imagine the gloating look of triumph in the yellow eyes staring at Cole, who had not moved a muscle. If anything, his face had taken on an odd blankness. Only Lucy, who knew Cole's moods as well as her own, saw the movement behind the glittering eyes, a flame burning

401

wickedly, as he lifted his gun and pointed it at Lucy. "Go ahead and shoot, Harry," he said softly. "Only you'll be dead exactly one second later."

"You're bluffing." Harry's voice rose shrilly. "Damm-it, you're bluffing."

"Sinclair may be bluffing, but I'm not. Let the girl go, Appleton."

The second voice coming from the small side door leading from the study into Black Oaks' formal draw-ing room made Lucy forget for one shocked moment the gun at her neck. She half turned. A moment before, the door had been shut. Now, moving so quietly that no one in the room had heard him, Jephthah stood in the door, a revolver in his hand. For just one second his steel-gray eyes met Lucy's, and he nodded, almost imperceptibly.

After that, Lucy would never be sure of the exact order of events. She remembered dropping to the floor, a double explosion thundering in her ears, Harry's gun and Jephthah's firing almost simultaneously. Only Harry's ball plowed into the door frame, an inch from Jephthah's head, sending chips of wood flying, and Jephthah's bullet found its target of flesh and bone.

Lucy saw Harry's head jerk backward, an expression of furious disbelief in his eyes, then his face seemed to shatter into nothingness before her horrified gaze. She watched Harry fall slowly to the floor, almost on top of her. And she remembered thinking vaguely that Harry was lying almost exactly where she had found her grandfather, dead, that long-ago morning in this same study.

Hands were pulling her to her feet, Jephthah's voice asking anxiously, "Lucy, are you hurt?"

She didn't understand. Why should he think she was hurt? Then, looking down, she saw her blood-splattered dress. Harry's blood. And not just his blood, she real-ized, sickened. There were bits of flesh clinging to her gown.

She clung dizzily to Jephthah's callused hand. I won't be sick, she thought. I won't make a fool of myself.

But the nausea rose, sour-tasting in her throat, and pressing her hands to her mouth, she fled helplessly from the room.

27

"Are you feeling better, sis?"

Lucy was standing staring out of her bedroom window at the gray-black storm clouds gathering over the hills in the distance. She turned and smiled at her brother. "Yes, thank you, Matt."

She had bathed and changed her clothes, then brushed her hair until her arms ached. In her white flannel robe with blue ribbons running across the bodice, and her hair hanging loose over her shoulder, Matt thought she looked all of sixteen. In a surge of brotherly affection, he said, "I'm sorry about what happened . . . about Cousin Harry."

"Yes," she said, a slight shudder passing through her body, remembering that last look on Harry's face turned upon her, wondering if she would ever forget those furious, glaring eyes. Her hands clasped tightly together to stop their sudden trembling, she asked, "Where . . . where is Harry now?"

"Jephthah and I . . ." Matt spoke with a new unconscious authority, a timbre in his voice reminding Lucy of her father. "Well, we talked it over and decided there was no need to bring the authorities into this. It would only destroy Harry's reputation, and there's no point to that now. I told Jephthah how Cousin Harry had planned to make our deaths look as though we'd been killed by bushwhackers." Matt grinned coldly. "We decided we'd do the same for Cousin Harry. We're going to take him a mile or so down the road and leave him by the branch that leads into Cold Brook, make it look as if he'd been killed for his horse and money." He hesitated. "Only Jephthah said that I should make sure first you had no objections."

"No . . . no objections." Lucy, however, wasn't thinking of Harry's reputation but of her Aunt Clare. This way Harry could be buried honorably, beside his mother in Appleton ground, as Aunt Clare would have wanted. When her brother started to turn away, she blurted, "Matt, wait." Then, more slowly, "Where is Colonel Sinclair?"

Matt turned back, frowning. "Cole left a half hour ago, without a word to Jephthah or me. He just took off." He glanced at his sister, a flush rising in his face as he asked, "It wasn't true, was it, sis, what Cole said in the study about your killing four of his men?"

"No, it wasn't true."

Her brother smiled, relieved. "I was sure it wasn't. I'm going to tell Jephthah what Colonel Sinclair said and see if he can make any sense out of it." Then, casting a quick look out the window at the threatening clouds, "We'll be back as soon as we can. It looks like that storm will be breaking soon."

Lucy could hear his footsteps bounding down the steps, two at a time, and finally the front door slamming. A few minutes later, she heard horses riding off and knew that Cousin Harry was leaving Black Oaks for the last time. Still, she remained in her room, as if hesitant to leave its sanctuary. Then, knowing she was foolish—she would have to reenter the study someday, she might as well get it over with—she walked slowly down the stairs and through the hall corridor to the study.

The storm clouds had already darkened the room, so that it was as dimly lit as if it were dusk. She could hear thunder grumbling in the distance as she hesitated in the doorway, looking at the floor by the desk where Harry had fallen. Jephthah or Matt must have taken up the rug, she saw thankfully. There was only the trace of a bloodstain left on the hardwood floor, the only indication that a violent death had taken place in the room just a short time before.

"I've been waiting for you."

Cole rose from the winged chair beside the fireplace. A lazy smile played across his mouth as he saw the consternation flood Lucy's face.

405

"Matt . . . Matt told me you'd gone." Lucy heard the fear trembling in her voice and fought against it, but she was all too aware that, with Matt and Jephthah gone, she was completely alone in the house.

"I wanted him to think that. Otherwise, how could I get you away from your watchdogs?" Then, as Lucy edged uncertainly toward the door, he said idly, "I wouldn't try running. You wouldn't get very far." He walked slowly toward her, the smile tightening like a death mask on his face as his gaze caught and held hers. She felt pinioned by that glance, as if she could not have moved if she wanted to. Her limbs felt oddly heavy, frozen.

"I didn't set up that ambush, Cole," she cried. "You have to believe me."

"Why should I?" he asked coldly, his hand reaching out to pick up a coil of blue-black hair, then wrapped its silken softness, like a noose, around her neck, pulling her closer to him. "Why should I believe anyone who can lie as expertly as you do?" he demanded. "That was the white rose's main stock in trade, wasn't it, lies and deception? What a joke it must have been for you and your friend Jephthah, how easily you fooled me. Did you have a good laugh over my blindness? Even when we were making love," he said suddenly, savagely, "that was all a lie, too, wasn't it?"

"No, I swear." Her voice trailed off helplessly. What was the use? He would never believe her.

"Sometimes I wonder if everything about you isn't false," he continued, his hand moving to her chin, tightening, so that she had to look full into that accusing, merciless gaze. "Is there any real Lucy Appleton at all underneath all that make-believe?"

"Please, Cole. The war will soon be over. Whatever happened, it's finished."

"Oh, no, it's not finished," he said softly. "Not between us, it isn't." Not until he stopped hearing the screams of his men in his nightmares, he thought, not until the memory of their dying before his eyes stopped haunting him. Dead, he thought bitterly, because he

406

had been besotted by a deceptively beautiful face and a lying, softly seductive body. Fleetingly he found himself wondering if his hatred wasn't directed as much at himself as at Lucy.

No matter, he thought, quickly and expertly imprisoning Lucy's arms behind her with one hand while the other brushed aside the ruffles of her robe, sliding a hand roughly beneath the beribboned bodice to cup a softly swelling breast. He had sworn she would pay for betraying him, for setting up the ambush that had killed his men. And one way or the other, pay she would!

Deliberately his hand tightened cruelly around that petal softness. He watched the black eyes flare wide, saw the look of shocked pain filling them, and something else. In that first moment his hand had touched her flesh, he had felt the slight, but instantaneous, shiver of passionate response ripple through her body. Flecks of gold swam deep in the darkness of her eyes, reminding him of another time, another place, before his face descended, crushing her mouth savagely with his own.

When his lips and his hands finally released their painful grip upon her mouth and breast, his one hand still held her while the other pulled loose the sash tying her robe. As it fell open, he saw that she was wearing nothing beneath the robe. Gazing down into the dark warm valley between the perfectly formed breasts, watching the firelight caress the creamy skin, he felt the swift onslaught of desire, stabbing knife-sharp in his loins.

As he shed his own clothes, he half expected she would make a dash for freedom, but she made no move to escape. When he turned to her, stripping the robe from her unresisting body and tossing it to one side before forcing her to the floor, she made no protest. Even when he thrust her long, slim legs apart and took her without waiting, he was still expecting her to struggle, to fight against him. Instead, except for one sharp cry, she made no sound. Her body lay still, motionless, beneath his, her face wiped blank. Only her eyes, wide open and darkly brilliant behind the thick fringe of her lashes, stared up at him with an expression he could not fathom.

Unexpectedly he found himself remembering the last time he had held her in his arms, that last night at Black Oaks, remembered the sweet, yielding passion of her body unfolding beneath his, the slender arms and silken thighs tightening around him, the warmth of her mouth moving softly against his, the apple-sweet fragrance of her skin and hair in his nostrils as he had buried himself in her arms. Even the look of wonder and joy flooding her dark eyes as their passion had lifted and carried them together....

Cursing himself for his weakness, yet unable to stop himself, only knowing that his need to know and share that same ecstasy again was all at once stronger than his need to hurt her, to avenge himself, he found his hands reaching out to her. Tenderly he stroked the silken inner flesh of her thighs, his hands playing gently over the curve of hip and lingering on her breasts, while his kisses covered her face, until he felt her body come alive, begin to move in a sweet, delicious rhythm with his. She murmured his name, and then repeated it, more urgently, while her hands caressed the nape of his neck with soft, feather strokes, then her lips sought his mouth, their warmth like a flame burning against his.

Outside the partly open study window, Lucy was only dimly aware of thunder like a cannonade crashing into the valley, of lightning fitfully illuminating the window. Her own heart was thundering too loudly in her ears. Whatever the violence of the storm raging overhead, it was only a counterpoint to the raging turbulence in her own blood. She heard Cole whisper huskily, "Sweet, sweet..." Then they were both being swept into the passionate vortex of their own private storm, and afterward, when she lay, happily spent, cradled in Cole's arms, she discovered, to her surprise, that she was crying softly.

Bemused, Cole gazed down into her tear-smudged eyes, thinking wryly of how he had planned to punish her betrayal by brutally raping her and instead had ended up seducing her all over again.

Gently he smoothed the unruly mane of blue-black hair away from her face. "Arabella was right, you know," he drawled. "You are a witch, a black-eyed witch." He grinned teasingly. "Only I don't believe 'witch' was the word she used."

Lucy searched his face anxiously. "You don't still hate me, darling?"

His face was suddenly closed to her. He put her aside and rose to his feet. "No," he said wearily, "I don't hate you. I don't suppose I ever did. It would be like hating a part of myself. I can't forget what happened, but I know now that nothing I do to you will bring my men back."

She scrambled to her feet, staring at him incredulously. "You still believe that I deliberately sent you and your men to your deaths?" she demanded.

The truth was he didn't know what he believed, Cole thought. His coldly logical mind told him that it had to be the white rose who had arranged the ambush, but in his bones and blood and sinew he was just as sure that the vibrant, loving woman he had held in his arms could never have betrayed him.

Before he could answer, they both were startled by the sound of hoofbeats racing up to the front of Black Oaks, spattering gravel, then the front door slamming open and footsteps pounding down the hallway.

Lucy had just managed to slip into her robe. Cole, his face instantly alert, was reaching for his pistol when the door to the study was flung open. Jephthah stood in the doorway, a drawn revolver in his hand. Behind him, Matt came to an abrupt halt, his young face turning scarlet when he saw his sister and Cole Sinclair, together, only partially clothed.

Jephthah's glance moved directly to Lucy as he growled, "Are you all right?"

She nodded without speaking, gazing unhappily at

Cole, then away, as she tightened the belt of her robe around her. Jephthah's shrewd, measuring glance turned to Cole, his voice sharp. "Young Matt told me about the wagon raid outside of Cold Brook, that somehow you had the fool notion that Miss Appleton here was involved in the trap you and your men fell into."

"Who else knew about the raid?" Cole asked, scowling.

"Harry Appleton, for one," Jephthah said dourly. "Matter of fact, as I remember, the raid was his idea. He even suggested to your General Early that you be the one to lead the raid. Then after it was all planned, naturally he turned around and sold the information to us." Jephthah's long mouth twisted sardonically. "I'd say Appleton was more than a mite disappointed when you didn't end up getting yourself killed in that ambush, Sinclair."

When Cole stood stiffly, without speaking, Jephthah shrugged, disgusted. "Ain't no law says you have to believe me." His gray gunmetal eyes lingered on Lucy's face for a long moment, as if he were imprisoning its loveliness forever in his mind, then he said, quietly, as if he and Lucy were alone in the room. "I'll be going now, Miss Appleton. The boy and I took care of your cousin. I reckon there's nothing more to hold me here."

He had strode out into the hallway, was at the front door, when Lucy's hand on his arm stopped him. When he turned, she was smiling gratefully up at him, her dark eyes glowing fondly. "Thank you, Jephthah, thank you for everything."

For a moment a bleakness brushed his face as he gazed down at her, then it was gone and he jerked his chin grimly back toward the study. "I wouldn't be too hard on the colonel," he said gruffly. "A man can make all kinds of a fool of himself over a woman."

She nodded, blinking back tears, as she looked up into the long-boned, homely face, so very dear to her. She remembered the perilous times they had shared, how they had gleefully flaunted death, riding together with danger riding in their shadow. "Oh, Jephthah," she blurted wistfully. "I know it sounds awful, but I'm going to miss it all, you and the courier route, and even the excitement of being the white rose."

Jephthah grinned crookedly, understanding. "Yes, ma'am, I reckon I will, too, at times. I ain't never been one for the quiet, tame life." A glint of amusement touched the gray eyes as he reflected that knowing only too well the reckless, impetuous nature of Lucy Appleton and the equally headstrong temperament of Colonel Sinclair, he didn't suppose their life together would exactly be placid.

Lucy reached up on tiptoe to drop a soft kiss on Jephthah's grizzled chin. "I'll never forget you," she whispered. "Never."

Then Jephthah was gone, and Lucy walked slowly back to the study. Matt had discreetly disappeared. Cole was alone in the room. He had finished dressing and had his hat in his hand when she entered. Although her bare feet made hardly a sound, he turned immediately. She saw the relief rush into his eyes, before his face became once more carefully blank and he said, "I'll be on my way, too, Lucy."

She closed the door behind her. "Why, Cole?" she asked, dismayed. "Why must you go? You gave Jephthah your parole, and the war is sure to be over in a few more days."

Cole stared at her, frustration and bitterness mingling in his voice as he demanded, "For God's sake, Lucy, do you think I want to go? Even if the war is over, what do I have to offer a woman? Gray Meadows is burned to the ground. Every cent I had went into Confederate bonds. I can't even afford to pay the debts I owe, much less the taxes on Gray Meadows. How could I support a wife . . . children?"

"There's Black Oaks," Lucy said stubbornly. "We can live here."

Cole's mouth tightened. "No," he said curtly. "Black Oaks belongs to Matt and you. I won't live on Appleton charity."

From beneath her thick, lowered eyelashes, Lucy

thoughtfully studied Cole's set, proud face. Then she sighed to herself. Oh, dear, this was going to be more difficult than she had thought. She should have remembered the Sinclair pride, not to mention Cole's own natural stubbornness. Then her eyes flashed mischievously. Well, the Appletons could be stubborn, too. And she wasn't forgetting her own special talent.

Casting her glance downward, her lower lip trembling piteously, she murmured bravely, "Of course, Cole, you must do what you think best. It's only ..." She broke off, as if unable to continue, tears glistening in the blue-black eyelashes, tracing silver paths down the soft curve of her cheeks. She gave a low, despairing cry. "It's only that I don't know how I'll manage all by myself here at Black Oaks. Matt's a dear, but he's just a boy. He doesn't know anything about planting or harvesting or running a plantation, any more than I do."

Now the tears were racing unchecked down her face, her breasts rising and falling in her agitation as she sank into a chair and buried her face in her hands. Her small body was racked with helpless sobs.

Cole stared at her, aghast. He had never seen Lucy so helpless, so defeated, before. Somehow, without quite knowing how it happened, he was in the chair and she was cradled in his arms, her face buried against his chest. Her tears dampened his shirtfront while he patted her trembling shoulders and made soothing, ineffectual noises.

Finally she lifted her lovely, tear-stained face to him, hiccuping childishly as her sobs lessened. "I'm ashamed to be such a coward, Cole. It's only I'm so tired, and so frightened of being left alone again."

"Hush," he said, his hand gently smoothing her hair away from her damp face. "Hush, my darling." His arms tightened around her protectively, as if she were a child to be held close and comforted. Except at some point, he wasn't sure when, the robe had slipped away from Lucy and there was nothing between her satiny skin and his hands soothing and caressing her quiv-

412

ering body. And the feelings surging through him were not at all fatherly.

Lucy sighed contentedly, and lifting her wide, brilliant eyes to him, she murmured, "You won't leave, Cole. You promise?"

"I promise," he said hoarsely, because the trembling of her body in his arms was no longer from tears, and his hands were suddenly no longer gently caressing but hard and demanding on that satin skin. He watched the firelight play across her face, her eyes shut so that the lashes lay fan-shaped on the peach-white skin, the softly curved mouth half-smiling. . . .

There was something about that smile that all at once aroused Cole's suspicions. Wasn't it too smugly self-satisfied? Now that he thought about it, even Lucy's behavior, the very personification of the helpless, clinging female, seemed suspect. Lucy, helpless! he thought, frowning. That would be the day!

He rose to his feet so abruptly that she tumbled to the floor, her eyes flying open, startled. "It was all an act, wasn't it?" he demanded, outraged. "All that weeping and wailing and poor little me. Dammit, you tricked me again, didn't you?"

She could not meet his accusing gaze, and getting to her feet, she snatched at her robe and tied it around her. A raw, genuine fear was making her heart thud against her rib cage. "I couldn't let you go," she said, her voice miserable. "I couldn't lose you again."

Hesitantly, she lifted her gaze to Cole's, wondering, frightened, whether she would glimpse that familiar, devastating anger in the icy blue-green eyes, that lazy, sardonic smile which covered, she was only too well aware, a streak of ruthlessness, as well as a teasing, gentle warmth.

Then suddenly, unexpectedly, as if unable to help himself, Cole threw back his head and began to laugh, laughed so loudly that the sound echoed against the walls and set the bibelots on the whatnot shelf to trembling.

Lucy gave a sigh of relief. It was going to be all right

after all, she decided, snuggling happily once more into Cole's arms. "I've been thinking, darling," she said thoughtfully, when the last peal of Cole's laughter had died away. "We should start planting right away. The English mills will be crying for our cotton now that the war's over. We can ask Sam and Jane and the children to come back and help us, and sell Aunt Clare's jewelry to buy seed."

Cole listened, amused, and lifted a quizzical eyebrow. Which Lucy was this? he wondered. The practical, efficient chatelaine, the fragile-appearing Southern matron who yet somehow, like his mother, had managed to run a huge plantation without apparently lifting a finger?

Lazily, deliberately, he reached down and with a well-placed kiss stopped the flow of Lucy's chatter. Finally, she drew away, her eyes, wide and gold-flecked, staring, smiling, into his.

"Take off that silly robe," Cole said.

As he gathered her warmth once more into his arms, he reflected ruefully on the many Lucys he had known. The saucy actress he had first seen on the Washington stage, the captivating colored maid Sukey, the mysterious Union agent called the white rose, even the gray-haired plump widow taking her son's coffin home.

Lucy saw the amusement gathering in Cole's eyes and asked suspiciously, "What is it? Why are you smiling?"

Cole laughed softly, running his hands slowly, caressingly, the length of her softly yielding body. And this Lucy, he thought, the woman who filled his arms and heart with her sweet passion and who would never change.

"I was just considering," he drawled, grinning wickedly at her before his arms once more pulled her close, "what an interesting life it's going to be, being married to all of you!"

NEW FROM FAWCETT CREST

CLASSIC BESTSELLERS
from FAWCETT BOOKS